HER
SILENT
PRAYER

BOOKS BY M.M. CHOUINARD

HER
SILENT
PRAYER

M.M.CHOUINARD

bookouture

Published by Bookouture in 2022

An imprint of Storyfire Ltd.
Carmelite House
50 Victoria Embankment
London EC4Y 0DZ

www.bookouture.com

ISBN: 978-1-80019-991-0
eBook ISBN: 978-1-80019-990-3

For Neo: The truth is, **you** *saved* **me**.

PROLOGUE
AUGUST 6TH

Diana Montauk's hand brushed Bennie Moreno's as they stared together at the stone foundations of the ruined Sutro Baths, tucked silently on the edge of the Pacific Ocean. The crash of the waves below lulled her, and she closed her eyes for a moment, filling her lungs with the invigorating brine of the sea air.

Bennie, the man she'd been dating long-distance for the last two months, playfully pulled her closer, but his smile failed to hide his impatience. "It's getting dark, and I'm getting cold. Wanna head back to the hotel?"

She nodded, then gazed back out to the ruins slowly being swallowed by the darkness. Images of Naya, Bennie's ex-wife, sprang up amid the shadows: of Naya's left eye swollen shut, puffed red and purple. Of dried blood flaking around her broken nose and smeared down her chin below a split lip. Of the desperation and hopelessness crying out from the single brown eye still able to peer into the camera, begging for the nightmare to be over.

Gazing up into his too-handsome face, she shifted him

gently in front of the expansive ocean. "I'm so glad I found you. I can't imagine another man I'd rather be here with."

As she stood on her tiptoes to kiss him, she stoked the rage evoked by those memories of Naya's face, allowing it to invade every cell in her body. When he deepened the kiss, she checked that his eyes were closed. Once she confirmed they were, she took a mental snapshot of the lust on his face.

Then she pulled the syringe of black-tar heroin from her purse and plunged it deep into his carotid artery.

The shift in his expression from confusion to realization sent her heart thumping, and she quickly took another mental snapshot. When his face began to slacken, she braced her feet firmly into the ground, then shoved him back over the ledge of the observation deck. She watched his body disappear into the darkness, listened for his muffled landing, then crossed the paved observation deck back to the path. Over her decade of kills here, the topology of the paths and observation decks had shifted—some paths and tunnels closed, new ones opened—but that kept her vigilant. She enjoyed changing things up, as long as the change wasn't too big. She bent to pick up a small rock, then slipped it into her purse alongside the now-empty syringe.

She pulled her scarf from her neck up over her dark hair—despite the rapidly falling darkness there might be a straggler or two, and the scarf helped hide her face. With a practiced calm gait, she strolled through the ghostly cypress trees toward the Legion of Honor. On the way, she disabled her burner phone and tossed it into one trash can, then tossed the SIM card into another. She powered up her real cell, climbed into her rental car, and headed out of San Francisco.

CHAPTER ONE

AUGUST 17TH

Melissa Rollins opened her eyes—or thought she did. The world around her remained black.

But she wasn't in bed—she was upright, head and torso propped up against a hard surface, the air around her so oppressively hot it felt like an invisible blanket. She shifted—pain shrieked through her head, but when she reflexively raised her hand toward it, she met resistance—her hands were tied together behind her back, numb, now buzzing with the stabs of a thousand tiny daggers. She tried to shift her legs—also tied together. She tried to straighten them, and hit another hard surface a few feet in front of her. She tried to swear, but a wad of fabric in her mouth swallowed the sound.

Fear clenched her chest like a vice. What the hell was going on? Where was she?

She studied the darkness, willing her eyes to adjust. She ran her fingers along the surface behind her, then below her. Smooth and true with a light texture—like her walls. Below that, a grainy, lined floor—hardwood floors. She shifted again, ready this time for the pounding in her head, and inched forward on her knees. Three walls, then wood with panels—a door. She rocked forward onto her feet and raised herself to where the knob should be. But there was no knob—only a backplate with no latch.

That meant a closet. *Her* closet? She'd installed a one-ended knob like this in the upstairs hall closet. Was that where she was? She frantically felt the walls and floor again, and traced the vague shape of the space, including the dent in the baseboard that had always annoyed her. Yes, her closet, but—what did that mean?

"Help!" she screamed despite the gag, flinching as the pain stabbed through her head. She screamed again, louder this time, trying to fight back her fear, then leaned back against the wall, hoping to hear something, anything. Sweat pooled at the small of her back.

The vice on her chest tightened and she struggled to breathe, gasping to take in the sweltering air around the fabric. She forced herself to slow down, to breathe slowly and deeply. If she didn't short-circuit the panic attack, it would overwhelm her.

How? How did she get in here? She remembered arriving home, relieved to be done with an exhausting workday. On the way home she'd picked up Vietnamese food for dinner, and flirted with the idea of opening a bottle of wine to go with it. She'd been looking forward to a peaceful evening on her own because everything had been so difficult with Avery since the judge had approved split custody—her daughter had always been rebellious, but now, when she could escape to her father's half the time, it was so much worse, and with school starting up again, all Melissa's spare time would go to PTA responsibilities and monitoring homework. She remembered parking and unlocking the front door while dreaming of comfort food, a good book, and a sheet facial mask... but she remembered nothing after. The time in between was just—gone.

Except—her memory flashed—a doorbell ringing? Someone she hadn't expected.

She squeezed her eyes shut, searching for anything else.

A flash of pain, like a prick in her arm?

Her eyes flew back open. Had someone drugged her? Then tied her up and threw her in the closet? But why? Had it been some sort of home invasion? Maybe she'd interrupted a burglary in progress?

That made sense—hers was the fanciest house on the block, a natural target for a robbery. And since she couldn't hear anything, that meant they were gone now, she'd be okay, she just had to get out and everything would be fine. Tears of relief welled in her eyes.

Except—how? Without a knob she couldn't open the door from the inside, she knew that all too well. And even if she managed to wriggle the gag out of her mouth, nobody would hear her scream. She'd chosen this house for just that reason— the large lot with trees and shrubs around the perimeter to keep out prying eyes, and the solid, nearly soundproof walls and windows. She'd tested it herself—you couldn't hear what was happening on the third floor from the first. And nobody was due until Sunday evening anyway, when Travis dropped off Avery.

Avery's soccer game! When she didn't show up Sunday morning, Travis and Avery would notice. But—would they bother to come looking for her? And even if they did, Tuesday night to Sunday morning was more than four days. Four days without food and water, in heat so thick she could taste it.

The hysterical panic bubbled up again, and she clenched her teeth and fists against it. She wouldn't give in to it. She had to stay calm. She had to figure a way out. Focus on one thing at a time, mind over matter, put all her mind and energy into each step, and she'd come up with something.

First thing: she needed to free her hands, or at least get them in front of her. She'd always been flexible, and she did yoga religiously. She could do it.

She pulled her arms down as far as possible and wiggled her rear between them. Her arms were just a shade too short. She maneuvered onto her back, bent her legs toward her chest, and yanked her arms up. Her left shoulder wrenched and pulled, like a drumstick refusing to release from a chicken. She screamed as it popped out of joint—but her arms cleared her legs, now in front of her again. She writhed on the floor, moaning into her gag.

When the pain receded enough for her to move, she tugged the gag from her mouth and pushed herself upright. She searched the closet, knowing she'd find nothing. She grabbed at the edges of the door, the hinges, trying to find anything she could get a grip on, nails digging into the wood. She pounded with her right hand, gritting her teeth against the jolts up her injured arm. It didn't budge.

She collapsed against it, tears mixing with the sweat pouring down her face. Her legs were stronger, maybe she could kick it down? But she'd have to free her feet first. She dropped to the floor and groped her ankles. Not rope—a zip tie. Could she chew through it?

Where her ankles met up, she could pull the tie a tiny bit away, just far enough to get her canine onto it. She bit down, and chewed.

The plastic was solid, with almost no give. But she kept going, as hard as she could, hoping the repetition would wear the material down. Her jaw tired and she switched sides. When she had to take a break completely, she worked the plastic with her hands, trying to fatigue it.

Finally, after God only knew how long, the tie snapped off, and a burst of adrenaline shot through her. She could do this. She *would* do this. Unlike the plastic, the wood had give, and she could splinter it off the lock mechanism.

She rubbed her ankles to restore the circulation, then carefully righted herself. She turned her back to the door, braced, and kicked as hard as she could in the limited space.

It didn't budge. No give, not even a vibration. Like kicking concrete.

"Help! Help! Help!" she screamed, turning it into a mantra like a karate kiai, kicking wildly with increasing desperation.

Until a sharp pain shot up her leg. When she tried to put her weight on it, pain sheared through her. No way could she kick any more, or even stand.

With that, something in her soul ruptured. She dropped to her knees and curled up into a ball, sobbing, praying someone would come looking for her before it was too late.

CHAPTER TWO

"Good morning, darling."

Detective Josette Fournier opened her eyes slowly to find Matt Soltero, her boyfriend of several months, standing over her bed with a steaming mug and a loving smile. She propped herself up, returned the smile, and relieved him of the mug. "What a lovely way to wake up. Thank you."

He waited while she took a sip. "How is it?"

"Mmm." She closed her eyes to savor the warm, velvety mocha. Almost instantly they popped back open. "Cayenne?"

His smile broadened. "And a hint of nutmeg. I'm calling it the Soltero Special."

"I love it." She took another big sip to punctuate the point. "What brought on this bout of creativity?"

He sat on the edge of the bed. "The need to butter you up. I just got called in to work. Dr. Patel herniated a disc in his back, so we now only have two neurologists to cover the hospital and I have to go in. I'm so sorry, I know how much you were looking forward to the Oakhurst Music Festival."

Jo's warm glow dimmed slightly, but she kept the smile on her face. "That's what you get when you date a busy, important neurologist. And since I can't count the number of dinners my job has interrupted, it's only fair."

"Very true. But I still feel obligated to make it up to you. Shall I make you my guanciale carbonara tonight for dinner?"

"Only if we can work off the calories afterward." She grinned.

His eyebrows shot up. "Oh, that's *done*."

She scooted back down into the warm covers and watched him change into the set of work clothes he kept in her bureau. At forty-five, he still moved and looked like a professional athlete, tall and muscular, with no hint of the thickening belly that caught up with most men by that time. So far his black hair was untouched by gray, but his warm dark-chocolate eyes crinkled with crow's feet that somehow made him look worldly and sexy.

When he finished, he bent down to give her a kiss. "I don't mind if you go without me."

She waved him off. "It wouldn't be any fun without you. Now go, someone needs you."

"Yes, ma'am." He kissed her again, then headed out.

As the front door clicked faintly behind him in the distance, the tiniest something twinged inside her. She'd meant it when she said the festival wouldn't be fun without him, and that was strange enough. But even if they hadn't had concrete plans, she'd miss him. She was becoming used to spending the weekends with him, and she hoped that wasn't a mistake.

She rolled her eyes and threw back the covers. Sneaking periodic sips of the spicy mocha as she showered, she considered what to do with the day now lying wide open in front of her. She'd gone to the shooting range the day before; going two days in a row wasn't honing your skills, it was obsessing. She briefly considered calling Sophie, her sister, and asking if her nieces, Emily and Isabelle, wanted to go to Magic Wings Butterfly Sanctuary, but remembered they were away visiting

Sophie's in-laws in Braintree. Ultimately, she decided to make herself an omelet, then curl up with the deliciously lurid serial-killer thriller she'd picked up the week before.

As she pulled out her omelet pan, her phone chimed with an email notification from a flagged address. She clicked on it. Her monthly compilation of information about recent Golden Gate Bridge suicides from the San Francisco Police Department.

Her mind balked as she stared down at the attachment. For over eight years she'd been obsessing about the death of Martin Scherer, a serial killer who'd preyed on married women in the online game World of Warcraft back when she'd briefly served as lieutenant of the Oakhurst County State Police Detective Unit. She and her makeshift task force had been just hours from catching him when he'd unexpectedly thrown himself off the Golden Gate Bridge—supposedly. Something about his death never sat right with her, but nobody else in the unit, not even her partner Bob Arnett, thought there was anything suspicious about his death. They were all convinced she was chasing a phantom, but she couldn't shake the feeling that something strange—and dangerously important—had happened.

Since his death, she'd arranged to have information about all Golden Gate Bridge suicides sent to her, and earlier in the year she'd used an entire two-week leave compiling and organizing nearly five hundred suicides into a spreadsheet in hopes of spotting some pattern. She'd been interrupted by a case just as she settled in to analyze it all, and had been too busy since to return to it. So much had changed in her life over the last few months, from her father's cancer to her own miscarriage and nearly losing her niece; in the process of it all, several things deep inside her had shifted. Was her certainty that something was amiss with Martin Scherer's case just one of many things she'd clung to for all the wrong reasons? If so, it was time to let it go.

But her pulse sped as her finger hovered over the screen and she tried to talk herself into deleting the email—this might be the batch of data that contained the clue she needed. It went against her nature to not at least *look* at the reports inside. After all, it was only eight in the morning, and her day now lay open, beckoning: *Why not take one final look?*

Fine, she told herself, she'd give it one more shot—on the condition that if she didn't find anything, she'd toss it all away.

———

With another mocha in hand and humming a zydeco ditty, Jo settled in front of her laptop. The file contained five new cases; she printed them out and grabbed a highlighter. She screeched to a halt at the second name listed: Ben Moreno, from Oakhurst, Mass.

That was strange enough to start with—only a small percentage of the suicides off the bridge weren't locals, and Martin Scherer also hadn't been from San Francisco. But stranger still was that Ben Moreno, again like Martin Scherer, had washed up on Ocean Beach, an area located on the San Francisco side of the Golden Gate Bridge. The vast majority of suicides washed up on the Marin County side of the bridge, and most of those that didn't made their way to China Beach, directly south of the bridge. To reach Ocean Beach, a body had to find its way around a corner of the peninsula that jutted out into the ocean. Highly uncommon, she'd been told by the expert she'd consulted, but not impossible. You just needed the right conditions and the right timing. How likely was it that two out-of-towners would both also happen to wash up on Ocean Beach?

Luckily, both the home address and the wash-up location of each jumper were variables she'd coded into her spreadsheet. She quickly sorted out everyone who wasn't from the San Francisco Bay Area, and found only fourteen individuals who weren't locals. Next she pulled up everyone who'd washed up on Ocean Beach, and found fifteen results.

Thirteen of those fifteen were out-of-town tourists. Which meant all except one of the non-local jumpers had washed up on Ocean Beach.

She didn't need to be a statistician to know that couldn't have happened by coincidence.

CHAPTER THREE

After a quick scan of the information on the suicide sheet, Jo located Ben Moreno's next of kin, Naya Moreno. Although listed as his wife, she had a separate address in Holyoke. Jo glanced at the time on her computer and made a quick decision. She threw her chestnut hair into a sleek ponytail and changed her clothes. A wall of sticky heat greeted her as she dashed to her Chevy Volt, and she thought wistfully of the jean shorts and T-shirt she'd just abandoned in favor of work slacks and red blouse. Hot, humid air usually reminded her of her childhood in New Orleans, but even that nostalgia lost its shine once the temperature rose past eighty-five, and the day was already pushing ninety. For the fourth day in a row.

She pulled up to Naya's apartment complex half an hour later. The clump of seven two-story red-brick boxes lined a courtyard, each facade broken up by a strip of wood paneling and balconies that could cave in at any minute. She located building D and pulled open the entryway door. Stale air tinged with urine assaulted her as she carefully threaded her way up stairs laced with ragged toys.

The door to apartment D13 opened to reveal a petite, late-twenties Latina woman in jean cut-offs and a coral tank top with a diapered baby on her hip. Jo guessed she was about nine months old.

"Naya Moreno?" Jo asked.

The woman looked her up and down with slightly narrowed eyes, and shifted the door closer to her. "Depends who's asking."

"I'm Josette Fournier from the Oakhurst County State Police Detective Unit. I'd like to talk to you about Ben Moreno."

Her expression changed from suspicious to annoyed. "You're too late. He killed himself two weeks ago."

"That's what I'd like to talk to you about. Do you mind if I ask you a few questions?"

The baby squirmed against Naya's side, dividing her focus. "What do you need to know?"

Between the antsy baby and the hostility, Jo wasn't going to get what she needed. She smiled at the little girl. "She's adorable. What's her name?"

Naya glanced at her daughter with pride and her face relaxed. "Rosa."

"How old is she?"

"Eight months. Big for her age, and very heavy."

"That's a fun time, before they learn to walk and say 'no,'" Jo said.

Naya laughed. "You got kids?"

"No, but I have two nieces. The lights of my life."

Rosa squirmed again, and let out a squeal. Naya stepped back into the living room and waved Jo in. "D'you wanna come in? I need to put her in her playpen."

"Thank you."

Jo glanced over the living room and the kitchen visible just beyond. Both were furnished sparsely with old dilapidated furniture, probably acquired at thrift stores or picked up from the side of the road. Naya pointed to a couch held together by several strips of duct tape. Jo sat cautiously.

Naya gently placed Rosa in the playpen, then sat on a stained armchair. "I'm not sure how much I can tell you, I left Bennie around six months ago, right after Rosa was born, and filed for divorce."

"Oh, sorry—you were listed in his file as his next of kin," Jo said.

Naya reached for the pacifier on the coffee table, then stuck it in the baby's mouth. "Right, yeah. His parents are dead and his sisters won't talk to him. One of them has a restraining order against him, even."

"Restraining order?"

Naya eyed her appraisingly. "Look, lemme cut to the chase. Bennie liked to beat on women. I let him get away with it for years because I thought I deserved it. But one day when Rosa was crying he slapped her, and it was like something in my head exploded. Because it's one thing to hit me, but my baby? Not while I have breath, I'm here to tell you that. So when he went to work the next day, I ran with what I could carry in a couple of suitcases. He came after me."

"Why didn't *you* get a restraining order against him?"

"What was I gonna say? I didn't take no pictures or go to the cops when he hit me, and I couldn't prove he hit the baby. She had a welt on her face, but he would have said I did it. I told him I was gonna get one, though."

"And that stopped him?"

"Nah, he just got smarter about it. Did stuff I couldn't prove, like calling me and hanging up, but from different numbers. And hang out in his car at the end of the street watching us, just far enough away I couldn't do anything. Then, about two months ago it just stopped."

"He just got tired of it?"

She laughed and rolled her eyes. "Yeah, right. I heard

through friends he started dating some chick. Fine by me if it gets the attention off me, ya know?"

"Do you know who the woman was?"

"I don't, because I didn't care. But my friends didn't know anyway. He wouldn't tell them anything about her. I guess they were on his ass about it, so he zipped up."

"It doesn't sound like he was heartbroken over the divorce— so do you know why he wanted to kill himself?"

Naya reached down to retrieve a toy Rosa had thrown out of the playpen. "No idea. At first I thought my friends were pranking me. I cussed out the man on the phone real good. Because Bennie was the kind of guy that if things weren't going well for him, he blamed *you*. I'd expect him to shoot up a mall before he'd kill *himself*."

"So he wasn't ever depressed? Had he had any bad luck, like losing his job?"

"I never saw him depressed. And if he lost his job I would have heard about it, 'cause he works for my cousin. That's how we met in the first place."

"Your cousin didn't fire him after what he did to you?"

She shrugged. "Nah. If Bennie didn't have a job, he wouldna been able to pay child support."

Jo glanced around before she could catch herself.

Naya spotted it. "Yeah, you're right—I only ever saw one payment. He had this attitude like if he didn't get to see her unsupervised he didn't have to pay. I went to the court but he went and offed himself before they could pull it out of his paycheck." She tilted her head. "Or whatever happened to him, if he didn't kill himself. My guess is he pissed off the wrong person."

"Did he have enemies?"

"Depends what you mean. Nobody special I know of, but he had a temper and never had no problems throwing a punch if he didn't like your vibe."

"I couldn't find any criminal records for him. Was he involved with sketchy people?"

She scrunched up her face. "He was an asshole, but he wasn't stupid. He wasn't trying to end up in jail. He didn't do drugs or nothing like that."

No, he got his kicks out of beating up on women. "Do you know why he went to San Francisco?"

She threw up both hands. "No clue. He never used to take me anywhere, not even to Florida to visit my aunty."

"Did he play World of Warcraft?"

Naya's brows squeezed together. "What's that?"

"It's an online game."

Her face cleared and she waved her hand in the air. "No way. He thought video games were stupid. His time went to hoops and porno."

Jo's hopes dipped—but then, just because Martin Scherer found *his* victims that way didn't mean it played a role in his own death. "Do you know what happened to Ben's belongings? Anything he left behind?"

Naya's head bobbed backwards. "Tch. He didn't leave nothing behind. A hundred-fifty in his bank account, and that's it. His landlord shoved everything into storage so she could get the apartment ready to rent by the end of the month. A couple of my cousins are gonna help me move the furniture over here so I can get rid of this crap, but they can't do it until next weekend."

"Did he leave any devices behind? Phone, tablet, laptop?" Jo's phone buzzed in her pocket, and she checked it surreptitiously. Work.

"Cell phone was on him when he jumped. But yeah, he had a laptop. Why?"

"Would you be willing to let me take a look at it?"

She laughed derisively. "Sure, if you want to sort through a big bundle of porn links. Why?"

Jo considered her answer carefully—she wasn't sure what she was dealing with. "I'd just like to be sure his death is what it seems. Would you be okay with me looking at the contents of his apartment, too?"

"Sure." But Naya's face paled, and she shot a look at Rosa. "Was he in trouble? And is that trouble gonna come after us?"

Jo put on a reassuring smile. "No, I don't think it was anything like that. Like you said, I think he may have angered the wrong person."

Naya didn't look convinced, but got up. "Hang on, I'll get you the computer."

Jo nodded, then slipped out her phone to check the full text. She was needed on a crime scene in Greenfern.

Naya reappeared, carrying a laptop and a sheet of paper. "I wrote down the password, and his landlord's name and number. Agnes Gerardi. I'll call her and let her know you're coming."

Jo rose to her feet, and pulled a card out of her pocket. "Thanks so much. If you remember anything you think might be relevant, will you let me know?"

She stared up into Jo's eyes. "You'll tell me if me and Rosa are in danger?"

Jo nodded. "If I find any reason to think you're in danger, I'll let you know immediately."

Naya took the card without saying anything more.

CHAPTER FOUR

As Jo walked back out to her car, she sent a quick text to Bob Arnett, her Oakhurst County State Police Detective Unit partner, letting him know she was heading out to the crime scene.

He responded almost immediately. *Can you pick me up on your way?*

Sure, she responded. *But why?*

Long story. Kylie's car broke down, and she borrowed mine. I don't want to take Laura's and leave her without any transportation.

That made sense; Arnett's daughter Kylie was notoriously irresponsible and his wife had a fiercely independent streak. *OMW. ETA twenty minutes.*

When Jo pulled up to Arnett's house twenty-one minutes later, Laura rose from tugging weeds out of the flowerbeds fronting their robin's-egg blue colonial, brushed off her knees and straightened her gray shorts, then headed toward Jo. A familiar confusion of feelings crept over Jo. She and Arnett had been partners and friends for twenty years, and Jo used to be friendly with Laura too. Ultimately she still was, but her fondness for Laura had been bruised when Laura cheated on him.

Not that Jo saw infidelity in black-and-white terms—it was rarely just one partner's fault when there were problems in a relationship. Arnett had owned up to his side of those problems: he'd descended into workaholism once they'd become empty nesters, and even at home had a habit of shutting down rather than talking to Laura about the stresses of the job. They'd gone through counseling and both made a continuing effort to rebuild their bond, and they'd been on a good path since.

But Jo still remembered the pain in Bob's eyes after he found out about the affair, and then when Laura asked for a divorce. She remembered the defeat in his posture, and how close she thought he'd been to giving up on everything. To this day, nearly a decade later, whenever she looked at Laura, that's what sprang to mind.

Laura reached out her arms for a hug. "Jo! How have you been?"

Jo returned the embrace. "I'm well, how are you?"

Laura's wide smile lit up her face. "Bob keeps telling me about this man you're dating. For several months now? You've even taken him for dinner at your mother's house?"

Jo smiled. "Guilty. His name's Matt. He's a good man."

Laura placed her hand on Jo's forearm. "That's what Bob said. So I told him I want us to all go out for dinner together. Maybe next weekend?"

Jo hid her surprise. "That sounds like fun, but he's covering for an injured doctor and I'm not sure how long that will last. He was supposed to be off today and Wednesday."

"Oh, if he is off Wednesday, that would be perfect. I was supposed to have my painting class, but the instructor had to cancel for the next two weeks."

"Ah, okay. I'll talk to him—"

Arnett pushed out of the front door. "Thank God I looked out the window. How long have you been here?"

Jo started to answer, but Laura beat her to it. "She just got here. I was asking her about all of us having dinner."

Arnett crossed to Laura's side, and Jo half-smiled at the odd couple they made. Laura was petite, trim, and always elegant in pastel shades that accented her pale, blonde coloring—even while gardening in ninety-degree weather. Arnett was perpetually twenty-five pounds overweight, always wrinkled, and his dark salt-and-pepper hair was unkempt even right after a haircut. Nobody would ever match them up, but here they were, still married after thirty-odd years.

Arnett leaned down and gave Laura a brief kiss. "Can't talk about it right now. We gotta move."

Jo leaned in for another brief hug. "Great to see you, Laura."

"I'll call you soon," Laura answered.

Once they'd buckled up and started down the street, Arnett turned to Jo. "Sorry about that. Don't worry, I know it's intrusive. I'll make some excuses for you."

Jo signaled her turn. "What was that about out of nowhere?"

"You used to come over for dinner now and then." Bob stared out the windshield.

When he didn't say more, Jo shot him a look.

Bob sighed, ran a hand through his hair, and glanced briefly toward the heavens. "She decided we need more couple friends."

Jo swallowed a laugh. "More?"

"Okay, *some* couple friends."

"And *I'm* what she came up with?"

He rubbed his brow. "My guess is she figures she'll have more luck asking someone I'm comfortable with. Like I said, don't worry. I know it's not your thing."

"It's not *not* my thing. And I think Matt's starting to wonder about my friends—the one time he met Eva she was in the middle of a breakdown because one of her kids was in the ER with a head injury, and the one time he met Lopez—well, let's just say he doesn't quite know what to make of her."

"Nobody quite knows what to make of Lopez."

"You'll only be able to put Laura off for so long, anyway, so let's just do it."

He searched her face. "You sure you're up for it?"

"I didn't say all *that*. But I'll give it a go."

He laughed. "Okay, then. She wants to try that French place downtown, Le Poulet Bleu. Would that work?"

"Perfect."

Bob tuned the radio to an eighties metal station. "Sorry your day with Matt got cut short, I know you were looking forward to the music festival."

"Not a problem actually. He got called in to work this morning."

"So what took so long getting to my place?"

Jo hesitated. Bob was unfailingly supportive in most areas of her life, but he'd never understood her dissatisfaction with the way the Martin Scherer case ended. Since she wasn't quite sure herself why it lurked in her psyche, she wasn't sure she was up for justifying it all. Still, she didn't want to lie to him. "I was following up a lead."

"Which case?"

She cleared her throat and kept her eyes forward. "The Martin Scherer case."

His head whipped toward her. He said nothing at first, and she knew him well enough to know he was carefully weighing his response. "Since when do we name cases after the murderer instead of the victim?"

Her shoulders tensed. "What if he was both murderer *and* victim? It never made sense that he killed himself. How many serial killers do you know who do that?"

He shrugged. "We were on to him. He probably knew it. Why is this coming up again now?"

She summarized quickly for him.

He sat a moment, considering. "So because all the Ocean Beach wash-ups were out-of-towners, something odd is going on? Maybe they just used the wrong end of the bridge."

She glared at him. "So, what, there's some secret, insider knowledge about the proper way to jump off the Golden Gate Bridge? And you're either born with it or they hand you a pamphlet as soon as you take up permanent residence there?"

"Fine, but you get what I'm saying. There could be some reason that happens to the out-of-towners."

"Exactly my point. There's a reason it happens to them and only them, and I want to find out what that reason is."

He held up both hands. "Fair enough. But the ex-wife's say-so isn't reason enough to believe he wasn't suicidal."

"That's why I want to take a look at the computer, and at his belongings. Don't worry, I'm doing it off the clock. Purely my own issue."

Bob scowled. "Oh, stop. You know I'll back you up. But I'm also gonna tell you when I think you're pissing in the wind."

"I appreciate that." Jo signaled a turn.

"But don't let Lieutenant Hayes catch you doing it." Arnett didn't make eye contact.

For the past nine years, the Oakhurst County State Police Detective Unit had struggled to keep a permanent lieutenant in place, and interim lieutenants had come and gone on a regular basis. Two months before, Lieutenant Lindsay Hayes had been promoted away from a department in upstate New York, and had wreaked all brands of havoc since arriving, including an odd insistence that she be updated immediately about new investigations. And, for reasons Jo didn't understand, Hayes had it in for her and didn't care who knew it.

"That's why I'm doing it on my own." She pointed down the street. "And if I'm not much mistaken, that's our crime scene."

CHAPTER FIVE

Jo soaked in the upper-middle-class neighborhood as she slid behind two patrols parked in front of a large three-story white neo-Victorian, complete with wrap-around porch. She remembered coming out to Greenfern as a teenager to pick apples from the orchards, but much of that land had now been turned into generous parcels surrounding beautiful, mostly modest, homes. Many didn't have fences and were separated only by plentiful trees and shrubs, but this particular property, and several of those neighboring it, also had an eight-foot chain-link fence. Not only was it easing the job of securing the scene for the responding officers, it also limited the perpetrator's possible escape route. A line of crime scene tape faced the road, while a second secured the front of the house set back across the vast lawn.

"Ugh, I'm already sweating." Bob slammed the car door and tugged at his collar. Jo grimaced her agreement, and tried to put it out of her mind.

They walked up to the officer guarding the outer perimeter, a tall, solid, brown-haired white man whose nameplate identified him as *H. Stromm*. She introduced herself and Bob. "What are we looking at?"

"Occupant, Melissa Rollins, didn't show up for her daughter's soccer game this morning. Rollins' friend, Tinsley Sparks, also has a daughter who plays on the team, and was worried when the daughter and the ex-husband showed up but Melissa didn't." He nodded toward a patrol car where an officer was trying to calm an early-thirties white woman with huge brown eyes and an anemic blonde ponytail. "After the game she came to check on her, and when she saw Rollins' car in the driveway but nobody answered the door, she called us in hysterics to do a welfare check because supposedly Ms. Rollins would never miss her daughter's game."

Jo winced at the use of 'hysterics.'

"We contacted the ex-husband, still half owner of the house, who agreed this wasn't usual for her. Front and back doors both locked, so we forced an entry. As we cleared the premises, we smelled decomp. We followed it to a dead woman inside a closet, partially bound."

"Is the ME in there?" Jo asked.

"Dr. Keyes was here but had to hurry out, the ME's office is overwhelmed with the hot-weather crime spike. I'll never understand why people lose their minds when the weather gets hot. He was just here long enough to determine the death'd have to be investigated as a homicide. As if we couldn't already see that for ourselves. Techs arrived before he did."

Jo nodded. "Thanks, we'll head on in."

"I'd recommend an anti-putrefaction if you have one."

Jo shot a look back at the trunk of her Chevy Volt. She always kept a basic kit with enough gear for her and Arnett, but the thought of putting on a restrictive mask in ninety-degree heat was deeply unappealing.

Arnett must have felt the same. "We've dealt with decaying bodies before."

"You've been warned." Stromm looked amused as he lifted the tape to allow them to duck under. "Third floor."

———

Jo and Arnett followed the gravel driveway that led across the vast lawn, then circled the blue Toyota Sienna.

"Thin layer of dust." Arnett pointed to the windshield. "Hasn't been driven anytime recently."

The gravel turned to crazy-paved slate stones that led to the porch, which responding officers had used as the demarcation for the inner perimeter. After Jo and Arnett kitted themselves in PPE, another officer, an Asian woman whose nameplate identified her as *A. Park*, led them into the house.

Jo didn't realize she'd been expecting a blast of cool air when they entered until the opposite happened—a wave of stuffy, oppressive heat and the stench of decay hit her lungs and attached like a lead vest. As they made their way to the third floor, she examined the interior. Clean in a way that spoke to the neat-freak in her, the rooms simultaneously alienated her— they weren't decorated, they were *appointed*, and the pastel color schemes looked like they'd attract whatever dirt by magical magnetic force. It took her back to her mother's 'parlor,' a room reserved for visitors that was never *ever* to be played in. They'd had a similar parlor in New Orleans before her parents' divorce, and Jo could remember standing in the doorway as a child staring at the perfectly spaced furniture, feeling sad for the tables and chairs because they must be lonely.

"Get ready," Park muttered before turning and heading back down.

As they turned onto the third floor landing, Jo spotted Janet Marzillo, head of the Oakhurst County SPDU's crime-scene investigator lab, kneeling carefully in front of a closet. Hakeem Peterson, who'd already distinguished himself despite having been with the lab less than a year, was hanging back, assisting Marzillo as needed.

"Fournier. Arnett." He nodded his head in acknowledgement.

Marzillo turned and stood. "I guess you two got called in on your weekend off, too?"

"Yep. Did Zelda manage to get moved back in okay?" Jo asked. Marzillo had briefly broken up with her long-term partner, but they'd recently reconciled.

"Mostly. That was the only good thing about getting called in today—I didn't have to help unpack the boxes."

Jo half-smiled and stepped forward toward the huddled figure half-leaning in the closet. The smile disappeared and her stomach turned as another intense wave of decomp hit her, this one tinged with urine. The woman appeared to be average height, although the cramped position of her body made it hard to judge. She wore business attire, a red button-down shirt and a knee-length black skirt. Puddles of urine had crystallized on the floor, and her hands and feet were crusted with blood. Her brown hair, once twisted into a tight chignon, now flailed tendrils into a lopsided lump. Red lipstick and mascara smeared her face. Her eyes were closed as if sleeping, but both her expression and posture had a strained quality, as though she was having a disturbing dream. Jo was flooded by an impulse to wake her, to end the nightmare and assure her everything would be okay—but it wasn't, and it never would be again.

"What are we looking at?" she asked.

Marzillo gestured toward the woman. "Late thirties Caucasian victim identified as Melissa Rollins, lives here with her daughter. Hands bound, gag around her neck. Feet aren't now but were at some point, based on the marks on her ankles and a zip tie we found in here that had been chewed through. She pointed toward the evidence as she cataloged it. "Antemortem shoulder dislocation and abrasions on her feet, but no other injuries we can detect so far."

"So she was alive when the killer put her in here?" Jo asked.

"Most definitely. Take a look at this." She pointed to the inside of the door, which was now open and flush against the wall.

"Blood smears?" Arnett asked.

"Yes. I have to do some testing, but there's blood on her feet and the smears seem to be at about the same height she'd reach trying to kick the door down. Then there's this." She pointed to gouges around the edge of the door.

Jo leaned in to examine them more carefully. "Is that part of a fingernail?"

Marzillo nodded. "Yes."

"She tried to claw her way out?" Arnett asked.

"Looks like. There's matter under her nails that seems to match the wood on the door. And, whoever put her in here was motivated to make sure she couldn't get out. Despite locking the door, they also wedged that chair under the knob"—she gestured toward a chair covered with fingerprint powder, then to a pile of nails by the wainscot—"and nailed the door in place along the side and the bottom."

Peterson chimed in. "The responding officer said it took them almost an hour to get the door open."

Jo peered at the knob's backplate. "There's no way to unlock it from the inside. Isn't there normally some sort of safety mechanism to prevent people getting trapped?"

"In newer homes like this, usually," Peterson said.

Arnett stepped over to the nearby bedroom door, then leaned out to look at the other doors along the hall. "It's a different style entirely from the other hardware in here."

Jo looked Melissa over a second time. "Do we have any idea what the cause of death is?"

"There's nothing obvious I can see, although once we remove her we may find more. Based on the attempts to free herself and the urine everywhere, I'd guess she was alive in here for a fair amount of time. Hours definitely, maybe days. Given she's relatively young, the three hypotheses that spring to mind are that she died because she needed some sort of medication she didn't have, she had some sort of heart attack or stroke due to the heat in here, or she died of dehydration. And I'm leaning toward dehydration because of the emaciation—see how her eyes are slightly sunken into her skull?"

That was it, that was what Jo had reacted to—Melissa reminded her of pictures she'd seen of people who died of starvation or extreme conditions.

"How long would she have to be in there to die of dehydration?" Arnett asked.

Marzillo wagged her head. "That depends on a lot of factors. People have been known to last as long as a couple of weeks under ideal conditions. Under typical conditions, I'd say about a week to ten days. Far faster when it's hot, and it's sweltering in here. You can dehydrate in hours under conditions like these, especially if you have compromised health."

"What an agonizing way to die," Jo said.

"Not how I'd want to go," Marzillo agreed.

"So what, this is some sort of burglary gone very wrong?" Arnett's hands settled on his hips. "Someone broke in, locked her up not realizing she had a condition that needed medication?"

Marzillo pointed to the pile of nails by the side of the door. "Why nail the door closed in that case? Far faster to just grab what you want and go."

Jo squatted to examine the nail holes. "No, this wasn't a spur of the moment decision. You don't just decide to find some nails and a hammer and shut someone in a closet."

Arnett shook his head. "But why not just shoot her or

strangle her? Why risk she'll survive long enough to be rescued?"

"Interesting point." Jo stood back up. "Maybe they thought she *would* be rescued?"

"Why nail someone into a closet if you expect them to be rescued?" Peterson asked.

The four of them stared silently at each other, but nobody had an answer. Jo broke the silence. "Any idea how long she's been dead?"

"I'll have to do some calculations given the ambient temperature in here, but my off-the-cuff guess is about twenty-four to thirty-six hours based on the decomposition. That's taking into account the temperature acceleration, but it still might be a little less than that," Marzillo said.

Jo considered. "I'm not sure how much that really tells us anyway, if she was alive when her killer put her inside. We need to know when the initial event occurred. I'm guessing there aren't any clues to that?"

"That'll be extremely hard to narrow down. Once the ME gets a look at her medical history and gets back the blood and urine work, we may be able to take some educated guesses, but they'll still be guesses."

"Then we need something else to help us narrow it down." Jo looked up and down the hall. "Anything else we should know before we check out the rest of the house?"

Marzillo shook her head. "We'll be awhile up here, but Peterson already took pictures of the rest of the house, and we did a 3D scan."

"That was fast," Jo said.

Peterson shrugged. "You'll see why."

CHAPTER SIX

As Jo and Arnett checked each room, Peterson's point landed—
it was fast and easy to spot anything out of place when nothing
was. The third floor contained a guest bedroom, bathroom, and
some sort of piano music room, complete with sheet music on
the rack. The second floor had a master bedroom suite, another
guest room and bathroom, and a young girl's room.

"This must be the daughter's," Arnett said.

Jo peered in. "Based on the Barbie Dreamhouse and the
unicorn theme, I'm guessing she's not a teenager yet." She
crossed to the closet and opened the door. "But not too far off of
it, based on the size of these clothes." Like the rest of the house,
the room was too pristine, without a single object out of place.
Did the daughter take after the mother? She bent to look more
closely at the dollhouse and realized no—the contents were scattered and disorganized. An odd feeling she couldn't quite identify crept over her as they exited the room and made their way
to the first floor.

"Finally, signs of life." Jo pointed to a bag of takeout
containers on the dining-room table, next to a briefcase and a
cell phone. Once they processed the phone and the briefcase

and changed to fresh gloves, she carefully opened the containers. "Soup and spring rolls, both with a lovely topping of mold."

Arnett shot a series of pictures as she lifted the containers out and placed them onto the table. "There we go. Credit card receipt in the bottom of the bag," he said.

Jo waited for him to photograph it. "Tuesday at six o'clock, from a restaurant called Pho and Away. My guess is she got off work, picked up dinner, then came home but never got a chance to eat."

"Narrows things down considerably. Whatever happened must have taken place after six fifteen, six thirty, depending on how far away the restaurant is. Unless she wasn't planning on eating until later."

Jo pointed toward the kitchen. "If that was the case, she'd have put the food in the refrigerator. And she was still wearing her work clothes. The first thing I do when I get home is change."

"So probably looking at between six-fifteen and seven, then. Hopefully one of the neighbors saw or heard something."

Jo's face scrunched. "I'm not too optimistic about that with all the shrubs and trees around the lot. And, look, Park is talking to another officer right outside the window, and I can't hear a word they're saying. This house is solid."

"Yeah, but if she was kicking and clawing at the door, she'd have been yelling for help, too. Whole other ball of wax."

"Let's test it. Hang out here for a minute." Jo trotted up to the third floor, warned Marzillo and Peterson what she was going to do, then shut herself into the guest bedroom. She screamed as loudly as she could, then returned to the dining room where Arnett waited.

"Did you hear anything?" she asked.

"Not a peep."

Jo nodded. "So someone screaming upstairs wouldn't be

heard even downstairs, let alone outside. She could have screamed herself hoarse and nobody would have heard."

They moved carefully through the rest of the first floor—office, living room, some sort of conservatory that had been transformed into a morning room—but found nothing relevant.

As they turned into the entry hall, Jo peered at the thermostat. "The heat is turned up to ninety-five degrees."

"You sure that's not just the temperature reading?" Arnett's brows raised as he checked. "No way that's a mistake, nobody in their right mind has their heat on in this weather. Even in winter, who heats their house to ninety-five degrees?"

Jo's stomach flipped again. "So somebody purposefully locked Melissa in the closet *and* upped the heat. That sounds like a very personal agenda."

"I'll make sure Peterson dusts it for prints," Arnett said.

Jo glanced at the front door. "Stromm said both front and back doors were locked. So how did they get in?"

Arnett stepped back along the hall toward the stairs. "Either way, dragging her up those stairs all the way to the third floor would take considerable muscle."

"So a man or a very fit woman," Jo said.

"Or two people working together."

————

Jo and Arnett backtracked to the kitchen, then exited onto the back porch. Jo enjoyed the ironic drop in temperature as she surveyed the thick bushes and trees surrounding the property. "Pretty safe to say none of the neighbors can see back here."

Arnett looked down. "Lawn trimmed nice and close, so no footprints."

They circled the house, looking for any disturbance to the landscaping as they went. When they reached the front, Jo continued out to the driveway and stood behind the blue

Toyota. "Killer could have parked here. I can't see any of the houses except the one directly opposite, so they're the only ones who'd be able to see a strange car here. If our killer came on foot, they'd be even less likely to be seen."

"We could get lucky, someone may have seen a strange car turning in or driving down the street, or someone on foot." His expression was skeptical.

"We'll send some uniforms to canvas regardless." Jo pointed to the house across the street. "But I'd like to talk to *them* myself."

As they approached the facing house, the front-window curtains twitched. But when Jo rang the bell, the only response was the yapping of a small dog, and she had to ring a second time before a human answered.

The door finally opened to reveal a tall Asian man in his mid-fifties dressed in business casual attire, looking harried and trying to avoid tripping over the beige toy poodle threading through his legs. "Help you?" he grunted.

Jo introduced herself and Arnett, and explained why they were there.

"I haven't seen anything, but my wife might've. I could've sworn she was just in here." He turned and called into the house. "Chandra?"

A petite white woman in a tunic and yoga pants appeared behind him and made a show of wiping her hands with a kitchen towel. "Yes?"

"These detectives want to know if you saw anything weird over at the Rollins' house this past week."

"Particularly Tuesday night," Jo said.

"Tuesday night?" Chandra's brow furrowed, and she peered over Jo's shoulder. "No, I wasn't here, I play Bunko with my friends on Tuesdays. And it's been quiet all week. It usually is when Avery's staying with her father."

Jo hid her surprise. "You know her daughter's custody schedule."

Chandra shrugged. "Avery brings treats for Roxy on the Thursday nights she's here when she brings the garbage cans out to the curb, right before she goes to her dance class." She pointed down at the poodle.

Jo's brows popped up—nothing got by Chandra. "She sounds like a sweet girl."

Chandra nodded absently, glancing over Jo's shoulder again. "Why are you asking? Is everything okay?"

Jo kept her face neutral—if Chandra hadn't been watching every move out of the window, she'd quit detective tomorrow. "There's been an incident at the Rollins' house. Can you tell me the last time you remember seeing Melissa?"

Her eyes widened and she made a show of considering her answer. "I guess Monday around six thirty? I got back from the grocery store just as she got home, and I waved to her. I remember thinking she looked angry."

"Angry? Did she say why?" Arnett asked.

"Oh, I didn't speak to her. Just waved from the driveway. I don't think she saw me, because she didn't wave back."

They continued to press, but Chandra hadn't noticed anything else. Jo left a card with her, and they crossed back toward Melissa's house. Arnett nodded toward Tinsley, who was watching them pointedly from the car. "Ready to have a chat with her friend? Hopefully she can give us some sort of insight."

"I hope so, because I'm searching the darkest corners of my mind but can't come up with any reason why you'd kill someone by nailing them into an overheated closet to die a slow, painful death."

CHAPTER SEVEN

When Jo and Arnett approached the patrol car holding Tinsley Sparks, she jumped out and launched herself at them, brown eyes wild, tugging at the tan linen shorts stuck to her legs.

"*He* did this to her. Travis, her husband." She shook a bottle of water at them to emphasize her points. "I *knew* he was an asshole, but I never thought he'd go *this* far. You need to go arrest him, *now*."

Jo had seen just about every flavor of shock that existed over the years, and this one was all too common. She raised a hand and put on a serious, reassuring expression. "Officer Stromm mentioned you were the one who called in about Melissa Rollins? Can you walk us through what happened?"

Tinsley's arms crossed in a gesture that made clear it was *about time* they asked. "Melissa's daughter Avery plays on the same soccer team as my Heidi, and Melissa *never* misses a game. Not once, not even when she had a tooth abscess, because she takes—took—careful notes on Avery's performance. We're friends, and both our girls are in the same fourth grade class at Highland Elementary, so if something had come up she would have texted or called. But she didn't."

Jo weighed Tinsley's level of animation. "Of course."

"I called her several times and she didn't answer, and that's not like her either. So I came over here to see what was going on. The car was here"—she pointed to the blue Toyota Sienna in the driveway—"so when I rang the bell about a hundred times and got no answer, I called the police."

A vision of the doorbell short-circuiting as Tinsley stabbed at it flashed through Jo's mind.

"When was the last time you heard from her?" Arnett asked.

"At the game last week. We chatted while the girls played, then we all got ice cream together before she dropped Avery off with Travis." Her face contracted like she had a mouth full of lemon.

"You didn't talk to her at all during the week?"

A slight flush of red crept over her cheeks. "She works overtime most days when Avery is gone to make some extra money. Divorce isn't cheap."

"So Avery was at the game today with Travis?" Jo asked.

Tinsley glanced from her to Arnett, then back again. "Yes, Travis. The one who did this. Melissa has her for a week, then Travis has her for a week. This was Travis' week."

"Did Avery happen to mention when the last time she heard from her mother was?"

Tinsley shifted her weight. "Melissa isn't supposed to contact her when Travis has her unless it's an emergency, and vice versa. Avery can call them whenever she wants to, but she usually doesn't because she doesn't want anyone getting angry."

Jo watched Tinsley carefully. "That seems odd. Why would they agree to something like that?"

Tinsley's face twisted with anger. "She didn't agree, it was *forced* on her. From the minute she filed for divorce he set out to destroy her."

Arnett's pen flashed in Jo's periphery. She raised her hand. "Destroy her how?"

Tinsley's head shook back and forth incredulously. "Every single way he could think of. But the most vile, disgusting one was he accused her of child abuse. Divorce lawyers tell them to do that, you know—there's even some name for it. If you think you're gonna lose custody, accuse your spouse of child abuse. Just absolutely despicable."

Jo had heard of the strategy before, but usually as a way to combat a partner who'd leveled their own accusations of child abuse. "And the judge believed him without evidence?"

"Oh, that's the really evil part of it. He twisted the truth so there was enough reality to make her look like she was just making excuses. And he made sure it all got into *The Greenfern Daily*, so the whole town knew about it. A lot of people in town turned on her after that."

That surprised Jo—newspapers were fairly vigilant about avoiding lawsuits. "He got the paper to print things that weren't true?" Jo asked.

Tinsley stiffened, and her hands dropped to her hips. "They finessed it. Melissa has high standards for Avery, and what's wrong with that? She wanted Avery to *make* something of herself. So Travis accused her of being a quote-unquote *Tiger Mom*, saying her demands were psychologically abusive, and that she punished Avery unfairly. Total BS. The world is a competitive place, and you don't get ahead by sitting around playing video games all day. A parent's job is to prepare their child for life, *not* to be best friends with their kids."

As a lifelong overachiever, Jo understood both the impulse to reach for success and the downsides that came along with it. "But the judge must have had doubts if he granted joint custody."

Tinsley jabbed her finger in the air. "Oh, *no no no*, that was only after a battle royale with the Lawyer From Hell. Travis and his attorney took Avery away from her completely for four months. But she fought tooth and nail and his lies fell apart. She only *just* got Avery back, and Travis has been raging about it. I knew he'd do *something*, but I never thought he'd *kill* her." Tears sprung into her eyes. "You have to do something. You have to go arrest him."

Jo needed to refocus her. "We'll talk to him as soon as we're done here. But I have a few other questions I need to ask you first."

She wiped the tears from her face with one hand, and nodded. "Okay."

"Did Melissa's other friends know about all of this?"

The question seemed to surprise Tinsley. "Between working and taking care of Avery, she didn't have a lot of time for friends. I was really her only one. It's not easy you know, raising a child well. Making sure they do their homework and study for tests and practice their instruments. People don't get that, how hard it is on the parents, at least if you take it seriously."

Jo grimaced sympathetically. "What kind of work did she do?"

"She was a pharmaceutical representative. The kind that takes samples of meds out to different doctors."

"What company did she work for?"

Tinsley's brow creased. "I'm not sure."

"Did she complain at all about work, any issues she had there?"

Tinsley shifted her weight. "Not really, just normal stuff."

Jo pressed. "No problems with co-workers or anything like that?"

Tinsley's eyes narrowed. "Not that I'm aware of. Look, you're not listening to me. I'm telling you, Travis did this."

Jo recalibrated—she needed Tinsley to engage with her questions without feeling discounted. "I appreciate your patience with our questions, I know this has to be hard on you. He'll be the very next person we talk to. But we have to make sure we do a thorough investigation, otherwise we'll never be able to prosecute effectively."

Tinsley's anger ebbed slightly. "Right, I understand. But no, I don't know of anybody who would want to hurt Melissa. She was good at her job and she was very involved in everything at the girls' school." Her tears welled up again. "Always volunteering, always trying to help. She was loved."

Jo hid her frustration. Tinsley had shifted into hagiography —she wasn't going to get any more out of her. She reached into her pocket for a card. "Thank you so much for your help. If you think of anything we should know about, please call us."

Tinsley stared down at the card. "Will you let me know when you arrest Travis? I'll sleep better at night knowing he's behind bars."

"Has he threatened you?" Arnett asked.

"No, not me personally. But I personally heard him threaten to kill Melissa if she ever even raised her voice to Avery again."

———

As Tinsley sped away from the house, she tried to put a label on what she felt. Squirrelly, that was the closest she could come to capturing it. Like if someone whispered boo to her, she'd jump out of her skin.

Which is almost exactly what happened when her phone chimed.

She steered with one hand while she checked the text. A single question mark.

Her heel tapped frantically as she continued down the road. She had no confidence in her ability to fool anyone about anything. In high school when she'd tried out for the lead in the school play, she'd only been given a small speaking part—she could still remember the tears pricking her eyes as she stared at the casting sheet. The faculty sponsor had tried to reassure her: *Keep trying, it was actually quite good for a freshman to get a speaking part at all, nothing good ever comes without work and practice.* So Tinsley had tried again, but the same thing happened the next year. And the year after that. The story of her life—good, but not quite good enough, no matter how hard she tried.

So all she could do was hope she had enough basic acting skill to see her through this. Most of what she'd said was the truth, after all.

When she finally hit a red light, she typed her response, thumbs shaking: *Did my best. All I can do is hope she doesn't tell anyone.*

Tinsley stared down at the three dancing dots until the reply came through. *Why would she? She doesn't have reason to think it's related.*

Tinsley tossed the phone onto the seat and pulled back into the road, praying that was true.

CHAPTER EIGHT

Travis Rollins lived on the other side of Greenfern in an apartment complex that, painted as it was in industrial beige with rust accents, reminded Jo of a low-priced hotel chain. Cracked cement paths cut through patchy rectangles of grass, and external walkways led to each of the apartments.

"I'm guessing Melissa got the house in the divorce." Arnett firmly shut the passenger door behind him. "I'd be pissed too if I had to live here."

"No, it wouldn't be my first choice, either." A child's shriek rent the air, and Jo turned toward it. "But hey. It has a pool." She motioned toward the chain-link fence surrounding the small, leaf-ridden rectangle of water and the handful of children splashing in it. A single adult sat on a rusty, towel-draped lounge chair, her attention in a book.

Arnett shook his head as they continued through to Travis Rollins' apartment. When they knocked, the door opened to reveal a tall, lean white man in his late forties, whose proud demeanor and tailored suit were completely discordant with the surroundings. "Travis Rollins?" Jo asked.

"No. I'm Tom Fischer, Mr. Rollins' attorney. And you are?"

Jo shot Arnett a look—it hadn't taken Rollins long to get lawyered up—then introduced them both to Fischer. "We're investigating Melissa Rollins' death. We have a few questions we'd like to ask your client. Can we come in?"

"Please." Fischer waved them in.

The main room of the apartment split into a living room, dining room, and attached kitchen. A blue sofa dominated one half while a white laminate table dominated the other; the only decor on any of the walls or surfaces were a trio of small pictures featuring a girl in dance costumes. A square fan oscillated in the corner, moving thick air pointlessly around the room. The late-thirties white man hunched over the table had a generic, likeable, everyman appeal, thanks to the red shirt that set off his brown hair and brown eyes, and the hint of a sunburn splashed across his cheeks. The effect was ruined when his tongue darted across his lips.

"This is Travis Rollins," Fischer said.

Jo began to restate the introductions, but Rollins stopped her. "It's okay, I heard you at the door. You're here about Melissa. Please, sit down." Rollins gestured to the chairs across the table. Fischer sat next to him.

Jo expressed their condolences, then glanced down the hall that led to three closed doors. "Is Avery here?"

"She's with my sister. I didn't want her to hear this, she's in shock as it is. The officer that called with the news wouldn't tell us anything. What happened?"

"We can't release any details yet. We can only confirm that Melissa is dead, and that foul play was involved."

The blood drained from his face. He looked at Fischer, who nodded, and he continued. "I have an alibi—Avery and I went out for breakfast with my family, and then we went to her soccer game. And all day yesterday she and I were at Six Flags with two of her friends." He pushed forward several pieces of paper toward her. "That's the friends' parents' contact information, along with the receipts for everything."

He was so well prepared, he must have been a boy scout—but was he prepared for what was coming next? Jo watched Travis' face, and Fischer's in her periphery, carefully. "Where were you Tuesday evening?"

Travis balked. "Tues— Tuesday? What does it matter where I was Tuesday?" He turned to Fischer, who seemed as surprised as he was.

"Please answer the question." Arnett didn't beat around the bush once attorneys were involved.

Fischer motioned to Travis, who leaned and whispered his answer in Fischer's ear. Fischer nodded, and Travis' gaze shifted toward Arnett. "I was here, with Avery. I picked her up and took her to dance class, and waited there until she finished at five thirty. On the way home I picked up pizza from Pizza Palace, then after we ate I helped her with her homework—"

"She had homework in the summer?" Arnett asked.

"She goes to a supplemental program during the summer. Melissa's hoping—hoped—she'd get enough ahead to skip a grade and get into college sooner." Travis shook his head in disgust.

"And what did you do after that?"

"We watched a movie before she went to bed at ten."

"What movie?" Arnett asked.

"*Frozen*. It's her favorite."

"We'll need to confirm with Avery," Jo said. Not that it would mean much—most daughters would lie to protect their fathers, especially when their other parent had just died.

Fischer responded. "We can arrange that once the initial shock of her mother's death has passed."

Jo shifted in her seat—she couldn't get a read on Travis

while he was sitting in his lawyer's lap. She shifted gears. "You're aware that it was Tinsley Sparks who alerted the police that Melissa wasn't at the game?"

Travis' jaw flexed. "Yes. She was upset when Melissa didn't show up to the game."

"You weren't?" Arnett asked.

Fischer took over seamlessly. "Of course he was concerned. But Mr. and Mrs. Rollins went through a very volatile divorce and were still embroiled in a volatile custody dispute. They'd both been instructed to minimize contact as much as possible. They try not to even call Avery when it isn't their custody week, so as not to antagonize one another."

So Tinsley had been right about that. "Our understanding is Avery was initially taken away from Melissa, but the judge changed the order to shared custody."

"We felt that decision was premature," Fischer said.

"Tinsley mentioned there were accusations of abuse?" Jo asked.

Travis' chin rose slightly. "Her abuse is the reason I sued for full custody."

"She beat Avery?"

Fischer nodded to allow Travis to continue. "Beatings aren't the only way to abuse a child."

"Psychological abuse, then?" Jo asked.

Travis leaned toward her, face animated. "Oh, for sure psychological abuse, but that doesn't really capture what she did. Nothing was ever good enough for Melissa. She had to be the best at everything she did, top seller at work, best parent at Avery's school, which isn't bad in itself. Her work ethic was one of the reasons I fell in love with her. But from almost the day Avery was born, she put the same expectations onto her. Tried to teach her sign language before she could speak, claiming it was somehow better for her brain and would give her an edge up. Then flash cards as soon as she *could* speak. Avery would get frustrated and break down and cry. When I told Melissa I thought it was ridiculous, she went off on me, screaming about how Avery's brain was growing every day, and it was up to us to stimulate as much of that growth as possible."

That also tracked with what Tinsley had told them. "That doesn't sound pleasant, but it also doesn't sound like abuse," Jo said.

His eyes flashed. "Sure, and I backed off for that very reason. I figured ultimately it wouldn't *hurt* Avery, and I made sure she did fun things to offset it. But it all got worse as Avery got older. Melissa would ground her if she got a 'bad' grade on a test, or take away her favorite toy, or make her do extra chores, and by 'bad' I mean a B+. When those punishments stopped working, she turned to physical ones—making her kneel bare-legged on grains of rice on the hardwood floor, making her clean the bathroom with a toothbrush. And I'm embarrassed to say I let a lot of things go that I shouldn't have for far too long, because I just didn't know what to do. Melissa always justified it all, claiming Avery was lucky to have a mother who cared about her future, and would turn out spoiled and undisciplined and would have no future if I had my way."

"I see," Jo said. There wasn't anything wrong with wanting a good life for your child. The question was, how far was Melissa willing to take that?

Travis continued. "The end for me came when I got home early one day and found Avery upstairs sobbing while playing piano—because she'd peed all over herself. Melissa was sitting next to her in the room, watching her play, knowing full well what had happened. I turned on her and asked what the hell was going on, and she said that until Avery played the song right, she wasn't allowed to get up. No food, no water, no bathroom."

Jo struggled to keep her face neutral. That unquestionably veered into abusive—if it was true.

"I was completely floored, I didn't even know what to say. I told Avery to stop playing, but Melissa screamed at her that she better not stop, that she was messing up on purpose, that she knew how to play the piece and was just being stubborn..." He paused as his throat closed for a moment and his eyes filled with tears. "I pushed past her—I had to literally pick Avery up off the bench and carry her into her room to get her to stop playing, that's how terrified she was of Melissa. So, no, she never literally beat Avery that I saw, but what do you call it when someone terrifies their child to the point where they piss themselves?"

Jo nodded. "So if a judge determined that Melissa was abusive, how did she get her custodial rights restored?"

"I spent every dime I had on Tom here, because this is his specialty. The judge gave us full custody pending a more complete investigation. But then Melissa hired her own top-notch attorney, and she convinced the judge I was exaggerating and lying."

Fischer took over. "The judge felt a mother deserves the benefit of the doubt when there's no overt proof of physical abuse. And here we are."

Jo cleared her throat. "Tinsley said Avery is in the fourth grade, so she'd be about ten, right? Couldn't she just tell the judge what happened?"

Fischer spread his hands out in a who-knows gesture. "You'd think. But the subjective element to this type of abuse clouds things quickly. Melissa claimed Avery had been wanting to quit piano, and was angry that Melissa wouldn't let her. She claimed Avery just wanted to stay with Travis because he was more lenient."

Jo took stock. She generally had a reasonable feel for the truth of a story by the time she'd heard both sides, but this got more complicated the more she heard. "Surely with her father as a witness to Avery's testimony, that must have counted for something?"

Travis cleared his throat and looked down again.

Something clicked in Jo's brain. "Tinsley said *Melissa* filed for divorce. Why?"

Fischer paused, then answered. "Travis cheated on her."

CHAPTER NINE

Arnett broke the silence. "Let me get this straight. You cheated on your wife, and because of that, she filed for divorce. Then, coincidentally, after watching your wife abuse your daughter for ten years, you just happened to decide it was time to report her to the Department of Children and Family Services?"

Travis turned an impressive shade of puce, but Fischer held up his hand to prevent his response. "The piano-practice event precipitated Mr. Rollins' report. It happened two days before Mrs. Rollins filed for divorce, and we believe she used Mr. Rollins' infidelity as an excuse to act preemptively. She knew Mr. Rollins intended to take action against her."

"Did Travis tell anyone about his intentions to contact DCF before Melissa took action?" Jo asked, hoping some sort of confirmation would help untangle the morass.

"He did not. He kept his family business private while he chose his course of action. And with no contemporaneous evidence of his intention, Mrs. Rollins' attorney argued in court that Travis' motive was revenge."

"With apparent success," Arnett said.

Fischer spread his palms out. "Just because it works doesn't mean it's true."

"And the fact is," Travis blurted, "the reason the affair happened was the abuse had destroyed our relationship. I'd tried to talk to her multiple times about the way she treated Avery—"

Fischer raised his hand again and shot Travis an intense look. "Mr. Rollins knows his affair wasn't the best way to deal with the stress in his marriage. But adultery is far from murder."

"Was the best way to deal with that stress going to *The Greenfern Daily*'s crime and corruption section with allegations of abuse?" Jo asked.

Travis shot forward. "I did *not* go to *The Daily*. Do you really think I want Avery to have to deal with that at school and everywhere else?"

"Then who did?" Arnett asked.

"I don't know." Travis looked away. "Ask Rick Burke, he's the one who wrote the column."

"And I'm guessing you didn't have any witnesses to your wife's abuse?" Arnett's question was a bullet.

"We didn't," Fischer answered for Travis. "Mrs. Rollins was careful about what she did in front of whom. And of course she provided a character witness, Tinsley Sparks. But just because nobody witnessed discipline that rose to the level of abuse doesn't mean it never happened."

"Tinsley," Travis snarled the name, and blew out a derisive puff of air. "Tinsley would swear that Vlad the Impaler was a humanitarian pacifist if it would get her what she wanted."

"And what did she want?" Arnett asked.

"What *didn't* she want? A job, first and foremost, since her husband lost his at the end of last year. I heard her ask Melissa about open positions at Gantry Pharma more than once. But other stupid little things, too, like positioning in the Highland summer showcase. Melissa oversaw it three years in a row and there's always a handful of mothers who kiss up to her to make sure their darlings get the slots they want."

"So Tinsley testified to curry favor with Melissa?" Arnett asked.

Fischer waved his hand. "Mr. Rollins isn't accusing anyone of anything, he's just providing information about Melissa's personal life in an attempt to be helpful."

Jo shifted gears. "Okay, then, who else had reason to want Melissa dead?"

Travis laughed, an ugly bark that almost made Jo jump. "Well, she never kept friends for very long, so that tells you something. And she was always on Avery's teachers' and administrators' cases about something—the classes weren't hard enough, there wasn't enough homework, they weren't giving Avery the attention she deserved."

The insinuations didn't sit right with Jo. "She has Tinsley, isn't she a friend?"

"Not a 'friend' as much as an understudy. Tinsley's just as type-A as Melissa, but isn't nearly as good at keeping her balls in the air. They have the same approach to parenting, so of course she idolizes Melissa's methods."

"She abuses her daughter?" Jo asked.

"I have no idea. I doubt Melissa told her about the *really* harsh things she did. But for the rest, the expectations about grades and extracurriculars, Tinsley raises her daughter exactly the same way."

"So you can't think of anybody specific who'd want Melissa dead?" Jo said.

Travis rubbed his eyes in frustration. "No. Isn't some sort of break-in the most likely answer?"

Jo stood up and Arnett followed suit. "We'll need to speak with Avery as soon as that's possible. Would sometime tomorrow work for you?"

Travis glanced at Fischer, who answered. "Avery gets home

from her summer tutoring at two. I can be here at two thirty tomorrow afternoon, and Travis works from home. Will that work?"

Jo nodded. "I appreciate the flexibility. What sort of work do you do, Mr. Rollins?"

"I'm an administrator for a medical insurance company. I work half the time from the office and half from home, which allows me to take care of Avery most of the time."

Jo nodded. "Right. Thank you. And if you think of anyone who might have wanted to hurt your wife, please let us know."

———

"What'd you think about all that?" Arnett asked Jo as they left Travis Rollins' apartment.

Jo took a deep breath. "I'm getting very conflicting messages. Both Tinsley and Travis are vehement and emotional —they're both genuinely upset, but I'm not sure about the source of the emotion. In Travis' case, maybe Melissa really did do those things, and he really was horrified and protecting his daughter. Or maybe he was just pissed at his wife for divorcing him, and he's gotten so good at telling the story that he's perfected it."

Arnett scratched his chin. "You're not the only one. Not common for a judge to take away custody only to give it back."

Jo's brow creased as she continued on. "And I'm confused about why Fischer would let him rant about it like that. He had to realize Travis was giving himself a motive for murder."

Arnett pulled open the passenger door of the Volt. "Maybe he figured it's all public record anyway, no point hiding it?"

Jo ducked into the driver's side, tugging at her necklace. "Sure, but Fischer himself would have been far more effective explaining it all in a neutral way. Because after seeing the response, I'm left with a motive for murder either way. If his wife was really abusing Avery, he seems passionate enough about it to do whatever he needs to do to protect Avery. And if he's lying, he seems bitter enough to take revenge on Melissa."

Arnett pulled on his seat belt. "The extremes our killer went to—nailing Melissa into that closet—that definitely speaks to deep-seated emotion."

Jo fired up the car and eased into the street. "So, next steps. Talk to Avery, of course. And we'll need Lopez to crack that laptop and phone so we can get a look at her texts and calls, and hopefully her schedule. Something that keeps tugging at me is what Chandra said about Melissa looking angry the day before she died. Probably a coincidence, but I'd still like to see what all was on her plate."

"Job doesn't seem like it plays in, but maybe talk to her boss regardless," Arnett said. "And we need to see the DCF file on Avery, and hopefully the court transcripts from the custody hearing. Also not possible until tomorrow."

Jo's phone chimed a notification, and after she eased to a stop at a red light, she slipped it out of her pocket. "Oh, dammit. I ran out to talk to Naya Moreno then got the call to come here and totally forgot to tell Matt I wasn't home. He's off work and wondering where I am."

"Go salvage the rest of your evening. A nice dinner, at least," Arnett said.

She dropped Arnett off, but didn't head for home. As hungry as she was, she was also itching to get her hands on Bennie Moreno's personal effects. With a new homicide on their desks, she wasn't sure when she'd get another chance.

CHAPTER TEN

I snapped off the television and leaned back on the couch to savor the moment.

The last five days had been excruciating. My rational side told me there was no way Melissa was going to get out of that closet alive, that not even Houdini could have managed it the way I'd doubled- and tripled-down on the precautions. But there was a small but stubborn part of me, the emotional part, that needed to know for certain she was dead, to see it with my own two eyes. Until that happened, I'd been a ball of stress. I couldn't sleep, I was barely able to eat, I even had trouble focusing during my evening rosary. But now, finally, I could breathe.

I got up for a glass of water. Just thinking about it all made me thirsty.

The news anchor didn't say how Melissa died, only that she'd been found dead and the police were investigating. That part was disappointing. I put so much thought and planning into making every step so fraught with significance, it would have been nice to see that acknowledged. But, that was my pride talking. This wasn't about me. Melissa knew what I'd done and why, and that's all that mattered.

The rest of the news report was better than I could have hoped, at least. I was worried they'd slap on that ridiculous patina of flawlessness they give to victims, portray her as some loving mother and claim it was a tragedy Avery had lost her. Thankfully, they did their jobs well, and even reported the controversy: "Melissa Rollins had recently regained partial custody of her daughter after an ugly custody dispute where she'd been accused of abuse." *Because the community shouldn't waste a moment's time grieving her. She was good at hiding her true self. At fooling people into thinking she was something she wasn't. Masterful, in fact; a natural chameleon and a talented liar.*

Back on the couch, I rolled the cool glass over my forehead and replayed it all in my mind. Her limbs limp and helpless in my hands as I bound her, hands, feet, and mouth. Nailing the door closed, five nails each across the bottom and the sides, the recoil from every strike traveling up my arm as I said my prayers. Bumping up the thermometer, delighting in each beep as the degrees climbed. The memories brought back the adrenaline, and the dopamine, and I closed my eyes to enjoy the rush through my system. This world can be such an uneven, unfair place. You have to grasp onto those rare moments of triumph and wrestle out all the joy you can.

Then I took myself to bed a little earlier than normal. I had to catch up on my sleep—the detectives were already hard at work, so I'd need to keep my wits about me.

Especially since I had my own surveillance to do.

CHAPTER ELEVEN

Gina Purcelli sat upright and stared at the TV. Melissa Rollins, killed? How was this even possible?

She *knew* Melissa Rollins. Well, she didn't *know her* know her, but she knew *of* her. Nobody whose kid went to Highland Elementary *didn't* know her, because she was everywhere. She was legendary, the mother of all mothers, the one everybody was envious of and wanted to be, including Gina. Melissa had her act together—she helped out on the PTA, managed the spring showcase, had a daughter who aced everything, all while working a full-time job. So different from Gina, who could barely manage to convince herself to get out of bed in the morning. Melissa had been an inspiration for her, because if Melissa could make it all work, maybe she could become at least a decent mother, too.

Yes, Gina had been shaken when Melissa's life had exploded. Cheating husband. Divorce. An article in the paper about the abuse. Custody battles. But then Melissa got her daughter back, and everything was golden again.

Sure, there'd been plenty of whispers flying through the Highland halls about whether or not justice had been served,

but that just pissed Gina off. She believed Melissa was innocent, that she was a good mother who was just misunderstood.
She *needed* to believe that, to keep her faith, more than she
needed oxygen.

But now Melissa was dead. Murdered.

Gina snapped off the TV and listened to the silence. Rafael
was long since asleep, but suddenly she needed to see him. She
jumped up, strode to his room, cracked open his bedroom door.
Yes, he was there, covers kicked off, little chest rising and falling,
sweet as the day was long. Her little cherub.

Regret gripped her heart and squeezed, the way it had
hundreds of times before.

She wrapped her arms around her waist. Was she just
kidding herself? Maybe she couldn't do it. It was all so hard—
beyond agony. The thought of never again—

She shut the thought down. If she worried too much about
the future she'd drive herself nuts. What was important was the
here and now, just getting through today. She'd worry about
tomorrow when it arrived—that's how she'd managed so far, one
day, one evening, one hour at a time. Sometimes even just one
minute.

She needed to be smart. And the smart thing to do was go to
sleep and not think about any of it any more.

CHAPTER TWELVE

Jo slid up to Bennie Moreno's apartment complex twenty minutes after dropping off Arnett. In the dark the building looked bleak and oppressive, like a mid-century Fascist complex staring down her soul. She doubted it'd be much cheerier in the light.

Agnes Gerardi had been expecting her—Naya Moreno had called earlier as promised. She shuffled from the manager's apartment to the storage areas in her housecoat and slippers, unlocked the wire mesh divider, and left Jo alone while she got back to her TV show.

Naya was right that Bennie's furniture would be an upgrade from her own, but the rest of the contents were bleak. A bare-bones assortment of kitchen equipment melded with a similar selection of toiletries and linens. Bennie either trashed documents as he went or Agnes hadn't felt they were worth holding on to, because the only personal paperwork present was a handful of unopened bills. As Naya hinted, the general paucity was offset only by an abundance of porn across a variety of media—DVDs, magazines, and even dirty books. Disappointed and dissatisfied, Jo re-secured the divider, dropped off the key, and headed over to Matt's place.

He greeted her at the door with a warm, slow hug, then led her into the kitchen.

"I made dinner." He slid a plate of carbonara out of the refrigerator and into the microwave, then put on a silly smile. "How was your day, dear?"

"No, you first. I can't eat while I'm talking."

As the food reheated and she dug in at his dining room table, he sketched out his day. After he described a seventy-year-old woman who'd had a major stroke, she swallowed and shook her head. "I don't know how you do it."

"Do what?"

"Look into their eyes and give them hope when life as they know it just changed irreparably."

He twisted his watch around his wrist, a sure sign he was uncomfortable. "I focus on reaching for the best outcome. Medical technology is always improving. Not long ago she'd never have walked or talked again with such a severe insult. What really kills me are cases like the five-year-old who came in today. In a coma, one I suspect was caused by a parent beating him. But I have no proof, so there's not much I can do except try to get him back to health and send him right back home with them."

Jo pushed away her empty plate. "I can relate."

The watch-twisting stopped, and he reached over to squeeze her hand. "What do you mean?"

She recapped the Melissa Rollins case as she washed the plate and set it in the drainer.

Matt shook his head. "And you wonder how I can do what I do? A woman nailed in a closet and left to die? That's horrendous."

She released a slow breath. "It really was. But, we have some strong leads to follow, so hopefully we'll get some answers soon. And, I made some interesting progress on a cold case." She summarized what she'd learned about Bennie.

His eyes lit up. "So he ended up dead in San Francisco. You think he met up with the wrong person?"

"Too early to say yet. But since so many people have died the same way, the signs are pointing to some sort of serial killer who targets out-of-towners."

"And you said the Scherer guy was also a serial killer? Very ironic if a serial killer coincidentally killed a serial killer." Matt scratched his chin as he considered this.

Jo tilted her head. "Maybe, maybe not. Serial killers have to lie about who they are, and they prey on people who have some sort of vulnerability, either societal or psychological. Two lying, damaged people might very well attract one another." She shook her head and wiped down the sink. "But if I think about that too long, my brain hurts. It's more likely two killers were working together and turned on one another. But Scherer lived in El Paso and I can't come up with a scenario where the two would live or work in different cities. So ultimately I think either someone is taking advantage of out-of-towners, or luring them in on some other premise. But no matter what, tomorrow I get to convince Lopez to search a computer for a case nobody else thinks is real, like she doesn't have enough to do with her time already."

"Still, it's exciting to find a pattern after so long. And if I read Lopez right, she'll be chomping at the bit to help you."

The enthusiasm on his face was sweet, and she smiled. "Oh, and I almost forgot. Laura wants the four of us to have dinner. She decided she and Bob need more couple friends."

His brows shot up, expression amused. "You look like you've been invited to a funeral. Bob's a great guy, so I'm guessing there's an issue with Laura?"

She caught herself and laughed apologetically. "It just feels a bit contrived, and I'm worried there's an agenda of some sort."

He reached for her hand and stroked it. "And you're still protective of your friend."

"Get out of my head." She stood up on her toes and kissed him.

He chuckled, wrapped his arms around her waist, and pulled her close. "Make me."

CHAPTER THIRTEEN

Diana Montauk was having a bad day.

After a full, satisfying day of work, she'd rewarded herself by settling in with a cup of cocoa to check the postings in her Facebook groups. Now she sat, frozen, staring down at Naya Moreno's post.

She read it for the fifth time, throat so tight she couldn't swallow.

> *You guys. Just when I thought I was finally free of Bennie, some police detective shows up at my door asking questions about him. I guess she thinks he was murdered. She wouldn't tell me much, but she asked a bunch of weird stuff like whether he played some game called World of Warcraft. How is Bennie still managing to be a huge pain in my ass even when he's dead?! Sorry for the rant, but it just never seems to end and I knew you all would understand.*

Prickling cold thrummed through Diana as she popped up from the couch. Cleopatra, her Sphynx cat, bounded off her lap onto the floor.

This was bad. Horrendously, fiercely, apocalyptically bad.

Diana paced the room and tried to convince herself that her fight-or-flight reflex was just overreacting, that this was just a coincidence due to an overzealous police department. But she couldn't get past the mention of World of Warcraft, because up until about eight years ago, Diana found her victims—stand-ins for the man who'd sexually abused her as a child—using World of Warcraft. *That* couldn't be a coincidence.

The last man she met there she'd known as Peter, character name Otthello. In the normal course of events, he'd have been nothing more than another engraved-rock trophy she kept in her jewelry-box drawer, another comforting memory to wrap around herself when her nightmares of the abuse returned. But as she monitored the San Francisco news coverage to be sure the police chalked his death up to an accident or a suicide off the Golden Gate Bridge, he'd turned dangerously anomalous— because the coverage reported he'd been a serial killer. Martin Scherer, Peter's real name, wooed women in World of Warcraft and met up with them in various cities to strangle them. The police had been closing in on him just hours before he washed up dead on the shores of Ocean Beach. The coverage also mentioned he'd been in the process of meeting his next victim, a woman whose World of Warcraft character name was Serylda.

Serylda was Diana. And while she'd known that Peter/Ot-thello/Martin wasn't a *nice* man—that was the whole reason she'd chosen him for her next kill—she'd been disturbed to find out he'd also been a killer, plotting to murder her at the same time she was plotting to murder him. Not because she was worried about him personally—he'd been arrogant and stupid and had underestimated her thoroughly. What disturbed her was how close she was to being caught in his crossfire. If the police looked closely into Martin's death, they might do blood tests and even look for the right metabolites, and if they did that, they might realize someone had murdered *him*. 'Serylda' would be the first suspect, and if the police knew her character name, they also likely had access to her chats with Martin, and the personal information associated with her account.

She always deleted her World of Warcraft account after each kill regardless, and always used a variety of tricks to make herself invisible—VPNs, alternating servers, everything she could think of. But she had no idea how long they'd been watching Martin in WoW and no idea what exactly they'd found. If they had her chat transcripts, they could do language analysis, and maybe even start trolling through all of WoW for matching anomalies. She wasn't even sure that was possible, but she knew it was the kind of program puzzle she'd love to try to solve, so surely someone else might, too.

To be safe, she left World of Warcraft completely behind her. What kept her alive was never assuming she was smarter than her nemesis, never assuming she knew all the answers, never underestimating whoever it was that might be looking for her. Paranoia was a friend she cuddled around in bed each night, and allowed to kiss her awake each morning.

But that left her in need of a new way to find victims. She'd briefly considered trying out another game—narcissistic misogynists abounded in online games—but the idea sparked the same fears, and she decided the safest way was to find a completely new method. After several weeks with no possibilities, she stumbled on the solution accidentally. While sitting in a café, sipping a mocha and finishing her day's work, she overheard a tense conversation. "I know he's beating you," one friend had said to another. The second woman broke down crying and told her friend she didn't know what to do, or how to get away. Among other excellent advice, her friend suggested she join a spousal-abuse support group. "They even have them on Facebook," she'd said.

Diana did two things when the women left. First, she followed the abused woman and identified her despicable husband for her next kill. Second, she created a fake account on Facebook and joined several spousal-abuse support groups, posing as an abused woman herself. Which was more than true, except that she'd suffered her abuse as a child rather than as an adult.

For years she'd hunted men like the one who'd wrecked her family—the man who'd had an affair with her mother, ripped apart her parents' marriage, caused her father's suicide, and turned his lust onto a very young Diana. The damaged, terrified little girl Diana had been still lived inside her, crying out through nightmares to be kept safe, and the only thing that assuaged her pain was to see similar men die. That day in the café, when Diana heard the pain in the abused woman's voice, the little girl inside her stirred. She realized a physically abusive man would do just as well as a stand-in.

Better, actually, because unlike the endless trawling on World of Warcraft, the abuse support groups were teeming with potential victims, like garbage cans filled with maggots. All she had to do was pick the woman with the most appalling story and trace back to her husband/boyfriend/partner. It wasn't hard—most people used their real names on Facebook, and very few of them thought to hide their friends lists. With a few hours research—usually less—she figured out who the partner was and what city he lived in. Then, with a little cyber stalking, she figured out a way to 'meet' them, and insinuate herself. Built into that was a blessed randomness—each man was from a different place and required different methods. Apps. Online communities. Posts to forums. In some cases, physical visits and accidental meetings.

Very helpful to incorporate that variety, because she couldn't change how she killed them. The little girl inside of her was very specific about that—she needed to watch them fall to their deaths in the depths of the Pacific Ocean, the same way her father had killed himself when her mother left him. Because

Diana knew repetition meant patterns and patterns were detectable, she compensated as best she could by ensuring their deaths looked like suicides or accidents. If anyone did ever suspect the deaths weren't suicides, they'd find heroin metabolites and most likely attribute the death to accidental overdose. She was also careful to leave no trace—she flew into Sacramento Airport, far enough away not to be included in any searches police might do, and drove a rental car into San Francisco from there. In and out the same day so there were no hotel reservations, and she only communicated with the victims via burner phone.

All of which made Naya Moreno's Facebook message absolutely incomprehensible. How could the local police in—where had he been from? Oakhurst?—have linked Martin Scherer to Bennie Moreno? That connection was the only reason for anyone to ask about World of Warcraft.

She strode into her office and fired up her laptop. She needed to know who was investigating Bennie's death. And she needed to know *now*.

———

Diana dove into the smattering of articles she'd practically memorized about Martin Scherer's death. They linked him in particular to a woman who'd been killed in the Oakhurst area, Jeanine Hammond. She googled coverage of Jeanine's murder and found a detective quoted in the first article: Detective Bob Arnett.

But Naya had mentioned a 'she,' so it had to be a woman. Maybe his partner? She googled Bob Arnett, and bingo—his name appeared repeatedly paired with a female detective, Josette Fournier.

Diana's search of Detective Josette Fournier sent her stomach into her colon. Detective Fournier was smart, with commendations and awards vomited all over the search results. She enlarged the two pictures of Fournier she was able to find, one an official portrait, one during a commendation ceremony. Fournier looked efficient, but didn't have the hard edge of the jaded. Her smile was enigmatic, and her green eyes were sharp. Something panged inside Diana's chest.

When she returned to the search results, something else caught her eye. Detective Fournier had once been *Lieutenant* Fournier, promoted in 2012, but was back to detective by mid-2013. Had she been demoted? Despite an extensive search, she found nothing that shed light on the change in status. What she did determine was the change happened around the same time as Martin Scherer's death. That also couldn't be a coincidence.

She dove back into her searches, this time seeking out personal information, anything that would give insight into who Josette Fournier was and what her weak spots might be. But the internet was frustratingly silent; Detective Fournier must be protective about her privacy. She couldn't find a Facebook account, no Twitter, no social media presence. Several pieces about charity work in connection with the department, but they yielded nothing. And the only other recent piece was about her current case, a woman called Melissa Rollins who'd been found dead in her home. Diana pushed the computer away in disgust.

She closed her eyes to help herself focus, and took herself back to the beginning. So what if Detective Fournier was suspicious about the deaths? There was absolutely no way to trace it back to Diana. She used different burner phones with every man, then dumped them as soon as they were dead. She never gave her real last name to any of them. Since Martin, she gave them a fake first name, too. Her World of Warcraft account was long since deleted, and Bennie had no connection to that, anyway. There was simply no way Fournier could find her.

Except those who assumed they'd thought of everything

were the ones who made fatal mistakes. She couldn't afford to just sit back and wait while this very real threat circled her.

Was it time to deploy her back-up plan?

No, not just yet. That was a difficult, complicated last resort, and there must be some other way she could get an upper hand on the situation.

She drummed her nails on the computer. Not only was the key to it all Josette Fournier, it was the only viable avenue she had to follow. That meant she needed to know more about Fournier—what she was doing to investigate Bennie's death, but also what her habits were, how she thought, what was important to her. If she came too close, Diana needed to know how to exert pressure. And since the internet wouldn't help her, she'd have to be more proactive about it.

Diana pulled the laptop back toward herself and started a different search.

CHAPTER FOURTEEN

AUGUST 23RD

Jo headed into HQ half an hour early the next day, hoping both to get in under the heat and to catch Lopez before Arnett showed up. Lopez had started a relationship with a fellow zombie-killing-game enthusiast a few months before, and had been adapting to his earlier schedule; sure enough, as Jo pulled up to the industrial-wasteland backside of the HQ building, she caught sight of Lopez's tall, slim silhouette slipping in through the door. Jo hurried in and sidled up to the desk just as Lopez was cracking open her first Rockstar of the day.

"Jo!" Lopez stared like she'd spotted a sea monster, and smoothed her long black ponytail. "Dude. It'd take a steel cable and a semi to pull me out of bed if I was waking up next to a snack like Matt."

"Oh, stop." Jo laughed. "Your Tony's pretty darn snacky, too."

"He's a five-course meal." Lopez's brows bounced up and down. "And he lasts just as long. One perk of him being nine years younger."

Jo groaned. "Okay, we're veering into TMI." She waved away the comment as her phone buzzed in her pocket. She slipped it out and checked the notification. "Ugh. Lieutenant Hayes."

"Ugh is right." Lopez took a big gulp of the Rockstar. "What does she want?"

Jo read off the text. "Need update on Rollins case ASAP."

Lopez glanced at the clock. "How does she even know about that yet?"

"She probably bugged my house and my car," Jo answered.

Lopez pointed the can at her. "Funny 'cause it's true. Why is she so obsessed with hating you? Did you piss in her Wheaties or something?"

Jo shoved the phone back in her blazer pocket and rolled her eyes. "Just lucky, I guess. I'll call her back when we're done. Silly me, thinking she'd prefer not to be bothered on a Sunday night."

"Micro managers." Lopez shook her head grimly, took another gulp of the Rockstar, then set down the can. "Anyway. What's up?"

Jo plopped into a chair, then pulled Bennie's laptop from her satchel. "I have a favor to ask you. Do you remember Martin Scherer?"

Back during the Scherer case, long before Lopez found her happy place as a tech wizard in the lab, she and Arnett had been assigned to investigate the death of Jeanine Hammond, one of Scherer's victims, while Jo served as lieutenant.

Lopez drew her legs up under her. "Sick fuck who strangled women with his own necktie and kept their wedding rings for trophies?"

"That'd be the one," Jo said. "You remember how that case ended?"

"'Course. He washed up on a San Francisco beach like the useless piece of garbage he was." Her gaze dropped down to the laptop, then back up to Jo's face. "Oh no. Please tell me you're not turning into *that* girl."

"What girl?"

"The one who chases a shadow even after she retires."

Jo laughed. "First of all, I hope I'm a long way off from retiring. And second, as a matter of fact, I've promised myself this is my last stab at figuring out what happened to him. And before you say we already know what happened to him, I have a lead that suggests he didn't kill himself." She tapped the laptop.

Lopez's eyes lit up. "Ooo, drama."

Jo summarized what she'd found among the Golden Gate Bridge suicides, and her visit to Naya Moreno. "So, I know you have a ton of cases you're working on, but I'd be deeply grateful if you could take a look at Bennie's computer for me. To look for a connection to WoW—he may have started playing it after Naya left him—or anything else that might help us."

Lopez reached for the laptop. "So you think someone killed Martin, and whoever killed him also killed Bennie Moreno?"

"That's the theory. I find it awfully coincidental that all out-of-town jumpers end up on Ocean Beach, and the others don't."

"Very strange. Don't suppose you have a phone for him?"

Jo shook her head. "Nope. It was in his pocket when he went into the water. But I'm going to grab his phone records from his provider."

"Sounds good. And if I'm remembering correctly, Marzillo texted me something last night about a laptop and phone you need me to crack for that vic you found nailed into a closet?"

"Melissa Rollins, yeah. That's a higher priority, of course." She cleared her throat. "In fact, we should probably keep the Scherer case on the down-low. I don't have an official okay to look into it, and I don't need another reason for Lieutenant Hayes to come after me."

Lopez winced. "Got it. I'll get back to you asap on both of them."

———

By the time Arnett arrived for the day carrying two Starbucks mochas, Jo had requested Bennie Moreno's cell phone records and had dived into the Melissa Rollins case.

She placed her hand over her phone. "I'm on hold with the Department of Children and Families. They're looking up Avery Rollins' case for me. Also, Lopez is cracking the computer and the phone as we speak, and I'm waiting for a call from Marzillo to catch us up on what they found yesterday."

"Sounds like you injected caffeine directly into your veins this morning," Arnett said.

A voice came over the phone. "Detective Fournier?"

She removed her hand. "Hi, yes."

"The caseworker assigned to Avery Rollins is Alison Choi. Do you want me to transfer you?"

"Can you give me her number before you do?"

"Sure thing."

After rattling off the number, the operator put through the call, but Alison Choi's voicemail picked up. Jo listened as the voice of a fortyish woman listed a series of numbers to push depending on the purpose of the call, then finally ended with "if you'd like to talk to Alison Choi, please leave a message at the tone." Jo did, then hung up.

"I'm thinking we just go over there," Arnett said.

"I'd rather talk to her in person, anyway—" Jo stopped as her phone buzzed. "Looks like Marzillo's ready for us. So maybe head to DCF after?"

"Let's do it."

As soon as they entered the lab proper, Marzillo waved them into her inner sanctum. Jo almost stopped short at the sight of her clothes—the black fit-and-flare Peter-Pan-collar dress over black leggings was a far cry from her typical sensible work pants under button-down shirts.

Lopez leaned over to whisper, "It's like Wednesday Addams took over our lab."

Marzillo re-tucked an errant black curl into her tight bun as everyone settled into chairs. "Jo, Bob. That was one of the strangest crime scenes I've ever seen, and that is *say*-ing *some*-thing." She stretched out the final words.

"Right?" Lopez said. "I've seen people stabbed, squashed, fallen from tall buildings and literally decapitated, but the pictures of that closet are gonna haunt me."

Jo shuddered. "Completely agree. Do we know anything more?"

"The ME confirmed Melissa died of organ failure—liver, to be specific."

"Dehydration?" Arnett asked.

Marzillo nodded. "Confirmed by the presence of what, for the sake of brevity, I'll refer to as toxic sludge in her blood, brought about by failing kidneys. Her liver beat them out, but not by much."

Lopez's face scrunched up. "Wouldn't it be kidneys first if it were dehydration?"

"Depends on the conditions. And with the high temperature in that house, conditions were bad." She turned to Jo. "You said you think she was placed in the closet Tuesday night?"

"Based on the take-out we found on the counter."

"It fits. She most likely died sometime late Friday, based on the best estimates we can make when we factor in conditions and decomposition. Which aren't very precise at all."

Jo nodded. "So, theoretically somebody could have just stuffed her in the closet during a robbery and forgot about her. But when you factor in the thermostat set so high and the nailed-shut closet door—"

'You get dark. *Very* dark," Lopez finished.

Marzillo tilted her head toward Lopez. "Exactly right. Because here's another thing to factor in. Look at *this*."

It took Jo a few seconds to recognize the picture that popped up on the monitor. A close-up of a quarter-sized bruise in the crook of Melissa's elbow, with two red dots in the center so close together they could almost have been one. "Is that an injection site?"

"It most definitely is. I couldn't find any track marks on her anywhere, so I'm guessing she's not a habitual intravenous drug user?" Marzillo looked from Jo to Arnett.

"I'm pretty certain her ex-husband would have mentioned that," Jo said.

"Screamed it from the rooftops, more like," Arnett said.

"Then, given the absence of defensive wounds or other signs of a fight, my guess is someone drugged her."

"You mean like a roofie?" Lopez twisted a ring on her thumb.

"I mean like a roofie. We'll have to wait for the tox screen, but I'm fairly certain we'll find something along those lines."

"So someone comes in the house, pulls out a syringe, then jabs her? How do you get away with that, especially in that area, unless someone's holding her down?" Arnett asked.

"But we're looking at someone strong regardless, because they'd have to fireman's lift her unconscious body up two floors," Jo said.

Marzillo wagged her head. "Not necessarily. A drug like GHB doesn't kick in for at least a few minutes. They might have coerced her upstairs before she passed out."

"Okay, my head just exploded," Lopez said. "None of it fits. Even with someone you trust, you don't just roll up and stick someone with a needle, *then* hang out until they pass out."

"And there's no possible explanation in her medical history?" Arnett asked.

Marzillo shook her head. "No condition that requires injections, and no recent appointments for blood draws or the like."

"Maybe somebody held a gun on her," Arnett said.

"If they had a gun, why did they need to inject her? They zip-tied her regardless, so why bother?" Lopez asked.

"Hang on. There are *two* dots there. They injected her twice?" Jo asked.

"Excellent catch. They pierced the skin twice, although that doesn't necessarily mean two injections. Possibly they weren't skilled at it, possibly something interrupted them."

Jo shook her head, eyes closed. "Okay, well. However they did it, someone got into the house, drugged and trussed Melissa, shoved her in the third floor closet, nailed it shut, and then bumped up the thermostat."

"What a horrible way to die." Lopez shook her head.

"Like being locked inside a running oven," Marzillo said. "There's a reason she looks desiccated in the pictures. She quite literally is."

Jo's stomach flipped, and she cleared her throat. "Right. Anything else we need to know about the autopsy?"

"Nothing more until the test results come back. We also sent out swabs from under her nails to test for DNA, so maybe we'll get something there."

Jo nodded. "I don't suppose we found any lovely intact fingerprints anywhere?"

"You mean that don't belong to Melissa or her daughter? Nothing, not even partials on the zip ties. My guess is the killer wore gloves. And we did find a few errant hairs that don't appear to be hers, but they could be her daughter's. We'll need to exclude them."

"Found directly on her, or elsewhere in the house?" Jo asked.

"Several on the floor inside the closet, and one nearby."

"Nothing else useful?"

Marzillo leaned against the desk. "You saw the place, it's practically hermetic. I'm not convinced actual people live there."

Jo half-smiled. "Okay, well. We'll see what we can drum up. Thank you." She turned to go.

Lopez cleared her throat. "So, what am I, chopped liver?"

Jo turned back. "You have something already?"

"Already? It's been an hour since we talked. How lame do you think I am?" Lopez winked.

"My bad." Jo laughed. "What did you find?"

Lopez held the folder out to her. "I cracked the phone and the laptop, got Melissa's schedule off her Google calendar, and printed out her recent call and text logs. Also, the top sheet has her sign-in information for her personal and work emails."

Jo took the folder and flipped through. "Amazing. Anything strange on her hard drive?"

"It's only been an hour. What do you think I am, a miracle worker?" Lopez raised her eyebrows and swigged her Rockstar.

CHAPTER FIFTEEN

"If you drive to DCF, I can look at these printouts on the way," Jo asked as they walked back to their desks.

"Can do." Arnett checked his watch. "And we should have plenty of time to finish before our appointment to talk with Avery."

"Thanks." Jo tapped a nail on the file as they diverted out of the building. "I'm hoping something in here will help clarify where the truth lies on the continuum between Travis' version and Tinsley's. Melissa's murder seems deeply personal, and they're the only two people close to her so far."

Arnett shot her a look as he pulled open the car door. "Travis' motive seems pretty clear-cut, and he certainly wasn't broken up over Melissa's death."

Jo climbed in. "True, and I'd be convinced if this were a spur-of-the-moment argument and he'd smashed her over the head, something like that. But to nail her in a closet and turn up the heat? That reeks of premeditation, and Travis doesn't strike me as stupid. He'd have to know he'd be the first person anyone suspected of killing her."

Arnett shrugged. "Sometimes the obvious answer is the

right one. We both know killers don't always think things through. And his alibi is weak."

Jo gave a 'maybe' head nod, and flipped open the file. "First sheet is Melissa's schedule for the week she died. Business appointments with doctors, including phone numbers and addresses. Nothing additional on the day she died. The day before, Monday, is when her neighbor said she looked pissed off, she did have an additional appointment with Alison Choi. But, that wasn't until seven, after Chandra waved to her."

"Maybe Melissa was angry about having the meeting at all," Arnett said.

"Very possible—as acrimonious as the whole thing was, any visit probably rankled. The week before was busier, with lots of notes about places she needed to drop Avery off and pick her up." Jo flipped through the pages. "Next is her call log. On the day she died, she had several calls that map onto the appointments she had, then finally a call to the Vietnamese restaurant."

"What about the day before?"

"Doctors' offices again, and then a call to Highland Elementary, and—well, lookie here—a call from Tinsley Sparks."

Arnett's head snapped around. "Who claimed she hadn't spoken to Melissa since Sunday. Was it before Melissa got home?"

"Chandra said Melissa got home about six thirty on Monday, and this call went from six oh three until six twenty. So probably while she was driving."

"And right after the call, Chandra said she looked pissed off."

Jo flipped to the next sheet. "There's also a text from Tinsley just before the call that says 'I need to talk to you.'"

"The plot thickens."

"Let me check her emails." Jo pulled out her phone and entered the login for Melissa's business account. "From what I can see, lots of boring business messages about quotas and sales numbers. Her relationship with her boss seems friendly." She switched accounts. "Yikes. Her personal email account is all Avery all the time. Extracurriculars, class work, school events. Calling her type-A and controlling is an understatement—she's already talking to the principal about plans for *next year's* spring showcase."

Jo continued to scroll, search, and periodically update Arnett until he turned into the DCF parking lot half an hour later.

He nodded toward the building. "I've never been to this particular branch before. Looks like some sort of industrial meat-processing plant."

Jo took in the sprawling single-story red-brick building topped with faux corrugated metal. "Probably not far from the metaphorical truth. How many kids do they have to find homes for in a given year?"

Arnett slid into the first open parking spot and switched off the ignition. "I don't wanna know. I have a hard enough time sleeping at night."

Jo shot him a skeptical smirk. "You'd adopt every single one if you could."

He waved her off and they crossed to the building. Once inside they asked for Alison Choi; the receptionist-slash-gate-keeper gestured them toward gray plastic chairs bolted together like paper cutouts.

Thankfully, Alison appeared quickly. A tall Asian woman in her forties, she had a willowy awkwardness that put Jo in mind of a newborn colt. She hurried them back through well-worn halls to a cubicle-delineated office space and pointed to two chairs facing her desk.

"You're here about Avery Rollins?" Alison slipped a file toward Jo. "You mentioned in your call you wanted to read everyone's statements, so I printed and copied everything for you. You said Melissa has been killed—I saw that on the news last night, but they didn't say what exactly happened?"

Jo reached for the file. "That's what we're trying to figure out. We understand you were assigned to oversee Avery Rollins' custody case?"

She wagged her head. "In essence. The first I was involved was when Travis Rollins called us to report his wife for abusing their daughter. He moved out and took Avery with him, and didn't want her to return to stay with Melissa. I wasn't aware of it initially, but she'd already filed for divorce at that point."

"What was your take on the situation?" Jo asked.

Alison's face scrunched up. "That's complicated. Travis claimed Melissa abused Avery with excessive and mentally cruel punishments, while Melissa claimed she was just a strict disciplinarian. Nobody claimed any physical abuse, and psychological abuse is far harder to prove. It's hard to even define, in fact."

"But Avery confirmed her father's story?" Jo asked.

Alison picked up a pen and flipped it over her fingers. "Yes. That's why we removed her from Melissa's custody initially."

"How did she end up back with her mother?" Jo asked.

Alison's eyes danced over the surface of the gray metal desk in front of her. "If a mother yells at her daughter for not trying hard enough on a spelling test, is that abuse? Most people would say no. What if the mother tells the daughter she's lazy and needs to work harder? That depends on wording, tone, and whether the child really does need to work harder. In some families a C is an acceptable grade. In others, it isn't."

Jo weighed how much conviction there was behind Alison's words. "Travis alleged Melissa made Avery kneel on uncooked rice during her time-out. That's intentional infliction of pain, so wouldn't that count as physical abuse? Or refusing to let a child go to the bathroom? Surely that counts as cruelty?"

Alison shifted in her chair. "Certainly, if there were proof.

Melissa claims—claimed—there was no rice involved in the time-outs, and that Avery exaggerated the length of the practice session. That's part of what makes it all so hazy—we're looking at similar versions of the same story. Melissa admits to telling Avery she needed to work harder, but says she never yelled or used words like 'lazy.' She admits she made Avery practice even when Avery didn't want to, but claimed that was because Avery begged to be allowed to play piano, and had to promise to stick it out for a year before they agreed to invest the money in a piano. Travis admits that part's true. So Melissa claims all she was doing was holding Avery to her promise, and Avery didn't like that. Her position is—was—that Travis was exaggerating out of revenge, and that of course Avery prefers to be with the parent who is more lenient. And it's a valid point—many children think that perfectly reasonable punishments are excessive. We get calls like that all the time."

Jo took a deep breath, tapping a nail on her leg as she did. "I'm sensing you didn't fully buy that argument."

"It doesn't matter what I think, it matters what I can prove."

"Right, we get that. But we'd like to know what you think anyway," Arnett said.

Alison studied both their faces before replying. "I believe Avery was being abused."

"What makes you lean that way?" Jo kept her tone soft—she sensed something fragile in Alison's response.

Alison shifted in her chair again. "There was an ease to Melissa's explanation that didn't sit well with me. Like she'd practiced what to say. When I listened to her, I didn't find myself asking whether or not what she was saying was true, but whether or not she *believed* what she was saying was true. And there were details about what Avery told me that felt very real."

"Can you give us an example?" Jo asked.

Alison's answer came quickly. "Sure. If Avery got less than a B on her exams, Melissa claims she sent Avery to bed without supper. But in Avery's version, 'sent her to bed' meant Melissa locked her in a closet until morning. Avery's description of what that felt like was very—"

Jo bolted forward, and her jaw dropped. "Melissa locked Avery in a closet?"

Alison's gaze ping-ponged between the two of them. "Allegedly. You didn't know?"

CHAPTER SIXTEEN

"Well, now we know the reason behind our convoluted crime scene," Jo said as they strode back out to the Crown Vic, the DCF file under her arm.

"Funny how Travis Rollins didn't bother to mention the closet punishments." Arnett's gait was long and fast. "That *really* pisses me off."

Jo's teeth scraped across her lower lip. "We need to know how widespread knowledge of the closet punishments were. Particularly if it was part of *The Greenfern Daily's* press coverage."

"You drive, I'll look it up." Arnett circled around to the passenger's side. "No point in going all the way back to HQ when we have to be back here at two thirty. Lunch?"

Jo glanced at her watch. "Sounds good. You know any place around here?"

Arnett didn't make eye contact. "We passed a McDonald's on the way in."

Jo sighed, and rubbed her eyes. Laura tried to keep Arnett away from junk food for health reasons, and Jo hated being an accomplice to his breaches. But she just didn't have the leftover energy to fight him while she sorted out the implications of the current revelation. She waved her assent and pulled away as Arnett tapped and scrolled.

"Found them," he said, and skimmed. "Yep, they mention several allegations, including that she locked Avery in a closet. It doesn't mention Avery by name of course, but you don't have to be Einstein to put two and two together."

Jo smacked the steering wheel with her palm. "Dammit. That blows our suspect list back up to the entire readership of *The Greenfern Daily.*"

"You think some random wacko read it and decided the evil mother just had to die?" Arnett asked.

Jo gave a sharp, frustrated shrug. "I don't think it's the most likely option, but it's possible and we have to consider it. At the very least, we can't use the information about MO as a litmus test in this case."

He nodded. "Fair. But how would a stranger get into the house?"

"How did anybody get in the house? With the rancor between them, I'm sure Melissa changed the locks when Travis left," Jo said.

"But Avery would have a key, right?"

"Good question. It doesn't look like Melissa allowed her to be a latchkey kid, but we should find out."

Jo pulled into the drive-thru and ordered, then grabbed a parking spot so they could tuck into their food. She lifted her burger out of the bag and inspected it. "Are Big Macs smaller than they used to be?"

"When was the last time you had one?" Arnett asked.

"Around twenty-ten?"

"Nope, you're just remembering wrong." He sunk his teeth into a Quarter Pounder and moaned with joy.

"I feel like I should leave the two of you alone," Jo deadpanned.

"Don't worry, I'll be done soon." He pointed at her. "And don't make any 'just like a man' jokes."

Jo gaped indignantly. "Who do you think I am, Lopez?"

He waved her off with one hand and dove back into the burger. True to his word, four bites and two minutes later, he crumpled up the empty wrapper and tossed it into the bag.

She took her time finishing hers, then wiped her hands on a napkin while Arnett programmed Travis Rollins' address into the GPS.

Before she could start the car, her phone chimed. She slipped it out and peered at it. "Oh, dammit."

"What?"

"Lieutenant Hayes texted me asking about the Rollins case and I forgot to respond. Now she's pissed."

Arnett clicked his tongue and shook his head. "You aren't doing yourself any favors."

"Yeah, well, the damage is done." Jo's thumbs tapped fiercely at the keyboard. "There."

"What'd you say?" He peered over at the phone.

"I gave her an uber-brief update and mentioned we're on the way to follow up with the husband and daughter now." Jo put the car into gear and backed out of the spot. The phone chimed again. "Nope, not looking at it," she said.

"Now, Jo," Arnett sing-songed, and picked up the phone. "It's not from Hayes anyway, it's from Lopez. *Finished Melissa Rollins' computer and phone. Nothing strange or of particular interest. Also finished Bennie Moreno's computer. No sign of WoW or any other game.*"

"Can you ask her if we can get Bennie Moreno's credit card transactions?"

"She say she's on it," he replied. "So you're all-in on this situation with Bennie Moreno? You're really that sure the same person who killed Martin Scherer killed him?"

"You're the one who taught me I needed to trust myself, right?" She turned to check his reaction.

He held up a hand. "I did. And you should. So what's the plan?"

"I don't have much of one yet. I'm hoping something will jump out at me. He went to San Francisco for a reason, and there has to be a trace of it somewhere."

"Did the info SFPD sent include where he was staying?"

"Yep. And he flew directly into SFO, which is also different from Scherer, who flew into Sacramento and drove down. So, no other communalities."

"Let me look at the files and I'll see if anything pops out for me," Arnett said.

She turned to look at him as she pulled up in front of Travis Rollins' apartment complex. "You're sure? Are you just burning to get on Hayes' bad side, too?"

He shrugged. "Where you go, I go."

Jo hid her relief as she got out of the car. "Speaking of, did Laura make the reservation for our double date Wednesday?"

"Indeed she did." He gave a believe-it-or-not headshake. "She's excited about it."

They made their way up the stairs and knocked on the apartment door. Again Tom Fischer answered, and again gestured to the table where Travis sat.

Jo glanced around the apartment as they took their seats. "No Avery?"

Travis glanced down the hall. "She's in her room."

"Ah. That works out well, because we have a question we'd like to ask you before we talk with her," Jo said.

Travis glanced at Fischer, who gave a quick I-don't-know-what-this-is-about shrug, then turned back. "Okay."

"We just spoke with Alison Choi," Jo said, not trying to hide her annoyance. "She told us you alleged Melissa locked Avery in a closet. You told us about flash cards and kneeling time-outs, why would you leave out something so much worse?"

Travis' glance flicked between them and landed on Jo. "I told you she did horrible things, and I told you about what I experienced directly. The torture during the piano practice—making Avery urinate on herself—that was the moment I decided I had to get full custody of Avery. At that point I didn't know about the closet."

The words were defensive, but Jo sensed a genuine confusion in them that gave her pause. Did he really not understand the relevance of the question? She and Arnett hadn't revealed the details of Melissa's murder to anyone—maybe he wasn't just playing stupid. "When did you find out about it?"

"When Avery and I were talking with DCF. When Avery had her initial discussion with Alison."

"How could you not be aware of your wife locking your daughter in a closet overnight?" Arnett asked.

Travis straightened. "She only did it when I was away. Once when I was on a business retreat, and twice when I was away at conferences."

"What exactly did she do to Avery on those occasions?" Jo asked.

Travis inhaled deeply and searched the ceiling. "Avery said she put her in the closet without dinner, and let her out in the morning."

"She didn't let Avery out to use the bathroom?" Arnett asked.

"She put in Avery's old kiddie toilet with her."

"The closet inside Avery's bedroom?" Jo asked.

His brow puckered slightly. "No, Avery's closet has sliding doors, all the bedroom closets do. Avery said she used the third-floor closet."

Fischer broke in. "What's the importance of the closet

incident?"

Jo quickly assessed what she could reveal without compromising the investigation, then watched Travis carefully as she answered. "That's where we found Melissa."

Travis' face screwed up and he opened his mouth to speak, but Fischer's hand shot up to stop him. "I think Mr. Rollins has helped you all he can. If you have any other questions, you'll need to submit them through me."

———

"Caffeine is imperative if I'm going to sort through all this," Jo said as Arnett pulled away from Travis' apartment complex. After Tom Fischer shut down the conversation with Travis Rollins, Jo and Arnett spoke briefly to Avery. She confirmed her father's story, including his alibi. Tuesday night they'd picked up pizza on the way home from her dance lesson, then spent the rest of the night together until she went to bed. And no, she didn't have a key to her mom's house, because her mom always picked her up from school.

"Agreed. Is there someplace close?" Arnett asked.

Jo clicked on Google Maps. "There's a Starbucks almost around the corner."

"Perfect."

Jo fiddled with her diamond necklace as she drove one-handed. "The problem is most of this abuse happened when nobody was around to see it. Like the closet situation—even Travis didn't witness it, it only came out after Avery told the caseworker."

"You think she was lying?" Arnett considered. "Her answers *were* hesitant."

"I'm not sure that's surprising, considering what she's going through. Even if she's telling the truth, the guilt of testifying against her mother must be crippling now that she's dead. And since that leaves her with only one parent and no extended family, she must be terrified of someone taking her father away too."

"True. She's old enough to get that if he goes to jail, she goes to a foster home."

"But I'm not sure it matters. If someone killed Melissa because they believed she was abusing Avery, the only thing that matters is they *believed* Avery was telling the truth."

"And the person most likely to fit that is Travis, so we need to confirm his alibi."

"Since he didn't keep the receipt for the pizza, I'll have Lopez check his credit card records." She pulled into the drive-thru and ordered their drinks, then typed the text to Lopez. "And I'd like to check to see if there's security footage of him picking up that pizza."

"On it." Arnett pulled out his phone and put through a call.

Jo corrected an error in the order and paid for the drinks during Arnett's quick call. As she handed him his, he hung up and turned to her. "The Pizza Palace keeps their security footage for seven days, and told us to come on over."

"No time like the present."

The Pizza Palace turned out to be a charming red-brick-oven pizza parlor with a counter surrounding an open kitchen, rustic wooden tables, and an attached room filled with arcade games. They'd hit the lull between lunch and dinner, so only one table was occupied, by a mother and two small children who'd managed to get pizza sauce all over their faces and shirts.

As Jo and Arnett crossed to the counter, she filled her lungs with a deep breath of roasting tomatoes and garlic, then glared at Arnett. "Good thing we had Big Macs instead of this."

"No regrets. They can't possibly be as good as Sal's." He strode past the two gangly teens in matching red polo shirts wiping down the already-clean counter, toward a blond man with thinning hair and a blue button-down shirt hunkered in the corner. "You Mike?"

The man glanced up from his clipboard. "That's me. You the guy that just called?"

"Detectives Arnett and Fournier, yes."

Mike waved them around and led them to a tiny office crammed with boxes labeled *canned olives* and *paper napkins*. He gestured Arnett to a folding chair across from the desk, then pulled out the office chair and passed it to Jo. He leaned over the monitor and shifted it so they could both see. "We've got a camera pointed at the front door, one on the back door, and one looking down at the registers. What time did you say you needed to see?"

"Last Tuesday, starting around five thirty," Arnett replied.

"Gotcha." Mike pulled open a drawer, selected a memory card, and stuck it into the computer. He opened the video file, which appeared as three panels in a split-screen, and clicked until he reached the target time. "You need me in here while you watch it, or do you mind if I get back out there? They work less and lean more when I'm out of sight."

"Whatever works best for you," Jo said.

"Right. Just let me know when you're done." He disappeared out of the office.

"I wish everyone was this accommodating." Jo raised her eyebrows at Arnett, then hit play, and sped the recording up to 4x. For the next hour they stared at the screen, carefully examining everyone who entered the restaurant.

"There," Jo exclaimed when Travis appeared. She clicked pause, and pointed to the time stamp. "He may have ordered the pizza earlier, but he didn't pick it up until seven thirty. Since he said he picked up Avery from dance class at five thirty, that leaves two hours unaccounted for."

"More than enough time to stop off, kill his wife, and nail

her in a closet." Arnett's jaw clenched. "Looks like we have a question to *submit* to Tom Fischer."

CHAPTER SEVENTEEN

After telling Pizza Palace Mike they'd need to keep the memory card with the security footage, Jo and Arnett returned to the car. Jo immediately put a call through to Fischer, but got his voicemail.

"Dammit." She threw the phone into her lap. "Should we drop by his office? It's getting outside of normal business hours, but somehow I think he's the sort who works late. Or we could go have a chat with Tinsley, because her lie's also sticking in my craw."

Arnett glanced at his watch. "Tonight's my salsa class with Laura."

"I didn't realize you were still dancing." Jo didn't try to hide her smile.

A light flush crept up Arnett's cheeks. "Don't razz me, Fournier, or I'll mention it to Matt on Wednesday in front of Laura and they'll both make *you* go, too."

Jo tucked her lips in and raised both hands, but the smile still played at the corner of her mouth.

Jo picked up her car at HQ, then wound her way home through the streets of Oakhurst as she turned Melissa Rollins' case over in her mind. They'd caught two people in lies so far—three, since Avery had also lied when confirming her father's alibi. That rankled and left her restless, but other than leave messages at Melissa's workplace and the Highland Elementary office, there wasn't much she could do until morning.

Her phone rang, pulling her out of her thoughts. As she eased to a stop at a red light, the caller ID flashed on the dashboard—Sophie, her sister. The familiar tightness tugged her chest at the sight of Sophie's name on the display, but this time fled again almost as quickly. Their relationship had improved steadily since Sophie helped Jo with a case the previous spring, one that ultimately ended with the suspect kidnapping Jo's niece, Sophie's daughter Emily. Jo had chased Emily and the kidnapper all the way into Connecticut, and had to shoot the perpetrator to recover her niece. She recovered Emily safely, and in the process of it all both she and Sophie had come to understand one another a little better. But, old habits were hard to break, and Jo worried the peace was fragile.

She tapped the console to accept the call. "Sophie. How are you?"

"Good," Sophie replied, sounding rushed. "Just calling to confirm dinner at La Rue Fondue Wednesday night. David's really looking forward to talking Corvettes with Matt."

Jo's eyes winced shut. She'd completely forgotten about the informal plans she'd made with Sophie when she agreed to dinner with Bob and Laura. And this was exactly the sort of thing that drove Sophie crazy—over the years Jo's work had forced her to regularly no-show at family events because of work obligations. If she canceled now, this would backtrack the relationship.

"You forgot." Sophie's voice went flat.

"I double-booked. Laura asked Matt and me out to dinner

and the invitation was so unexpected my brain apparently shut down."

"Laura? Bob's wife?" Sophie sounded intrigued.

"Yeah. They used to invite me over back when their girls were still living at home, but since the—" She stopped short. She didn't need to resurrect gossip about her partner's relationship.

"Since the affair, you haven't felt fully comfortable with her."

Trust Sophie to cut right to the chase. "Truth be told, I haven't."

"Don't take this wrong, okay?" Sophie said, and Jo winced again—nothing good ever followed that phrase from Sophie. "I'm asking not as judgment, but because I'm genuinely interested in your perspective on this. I've never understood your stance on infidelity. You were so angry at Mom for so long, but then you've always flitted from man to man."

Jo pushed down the instinctive defensive heat that rose up in her chest, reminding herself to take Sophie at her word, and to be grateful Sophie was willing to go deep with her. Instead of snapping, she considered her sister's words. She'd never thought of it in those terms, but yes, if she were honest, *angry* was the right word for how she'd felt about her mother's affair. "But I never cheat on them. I go to extremes to make sure they understand there's no exclusive commitment, and even so, I only ever see one man at a time." She paused before continuing. "And I guess as a teenager it was hard for me to understand that the death of a marriage is rarely due to one person only. Mom cheated, but Dad pulled her out of the only place she'd ever been comfortable and left her to fend for herself amid scores of his Louisiana relatives."

"If only things were as simple as we think they are when we're young." Sophie cleared her throat. "Anyway. So you're double-booked for Wednesday?"

"Well—" Jo's mind raced—she really didn't want to take this step back. "Maybe we can all six go out together. You've met Bob several times before, do you think David would get along with him?"

Sophie paused for a long moment. "You know what? Why the hell not? What I need right now is a night of adult conversation where I don't have to do any of the cooking, and I've always enjoyed talking to Bob."

Jo's brows popped up at Sophie's use of profanity. "You okay, Soph?"

She sighed. "I'm fine. Just tired, that's all. I'll call La Rue Fondue right now and change the reservation to six people. Seven o'clock?"

"Actually, Laura had her heart set on Le Poulet Bleu. Would that work?"

"Oh, that would be *lovely*. I've been trying to get David to go there for months. This way he can't argue." Her voice perked up slightly.

Jo considered pushing, but decided not to—Sophie didn't respond well to being pressured. "That's a relief. I'm so sorry I dropped the ball on this. Thanks so much for understanding."

"All's well that ends well. See you Wednesday." Jo could practically hear the shrug through the phone before Sophie hung up.

She stared down at the phone counting the strange aspects of the conversation. The last thing anybody would ever call Sophie was easy-going, and yet she hadn't even chastised Jo for forgetting the date, and actually seemed glad about the change of venue. *And* she'd asked Jo about something negative from their childhood without including some sort of insult?

Something was definitely wrong.

CHAPTER EIGHTEEN

As soon as the detectives left, Travis Rollins hurried Tom out of his apartment. Tom had wanted to go over everything with him again, but Travis played up how stressful the police interview had been for Avery, and said she needed some time alone to deal with it all.

As Avery worked on her tutoring assignment, Travis paced the small apartment, trying to figure out what to do, itching to send a text. But the walls were thin. If he got a call back, Avery might hear, and he couldn't risk that. She might even come out of her room while he was on the call, and he couldn't risk that, either. No matter what, he couldn't allow her to know the details of her mother's death.

It was hard enough for an adult to sort through both loving and hating someone at the same time, let alone for a child. He'd tried to assure her whatever she felt was okay, whether she was so angry with Melissa her little face turned red, or missed her mom so much during her weeks with him that she cried herself to sleep. If she knew everything, how would she ever come out of this halfway sane?

No—the text would have to wait until Avery was asleep.

He veered off into the kitchen and pulled out ground beef. Hamburgers and potato salad would have enough steps to keep him focused on something, but were easy enough that he really couldn't screw them up when his mind was scattered.

And yet, he did. He burned them, and the buns, and spilled the potato salad when trying to serve it up on their plates. He cut his finger when trying to open a safety-sealed container of ice cream, and knocked his Coke off the table all over the floor.

"Dad, are you alright?" Avery asked him.

He threw the wet paper towels into the garbage, then came over to kiss her head. "I'm fine, sweetheart. Do you want to watch a movie?"

She nodded, and went off into the living room to pick one from the on-demand menu while he did the dishes. Then they watched a movie about a variety of musician trolls, or at least Avery did. He tried his best to pretend he was interested and not to fidget or obsess about the text he needed to send for an hour and a half of what felt like being tortured in hell.

When it finished, he asked Avery, "Another one?"

Her brows drew together—he'd seen that crease so much in the last six months he worried it'd become permanent. "I'm really tired," she said. "Is it okay if I go to bed early?"

"Of course, honey."

"Do I have to go to tutoring tomorrow?"

"Not if you don't want to. I don't see any reason why you ever have to go back again."

She leaned over to give him a hug. "Thanks, Daddy."

He smiled after her as she padded off to bed, then forced himself to watch a half-hour sitcom while his left leg bounced enough to fly off. When the show finished he snuck carefully into Avery's bedroom and checked she was asleep. Her soft snore tugged at his heart, and he gently clicked the door back into place.

Back in the living room, he finally sent the text: *We need to talk.*

CHAPTER NINETEEN

Gina Purcelli glanced over her shoulder as she buckled Rafael into his car seat. Yep, the group of whispering mothers were still staring at her. They didn't even bother to glance away when she caught them.

The news about Melissa Rollins had blazed through the halls of Highland Elementary in hidden whispers by so-glad-it's-not-me hypocrites. It was hard to miss the rumor mill in high gear, even if nobody was talking directly to *her*. She caught snippets of conversations—*Melissa Rollins, found dead, police there all day, can't bring myself to feel sad about it*—and caught the side-eye that came at her from every angle.

She hurried herself into the car and pulled off down the street, telling herself it didn't matter what any of them thought. She checked the clock on the dash—if she could get Rafael over to her mother's house in the next ten minutes, she'd have time to get to her meeting. And with everything going on, she really, *really* needed to not miss her meeting.

So of course every light she hit turned red, and she managed to get caught behind every Sunday driver in Greenfern. She stopped her heel tapping the floor as she waited at her fifth red light, and reminded herself to hold it together. She couldn't control the traffic, she could only control her *reaction* to the traffic. She closed her eyes and took a deep breath, rubbed the side of her hand, and repeated her mantra.

As she started back up, a movement in her rearview caught her eye. A blue car changed lanes, slipping behind the car in back of her. Hadn't that same car also changed lanes when she did a few minutes ago? Was the car following her?

She took another deep breath and tapped next to her eyebrow five times. Melissa's death was getting to her, making her imagine things that weren't there, and she needed to pull it together. She tapped next to her eye, then below it, then on her chin.

She glanced back at Rafael and smiled—he'd already fallen asleep. If only she could find that sort of peace somewhere, find the ability to disconnect and zone out from the stresses of the world.

She glanced at the clock again, and prayed for the light to change.

CHAPTER TWENTY

The humidity cocooned Diana as the doors out of Hartford International Airport slid open. She closed her eyes to take the sensation in. It was auspicious, she decided—the embrace of a tropical vacation rather than a reconnaissance mission, like a hearty affirmation from the universe she was on the right course.

By the time she finished with the lines for her rental car, it was after five, most likely too late to catch up with Detective Fournier that night. But it didn't hurt to try—Fournier might be working late, and if so Diana might catch her on the way out. Either way, she needed to analyze the area she'd be staking out. She put her hotel check-in on hold and drove directly to the Oakhurst County State Police Detective Unit headquarters.

The set-up couldn't have been more perfect if she'd designed it herself, and she'd become quite the connoisseur of stalking while investigating the last few of the men she'd killed. The building sat on an unenclosed lot, parking in front for visitors, in the back for employees. Residential streets surrounded two sides, restaurants and stores the two others, giving her plentiful places to park and watch, all far enough away to avoid the security cameras rigged at regular intervals on the facade. She tried several spots, checking visibility while remaining unobtrusive. Nothing was perfect, but she had several options that would allow her to fade into the background, while preserving her ability to spot Fournier. She'd already memorized every line of Fournier's face, from the fringe of brown hair to her button nose to the slight curve of her chin.

Satisfied, Diana drove off. She had some research she needed to do at the local library and a few public records searches to complete, but she wanted to turn in for the night as soon as she could.

After all, the early bird got the worm.

CHAPTER TWENTY-ONE

AUGUST 24TH

A wave of already oppressive heat slammed into Jo as she left the house the next morning, instantly deflating her mood. If it was this hot early on, the day would probably top out near a hundred. So many days in a row was like a psychological beat down, deflating and demoralizing, and none of her professional clothes were scant enough to keep her from getting heatstroke. She sighed, pulled up an image of cozy snowdrifts, and whistled 'Baby, It's Cold Outside.'

Five minutes later she plugged her figurative nose and did the unthinkable: ordered her beloved mocha in iced form. As she took the first sip, Lopez texted to say she had information about Bennie Moreno; as soon as Jo handed Arnett's hot coffee to him upon arrival, she gestured him along to the lab.

Lopez did a double take when she saw him, and threw a questioning glance at Jo.

"I told him what I'm doing and why," Jo said. "But Hayes still doesn't know, so we need to keep it under wraps."

"Yes!" Lopez pumped her fist. "The OG band's back together. I have a feeling three heads are gonna be better than two."

Jo grimaced. "So, no clear-cut texts from his murderer explaining where he went and why someone wanted him dead?"

Lopez rolled her eyes. "These kids today. No consideration."

"So why are we here?" Arnett asked.

Lopez narrowed her eyes at him. "I forgot how much fun you are first thing in the morning. Jo allows me to unfurl my discoveries with the proper level of drama."

Arnett threw his hands up and dropped into a chair. "My bad. As you were."

Lopez gave a *that's-right* head swivel, then turned back to Jo. "So. A deeper dive into Bennie's laptop uncovered a smattering of San Francisco searches centering around topics like romantic restaurants and romantic outings."

The news joined up with the caffeine wending through Jo's system and clicked her brain into high alert. "Well, well, well. Bennie's trip to San Francisco was pleasure, not business. Unless there were searches about that too?"

"None I could find," Lopez said.

Arnett's slumped posture straightened. "And since he ended up dead, I'm guessing the romance soured."

Lopez met his eyes. "If we're doing cheesy one-liners, how about this one: he may have gotten lucky, but his luck ran out."

"Very nice." Arnett nodded his approval over his venti coffee black.

Lopez fist-bumped him, then handed them both a printout. "Anyway. His credit card records were a bust. He used his card to check into a hotel the same morning he died, then nothing. No meals, no shopping, just radio silence."

Jo cast her mind back to the files she'd reviewed the night before. "Martin Scherer also didn't have any charges on his credit card."

"Yep. Definite parallels between the two." Lopez handed

them another set of printouts. "His phone records were a little more interesting. Check out the texts first."

Jo and Arnett each skimmed the sheets. "Some standard work texts, some BSing with buddies, and then a whole lot of what I'll generously call flirting," Arnett said.

Lopez tilted her head at Arnett. "Aww, what a quaint, old-fashioned way to say *sexting*. All that's missing is a dick pic, and I'm still deciding whether I feel relieved or cheated about that."

Arnett grimaced. "Put me firmly in the relieved column."

"Noted." Lopez pointed to the papers. "And you'll notice that same number, listed in his phone as Lucia, occurs frequently in the call log, as well."

"Do we know whose it is?" Jo asked.

"We do not," Lopez replied. "It's a burner phone, purchased in Phoenix. With cash, from a Walmart, and the surveillance footage is long gone."

Jo fingered the diamond at her neck. "So no name, but something odd is definitely going on. What normal person uses a burner to start up a relationship?"

Lopez swigged her Rockstar. "I mean, I *guess* I can see someone doing that? But it takes paranoid to a really pathological level."

Arnett rubbed his face. "They talk about how they can't wait to meet in person, so he must have met her online somehow."

"I told Jo already, I checked everything obvious on his computer. No World of Warcraft, no dating apps I could see," Lopez said. "And after I got the phone records yesterday, I called two of the friends he texts frequently and asked them if they knew anything about his new girlfriend. They both said the same thing—he wouldn't talk about it, and he's not normally the discreet type."

"Naya said something about that," Jo said. "Also strange."

"So, the next logical step as far as I can see is to get a

warrant for the burner phone's data," Lopez said. "Not just the call and text records, but location data. That should at least be able to confirm the burner is from San Francisco, although I'm not sure how much that helps."

Jo tapped her knuckles on the desk. "I've been thinking about that, actually."

Both Lopez's and Arnett's brows popped up. "I'm intrigued," Lopez said. "Do tell."

"Okay, well, you're the expert, so you tell me if this is even possible. But. You know that meth bust you helped with a while back, where you knew one perp's license plate and you used automated license plate readers to figure out who else was involved?"

A smile burst across Lopez's face. "That was badass, if I do say so myself."

"If I understand right, because your confidential informant gave you the one plate, you were able to track each ALPR it hit on the way from Boston down to Hartford, and every time it hit, you looked at all the other license plates that also hit that same location within, what, fifteen minutes before and after?"

"Ten. And then we compared each of those ten-minute data aggregates to see which plates also hit the next plate reader, then compared that subset to the next reader, so on across Massachusetts. By the time they got to the border, we had it narrowed down to three other license plate numbers that were still in proximity to our target, and so were almost certainly accomplices. We stopped all those cars and busted everybody." Lopez's smile broadened wickedly.

That was pretty much what Jo thought she remembered. "I'm wondering if we can do something similar with cell-tower data and these suicides. If the killer had their cell phone on and we can somehow search the pings near the Golden Gate Bridge at the time of each of these suicides, the number should appear in each of those data sets. So, basically, if we can identify a cell phone number that's present at the time of all the out-of-town deaths, or most of them, that would be our killer."

"Ooo, *interesting*." Lopez's eyes lit up, and she stroked her long ponytail. "Okay, I see a few problems right off the bat. First is getting the data in the first place. With the ALPR system, we have access to that information in real-time already, but we don't for cell phone data. Since we don't know what cell service provider our killer uses, we'd need data from all five major US cell phone carriers, and since that's a lot of privacy violation, we'd need one helluva justification to get a warrant."

Jo bounced her palm on the desk. "I've been thinking about that, too. I think we may be able to get access if we agree to analyze the data anonymously, without knowing any identifying information until we isolate out potential numbers from the data that fit our criteria. If they only have to give us information for the numbers that pop up as potentially belonging to our killer, we aren't violating privacy for anyone other than probable suspects."

Arnett pointed at her. "Nice."

Lopez gave a *not-bad* smirk. "Okay, so assume we get access, then. The next problem is, we don't have a dedicated system like we do with the ALPR that can quickly analyze the data. But—" She paused to unleash another Cheshire-cat grin. "I bet I can write some code that'll do the trick pretty darn fast."

Jo grinned back. "If anyone can do it, you can."

Lopez wiggled her eyebrows in acknowledgment. "Then the next problem is we're limited by how long each company keeps data from tower dumps—"

"Tower dumps?" Arnett asked.

"Data on all devices making contact with a given tower at a particular moment in time."

"Perfect," Jo said.

"I'm fairly sure that T-Mobile only keeps that data for three months at a time, and I believe Verizon and US Cellular are the next shortest, at a year. So we need data from at least two deaths, but we'd only be able to get data from all five providers for Bennie's time of death." She glanced at a printout. "This next most recent suicide, Jim Dornan, was just under a year ago, Friday, October twenty-third, and we'd be able to get data from four out of five providers for that one. As long as our killer wasn't on T-Mobile, it would still work. T-Mobile has about twenty-five-ish percent of the market, so the odds would still be on our side."

"More likely than not the data would be present," Jo said.

"Yep, for sure worth taking a shot still. But, if we only have two data sets, we won't be able to eliminate much because we'll still have a lot of numbers that occur in both sets. For example, the farther you go back in time, the fewer residents you have living in the area at both times—but in less than a year, not many will have moved, and their cell numbers will be present in both sets. But—" She held up a finger while she thought, and took a big gulp of her Rockstar.

Jo and Arnett waited patiently as a minute clicked by on the clock hanging over Lopez's workstation. Finally, she shook her head.

"I have some thoughts on ways to deal with that, so let's see what I can come up with. I'm not sure they'll work, but it'd be fun to try." She tapped the printout. "The next problem is, if our killer was smart enough to not bring their phone along with them, of course they won't show up in the data."

Jo shrugged. "Nothing we can do about that. This is us hoping they *did* have their phone with them."

"Yeppers. But the biggest problem of all is, we don't have an exact time of death for either Bennie or Jimmy. That means we'd have to examine at least a day or two's worth of data for both suicides. That's a ton of data, and with nothing to help us filter out the noise, I'm not sure it's tenable."

"I may have a solution for that part, actually. Bennie

Moreno had his cell phone with him when he fell into the water, and I can check to see if Jim Dornan did, too. Since—"

"That's brilliant!" Lopez interrupted. "Phones don't last long underwater, so—"

"If we can see when the tower stopped receiving signal from the phones, we'll not only know which tower we're looking at, but we'll have almost exact times of death," Jo finished triumphantly.

Lopez held out a fist for Jo to bump, then made an explosion noise. "Yes! I can work with that, for sure. You get started on the warrant, and I'll start brainstorming ways to subtract noise from the data, and on writing a program to do it."

"Are you sure you have the time? I know they have you on a ton of cases right now..." Jo said.

Lopez waved her off, already jotting notes with her other hand. "Are you kidding? I hardly ever get to do cool stuff like this. Go get me some data to work with!"

CHAPTER TWENTY-TWO

"Meanwhile, back in Greenfern," Arnett said as they slid back into their desks.

A flashing red light on her landline caught Jo's eye. She dialed her voicemail. "Tom Fischer," she told Arnett as she listened to the message.

"Nice of him to call that line instead of your cell," Arnett said.

She grimaced. "I'm sure he didn't at all do that out of some passive-aggressive hope I'd miss the message for days." She finished listening, tried to ignore Fischer's smarmy self-satisfaction, and hung up. "He says he talked to Travis this morning, and Travis claims the night Melissa died he picked up Avery, took her home, they decided they wanted pizza, so he went out to get it while she waited at home. Fischer says he lied because he was afraid if he couldn't come up with a solid alibi for all of Tuesday night, we'd assume he had something to do with Melissa's death."

"And he'd be right," Arnett said. "More so now that he lied to us."

"The problem is still evidence. His fingerprints have every

right to be all over the house, and the same thing with any hair or fibers he might have shed. The officers who canvassed the area came back with nobody who saw anything suspicious—"

"Might be because they wouldn't have noticed Travis going in, since it was his house," Arnett interjected.

"True, but I doubt that'll be enough for the jury. We have a possible motive, and now we have him lying about his alibi. But a defense attorney is going to claim it's crazy to think he'd kill Melissa to keep Avery safe when DCF was already watching the situation. The ADA'll want more to overcome reasonable doubt."

"What about follow the money? That apartment he lives in is garbage. I'm thinking he has to inherit the house, or Avery does, and as her guardian he'd be the one controlling it?"

Jo's brows popped up over the coffee she'd just sipped. "Excellent point. It might be good to look into both his and her money situation, and see if she had any life insurance of any sort. I'll text Lopez."

"In the meantime, due diligence on other possible suspects," Arnett said. "Recap?"

Jo thumbed out the text. "Suspect number two, Tinsley. Because she also lied to us about the last time she talked to Melissa. Seems like they were fighting on that call, so it's possible she was angry enough to kill Melissa."

"Travis said she was a user, and she wanted a job at Melissa's company."

"Travis may be lying about that to shift attention off of himself. But we should call Melissa's boss, regardless." Jo jotted down a reminder. "And if Tinsley looked up to Melissa and found out she really *was* abusing Avery, she might have felt duped. It can be painful when your hero falls off their pedestal. And we should call Highland Elementary's administrators too, to get the lay of the land. I did get a few vibes from her emails that her micro-managing wasn't always appreciated. Nothing big, but it might be a good idea for us to go through them a little more carefully."

"Sounds good. And the final possibility: a random sicko who read about the abuse in the paper and got triggered by it all." Arnett's expression was skeptical.

"Maybe not random, maybe someone who already had reason to dislike her. Another good reason to check in with her job and the elementary school," Jo said. "And that brings up a question that's been floating through my mind. Does reporting a housewife's alleged child abuse feel odd to you? Like public shaming? I mean, I know it's legal as long as what he's saying is true, and that someone did make the allegations. But especially naming the mother, that feels a bit slimy, doesn't it?"

"What's newsworthy probably depends on the day," Arnett said. "And he wouldn't be the first journalist to put his career ahead of any sort of empathy for others."

Jo raised her brows in agreement, and tapped her leg. "I'm surprised it's newsworthy *any* day."

"You think Travis got the reporter to write about it?"

"Or the attorney." Jo pulled out her phone. "Or even a friend or neighbor who was concerned for Avery. What did Travis say the reporter's name was, Rick Burke?"

"Yep," Arnett answered. "But why? To start a town mob?"

"If you're about to lose a custody battle, getting your ex ostracized in the community might be worth a shot." Jo pulled up the paper and verified the name, then stuck it into the search engine. Nothing came back; the engine worked via content words, not author. So she tried again, this time searching 'child abuse.' To her surprise, twenty articles came back from the last five years. "I stand corrected. Apparently it's *not* uncommon for *The Greenfern Daily* to write about child abuse. But—all the articles are written by the same guy, Rick Burke."

"So it might be worth talking to him about that particular interest."

"Okay, so." Jo pulled her notes closer. "Lopez is looking into Travis and Melissa Rollins' financials and insurance. We want to talk to Rick Burke, but before we head back out to Greenfern, we should probably take care of the ground work with Melissa's job and school."

"You take the school and I'll take the job," Arnett said.

They dove in, stopping only for a quick vending-machine lunch. Jo read rather than skimmed this time, but found the interactions to be pleasant, and typical. Even those who disagreed with Melissa about choices she made for the showcase enthusiastically congratulated her on how well the show turned out.

"Here's something weird," Arnett suddenly said.

Jo scooted her chair over to his desk. "What's that?"

"This email from her boss, Leigh Peisen."

She craned her neck in to see. Arnett pointed to a postscript at the end of an email summarizing that month's sales numbers: *Thanks for giving me the heads-up about Tinsley. Very much appreciated. I'll find a subtle way to take care of it.*

"When's the date on this?" Jo asked.

Arnett scrolled up. "The Friday before Melissa was killed. I missed it the first time I read it because it's below the sign-off, out of sight unless you scroll down. I noticed the same thing on another email, so went back and checked the others to be sure I didn't miss anything else."

"Probably why I missed it, too." Jo reached for her phone and tapped in the phone number listed in Leigh Peisen's email signature. The phone rang several times, and just as Jo prepared herself to leave a message, a brisk, efficient woman's voice answered.

"Gantry Pharmaceuticals, Leigh Peisen."

"Hello, Ms. Peisen. My name is Josette Fournier and I'm with the Oakhurst County SPDU. I'm investigating Melissa Rollins' death."

Leigh Peisen paused awkwardly—a pause Jo had heard from a thousand people struggling with an unexpected death in their professional sphere. "I still can't believe she's just—gone. How can I help you, Detective?"

"We've been looking through Melissa's emails to see if there's any indication someone may have wanted to harm her. Do you know of any tension with her colleagues?"

Her response was immediate. "Not that I'm aware of. Melissa was very good at her job and consistently outsold the rest of my team, but she was also very willing to share her technique with everyone. In fact, I asked her to mentor our last two hires, and they've both sung her praises and risen to the top of the group."

"Ah. Based on what her husband told us, I got the sense she might have had a bit of an edge."

"Oh, don't get me wrong, Melissa was competitive," Leigh said, and her voice quavered slightly. "But only with herself. She always wanted to outdo her previous sales. It was about work ethic, about being excellent at what she did and beating her personal best. She saw helping others on the team as a way to raise all boats. She was straightforward and had high standards, but both of her mentees told me they preferred that. They always knew where they stood with her and her guidance allowed them to excel."

Jo nodded as she took the appraisal in—Leigh Peisen knew how to measure her employees' pluses and minuses and weave them into a strong team. "So no conflicts you're aware of?"

"None."

Jo wrote 'NONE' on her notepad and scratched through it. "Just one last question, then. In an email about a week and a half ago, you said, *"Thanks for giving me the heads-up about Tinsley. Very much appreciated. I'll find a subtle way to take care of it."* Can you tell us what that was about?"

"Oh, right, that. Very strange." Her voice sounded slightly

perplexed. "Her friend Tinsley had been haranguing her about a job on our team. I guess because her husband just got furloughed? Whatever the reason, Melissa asked me to interview her for a position."

"And you did?"

"Of course. I'd have hired her sight unseen if Melissa asked me to. But then a couple of days later she came to me oddly unsettled and asked me *not* to consider her for the position."

"Did she say why?"

The line went quiet for a moment. "I'm trying to remember the exact words she used, but I can only remember the gist. Basically she left me with the impression that Tinsley had done something unethical, and she didn't want to bring someone like that on board."

"Something she did to Melissa?"

"I'm not sure, she didn't want to get into details. I can't remember exactly why, but my mind flew to blackmail. And she implied Tinsley might have more of a temper than she realized."

Jo wrote down *blackmail?!*, then glanced up at Arnett. "And how did you handle the situation?"

"I figured the best way was to go through the phone interview as I normally would, then I told Tinsley that we didn't have any current openings but I'd keep her name on file for the future," Leigh said.

"When was that?"

"Monday afternoon."

Jo shot another look at Arnett. "How did she take the news there was no opening?"

"Funny you should ask." She laughed dryly. "At the time I got the feeling she wasn't fooled, but there wasn't much she could do about it. Then this morning she called asking if a position had opened up, with the implication that we'd need someone to replace Melissa."

Jo suddenly felt a line of ants crawling over her. "That takes hutzpah."

"No, brass *cojones* is what it takes. I don't mind telling you, I found it highly distasteful. Melissa was right to warn me about her."

Jo cleared her throat. "Well, this has been extremely helpful. If you think of anything else that might help us, will you let us know?"

"I will."

Jo ended the call and turned to Arnett. "I guess that explains why Tinsley didn't want us to know about that Monday phone call."

"And it's a damned good reason for Melissa to be angry Monday evening," Arnett said.

"I've had just about enough of people lying to us." Jo stood up. "Time for a very different type of chat with Tinsley."

CHAPTER TWENTY-THREE

Half an hour later they pulled up to Tinsley's lemon-yellow colonial and brushed past the dwarf echinacea that ringed the house. Jo rang the bell twice before Tinsley appeared at the door, with a smear of flour on her shirt and across her forehead. A vision of a 1950s housewife struggling to keep her head above water flashed through Jo's mind.

Tinsley didn't hide her surprise, and the aggressive posture she'd taken during their previous conversation was gone. Instead, she was hesitant and tentative. "Detectives. I'm sorry, you caught me at a bad moment. How can I help you?"

Jo wasn't in the mood to tiptoe. "A short time ago we got off the phone with Leigh Peisen, and we'd like to talk to you about that conversation."

Tinsley's face fell, but she valiantly recomposed herself and reluctantly stepped back. "I—um—the house is a mess. Do you want to come in?"

"Thank you." Jo and Arnett stepped into the open-floor plan and followed her through a beige-and-gray living room, past a beige-and-brown dining set, into a beige-and-white kitchen. Other than the in-progress baking, the house was nearly as spotless as Melissa's house had been, although the less-pristine furniture gave away the inconvenient truth that actual people used it.

Tinsley gestured to the kitchen table. "Feel free to sit. Do you mind if I keep working while we talk? I have to finish these cupcakes or I won't have a chance to frost them before Heidi's dance class," Tinsley said.

Jo's brows raised—her sister Sophie would be appalled. She'd mentioned more than once that 'approved' snacks these days had to be healthy, like fruit and raw veggies, or string cheese. But maybe the Greenfern community had different guidelines.

"That's fine." Jo and Arnett both remained standing. "When we spoke to you Sunday, you said the last time you'd talked to Melissa was the week before, at the girls' soccer game."

Tinsley's eyes remained on the tins she was filling. "That's right."

"But when we checked Melissa's call record, we saw you called her the day before she died."

Tinsley's eyes bounced up to Jo's, wide and innocent, then searched the ceiling. "Oh, right—I remember now. We did talk then. I'm so sorry I forgot."

"What did you talk about?" Jo kept her face passive.

Tinsley shifted her weight from one foot to the other. "Nothing, really. She'd arranged for a job interview with her boss. I just caught her up on how that went."

"How did it go?" Arnett asked.

Defiance suddenly flashed in Tinsley's eyes. "Since you talked to Leigh Peisen, you already know how it went. I didn't get the job."

"You seem angry about that," Jo said, remembering Leigh's comment about Tinsley's potential temper.

Tinsley set down the ice-cream scoop she was using to fill the tins. "Yes, fine, I was angry. To put me through the charade of a fake phone interview with her boss only to tank me? That wasn't very nice."

"What makes you think she tanked you? From what Ms. Peisen said, they didn't have any current openings," Jo asked.

Tinsley's eyes narrowed. "I may not have an advanced degree but I'm not stupid. One day there was an opening, and suddenly there wasn't. And the way Leigh talked to me—it was clear from word one she was humoring me."

"So you confronted Melissa, and the call got heated?" Arnett asked.

Tinsley's face shifted, and tears filled her eyes. "I was upset, and I told her I didn't appreciate what she did. But all friends fight. I didn't want her dead, I swear."

Jo watched Tinsley's face. "Why wouldn't she want you to have a job at her company?"

"That's what I wanted to find out." She turned to put the cupcakes into the oven.

She was stalling. Buying herself time to think? Jo waited until she turned back. "What did she say?"

Tinsley grabbed a sponge and swiped at the counter where the cupcakes had just been. "She denied she had anything to do with it."

Jo made a quick decision—it was time to go out on a limb. Jo waited silently until Tinsley looked back up. "Leigh Peisen seemed to think Melissa's change of heart was due to blackmail."

Tinsley's eyes flicked frantically between the two of them for a long minute—finally, her face crumpled. "You—you don't know what it's like."

Jo softened her tone and lowered her voice. "Tell me what it's like."

Tears flowed onto her cheeks. "It's *impossible*, that's what it's like. No matter what I do, it's never enough. Other women manage it—like Melissa, her house was always spotless and she was on the PTA and she ran the showcase and she managed to get Avery back and forth from three different extracurriculars and the freaking brownies she made for the bake sales were 'legendary.'" She put finger quotes around the word, then gestured a frantic circle around the room. "And she had a job! I can't manage half of that, and Heidi's the one who suffers. She didn't get a slot in the Highland showcase and that was my fault because I didn't push her hard enough. I let her miss some rehearsals at the dance studio because she wasn't feeling well when I should have made her go, and then she got pushed to the back row of the dance studio showcase, too. She's slowly losing ground, and I don't know how to fix it."

Jo took another guess. "So you blackmailed the dance teacher?"

She slashed her hands across the tears on her cheeks. "That's what Becca told Melissa. But I never *blackmailed* her, I just explained to her how important it was for Heidi to have that slot."

"Why did Becca feel the need to tell Melissa anything?" Jo asked.

Defiance flashed in Tinsley's eyes again. "Look, I'm not proud of it, okay? But I didn't appreciate Becca acting all high-and-mighty, like she never makes mistakes. I explained to her that Heidi's performance was my fault, that I was the one who had made the decisions about allowing her to miss. But she didn't care, and so I told her that she should show a little more compassion, and that she was lucky I wasn't the same sort of bitch she was, because if I were, I'd go straight to her husband and tell him I saw her out with another man. Then I quit the school, because I knew Heidi wasn't going to have a fair chance there, and I knew I had to take her somewhere else where she could start fresh."

Jo's eyes narrowed—something wasn't adding up. "I'm still not clear on why Becca discussed the situation with Melissa.

Especially since I'd think she wouldn't want word to get around that she was cheating on her husband."

"That's exactly why—she wanted to cut it off at the pass, and convince Melissa I was lying. So she told Melissa *she* kicked *me* out of the school after I supposedly *blackmailed* her." She threw finger quotes around the word 'blackmail.'

It still didn't add up—Tinsley was either sanding off corners or flat-out lying. Had she really seen anything? Had Becca been the one to throw her out in light of the clumsy threat? "But you and Melissa were friends. Why would she believe Becca and not you?"

Tinsley's finger jabbed the air toward Jo. "*Exactly.* A *true* friend would have quit that trash school with me. But no, instead she took Becca's side and used it as an excuse to keep me from getting a job with her company."

"That's a crap thing for a friend to do," Arnett said. "My friend did that to me, I'm not sure I could stay friends with them."

Tinsley's jaw tightened. "*That's* why I didn't tell you about it, because I knew you'd think that. I was angry, yes. Friends get angry at each other, sometimes they even stop being friends. But it's not something I'd *kill* over."

Jo cleared her throat. "We'll need to know where you were Tuesday night."

Her voice went flat. "Tuesday night. Heidi has her violin lesson until five. I waited there until she was done, then we came home. I made dinner, we watched TV, then went to bed."

"Can anybody verify that?"

She pulled up a contact on her phone. "Here's the number for her violin teacher, she'll confirm I waited for Heidi. My husband was here when we got home, but then he went to play poker with his friends after dinner, around six thirty."

"Leigh Peisen said he just lost his job?"

She shook her head. "They don't play for money. And he was laid off nine months ago. His company relocated to Maine."

Jo ended the interview, and she and Arnett saw themselves out.

Arnett stared back at the house as Jo drove away. "I don't know about cupcakes," he said, "but she sure can whip up a batch of lies."

CHAPTER TWENTY-FOUR

"You mean you don't believe Tinsley's the injured party in the dance-school drama?" Jo deadpanned.

"Guess I'm just an old cynic," Arnett replied.

"Whatever happened, Tinsley did something unsavory." Jo slid to a stop at a red light.

"But just because she'd badger or blackmail a teacher into giving her daughter a dance slot doesn't mean she'd kill over it."

Jo wagged her head. "Between my sister and what we saw at Briar Ridge a few months ago, I've learned not to underestimate the pressure parents are under with respect to their kids. You saw how emotional she got in there—she's not in a good place, and if you add on that she needs a job and feels like her friend betrayed her, it might have been one bridge too far."

"Except that doesn't explain why she'd nail her into a closet," Arnett said. "And she doesn't look strong enough to do it."

"Unless she did it to frame Travis," Jo said. "And haven't you learned after everything that happened at Briar Ridge last spring that you should never underestimate soccer moms?"

"Fair enough. But I'm still thinking there's more we need to learn from the people at Highland Elementary. I'll call while you drive."

But after talking to the principal, Avery Rollins' teacher, and several parents Melissa worked with on the showcase, Arnett couldn't dig up anything else relevant.

Jo's phone rang. It was Lopez, and Jo put her on speaker. "What's up?"

"Good instincts on the Rollins' financial situation. He came out with the short end of the stick in the divorce, and since they haven't sold the house yet, it goes right back to him now that she's dead. And, I checked with HR at Gantry Pharma, and it turns out she has a life insurance policy that's going to pay out a hundred and fifty thousand bucks—to Travis. He's still named as beneficiary."

"Great job, thanks so much," Jo said.

"I live to serve," she sing-songed, then hung up.

"Yeah, this is starting to feel like an if-it-looks-like-a-duck situation," Arnett said. "Except for that pesky lack of physical evidence."

"So we keep digging, even if we have to settle for a death-by-a-thousand-cuts approach. Travis had motive over custody of Avery, and now he stands to benefit financially. If we find out he asked Burke to write the articles about Melissa, we'll have another piece for the ADA to slip into place." The GPS announced their arrival, and Jo pulled over to the curb.

Arnett peered out his side window. "This is *The Greenfern Daily*'s offices?"

"I think so." Jo studied the building in front of them, set back on a large parcel of land. The design was oddly asymmetrical—the left third consisted almost entirely of glass while the right portion was compressed rocks with slivers of window and metal supports peeking out. A large rectangular overhang jutted over patioed steps and a circular drive. "Either that or a portal burst open and vomited up the 1970s."

"Absolutely no identifying information whatsoever. Very helpful," Arnett said.

Jo considered. "Maybe they don't want to advertise to disgruntled members of the public where they should show up to express their displeasure?"

"Sad, but probably true." Arnett released his seat belt. "Guess we'll find out soon enough."

After pushing through the building's massive glass door, Jo spoke with the receptionist. He pointed toward a row of grungy chairs against the wall that made Jo's glutes cramp on sight; she and Arnett elected to remain standing.

An average-sized white man appeared a few minutes later, with brown corduroy pants, a ponytail of frizzy black hair, and wire-rimmed John Lennon glasses that all matched the building's design so perfectly Jo had to fight an unsettling sensation she'd stepped back through time.

"You're the detectives?" he asked.

Jo considered his rudeness as she slid over her blazer to reveal her badge. Someone had almost certainly warned him they were coming—so why let them see his discomfort with their visit? "Detective Jo Fournier, and my partner Detective Bob Arnett. We're here about the Melissa Rollins murder."

"I have a few questions of my own about that." He looked them both up and down. "The police haven't been very forthcoming. Follow me."

As soon as he turned his back, Arnett shot Jo a look. She responded with an amused grin—she'd dealt with egos like Burke's before, and they almost always underestimated her.

Burke led them to what Jo assumed was a desk under the jumble of files, clippings, notepads, and coffee cups. He dropped into an office chair personalized by a variety of stains, then pointed at two folding-chairs in the corner of his cubicle. Jo grabbed them and passed one to Arnett. Burke swung his chair back and forth in a half-arc, appraising them.

"Thanks so much for talking with us," Jo said. "We'd like to ask you about your coverage of Melissa Rollins. I've never seen that type of issue included in a paper's crime beat before."

"Crimes are crimes." He leaned forward again and pulled a pen and pad toward him. "The official press report on Melissa Rollins' death says she was murdered. Why do you believe that?"

"Allegations of child abuse in the course of custody battles are a bit more complicated than other situations," Jo said.

He smirked. "I guess that depends on your perspective. I'm always careful to make sure I state they're allegations. But once the judge takes away custody, that's a pretty clear ruling that the allegations have been substantiated, wouldn't you say?"

Jo ignored his attempt to bait her. "Not always. My understanding is the custody rights in this case were temporarily revoked pending investigation, and then reinstated."

"And when that happened, I printed it." He thwacked the pad repeatedly with the pen. "How did Melissa Rollins die?"

"My understanding is many journalists feel they have an ethical obligation to be circumspect when it comes to reporting details about child abuse cases. But you print the parents' names, and details about the abuse."

"Was there a question in there? Not only is it legal to print that information, I believe it's a moral imperative. Child abuse is an epidemic in this country, Detective. Every year *four million* cases are reported to child protection agencies throughout the country. Those children suffer irreparable physical and psychological damage they carry with them their whole lives—and those are the children who don't die in the course of the abuse. Thousands do. I believe journalists have an ethical obligation to call out such abuse."

Arnett stirred in his chair, and Jo shifted her weight toward him in silent reassurance. As much as Burke's smarmy attitude annoyed her, she knew it was nails on Arnett's mental chalkboard, and she needed to keep careful control of the emotional tone. "We noticed only a subset of abuse cases end up in your column. What caused you to pay attention to this particular one?"

"I can only report on cases that are brought to my attention and come from reliable sources. But in this case, I couldn't ignore the egregious nature of the abuse. Was Melissa Rollins killed in a home invasion? A source told me a friend went to her house when she didn't show up to a..."—he made a show of shifting several folders to uncover a legal pad—"soccer game."

Jo raised her brows in a carefully calculated arch. "Interesting you consider this abuse notably egregious. I've seen children beaten to the point where they had to be hospitalized. And as you say, some even killed."

Burke's eyes narrowed, and his jaw flexed. "The *unusual* nature of the abuse, then."

She'd hit some sort of nerve—time to double down. "Timeouts kneeling in a corner. Restriction when her grades weren't good. Hardly seems worth mentioning in a news article." She shrugged with studied nonchalance.

He leaned toward her, red creeping across his cheeks. "Making a child piss herself if she didn't get a song perfect. Locking her in a closet overnight. Telling her she's worthless. You find that acceptable?"

"How did you find out about those incidents? DCF can't disclose that to you, and we couldn't find any public records regarding the custody decisions."

He held her gaze. "Interesting."

Jo refused to break the eye contact. "So how did you learn about them?"

His smarmy smile returned. "Tsk, tsk, tsk. You know I can't give you my sources, Detective."

"You choose whether to reveal your sources, and in this case, whoever leaked that information to you had an agenda.

They used you, and they may be responsible for Melissa Rollins' death."

"Oh, come now, Detective." He crossed his legs. "You can't really expect me to identify them after you've told me you consider them a suspect?"

She widened her eyes ever so slightly. "I'd expect that if justice is as important to you as you've hinted, you'd want to help us find Melissa's killer."

"That assumes I believe justice hasn't already been served."

"So you think Melissa Rollins deserved what she got," Arnett broke in.

Burke's gaze shifted to Arnett. "How would I know? I don't even know how she died. Was she shot? What makes you think her death was related to her custody fight?"

He was trying to regain control of the interaction. Too little too late—she'd seen his Achilles' heel. She tilted her head and put on a little grin, then bent toward him conspiratorially. "You didn't get Melissa's information directly from the family court docket. Since you seem to have a fondness for writing about child abuse cases, I have to wonder—why is this an important enough issue for you to have a source embedded in the probate-and-family court?"

This time the red didn't just tinge his cheeks, it crept full on across his face and neck. He stared at her for a long moment, the muscles at his temples clenching and unclenching, then stood up. "I think we've been as helpful to one another as we're going to be. I'm sure you can find your way out?"

Jo and Arnett both stood. "I'm sure we can," Jo said. "But before we go, we need to know where you were on the evening of August seventeenth."

One of his hands clenched into a fist—he noticed her gaze flick down, and he released it. "I believe I was here working on a story that night."

"Can anyone verify that?" Arnett asked.

Burke held up his hands in a mocking gesture. "No idea. I guess you'll have to do some detective work and find out."

Arnett's hand twitched.

Jo hurried to step in. "We'll take that as a no, Mr. Burke." She pulled a card out of her pocket and flicked it up through her fingers. "If you find someone who can corroborate your story, have them call us. And if you come across information that might help us, we'd love to hear from you."

He took the card and tossed it into the chaos on his desk. "And I'm sure that as soon as you have information to disseminate, I'll be the first person you call."

Jo turned and strode away, Arnett at her side.

Once they were outside the building, she turned to him. "Mr. Burke seems to have a *very* sensitive spot when it comes to issues of child abuse, wouldn't you say?"

"Sure does," Arnett said. "I think we need to find out why that is."

CHAPTER TWENTY-FIVE

Burke waited for a full five minutes, pretending to write on a notepad, until he looked back over his shoulder.

How fucking *dare* they?

There was no law against reporting on child abuse cases, as long as the children weren't named. And was he supposed to feel guilty about calling out the abusers? Horrible, despicable people that deserved whatever consequences came their way? And they were going to insinuate *he'd* done something wrong?

If they'd seen the things he'd seen. Gone through what he'd gone through. Watched the insidious, destructive way abuse threaded its tentacles through children's souls.

You have to be careful, the voice in the back of his head whispered to him. *She saw it in your face. She's smarter than you expected.*

He strode to the window, and watched the detectives get in their car and drive away.

He couldn't lose his cool like that again.

CHAPTER TWENTY-SIX

"My guess is Burke watched someone he cared about get abused, was married to an abuser, or most likely, was abused himself," Jo said as they rounded the corner away from *The Greenfern Daily* building. "Whether he's our killer or not, he's got a personal agenda here."

"If he was, he may be associated with a file somewhere in DCF." Arnett signaled a turn.

"And likely to have at least one long-term, intimate contact there." Jo smiled. "Don't you have a contact relatively high up in DCF?"

"Yeah, but she's out in Springfield."

"He might not be from Greenfern anyway, but aren't all the systems interconnected?"

"I'm not sure." He pulled over and took out his phone, scrolled for a minute, then tapped.

The phone rang, then a middle-aged woman's voice picked up. "I'll be damned, Bob Arnett. Haven't heard from you in a while, so this must mean trouble."

He broke out into a grin. "How goes it, Loretta?"

"Can't complain. Or, I could, but it wouldn't do any good, so why waste my breath? You?"

"Not bad, not bad. But you're right, I have a favor to ask."

"Aw, geez. Hit me with it," Loretta said.

Jo stared over at Arnett, hiding her smile.

"We're investigating a murdered woman. I'll give you the details if you want, but what it boils down to is we need to find out if a man named Rick Burke came through the system in any capacity, most likely as an abused kid."

Computer keys clacked in the background. "When would this have been?"

Arnett turned to Jo. "He's, what, about thirty-five? So if he were the abused party, at least fifteen years ago. Probably more like twenty."

Jo nodded, and continued to listen in amused silence.

The clacking stopped. "In Springfield?"

"Not sure. Most likely Greenfern."

"Can't help you then. That long ago, especially if it happened before his teen years, the file wouldn't be in the computer. I'm happy to dig through the boxes here for you, but if it's out in Greenfern, you're gonna have to talk to someone there."

"Don't suppose you can hook me up?"

"Renata Cruz. Straight shooter, doesn't take any crap from anyone. Tell her she still owes me for Pence Strictland."

"Pence Strictland?"

"Never you mind." She hung up.

Arnett chuckled, then looked up and noticed Jo's stare. "What?"

"I didn't know you had a sister," Jo said.

"So funny I almost forgot to laugh." He tapped at the phone again.

A minute later someone answered. "Department of Children and Families."

"Is Renata Cruz available?"

"Hold, please."

After a long stretch of 1960s muzak, an efficient-sounding older woman came on the line. "Renata Cruz."

Arnett quickly summarized why he was calling.

Again the sound of typing came over the speaker. "Nothing's coming up for me under that name, but that doesn't necessarily mean anything. Loretta's right, depending on how old he was when the investigation was opened, it's very possible the file wouldn't have been computerized. I can dig in our archives and get you an answer by tomorrow afternoon if that works?"

"We'd appreciate that very much."

"Not a problem. I can call you back at this number?"

"That works perfectly. Thank you. And Loretta says you still owe her one for Pence Strictland."

Renata barked a loud laugh. "I'll be in touch, Detective. Have a good evening."

CHAPTER TWENTY-SEVEN

I was five the first time I remember my mother hitting me. I can still feel the shock of it, the deep sense that I'd been betrayed. Ridiculous because I should have been prepared—I'd seen her beat my older sister often enough. But I guess I never thought she'd do it to me, that I was somehow special.

We were in church, and I had to go to the bathroom. She told me to hold it, that I had to learn how to be still during the homily. But it was urgent and I couldn't help squirming, and the people around us started to stare. So she bundled my sister and me up out of the pew and into the church bathroom, her hand clenched around my arm the entire way.

I remember the physical pain, of course. The explosion of agony that bloomed across the side of my head when something— to this day I'm not sure what—struck me out of nowhere. How it then enveloped all of me as she rained blows down my back, my shoulders, and sides when I curled into a protective ball.

The physical pain faded, of course. What didn't fade, what haunted me for years, was the helplessness. Knowing it could happen again at any moment, without reason or warning. The intense panic when her face shifted, when her mouth screwed up and her cheeks flushed and she'd seem to grow ten times her normal size, looming over me, screaming until white flecks formed in the corner of her mouth. Dragging me, hitting me with whatever convenient object she could reach. The feeling I was never safe, that the person who was supposed to protect me was the one I needed to fear the most, and that left me no safe place to hide except inside myself.

But the worst is the guilt that haunted me, and still haunts me. Guilt that I couldn't do anything but watch or hide when it happened to my sister, and guilt that I didn't stop it in time. But worse—guilt that when she beat my sister my first and strongest emotion was relief that it wasn't happening to me.

To this day when I look at myself in the mirror, I think of her and I see a selfish, unforgiveable coward.

CHAPTER TWENTY-EIGHT

Picking up Fournier's trail was easier than Diana had dared hope. She'd identified Fournier's address the night before, and waited far down her street for her to emerge before dawn broke the next morning. Fournier was a responsible driver, signaled all her turns and didn't speed, so Diana had no trouble following at a far enough distance to not be detected. She pulled into one of her scouted spots as Fournier parked and had plenty of time to get a good, long look at Fournier in three dimensions.

Diana cocked her head as she watched. Fournier had been pretty in her picture, but was even more attractive in the flesh. There was something Diana couldn't put her finger on—the way she carried herself, her presence. The way her clothes hung on her, the way her hair bounced. She walked with confidence but not swagger, had a quiet strength that was powerful without being menacing.

Something about her was familiar, but Diana couldn't quite place why.

Something else tugged at her. She liked this woman, she realized. An odd reaction to someone who was an existential threat, because she'd have to slit Fournier's throat if she got too close. But nonetheless, she felt sure somehow that under different circumstances, she and Josette Fournier would be friends.

Once Fournier disappeared inside, Diana had settled in to wait. She had no idea what a day in the life of a police detective looked like, so no way to predict whether Fournier would leave again in ten minutes or ten hours. Her research told her most detective work was done from behind a desk, so she'd prepared for a long wait: healthy snacks, caffeine, and a special bottle with a funneled top in case she needed to urinate. She glanced over at it and sighed—a necessary evil on stakeouts, but she'd never fully get used to it.

Half an hour turned into an hour, then two, then six. Just as she began to think she must have missed Fournier somehow, she appeared. Along with a kind-looking man with a dad bod and just enough gray to look distinguished if he'd get a proper haircut—from the research she'd done, had to be Arnett.

She followed them at a careful distance, hoping that detectives were more used to tailing people than detecting tails. They wound their way into a suburban haven called Greenfern, a town that instantly transported Diana to the mini-metropolis she'd grown up in. When they pulled up in front of a sweet little colonial, she watched through binoculars, a block and a half away. A frantic, guilty-looking little woman twitched like a little mouse as soon as she saw them—she had something to hide, and even the most brain-dead of detectives would realize that immediately. Diana smiled as Fournier took the lead.

The visit was shorter than she expected, and she hurried to start up again when they abruptly appeared. Next they headed to a far-west section of town, where they parked in front of an ugly industrial building set out in a field. Nearly impossible for her to follow without being noticed, so she passed by, did a U-turn, and parked along the next side street. She peered around for some sort of identifying information, but finally pulled up the location app on her phone. After a little sleuthing, she came up with a name—*The Greenfern Daily*, the local newspaper. Interesting, and unexpected.

After finishing their business they drove back to Oakhurst. Diana almost cheered when the pair reemerged an hour later, each heading to their respective cars—the work day was over, and Fournier would be heading out to a personal life. Anticipation tingled through Diana's chest as she considered the possibilities. She found articles reporting Fournier had been shot in the line of duty, and had faced down multiple murderers—she wasn't the sort of person who'd be intimidated by a personal threat. But she'd thrown all personal and professional caution to the wind the previous spring when someone had kidnapped her niece, an instinct Diana very much understood—so the way to kneecap her would be through the people she loved.

Fournier stopped at an Italian restaurant named Sal's, and appeared twenty minutes later carrying a white plastic bag. Then she drove back to her quiet house on her quiet street, while Diana watched the way her head tilted, and the way her fingers drummed the steering wheel, and the way she periodically reached up to her throat. All somehow endearing, although Diana couldn't quite figure out why, and again the sense of familiarity came over her. She again parked a block and a half back and watched through binoculars. But nobody came or went, and three hours later all the lights in the house went dark.

Diana grabbed food at a drive-thru and considered what she'd learned. The trip to Greenfern wasn't relevant to her, it was about the Melissa Rollins case. But before that, whatever Fournier had done inside the police building could have been about anything. That meant she hadn't achieved either of her objectives so far: to determine whether Fournier was still investigating Bennie's murder, and to obtain some form of personal leverage against her.

She peered through the darkness at the sweet college town, and made a decision—not the worst place to have to stay for a few more days.

CHAPTER TWENTY-NINE

AUGUST 25TH

Jo met the next morning groggy and grumpy. With Matt working extra hours, she'd slept alone, and as much as she didn't want to admit it to herself, the bed felt empty and cold without him. It left her disconcerted in a way she wasn't sure how to process, so she headed in early.

A triple mocha—iced yet again—helped raise her spirits, and once she settled into her desk she dove in, drilling deep into Rick Burke. But, try as she might, she couldn't find anything even vaguely of interest—he didn't have as much as a parking ticket, he carried no balance on his credit cards, and he seemed to be well respected within his field. He'd worked for *The Greenfern Daily* since he interned during college, and had progressed steadily from less important pieces into the crime beat. If he was a vicious murderer, he was very good at keeping his outsides squeaky clean.

Arnett handed her a fresh mocha when he arrived, this one hot. "Laura sends her love, and says she's looking forward to seeing Sophie again, and meeting Matt."

"Thanks for the reminder. I never texted Sophie a confirmation." Jo grabbed her phone and tapped out the text.

"Also, I got a call on the way here from Renata Cruz. She found a file for Rick Burke last night. She's out of the office today, but said she left the file with Alison Choi last night for us to pick up."

Jo cradled the beverage gratefully, soaking in the scent, and said goodbye to HQ's air conditioning. "Let's head over."

"Whoa, Nellie." He laughed. "You really do have a mental block when it comes to Hayes. You're forgetting the Wednesday mandatory departmental meeting."

Jo slumped back into her chair and rubbed her face. "Oh, God."

One of the many changes Lieutenant Hayes had made upon arriving from upstate New York was to institute an additional mandatory meeting each week on each shift, and she herself attended every one. The stated goals for the meetings were to get to know each of her detectives, and to familiarize herself with the workings of the department. Her real goal had been to mark her territory by putting her fingers into everything.

"I know, I know." Arnett shook his head in faux sympathy. "I gotta say, you're so good at dealing with hierarchy, it's refreshing to see someone get under your skin. Makes you seem more human."

Jo flashed him a dirty look. "Just wait 'til she comes for you, Golden Boy."

He bowed slightly and swept his arm out in front of him. "After you."

With a pointed grimace, she grabbed her coffee and forced herself up. Lopez and Marzillo were already sitting in the back of the briefing room, absorbed in pictures of blood spatter across two walls and a floor.

Jo slipped into a chair next to them. "That for Paletta's double homicide?"

"Yep." Marzillo's glance flitted over her face. "What's wrong?"

Jo pursed her brow indignantly. "Nothing."

"Tell that to your face," Lopez said. "I'd think you'd be happy, just before we headed in here I saw we got the go-ahead with the warrants on Bennie Moreno's case. I hope to have some cell data to analyze in the next few hours. But." She glanced up at the door before continuing, and her voice dropped. "Hayes came in earlier and before I could cover it, saw Bennie's computer *and* the documentation I had attached to it. I'm telling you, that woman's eyesight is like a hawk got bitten by a radioactive spider after eating a bucket of genetically modified carrots. She asked me what it was for and I kinda had to tell her."

"It's a myth that carrots are good for your eyes," Marzillo said, eyes back on the pictures.

"Dammit. What did she say?" Jo whispered, one eye watching the door for Lieutenant Hayes.

As Lopez started to respond, the door flew open and Hayes marched in with clipboard clasped to her side, her blonde bun sleeked back so tight it made *Jo's* scalp ache. She slapped the clipboard onto the podium. "No time to waste, let's get started. We'll shake things up by starting from the back. Marzillo?"

Marzillo gave a brief, general update on the state of the lab, including a weekly plea for additional equipment that would help her get results back to the detectives faster and more effectively. Hayes "took it under advisement" and moved on.

"Arnett and Fournier," she said.

Jo responded. "We're still waiting for DNA results for the Trinchian murder and Sanford rape cases. The ADA is moving forward with charges on the Gonzalez murder. Sunday we were called out to a new homicide, Melissa Rollins." As she gave a quick summary, she watched Hayes' glare turn withering.

"Leads?"

"Strongest suspect is the ex-husband, Travis Rollins." She laid out the reasons why.

"Why haven't you arrested him?" The question was a bullet.

"We have no conclusive evidence to put him at the scene. And, there's at least one other suspect any defense attorney could make into persuasive reasonable doubt." She laid out the case against Tinsley Sparks. "And because the MO is strange and the alleged abuse was reported in the local paper, it's also possible a person or persons unknown attacked Melissa."

Peter Lee, a relatively new detective in the department, jumped in as soon as she finished. "Did you say there was an injection site on your vic's arm, but no other signs of IV drug use?"

"Correct." Jo held her breath as Hayes' death stare swiveled to Lee—Hayes did not like to be preempted.

"To be precise, two injection sites nearly on top of one another," Marzillo added.

"Probably doesn't mean anything, but we had a case like that, what, about a year ago?" He shot a glance at his partner, Dave Ortiz. "Also in Greenfern. Louisa Pryzik. Head caved in during what looked like a robbery gone bad, but had an injection site on her arm despite no drug history and no recent trip to the doctor. I didn't think much of it, but it's hinky your case has the same thing. The case had almost no leads from the start, and the few we did have fizzled out. We put it in deep freeze a few months ago."

Arnett sat up in his chair as Lee spoke. "Mind if we take a look?"

"Have at it."

Hayes seized the opportunity to regain control of the conversation. "See, boys and girls? This is what happens when we all play well together. Guess these extra meetings aren't a waste of time after all." She shot a look at Fournier, then moved on to the next pair of detectives.

Jo's fist bounced against her thigh for the next hour as the detectives went over their cases, until Hayes dismissed everyone. Jo rose to head for the exit, but Hayes shot out a hand toward her. "Fournier. Please hang back."

Jo froze, surprised, and Arnett drew up next to her.

"Just Fournier." Hayes waved him on.

Jo's mind flew to the DCF file waiting for her in Greenfern —she didn't have the time or the inclination to deal with this. Her pulse raced, and she chastised herself. She was a grown woman in her early forties, not a teenager summoned to the principal's office. People only had the control over you that you allowed them, and she was giving this woman far too much.

Once the last person filed out, Hayes turned to her. "We seem to have some sort of problem."

Jo kept her face pointedly neutral. "I'm not sure what you mean."

"You've ignored my requests to be apprised of all new investigations in a timely manner. I have to follow up texts in order to get you to respond. But even more worrying, you seem to have taken it upon yourself to direct *my team* to run analyses on computers that have nothing to do with your assigned casework."

Jo ignored the heat that crept up under her shirt. It wasn't worth objecting that she'd informed Hayes about the Rollins case in less than twenty-four hours. It also wasn't worth getting into an explanation of how the Scherer case was related to a previous murder in the area. Whatever was going on here, it wasn't actually about any of that, and Jo had lived long enough to know that when people were baiting you, the stupidest thing to do was bite.

"I apologize for the oversight. I'll make sure to run everything by you first."

Hayes narrowed her eyes. "You've been a detective for twenty years and you only just now understand we're working with limited resources and you're not the only detective whose cases matter? Not surprising you weren't able to hold on to the lieutenant position with that sort of self-serving outlook."

Jo practically heard the pieces click into place, and the tension drained from her body. Hayes had hoped to deliver a death blow, but instead she'd revealed her hand.

When she didn't respond, Hayes continued. "Lopez told me this had to do with a serial killer who turned up dead eight years ago, while you were lieutenant, who you weren't fast enough to catch. I get that you can't let go that you screwed up the case, but that doesn't give you the right to channel resources into some fool's errand when we don't have enough man hours to work the actual cases we have, especially given the summer spike. Maybe if you weren't splitting your attention on matters that aren't in your caseload, you'd have a decent lead on the Rollins case by now. Don't let me catch you pulling a stunt like this again unless you want to find yourself back in a uniform."

Jo kept her tone even. "I understand. Is there anything else?"

An amusing blend of confusion and annoyance plastered Hayes' face. After a pause, she took a last shot. "Yes. In future, respond to my communications in a timely manner. You'd do well not to mess with the bull, Detective. Now go."

As Jo turned out of the room, she barreled directly into Lopez, who grabbed her wrist and hurried her around the corner into the lab.

Lopez gaped at her, eyes wide. "Please tell me the Wicked Witch of Schenectady did *not* just quote *The Breakfast Club* at you."

CHAPTER THIRTY

Half an hour later, Jo chased away the stress of her tête-à-tête with Hayes by sinking her teeth deep into a meatball sub, then closed her eyes to savor the melange of Italian bread, spicy tomatoes, gooey mozzarella, and thick meat. She swallowed, and washed it all down with her Diet Coke. "I can't thank you enough for cutting out early for lunch."

"Like it's so hard to talk me into Sal's," Arnett said, mouth full of his own sub.

"Ten thirty's early even for you. Thank goodness they were willing to dip into the lunch menu for us. Eggs and pancakes just wouldn't have cut it."

"As much money as we spend here, it's the least they can do." He dove back into the sandwich. "And don't let Hayes get to you. It's not like you, me, and Lopez don't know how to get things done outside of official channels."

She nodded, but didn't respond—it was one thing to put her own career on the line, but dragging Arnett and Lopez in made her antsy, even if they had all done it before. She sighed—maybe she should just drop the whole thing, for everyone's sake.

When she'd finished her sub, she pushed her plate out of the way to make room for the file Lee had alerted them to. "Louisa Pryzik, thirty-two-year-old white woman, found dead in her home in Greenfern on October fifteenth of last year. Someone tied her to a chair in her kitchen, then bashed the front of her head in with a frying pan, which was found nearby with hair and blood on it. She also had several other bruises, and the injection site Lee mentioned on her left arm."

Arnett held up a hand. "Wait. Tied up and *then* smashed in the head?"

"Apparently." Jo rotated the file so he could see the crime scene photos. They showed Louisa tied to the chair with cord around her chest and feet, head lolling to one side and blood trickling down her neck and shoulder.

"That makes no sense. And if you wanted to kill her, why go through the hassle of tying her up? And if you just want her contained, why kill her *after* you have her secured?"

Jo's brow creased. "Maybe there was a struggle, and the killer was just trying to subdue her? Then once they thought they'd knocked her out, they tied her up and didn't realize they'd hit her hard enough to kill her?"

"Possible," Arnett said, but didn't look convinced. "Then why the injection?"

Jo swiveled the file back around and flipped through. "The ME wondered about that, too, and was very thorough with the tests. They found GHB in her system. She was drugged."

"Which is what we suspected happened to Melissa Rollins," Arnett said. "Although she had two injection sites, and Louisa only has one?"

"Yes. Maybe they missed Melissa's vein with the first attempt? That happens to me all the time when I get blood taken. Apparently I have very dainty blood vessels." Jo flipped back to the crime scene pictures. "But the GHB makes even less sense to the scene, because why knock her out if she's already tied up? Or, why bother to tie her up if you already have her knocked out?"

Arnett pointed at the file. "Lee said it seemed like a robbery gone wrong, and they ultimately decided it was staged?"

Jo nodded. "Her purse was found rifled on the floor, with no cash or credit cards in her wallet. But there was a jewelry box and a laptop in the bedroom that wasn't touched, and her phone was found on the counter."

"Right." Arnett scratched his chin as he thought.

Jo kept reading. "The initial suspect—well, the only suspect they ever had—was Louisa's ex-boyfriend, Dustin Heidami. He was the father of Louisa's daughter, Raina—" She stopped short, shoved the folder back toward Arnett, and jabbed a finger at a passage on the page. "And Heidami had filed a report with DCF alleging Louisa was abusing her. The initial investigation was 'supported' and Raina was placed with Heidami. But Louisa requested what they call a fair hearing, and the decision was then reversed to partial custody."

Arnett bent to read. "Another borderline case of psychologically harsh discipline?"

"Nope. These allegations were flat-out physical abuse. Supposedly Louisa beat Raina."

"So how was she able to get the decision reversed?"

Jo skimmed, looking for the information. "The file doesn't go into detail about that. I don't think Lee and Ortiz felt it was relevant."

"Not sure I would have, either."

"But, it does say Heidami had an alibi they couldn't get around. He worked overtime the evening Louisa was killed, witnessed by at least twenty other employees and his boss."

"Where was the daughter?"

"With Heidami's father, who watched her after school

during the weeks when Heidami had her. He and Louisa shared custody."

Arnett waved at the waiter. "Time to take that trip back out to Greenfern."

————

When they asked Alison Choi to look up Raina Pryzik's file, she was understandably confused. "I thought you were here to pick up the Burke file?"

"We are, but we think Raina Pryzik might be related to it all," Jo answered.

"To what all?" Her eyes bounced back and forth between them. "What's going on, detectives?"

"We're not quite sure. Are you familiar with the name?" Jo asked.

She shook her head. "That's not one of mine. How do you spell it?"

"P-R-Y-Z-I-K."

Alison scanned the monitor. "Found it. That was one of Steve Brodlin's cases. Let me print you out a summary and pull the physical file for you."

As Alison exited the cubicle, Jo flipped open the file on Rick Burke and scanned it. "The initial investigation on Burke was opened when he was eight. Apparently one of his teachers reported noticing on repeated occasions that he had more bruises than he should have."

"Who was the social worker on the case?" Arnett asked.

Jo flipped back and located the name. "Someone named Lila Doug. From what I can tell here, there was an initial decision to remove Rick from his mother's custody, and he went to live with his grandmother. But..." she went quiet for a moment as she skimmed and flicked through the file "... Rick's mother objected to that decision and asked for a fair hearing. The decision was reversed because they couldn't prove definitely that the mother had caused the abuse, but the whole situation went back and forth for several years."

"So, just like with Melissa and Avery, and Louisa and Raina."

"Definitely an odd coincidence, and definitely the sort of history I'd expect for someone triggered by child abuse. Oh, this is interesting—hold on a sec."

Arnett bent toward her to read the file from the side.

"It says here Rick's mother threw him out when he was sixteen."

"Threw him out?"

Jo pointed to the file. "According to this, she tried to punch him, and he defended himself—he didn't hit her, but he blocked the punch by grabbing her hand and when he wouldn't let go, she freaked out and told him to get out of her house."

"Guess that's what happens when the kid you've been abusing for years finally grows bigger than you."

Jo raised her eyebrows in agreement. "He went to stay with a friend who was two years older and had his own place. The mother must have realized that wasn't going to look very good, so she went to the police and reported him as a runaway, and they told DCF."

"Let me guess, they drug him back?"

"No, actually." Jo's brow knit. "I'm trying to read between the lines here, because the notes are strange. The upshot is, Rick's mother agreed it was best for him to live with his friend until he went away to college. He got a part-time job at McDonald's to help pay his way with his friend, and then graduated and enrolled successfully at Oakhurst U."

Alison Choi appeared back around the cubicle with a file folder in her hand, and picked up the waiting printout. She pushed them both toward Jo and Arnett. "There you go."

"Thank you so much," Jo said. "Is there any chance we can talk to Lila Doug?"

A shadow passed over her face. "Lila was my mentor when I started here. She passed away about a year and a half ago."

CHAPTER THIRTY-ONE

"Coincidence his caseworker died recently?" Arnett said as he pulled open the driver's side door of the Chevy.

"Very interesting—if we're looking for a *why now*, having his guardian angel die could have triggered him to start killing. I'll text Lopez to find out how she died." Jo gasped as she slipped into the passenger seat. "Sweet hell, it's like Satan's hot tub in here. That's what I get for not parking in the shade."

"Cranking up the air conditioning, stat.," Arnett said. "And, I'm gonna need something to drink. Iced coffee from Starbucks?"

Jo did a double take. "Who are you? Wasn't it just yesterday that you told me—and I quote—'*Iced coffee is for teenaged girls at the mall?*'"

Arnett shrugged. "That's what happens when I start sweating in places I didn't even know had sweat glands."

"Thanks for that visual." Jo grimaced. "And if you order anything with the word 'frappa' in it, I'm checking you for body snatchers."

"Too bad Lopez isn't here to appreciate your delightfully retro reference." Arnett fired up the engine.

"So sad when wit is wasted." Jo shook her head and looked down at her texts. "Lopez says she'll get right on it, and Sophie texted a thumbs-up to my confirmation of tonight's dinner. I never know what to do with a thumbs-up. You don't do that when you're happy about something, right? So is there a message in it? Is it passive-aggressive?"

Bob shot her a clueless look. "Beats me."

She sighed and opened up the case file. "The original DCF investigation was opened by a complaint from Raina's father, Dustin Heidami. He came home to find Raina crying and holding her arm. She told him that Louisa had hit her with the vacuum cleaner—"

"How do you hit someone with a vacuum cleaner?" Arnett asked.

"I'm assuming it's one of those new Dyson-style ones that's just a long tube," Jo answered. He nodded, and she continued. "She had a big lump, and Dustin rushed her to the hospital. He reported what happened to the nurse and the doctor, who helped him file the report to DCF."

"That seems pretty straightforward," Arnett said.

"Apparently Louisa claimed Dustin was lying, and the whole situation got muddied because there was a bad history between them."

"Did he cheat on her?" Arnett asked.

Jo's brows popped up. "Good callback. Maybe so, although it doesn't specify here, just says they had a volatile relationship with lots of fights and lots of on-again off-again. Louisa dated one of his friends at one point."

"Ouch. That never feels good." Arnett grimaced as he turned into the Starbucks drive-thru. He pulled up to the speaker and placed the order for their drinks.

"Oh, this is interesting. As part of the investigation, they requested Raina's medical records, both from her pediatrician, and from the hospital in Greenfern. Apparently she'd been seen in the emergency room on another occasion, and that doctor also found her injury suspicious."

"So not just the father lying, then," Arnett said.

"No." Jo continued to skim. "Louisa claimed Raina had always been a clumsy child, and both incidents were a result of her falling. Once in the bathroom, she claimed, and the other time she'd supposedly fallen while climbing a tree."

"Hard to disprove."

"Exactly—I know I fell out of more than my fair share of trees as a child. So while they removed Raina from the home after the initial determination, Louisa protested, and ultimately they restored Raina to her when she agreed to conditions that included monitoring and mandatory counseling."

"Counseling," Arnett grunted. He pulled forward, paid for the drinks, and handed an iced coffee to Jo.

She sipped as she read. "That seems to be the end of it— except, hang on," Jo said.

"What?" Arnett asked when she didn't continue.

Jo's mouth dropped as she read. "Oh my God. When they talked to Raina about the two incidents that sent her to the hospital?"

"Yes?"

"She corroborated her father's story about her mom hitting her with the vacuum cleaner. And the previous visit was for a head injury—Raina claimed her mother hit her on the head with *a frying pan*."

CHAPTER THIRTY-TWO

"Holy shit." Arnett braked for a light and stared over at her. "So in both cases, the murderer killed the women in a way that mimicked their alleged abuse. No way is that a coincidence."

"Not likely." Jo tapped her fingernails against the files. "But, it *is* possible. They tied Louisa up in the kitchen—maybe they injected her to keep her quiet, but miscalculated the dose and she woke up screaming. If they had to shut her up quickly, a frying pan might have been the closest thing at hand."

Arnett tossed her a skeptical glance.

"I'm just saying it's possible, and we have to keep it in mind." She grabbed her phone and frowned down at it as she typed and scrolled. "Rick Burke reported on the Pryzik case, and he covered the alleged frying pan incident."

"So, what, we're looking at a serial killer who targets alleged abusers? Like Robin Hood for abused kids?"

"Possibly. But why tie her up first? Raina wasn't tied up. The doctor's exam was thorough because of their suspicions, and they would have noticed if so."

"Torture. If this was about punishing the women for the

abuse, the killer may have wanted them to know what was happening." Arnett started back up as the light turned.

"Could be." Jo reached up and twisted her necklace. "No matter what, it turns everything we've been thinking on its head. Travis may be the most obvious suspect for Melissa's murder, but it makes no sense that he would kill another woman months before he found out Melissa was getting custody of Avery back."

"Unless the families were friends?" Arnett said. "Same problem with Tinsley as our killer, unless Tinsley also had a dysfunctional friendship with Louisa Pryzik."

"Good point. According to this, Raina Pryzik went to Martin Luther King Jr. Elementary, but Louisa and Tinsley could have known each other another way, especially with all the extracurriculars Avery and Heidi are in. No matter what, unless the frying pan was a very strange coincidence, this changes up the motive. Someone's taking out child abusers."

"Rick Burke's background puts him in the lead of the pack," Arnett said.

"Agreed, but we still have to consider that it could be just about anybody who reads *The Greenfern Daily*—Burke's articles may have triggered someone else."

"Could also be someone in the family court system."

Jo nodded. "I say we ask DCF for a list of all children in the area in the last, say, thirty years who were allegedly abused by their mother, then returned to her. It can't be a coincidence our victims are all women."

"That's a tall order, and would completely miss anybody from out of the area."

"We can't avoid that. But we could offer to send one of our people down there so they don't have to devote resources," Jo said.

Arnett's head bobbed. "Worth a shot."

Jo jotted down a note. "And we're looking to see if there are any other murders that fit this methodology, or who were accused of child abuse. As for Travis and Tinsley, we need to look for some connection between their families and Louisa's."

"For all we know, Louisa might have been the woman Travis was having an affair with. Maybe she threatened to go to his wife, and he killed her in an attempt to keep it quiet."

"Lopez is already combing through the Rollins' and Sparks' phone records, but I'll let her know to look specifically for contact with Burke or the Pryzik family. And I think we need to cast a broader net, look into their backgrounds for any other similarities." Jo tapped out a text to Lopez.

"We should ask Travis for a list of Avery's extracurriculars over, say, the last two years." Arnett stepped hard on the brakes to avoid hitting an Audi that cut him off. "Their credit card and bank records should help with that, too."

Jo glanced back into the file. "Both girls had different social workers, but I'm guessing they had to go physically to the DCF building regardless. If they had appointments near the same time, it's plausible someone struck up a conversation, and a friendship."

"That should show up in phone calls or texts," Arnett said.

"Maybe." Jo's hand flew back to the necklace.

Arnett turned to study her face—he knew better than anyone that when she played with the diamond, taken from the ring her murdered fiancé had proposed with, her mind was making important calculations. "What are you thinking?"

"I'm not sure. What was that old movie—*Strangers on a Train?*"

Arnett's brows popped up. "So, what, Travis and—what's the other one's name?"

"Dustin Heidami is Raina Pryzik's father, but wasn't married to Louisa."

"So Travis and Dustin hatched a plan to kill each other's baby mamas?"

"Highly unlikely, I admit." She pulled out the notes she'd taken on Avery's file. "But, there is a small time overlap between the DCF's investigation of Melissa Rollins and Louisa Pryzik's death."

"I say we go have a little chat with Dustin." Arnett glanced at his watch. "Three thirty. Does the file say anywhere where he works?"

"Hold on a sec, it was some paper mill—found it. Pen and Ink Industries, about fifteen minutes east of Greenfern, out along Millers River up the Mohawk Trail." Jo reprogrammed the GPS. "Let's do it."

———

Pen and Ink Industries was a blue corrugated hull of a building complex, all squares and rectangles of different sizes sprawling between the highway and the river, belching never-ending columns of what Jo hoped was steam.

After following a winding byway to a large parking lot at the rear, Jo and Arnett cleared themselves through security and stepped inside a clean, if worn, reception area with a line of gray padded chairs and a surprisingly cheerful receptionist. When Jo explained why they were there, however, the receptionist's expression dimmed. Without a word she lifted the phone and whispered a call, then a tall, silver-haired white man in a polyester suit stepped out from the office behind her.

He stuck out his hand to Arnett. "Joe Weiss. You need to speak to one of my employees?"

"We do," Jo said as Arnett shook his hand.

Weiss glanced awkwardly at her, then hurried to shake her hand. "Is Mr. Heidami in some sort of trouble?"

"No, not at all. We just need his help," Jo answered.

Weiss paused, his face showing the struggle to get more information. He stepped forward. "Follow me."

After giving them neon-orange hard hats and safety vests, he led them out to a multi-floor, open-area space. Yellow railings cordoned off machinery of various types, all thrumming an overpowering roar in unison.

"Over here," he yelled, then made his way to a brown-skinned, dark-haired man in an identical hard hat and vest, but worn over blue industrial coveralls.

The man pulled out his earplugs when he noticed them approaching, letting them drop and dangle from the cord around his neck. "What's up?"

Weiss leaned in and yelled something to him Jo couldn't hear, then turned around and raised his voice. "This is Heidami. Have at it."

"Any chance we can talk somewhere quieter?" Arnett asked.

"Nope. Can't disrupt the workflow." Weiss clamped his arms across his chest and didn't bother hiding his smirk.

Jo suspected Heidami wouldn't be interested in discussing personal business in front of this man. She met his eyes. "We have a few questions we need to ask you about Louisa Pryzik's death."

Heidami shot a look at Weiss. "I'm late for my break, 'cause I was trying to get that pulp cleared through before I went. I should probably take it now before OSHA shits a brick." He threw up a hand and motioned across the open space toward someone Jo assumed was the foreman. The man nodded and Heidami stepped away. "Break room's this way."

Weiss attempted to follow them, but Jo held up a hand. "We appreciate your help, Mr. Weiss, but we'll be fine from here. Mr. Heidami can show us back to your office when we're done."

Looking like a pressure valve about to erupt, Weiss turned and stormed off across the cement floor. Heidami threw her a grateful look. She hoped it would buy them some goodwill—they were going to need it.

Two rows of plastic folding tables ran down the center of the long gray break room, and a coffee machine, microwave, and two vending machines lined the back wall. As the door clicked into place behind them, Heidami pointed to the nearest black folding chairs and plopped himself down into one.

"You're not the detectives I spoke with before. Do you finally have a suspect?" he asked.

"We have a new line of inquiry," Jo answered. "We think Louisa's death may be related to another murder. Do you know a woman called Melissa Rollins?"

His eyes flicked between them. "I've seen her name in the news the last few days."

"But you didn't know her personally?"

"I don't."

"We understand you filed a child abuse complaint against Louisa and that you received sole custody of your daughter Raina for a time, but that Louisa ultimately regained her custodial rights?"

"That's right."

"The same thing happened with Melissa Rollins."

Heidami glanced at his watch. "I'm not sure what you're asking me."

No, apparently getting rid of Mr. Weiss hadn't bought them much goodwill at all. "We think someone may have murdered them both, believing they were child abusers."

Heidami's expression turned wary. "Louisa *was* a child abuser."

"Did Louisa know Melissa? Was Raina friends with her daughter, Avery?"

His face didn't move. "Not that I'm aware of."

"Can you tell us what activities your daughter was engaged in around the time of her mother's death?" Arnett asked.

"She did dance classes. Still does."

"Where?" Arnett asked.

"Jackie's Jazzy Jewels, over on Franklin."

Arnett jotted the name down. "Anything else?"

"I have a hard enough time paying for that," Heidami said.

"Girl scouts, even?"

"Nope."

"Your father helps you watch Raina when you work, is that right?" Jo asked.

His chin twitched. "My father passed away two months ago."

Jo's heart panged—the pain in his face was real. "I'm so sorry for your loss."

"Thank you."

"Who watches her now? Other family?" Arnett asked.

He shifted in his chair. "I don't have any other family. I had to hire a babysitter."

Jo tried to keep her voice neutral. "Can you tell us where you were last Tuesday night?"

Heidami stiffened. "Why?"

"We're not at liberty to explain at this time, but we do need to know," Jo answered.

Heidami's expression turned borderline hostile. "You know I had an alibi for Louisa's death, right?"

"We do. We still need to know about Tuesday."

He stared at her for a long moment, then stood up. "After work I was home with Raina all night. If you have any other questions, you can talk to my lawyer."

Jo nodded and stood, as did Arnett. "Who's your lawyer?" he asked.

"Tom Fischer."

CHAPTER THIRTY-THREE

My father never realized my mother was abusing us.

He worked long hours, and while he was gone, she drank—after she spent the morning in prayer. Sometimes straight from her omni-present jug of Gallo wine, one finger threaded through the handle on the side of its neck. She'd drink until she reeked of it, but because he worked late, he'd assume she only had a glass with dinner.

I still recoil whenever I smell red wine on anyone's breath. I can't even bring myself to take it during Holy Communion.

When he did notice a bruise on either of us, my mother passed it off as our clumsiness, or blamed school fights. Easy to believe—children hurt themselves all the time. How could he know my bruised arm wasn't from a fall when I climbed our tree?

I did try to tell him once, when I was about eight. She told him I was lying out of revenge because she wouldn't let me go to see an R-rated movie with a friend. When my father turned back to me, my mother stood behind him, mouth twisted, eyes narrowed, jaw tight. The message was clear: I'd be alone with her when he left for work in the morning, and I'd have hell to pay. So

I recanted, told him I'd lied, hoping he'd read the truth in my eyes. Instead, he punished me.

After that, I didn't have the courage to try again. Regretfully, my sister did.

She was smarter about it. She picked an injury that was harder to explain: a bruise in the shape of fingerprints on her arm. My father listened, and did something I wish I'd known he'd do—took us away from our mother that very moment, to his own mother's house.

In today's world, everybody knows what to do if something like that happens. Go to the authorities, take pictures, document everything. But back then, neither my father nor my grandmother knew what to do, and their delay was fatal. My mother immediately called the police and told them my father was the abuser. That when she threatened to leave with the kids if he did it again, he'd kidnapped us.

The police didn't know who to believe. On the one hand, we corroborated our father's story. On the other, my mother said we were lying because we were terrified of him. Since she was the one who contacted the police, they were inclined to believe her—especially when she produced marijuana paraphernalia she said was his. They placed us in foster care while the system investigated. Both my mother and father hired lawyers. But the reality was, mothers were almost always awarded custody back then. Most often they still are.

We were returned to our mother, and the abuse intensified. But she'd learned her lesson—she couldn't risk overt signs of abuse. So she shifted tactics. She claimed our rebellious, disrespectful natures were because she hadn't raised us with enough fear of God. She enrolled us in a Catholic school for 'difficult' children, and told the nuns we were liars and delinquents; she also told them my sister was 'too fond of boys.' She woke us at four each morning to do chores and attend morning Mass. After school my sister made dinner and I did yard work. When we finished, we said a novena while she watched, nine complete rosaries while kneeling on the hardwood floors. We rarely had enough time to finish our homework before bed, but were punished further for our bad grades. We didn't go out. We didn't have friends.

Of course we told our father and our grandmother. But what could they do? What could possibly be wrong with chores and church? Children always complained about such things. And nobody was willing to challenge my mother's constitutional right to raise her children according to the strictures of her religion.

Ironically, the prayers actually saved my sanity by transporting me directly to God. They gave me peaceful escape inside myself from this world into the next, and I came to understand I was suffering for a reason. I had complete faith the purpose of it all would become clear eventually.

Faith didn't work for my sister. She found no such peace.

She ran away after several months; the police found her and brought her home. Mother scissored her long, beautiful hair into a purposefully ragged cut, then took my sister's cat Bella and got rid of her. In front of us.

About a week after that, my sister didn't emerge from her bath after her allotted fifteen minutes. The door was braced from the inside, and Mother had to break it down with an ax.

Until the day I die I'll have nightmares about the sight of my sister lying dead in a tub of dark pink water.

They gave custody of me to my father after that. Too little, too late.

CHAPTER THIRTY-FOUR

Tom Fischer was Dustin Heidami's lawyer.

Jo kept her face blank as they followed Heidami back out to Weiss' office, despite the thought echoing continually in her head. But as soon as they cleared the building, she turned to Arnett. "There's our connection, right there."

Arnett punched into his palm. "Can't believe I never even thought about the lawyer."

Jo climbed into the driver's seat and started the engine. "Do we call Mr. Fischer, or just drop on by?"

"I vote drive-by." Arnett pulled out his phone and tapped at it. "Based on these search results, his reputation precedes him. Pages of press coverage about the cases he's won—mostly for fathers."

"Either he cherry picks his cases, or he's damned good."

Fischer's office turned out to be housed in a sleek gray office building in the middle of downtown Greenfern. "Swanky digs," Arnett said.

After an elevator ride up to the third floor, a middle-aged silver-haired white woman greeted them while emanating waves of efficiency like expensive perfume.

"Mr. Fischer's not in right now. He's at a deposition with a client." She peeked at them from over her glasses. "And I don't expect him back tonight. Can I take a message for you?"

"If he won't be back tonight, it might be best for us to call him directly," Jo said, and thanked her.

Jo put through the call once they were back in the car, but wasn't surprised when she reached Fischer's voicemail. "We could always hunt down his residence and show up there?"

"Not tonight we can't. We have our triple date." Arnett pulled into traffic.

Jo facepalmed. "What is *wrong* with me that I keep forgetting about that?"

Arnett shot her a curious look. "Things not going well with your sister?"

No way was she going to mention her hesitations about Laura. "No, Sophie and I are getting along surprisingly well. Or at least I think we are. I wonder if—" Her mind flew to the tension in Sophie's voice when she mentioned David.

"What?"

She shook her head vigorously. "Never mind. My mind is making up problems that aren't there. So I'm just gonna focus on the amazing calvados soufflé I hear Le Poulet Bleu has, and put the rest out of my mind."

———

Le Poulet Bleu's decor was rustic French farmhouse fused with modern flair. Exposed beams and brick dominated unfinished pine chairs and spindle tables, while the hanging chandeliers and place settings provided flashes of brilliant cobalt blue. Square metal stools lined the naked pine bar where Bob and Laura waited when Jo and Matt arrived.

"Bob says you met Jo when the two of them were investigating a Jane Doe case this spring," Laura asked Matt after initial greetings and drink orders.

Jo smiled vaguely and glanced over her shoulder toward the entrance. Sophie and David were late—but Sophie was *never* late.

"That's right," Matt said. "My official introduction to her was a warning from an emergency room doctor."

Arnett laughed, and heat licked at Jo's cheeks.

"What?" Laura smiled conspiratorially.

"I'd, uh, been a little brusque with her," Jo said.

Arnett waved a hand dismissively. "Handed the woman her own ass is what you did. Fully deserved, because she'd screwed up evidence collection. Jo did her a favor, because if she'd kept that up, the ADA would've taken it up with her boss."

"One hundred percent right." Matt swirled his wine. "And the upshot is, before I even laid eyes on Jo I was impressed and intrigued. She turned out to be empathetic, sharp, and beautiful on top of it all."

Thankfully, Sophie and David stepped through the entrance door and preempted the need for Jo to respond—but they both had storms on their faces. Jo raised her hand to get their attention; Sophie's face cleared when she spotted Jo, and she waved back.

Jo made the introductions. The men shook hands and clapped each other on the shoulder while Sophie hugged Laura.

"I absolutely love your dress." Laura gestured to the sage-green sweater dress that hugged Sophie's lean figure and set off her green eyes.

Jo measured Laura's compliment as Sophie reciprocated with one about Laura's dress—was it genuine, or was this the sort of double-edged girl chat Jo had never been able to fully understand?

"I apologize for being late," Sophie said, and shot a look at David. "I hate to keep people waiting."

David's blue eyes flashed across the room and he raked one hand through his short black hair. "We'd have had plenty of time if I'd known we were coming to a restaurant that required formal wear."

Jo winced. As much as Sophie didn't like to be late, she hated conflict in front of strangers far more—and David knew it. Jo anticipated the broad smile and the *aren't-men-terrible* eye roll Sophie normally put on to gloss over any such tension.

But Sophie's smile pinched, and her tone became clipped. "I suppose the three times I told you we'd changed venue to Le Poulet Bleu wasn't quite enough. Funny, you change in no time flat when it suits you."

David's mouth dropped open, then clamped shut, and his neck reddened.

Laura filled the silence. "That's my fault, I'm afraid. I've been wanting to come here for so long, and—"

"Nonsense," Matt's smooth voice cut in, and he signaled the hostess. "I've also been looking forward to this, and I'm glad you suggested it. We're all here now, should we go in?"

Once seated at their table, focus settled into pleasant chatter about the offerings. When David made increasingly dissatisfied noises at the menu, Sophie stiffened.

Jo hurried to distract her. "Are the girls with Mom tonight? How are they?"

Sophie's face softened. "Isabelle is absolutely delighted she didn't have to go to camp this year. It really was the best decision because Emily finally slept through the night every night this week. And she's back to her cheery self, almost like nothing ever happened."

Toward the end of spring, Emily had been kidnapped by a murderer. Jo recovered her within hours, but Emily had been understandably terrified by the situation, and was still struggling with it. Sophie had decided it was too soon for her to spend a week sleeping away from her home and parents.

Jo tugged at the tablecloth hanging over her lap. "I'm so glad to hear that. And I'm glad you're keeping a close eye on her—the women in our family have a special gift for keeping our pain hidden."

Sophie's pinched smile returned, and she glanced at her menu. "That we do. You know what? Who cares if I fit in my slacks tomorrow, I think I'll have the soufflé, too."

———

"So that was interesting," Matt said as he eased out of the restaurant's parking lot.

Jo grimaced. "You mean the awkward tension between my sister and her husband?"

"Partly that. David didn't engage about the Corvettes I'm considering for my restoration project, and while I admit I've only known him for a few months, that doesn't seem like him."

Jo sighed and stared out into the darkness. "No, it is not. They must have had one doozy of a fight on their way to the restaurant. I'm starting to worry about them."

"You think it's serious?"

"It might be. Sophie's never been one to talk about her problems, especially to me, but I've noticed an escalation in the past year or so. It's possible I'm imagining things because of our dynamic."

Matt chuckled. "I'd never bet against you when it comes to reading people."

Jo placed her hand on his thigh. "Thank you."

"And that's why I also found the way you interacted with Laura tonight very intriguing."

A sliver of ice pricked at Jo's chest—she'd been so sure she'd hidden her hesitation. "Was I rude without realizing it?"

He dropped one hand to cover hers, and squeezed. "Not at all. You were kind and attentive, like you always are. But there was a—caution? Like when someone speaks to a great-aunt or great-grandmother, respectful to someone they love, but can't be their full natural self. Not like you were talking to someone in your circle of friends."

"Damn. The last thing I wanted to do was make her feel uncomfortable."

"I don't think you did. It was subtle, and another night I'd have attributed it to the dynamic between two newly introduced couples. But that wasn't it, was it?"

"No, it wasn't." She launched into a quick history of Laura's infidelity. "I really don't mean to be judgmental about it all, and I've been rolling my hang-ups around in my head since Sophie asked about them. I think my issue is there doesn't seem to have been any consequences for her. *Consequence* isn't the right word, though. What I mean is, Laura acts like it never happened. Like she took an eraser to a chalkboard and thinks there isn't any residue left. But a lot of things are different because of it, and Bob's different, and— I don't know." She threw her hands up and let them drop into her lap. "Now I'm just babbling."

"No, I get it, I do." He nodded, his expression somber, and paused for a long moment before continuing. "I told you I was engaged once."

"You did." By unspoken agreement, neither of them talked much about past relationships. She'd told him about Jack, her fiancé who'd been shot in front of her in a Boston alley, but not really anything more. And she'd been content to let his romantic history remain in the shadows.

"But I didn't tell you how it ended."

"No."

He stared straight out of the windshield. "Her name was Iliana. She was five years younger than me, and while that doesn't necessarily mean two people are in different places in their lives, it certainly meant that for us. But I loved her fiercely, and ignored the ways we didn't mesh. About six months after I proposed, I found out she was cheating on me."

"Ouch." Jo studied his face.

"I should've sat down with her and had a mature conversation about it. Tried to determine if there was a problem in the relationship that she just wasn't communicating to me, or if it was just about who she was. But that's the wisdom of hindsight, learned the hard way. At the time all I knew was my heart was broken."

"Of course it was."

"I know now my ego was shredded, too, and that's where my reaction originated. I confronted her about it, angrily. She denied it, said that the friend who told me they saw her with another man must have been mistaken. She didn't know I'd refused to believe it until I saw it with my own eyes, and that I'd followed her to be sure. I didn't tell her that, and I didn't immediately break up with her. Instead I went out the next weekend with friends to drown my sorrows, and spotted a beautiful girl across the room watching me."

"Oh." Jo's stomach twisted.

"Yes, precisely. I flirted, she flirted, and we ended up in bed together. I think I hoped to feel re-empowered somehow, or that the attention would help patch the damage Iliana had done to me, but of course it didn't. I spent the next day vomiting, and even though I'd only had two beers the night before, I talked myself into believing it was due to a hangover. The next night when I picked her up for a dinner party we were supposed to go to, I told her what I'd done. I expected to feel some sort of justice, like some sort of karmic rebalance. I didn't, but Iliana did—by the end of the conversation she said she was glad I'd done it, because now we were even and could start over fresh like nothing had happened."

Jo remained silent as she watched his face.

"And maybe I'd hoped for that too on some level, but as she said it to me, I realized no, we couldn't start over fresh. Her face at that moment is seared into my memory—a strange blend of relief and forgiveness. And I got angry, because it was up to *me* to forgive *her*, not the other way around—but even as I thought that, I realized it wasn't true anymore. I'd allowed myself to become something I detested, and she was right, we *were* 'even'—now she wasn't the only despicable one, I was despicable, too. But for her that equivalence meant everything was alright. For me, it meant everything was all *wrong*. And if we'd both seen it that way we might have been able to rebuild the trust from there, but since we saw it so differently, there was no place to go. So I ended it."

Jo nodded, and thought for a long moment. "It might have actually brought you closer if you'd agreed to fix it together."

"We'll never know." Matt scratched his chin with his thumb. "As I'm listening to your thoughts, I'm realizing sometimes the two people in the relationship aren't the only ones who lose trust, but that loved ones outside the relationship have no choice in the matter and no recourse to work on rebuilding that trust."

Trust. The word reverberated around Jo's skull like an echo in a canyon, getting louder with each pass. She'd spent years learning how to trust herself again after being unable to keep the two men she loved from being killed, and had finally had a major breakthrough when she'd rescued her kidnapped niece. But like a stalker that wouldn't go away, here trust was again, rearing its ugly head, pulling her back under. Would she ever get over it?

No, she heard her therapist's voice in her head—*you won't. Change isn't an all-or-nothing epiphany. It's good days and bad days and slowly thinking better and choosing better.* She and Nina had talked about how building trust in one area of your life didn't automatically transfer to all other areas. New issues would bubble up to propel her on to the next phase of healing.

She reached over and grabbed his hand again. "I'm sorry that happened to you."

He squeezed her hand back. "I'm not. It taught me a lot of things I needed to learn. Of course, it hurt like hell for a couple of years."

Jo shook her head in wonder. "It's amazing how easy-going you are about relationships considering what happened. You're the least possessive man I've ever known. You give me as much space as I want and you never make demands. I'd have thought a cheating fiancée would make you less trusting."

"Same lesson. Part of the reason it all happened was Iliana wasn't ready to be engaged yet. Deep down I knew that but I didn't want to believe it, so I proposed anyway. She didn't have the self-insight to realize she should have said, 'Not yet,' but as soon as I proposed, a lot of her behavior changed. So I suppose I learned there's no use asking people for what they don't want to give. They'll give it, or they won't. And, I learned that trust isn't a default, it's a choice."

Jo considered. "I guess I'm just not ready to trust Laura yet, at least not fully. And maybe my hesitation is because I feel like she's demanding it when I'm not ready to give it," Jo said.

"How long has it been?" Matt asked.

"Nearly a decade." Jo caught the sideways glance Matt shot her, and laughed. "Okay, it's possible I should've gotten over myself by now."

Matt smiled. "Maybe it's not something you'll ever get over completely."

Jo sighed. "That's not fair to Bob."

"Maybe." He tilted his head. "But I'm more worried about whether it's fair to you. Is that the person you want to be?"

She narrowed her eyes at him. "Message received, Obi-Wan."

His brow creased. "Obi-Wan?"

"He was quite the philosopher, didn't you know?" she said. "He said the truths we cling to depend very much on our own perspective."

Matt laughed. "A wise man, indeed."

CHAPTER THIRTY-FIVE

Diana sat outside Le Poulet Bleu, energized by the possibilities before her. Fournier had a male companion—and a handsome one at that. Fournier had a social life. Someone whose life she cared about.

And thus, a weakness.

After her first day following Fournier, Diana had spent an evening of furious computer research confirming what she thought she'd learned. The destinations in Greenfern all tied up well with the news coverage she'd been able to find about Melissa Rollins, both since her death and before—the horrible woman had been a child abuser, and got what she fully deserved.

Today had been largely the same. Another stultifying morning in the car waiting for them to emerge, but she'd long ago mastered a technique to keep focus during stakeouts: she channeled Cleopatra watching birds in the yard, became a hunter silently waiting for her prey. Endless Zen focus, almost like a literal sphinx, motionless except for a slight, intermittent, self-satisfied flick of her metaphorical tail. Magically the wait transformed into a revitalizing meditation.

Fournier and Arnett finally emerged, off again to the Department of Children and Families, then to some factory by the side of the river. A paper mill, she discovered as she waited for them to come out, but for the life of her, she couldn't find any connection to the Melissa Rollins case. She was fairly certain it didn't relate to Bennie Moreno, but she still wasn't sure. And she still hadn't found any leverage.

So when Mr. Handsome picked Fournier up for dinner, Diana's adrenaline spiked.

In her experience, beautiful men were the ones with the biggest secrets. They expected to get away with more, usually did, and she had yet to find one who wasn't trouble. Her eyes narrowed as she remembered and analyzed the body language between them—how serious was the relationship? How important was he to her?

She caught herself mid thought: was she actually *concerned* for Fournier?

Yes, she realized. She was. And in a rush, she also realized why Fournier had seemed familiar to her—she reminded Diana of herself. Now out of detective clothes and into a beautiful blue dress, hair pinned up and make-up done, the resemblance between them shone through more clearly. They were about the same height and weight now that Diana had finally dropped the extra twenty pounds she'd carried since her father killed himself. Josette's hair was lighter than hers, but they were both fair-skinned brunettes with lightish eyes. Close enough, really, to be sisters. And of course they'd both dedicated their lives to seeking out justice—so they were alike in mind, too.

She sat for a long time and rolled the implications around her brain. She didn't want to kill Josette—Diana didn't kill innocent people. Ultimately, she decided, it didn't change anything. If Josette didn't keep her distance, Diana would first deploy the back-up plan, but if Josette kept coming for Diana even then,

Diana would be forced to kill her no matter how alike they were. Either way, Diana's priority was now finding out everything she could about Mr. Handsome. Because she'd need to kill someone else before too long, and he'd do just as well as anybody else.

But—when he and Josette emerged, they weren't alone.

Diana sat up straight and peered at the other two couples laughing and embracing outside the entrance. Well, five of the six were laughing—one of the men looked like he was suffering from indigestion. She tried to parse out who the newcomers were. Mr. Handsome had his hand on Josette's back, and Diana easily recognized Arnett—he hadn't even bothered to change out of the suit he'd been wearing earlier. One of the women held his hand, a WASP-y matriarchal-type with hair the color of beaten straw. Obviously his wife. But the other two—who were they?

She leaned forward across the steering wheel, as though the six inches made any difference. The final woman was the youngest of the group, and had a face so similar to Josette's they must be related. Her sister? A cousin? But where Josette carried herself with a relaxed-but-vigilant ease, this other woman was a trap about to spring, and passive-aggressively pretending not to be focused on the man with indigestion. He was another handsome one—clean-shaven, dark hair, tall with broad shoulders. The two of them broke from the group and walked toward their car, and she tasted the tension as easily as if she'd been standing beside them.

Suddenly she had multiple options—several people who meant something to Fournier, who she'd make hard choices to keep alive. Diana just needed to find the best pressure point for her needs.

She fired up her ignition and made a quick decision. Her hope had been to follow Josette and her boyfriend to figure out who he was. But she'd be able to intercept Mr. Handsome at Josette's house another night, while she might not get another shot at this couple. And based on their interaction, something very important, and potentially useful, was going on.

They pulled out of the parking lot. Diana waited until they reached the end of the block, then followed them.

CHAPTER THIRTY-SIX

AUGUST 26TH

Jo woke the next day with an unsettled feeling she wasn't able to categorize. At first she hoped it was just waking up without Matt—he'd had to sleep at his own house to make an important early administrative meeting in the morning. But no, there was more. A sense that something wasn't quite right weighing on her like impending doom.

Her mother often reported feelings like that, but they usually turned out to be nothing, so Jo chalked them up to paranoia. Her aunt Odette down in Louisiana got them, too, and referred to them as *the sight*. What Aunt Odette saw was always vague, along the lines of "something bad's gonna happen," and younger Jo had never understood the point of *sight* so incredibly myopic as to be completely worthless. As Jo got older and recognized her own ability to see people in a way others couldn't, she'd decided that *the sight* was some version of the same thing—a sensitivity to people and situations that allowed Aunt Odette to pick up on undercurrents, even if she wasn't able to pinpoint what was wrong or how it would play out.

This was the first time Jo's intuition looked more like Aunt

Odette's, and she wasn't quite sure how to manage it. So, she prodded it as she showered, examining everything going on in her life, looking for a response akin to the dull ache of poking a bruise. The Rollins case? That left her with a sense of hurtling forward through a landscape only to find she'd been going in circles, but it wasn't responsible for the unease. The Scherer case? That felt like chasing a ghost, like some phantom force just out of sight, but it wasn't the reason, either.

The dinner last night? Her brain shrieked in response. That was it, then—she was worried about Sophie.

Every relationship had problems. But this felt different and she wasn't sure what to do about it, which made her feel help-less. Sure, she'd made gains in her relationship with her sister, but she wasn't at all sure Sophie would take kindly to Jo prying into her marriage, and it might even kick them into the weeds of their previous dynamic. The smart thing to do was probably leave it alone—but the tugging around the edges of her mind felt immediate and dangerous.

The rapidly cooling water pulled her out of her thoughts. She sighed, toweled off, and dressed for work as quickly as possible. When she strode up to her desk half an hour later, Arnett was already installed at his desk.

He nodded toward the mocha waiting on her desk. "I just left another message for Tom Fischer letting him know it's urgent that we talk to him today. I've also put together the warrant paperwork for his phone records and emails."

"Hopefully he'll think it's all about Travis." She grabbed the mocha and took a large swig. "In the meantime, I want to take a closer look at his history with DCF, and Rick Burke's, to see if they are connected with some sort of abuse situation."

"I'll take Burke, you take Fischer?"

"Sounds good."

Jo dug in. Fischer was born and raised in Worcester, then went to university at BU, followed by Harvard Law School. No criminal record—not surprising, since lawyers risked being disbarred if they misbehaved. No surprises among his case history; he represented both plaintiffs and defendants in family law cases, and had an impressive win record. Jo picked up her landline and dialed the DCF office in Worcester.

Expecting the office would have to search through hard-copy archives the way Greenfern had done for Burke, Jo was pleasantly surprised to be transferred to the social worker who'd handled Fischer's case. But she wasn't at all surprised to discover his case followed a familiar pattern—his father had petitioned for custody due to abuse, his mother fought it, and partial custody was restored to her.

She relayed what she learned to Arnett. "Amazing how many people associated with this case have the same strange history."

"I can hear Marzillo's voice ringing in my head—'*this number of co-occurrences are statistically unlikely to have happened by chance,*'" Arnett said.

"It's possible Fischer is acting out a vendetta against his abusive mother by cherry-picking cases from among his clients, so I'd like to know how Rollins and Heidami came to hire him. Same theory could work for Burke—he may be gathering information on alleged child abusers to identify those he feels needs to die."

"Fischer might be sourcing Burke's articles," Arnett said.

"We need to find out if they were in contact, or even knew each other. Phone records should help, but if one or both of them is our murderer, they may have made sure any such contact was on the sly. We should also check out the people in his law firm, especially the ones that work directly for him—they'd have access to the details of his cases, and could have been the ones in contact with Burke." Her hand flew to her necklace. "But wait. Let's not forget the obvious. Give me a minute."

She plugged both Fischer's and Burke's names into Google, and hit gold with the top result. She scoured the article, then turned her monitor toward Arnett. "Check this out. An article about an awards ceremony for The Precious Cargo Foundation, an organization that helps abused children, primarily by providing shelter to the children and their parent so they can escape an abusive partner. They help in other ways, including providing legal advice on a sliding scale, often pro bono. They gave Fischer a service award."

"What a stand-up guy." Arnett's eyes narrowed. "I'm assuming there's more?"

Jo grinned, and scrolled down. "Look who else was honored at the gala."

"Well, well, well. Rick Burke." Arnett slapped his desk. "Doesn't mean they spoke to each other at the time, but Fischer would surely have realized there was a sympathetic ear in the press."

Jo's cell chimed a notification. "Speak of the devil and he shall appear. Tom Fischer just arrived."

Arnett stood up. "Let's do this."

CHAPTER THIRTY-SEVEN

The thrill of peeling back the next layer of Josette's life was almost as exciting to Diana as hunting for a kill.

She'd followed Josette's sister home the night before, to an impressive house that flirted with the possibility of being a mansion. Almost as soon as they arrived, another woman left— an older woman who bore a distinct resemblance both to Josette and to the younger woman. Based on the ages, the safe bet was the older woman was Josette's mother, and the younger was her sister. She cursed the tradition that encouraged married women to drop their maiden names and made them so much harder to track.

She'd made another split-second decision and followed the mother, since she knew where the sister lived now and could do a property search on the address to find her married name. She crossed her fingers that the mother would also own her own home—if she turned out to be a renter, that would be harder to track. But, she had a variety of tricks up her sleeve that would help.

She needn't have worried. Josette's mother's house wasn't as grand as the sister's, but it was still impressive and unlikely to be a rental. The mother pulled into a two-car garage and parked next to a silver Audi. Based on that and the fishing equipment and tools along the far side of the garage, the mother had a partner. Possibly, but not certainly, a man.

The lights in the house went out less than an hour later, and Diana returned to the hotel to do her research. The owners of the mansion were David and Sophie Belleau, and Diana found Sophie's name in several articles about events at Briar Ridge Elementary School, and several others about local charities. Sophie must be a stay-at-home mother, the sort who prioritized her children and her community. The way Diana's own mother had until she'd decided to throw away her entire life to be with a twisted pedophile.

Was Sophie's husband one of the good ones, or one of the bad ones?

She'd plugged in David's name. He turned out to be the CEO of Branford Home Products, a company that specialized in personal hygiene and cleaning products. CEO was a stressful job, but that brand of stress didn't fit the body language she'd seen—the tension between him and his wife had been undeniable. Diana smelled difficult situations like a shark smelled blood, and her nose was pulling her to investigate further.

So she'd set her alarm for four in the morning and perched herself outside the Belleau home. When David emerged, she followed him to the offices of Branford Home Products, and parked within sight of his vehicle. She considered going inside the building to check out his office and his team to get a better sense of him—she'd become something of a master at drumming up excuses to accidentally meet the men she targeted. The company's website had touted their relationship with hotels nationwide; she could go in and present herself as a buyer for a hotel looking for more information about what they provided.

No, she decided. There were too many potential problems with that plan. She'd need business cards, and she'd need to know far more than she did about how both sides of such an arrangement worked. And if David Belleau turned out to be what she thought he was, work probably wasn't the best way to meet him. He might be on dating apps—it sickened her how many married men were. Or, she could bump into him somewhere more neutral that he frequented. Maybe a favorite restaurant where he ate lunch? Or maybe he went to the gym after work?

Her pulse was already racing at the thought. If he was what she thought he was, she'd be doing Sophie and Josette a favor. Maybe she wouldn't even wait to use him as leverage...

She snapped her thoughts away from that. First things first. She needed confirmation of what he was, and what tack she'd need to take in terms of leverage, before she risked being seen or wasted a burner phone on this trip. They were far too much work to acquire safely. She purchased them when on innocent work trips, then carefully cycled them out to be sure she never used one until at least a year after she'd purchased it.

She drummed her red-lacquered nails on the steering wheel as she decided. For now, the smart thing to do would be to wait for him to come back out—and hope the instincts that yanked her to him like a paper clip to a magnet were still sharp.

CHAPTER THIRTY-EIGHT

As Jo and Arnett strode into the interrogation room, Fischer's expression changed from bored malaise to concerned befuddlement. He stood to shake their hands. "Detectives. I was coming from a deposition nearby and thought it would be easier to just stop by."

"We appreciate you saving us a trip." Jo gestured to the chair Fischer had just vacated, and sat opposite him as Arnett pulled over another chair.

Fischer cast a pointed glance around the room. "I also received a call from Dustin Heidami telling me I might be hearing from you. Your messages said you needed to talk to me in person. I'm curious about why a phone call wouldn't have been sufficient?"

Because I want to see your expression when I do this. "We have a few questions we'd like to ask you personally, not just as a representative of your client. Or, clients."

And there it was—an emotion flashed across his face before he settled into his guarded lawyer expression, too quickly for Jo to identify, but enough to signal something was off. "I'm happy to help any way I can."

"As you mentioned, we recently spoke with Dustin Heidami, who told us you're his attorney."

He nodded. "He said you had questions about his ex-girl-friend's death, and that you wanted to know if he had an alibi for Melissa Rollins' death. He was understandably confused and concerned, as am I."

Jo imagined he was a lot of things, but doubted confused was one of them. "We took a close look at Louisa's death, and have reason to believe it's connected to Melissa's."

Fischer's expression didn't flinch this time, but he paled ever so slightly. "How exactly is that possible?"

Jo chose her words carefully. "We aren't at liberty to release all the details at this time. But what we can say is the circumstances of their murders suggest strongly that the motive behind both killings was their alleged child abuse."

Fischer exhaled slowly before answering, almost certainly a ruse to buy time. "I can assure you neither of my clients are involved. Travis has an alibi for the time of Melissa's murder, and Dustin has an alibi for Louisa's."

"Does Travis have an alibi for the time of Louisa's death?" Arnett asked.

"I'll ask him. But it was so long ago now, I wouldn't be surprised if he doesn't know."

Jo nodded. "We'd also like to know where you were on the evening of August seventeenth, and on October fifteenth of last year."

Fischer glanced back and forth between the two of them. "Am I a suspect, detectives?"

"In order to be thorough, we have to take a close look at anyone who is involved with both families and has a demonstrated interest in child abuse cases," Jo answered.

Fischer reached into the breast pocket of his suit and pulled out his phone. He tapped and scrolled, then answered. "I was at a deposition on the seventeenth that lasted until six. After that I met my partners for dinner at Rudolfo's at seven thirty. Back on October fifteenth, I was in court during the afternoon, then conferred with my clients right after. I went back to the office to deal with the relevant filings so they'd be ready the next day, and my billable tracking puts me in the office until eight that night."

"Can anyone confirm you were in the office until that time?" Arnett asked.

He shifted in his chair. "After this amount of time, I can't remember who else might have stayed late. My assistant may have, but she'll likely be refreshing her memory from the same schedule I am." He rattled off names and contact information.

"Thank you." Jo sipped her coffee, then continued. "We also noticed that a fair amount of your work revolves around child abuse cases, and that you do charity work around that cause."

"All lawyers do pro bono work."

"It's not mandatory," Arnett said.

"It is if you don't want to be a pariah." He slipped his phone back into his pocket. "But I'd do it regardless. I believe in giving back to the community."

"Why in this particular way?" Jo asked.

Jo caught a slight twitch in Fischer's temple. "For the same reason I went into family law."

"Which is?" Arnett asked.

Fischer's eyes narrowed. "I'm sure you already know the answer to that, otherwise I doubt I'd be here. My mother abused my sister and me, and my father went through hell trying to keep us safe. I swore that when I grew up, I wouldn't let that happen to any other child in that situation. That I'd do what-ever I could to help them"—he paused to pointedly make eye contact with each of them—"short of murder."

"We saw you won an award from The Precious Cargo Foundation," Jo said.

He nodded, but looked wary. "A safe place to stay is vital. So many abusers take away all of the social network surrounding their partner, exactly because it makes it almost impossible for them to leave."

"We also noticed Rick Burke works with the same foundation," Arnett said.

Understanding settled on Fischer's face, and he smiled. "We both use the skills we have to help where we can."

Jo winced mentally—she'd hoped he would lie about knowing Burke worked with the foundation, but he was too smart for that. "And is one of the ways you use those skills alerting him to parents accused of abuse?"

"That's a difficult question to answer."

Jo leaned forward toward him—he hadn't been expecting that, and she had to play this carefully. "How so?"

"It depends what you mean by 'alerting.'"

Ah, word games—always dangerous ground when dealing with a skilled attorney. "Have you spoken to Rick Burke about individuals accused of child abuse?"

Fischer sat straighter. "Of course. His job is to investigate, and my job is to speak for my clients. I instruct them to always check with me before they speak to anyone in the press."

Jo wasn't going to let him off that easy. "And do you ever initiate contact with him about such cases?"

"Again the wording's tricky. I initiate contact with the press when need be, for example, when one of my clients is misrepresented, etc."

Arnett scratched his coffee cup, a sure sign he was anxious. Jo lifted her pinky very slightly to let him know she was okay. "And did you ever tip Rick Burke off to abusers he wasn't already aware of?"

"I have." Fischer shifted in his chair again. "But not in the case of either Melissa Rollins or Louisa Pryzik."

Jo hadn't expected that, and it took her a second to recover.

As she did, Arnett asked, "So we wouldn't find any calls between you and Burke during the course of those cases, or around the times when he published his pieces about those two women?"

"I can't guarantee that. I work with any number of clients at a given time."

"Have you ever advised a client to reach out to the press, to initiate contact?"

"There have been occasions where I've advised that."

"Did you advise Travis or Dustin to do that?"

He leaned back in his chair, and his face relaxed. "You know that falls under attorney-client privilege, Detective."

Of course it did.

She studied his expression. He'd outmaneuvered them, and he knew it.

———

Tom Fischer laughed out loud as he pulled out of the police parking lot. *That* was amateur hour, and he'd enjoyed it.

Didn't they realize what he did all day long? That well-worded questions and picking apart definitions was how he made his bread and butter? That he could make a nun look like a pathological liar if he decided to? Did they really think they were gonna corner him on some bullshit definition and get him to admit something that could potentially get him disbarred?

They'd spin their wheels looking for something conclusive, but they wouldn't find it. And if they were stupid enough to come after him for the murders, they'd never make it past reasonable doubt. He could tell from their questions alone they were throwing everything at the wall trying to see what would stick. Most likely they hoped he'd be on the phone to Burke before he even started up the car, warning him.

Unfortunately for them, it wasn't his first day on the job, and he didn't just fall off the turnip truck. All everyone had to do was stay calm, and they'd all be fine.

CHAPTER THIRTY-NINE

Gina Purcelli dumped vomit-soaked napkins into a plastic grocery bag and shoved the bag down under Rafael's feet. Thank God in heaven she'd taken her mother's advice about Scotchguarding the interior of the 2015 Kia Soul—she'd figured as beat up as it already was, what was the point? Ten minutes she didn't have to clean it up instead of twenty, that was the point. She pushed back the tendril that had escaped out of her messy bun, then reached over to rub Rafael's belly.

"You feeling better, honey? You want a ginger ale?"

He paused his thumb sucking long enough to nod, then tucked his head into the side of the car seat.

She dashed to the rear of the car and pulled a can of ginger ale out of the groceries she just bought. She cracked it open and filled his sippy cup. As she dove back into the driver's seat, she glanced down at the to-do list on her phone and fought back the feeling that she was sinking into a pit of quicksand.

Why did everything seem to be such a struggle for her? Everyone else managed to get through their Thursday without a mini breakdown, why was she such a loser?

Don't do that, she told herself. *Being a single mother is hard and you're doing your best day by day. Cut yourself a break. It's about progress, not perfection.*

She glanced back at Rafael sipping his soda, forced herself to sit a little straighter, and searched for an upbeat song on the radio. She settled on Taylor Swift's 'ME!' and reminded herself that she could do this, she was enough, she deserved to be happy.

One thing at a time, and the next thing was returning the cable box. She couldn't afford it, and that was just that. Hopefully she'd get the raise at work soon, then she'd be able to get it back. In the meantime, whatever was on Netflix would have to do.

Except the weeks when Rafael was with his father were so lonely. She hated coming home to an empty house and rattling around in the quiet. Television filled the hours. Same when the insomnia hit—she could always count on some true-crime show or an old sitcom rerun to help her mind break out of the circles it liked to run.

Ah well. More reason to work hard and get that raise faster.

She sighed.

As she turned down Franklin, a text chimed over her phone. She checked it, then tossed the phone back down. She flipped a fast U-turn back toward Greenfern Liquors, and quickly pulled into the parking lot.

CHAPTER FORTY

I had to act fast. I had to kill Gina Purcelli as soon as possible, before things spiraled out of control.

Dangerous, because I'd been so careful with my timing so far. That had been crucial. I waited almost a year between Louisa Pryzik and Melissa Rollins so there wouldn't be any obvious connection between the two. I knew all along I wouldn't be able to take so long with the next, but had hoped to wait at least three or four months. But if I wanted to be sure Rafael was safe, I had no time to waste.

And that terrified me, because there'd be no hiding what was happening now. This would be the beginning of the end. I'd known it was only a matter of time, regardless—my personal ticking clock had been my directive—but I hadn't known when.

But—maybe there was a way I could deflect. Put the attention on someone else? Given Gina's history, I could make this one simple while still accomplishing my goal. With a few small adjustments, I could send the police in a completely different direction.

But I had to get my ducks in a row quickly. Rafael would be with his father the following week, so that lined up, at least. But I still needed to figure out how to slip in without being noticed. I pulled up Gina's house on Google Earth; the lots were small, with plentiful trees and shrubs lining the properties. I'd need to find out how active her street was—I might need to park a few houses away.

As I sorted out the details, my excitement built, like an IV slowly dripping into my arm. The planning was always invigorating, knowing I was about to make a difference in the world, about to become a guardian angel to a child in danger, about to do God's work. What better purpose could there be for my life?

Then, once I had the basics in place, I bowed my head to pray.

CHAPTER FORTY-ONE

Diana leaned in when David emerged at six that night, now dressed in gym clothes and wiping his face down with a towel—the corporate offices must have an executive gym. She followed him back to the house.

Family dinner at the Belleau house followed. Dining room curtains fluttering in the wake of central air gave intermittent glimpses of two adorable little girls chattering and smiling; Mommy and Daddy smiled back at them, but not at each other. Diana stared longer and harder than she should have—something about the girls made it impossible for her to look away.

As the sun set and he didn't come back out, she wondered if her intuition had let her down. Maybe what she'd seen was a typical, harmless marital spat—maybe Sophie had gone to Chanel on a spending spree, or he'd golfed all weekend long despite repeated promises not to. But none of that computed for her, and more likely David was being a good boy to make up for whatever sin he'd committed. If that were true, who knew how many days she'd have to spend following him. Luckily, men like that weren't good at delaying gratification.

But then, miracle of miracles, the garage door opened and

David, now in office-casual clothes, pulled out of the driveway and took off down the road.

Dread tugged at her stomach as she followed him back toward the office. Was that all this was, a widow of business married to a workaholic? Sad, but not tragic, and not the right type of sin for her particular skills.

But when he was half a mile from the Branford building, he turned sharply north.

Diana's heart thrummed like she was in love.

————

She almost lost him, trying to keep her distance, as he turned into a residential neighborhood of charming brownstones with wrought-iron fences that enclosed postage-stamp gardens of shrubs and flowers. He pulled over in front of one without signaling, and to keep from looking suspicious, she had to drive past him and double-back. By the time she'd done that, he was out of the car and turning up a flight of gray steps toward a set of carved-mahogany double doors. She pulled into the nearest parking spot as quickly as she could, then pulled out her Sony A7SII and started clicking.

Just in time, as it turned out. The moment he knocked on the door, it opened.

By a young woman, maybe twenty-five, with golden hair, sweet dimples, and twinkling blue eyes that openly adored him under the streetlights. She stood up on her tippy toes to kiss him.

As his lips met hers, his hand stroked the bump of her belly.

CHAPTER FORTY-TWO

AUGUST 30TH

The rest of the week flew by for Jo as she and Arnett chased down leads and dug into even the smallest of possibilities that could lead to conclusive evidence. Fischer's two law partners confirmed being with him the night of Melissa Rollins' death, but also confirmed their dinner finished early enough for him to leave and kill her after. They found nobody able to confirm he'd been in the office the night of Louisa Pryzik's death, or to claim otherwise. Nobody else in his office had any motive they could find associated with the case.

As an officer made slow progress through DCF files, Jo and Arnett verified that Tinsley Sparks had no connection with DCF as either abused or abuser. Lopez confirmed that Louisa had rented her home and had no assets or insurance to constitute a financial motive, and discovered that Lila Doug, Rick Burke's caseworker, had died of a heart attack. They revisited background checks for each of the primary suspects involved in the case, but couldn't unearth anything new, and couldn't find any conclusive connection between Tinsley Sparks and Dustin Heidami, but couldn't rule it out, either.

They did another walk-through of Melissa's house to be

sure they hadn't missed anything. They hadn't, but did verify that except for the one in the third-floor hall closet, all the house's doorknobs were made by the same manufacturer. After days of frustration they decided the best course was to give themselves some time away from the increasingly frustrating facts, and reconvene on Monday morning.

After spending the weekend trying to rid herself of the image of little Avery Rollins huddled in the darkness of that closet, Jo handed Arnett his latte and dropped into her chair. "I hope you managed to come up with something, because my brain refuses to cooperate."

"Should we recap?"

Jo swallowed a gulp of her mocha. "I'll start. We have five main suspects: Travis Rollins, Tinsley Sparks, Dustin Heidami, Rick Burke, and Tom Fischer. Of those, I think Tinsley's the least likely. Since we can't find any reason to believe she's obsessed with child abusers, she has no motive to kill Louisa Pryzik."

"Unless she was working with someone else for some reason," Arnett said.

"But nobody's phone records or anything else even hint that might be happening. We have similar issues with both Travis Rollins and Dustin Heidami, who may each have reason to want their own former significant others dead, but don't have motive for the other killing unless they've entered into some sort of *Strangers on a Train* swap. Which is logistically possible given their lack of alibis, but again we have absolutely no evidence they even knew each other."

"And last we have Tom Fischer and Rick Burke," Arnett said.

"Who fit the current facts best," Jo continued. "Both have histories of being abused as children that map on to Melissa and Louisa's situation, so they'd make sense in terms of a serial killer triggered by past trauma. The clearest fit to me is Fischer—it's possible he seeks out certain kinds of cases, and if he loses, kills the abusive parent. Both he and Burke have access to information about mothers who mirror their own abuse experience, and information about their lives. And neither have an alibi."

Arnett sucked air in through his teeth. "I just don't see a way Melissa or Louisa would let opposing council or press into their homes."

"Fischer could have shown up claiming to want to negotiate some sort of custody situation more to their favor."

"Possible, I guess. But with the sort of bad feelings we're talking about, I'm not convinced."

"That's fair." Jo nodded. "And, of course, we still have no physical evidence pointing to any one person. Which is a big problem, because any defense attorney will cry reasonable doubt, especially in light of our final possibility: a random citizen inflamed by Burke's articles to kill these women."

"Wouldn't be the first rage killing we've seen. So we keep searching the DCF files to see if we can find another suspect with stacks of zip ties, rope, and a hammer that just happened to pick up some of Melissa's DNA on it somehow," Arnett quipped. "And, keep interrogating and digging the suspects we have until we trip someone up in a lie."

Jo tapped her pen on her desk. "What I keep coming back to is the injection. It makes no sense, and I can't help but feel it's a key to the whole thing."

"Any of the five could have obtained GHB with next to no hassle," Arnett said.

"Sad but true." Jo's phone buzzed. "It's Lopez. She wants us to come to the lab."

Arnett pushed away from the desk. "Say a quick prayer she's got something that'll help."

When they rounded the corner into the lab, they found Lopez hovering over her printer, bouncing up and down on the balls of her feet.

Arnett pointed down. "Seriously, Lopez, that's not normal. You need to cut it out with those Rockstars."

"Geez, Arnett. It's like you've never seen an excited woman before." She tilted her ponytail to the side and frowned. "How sad for Laura."

Jo hid her smile behind her coffee. "What has you so excited?"

"Coupla things. First one relevant to TMK—"

"TMK?" Arnett asked, beating Jo to the punch.

"The Mom Killer." Lopez's eyebrows shot up. "All the good ones have a name, right? And an acronym is even better. The point is, it's about Travis Rollins, and I'm pissed off with myself on this one." She sorted the printouts into stacks as she talked, swiping her highlighter across several pages of each. "When you found the possible connection with the Louisa Pryzik case, I went over his phone records again to see if we could establish a connection between him and Heidami, but didn't find anything."

"Right. That's what you told us." Arnett picked up an unopened can of Rockstar and frowned down at the ingredients.

"Right. But as we've been sorting through everyone's backgrounds, I did what I always do when I can't find anything— start from scratch and check everything again. To be thorough, I requested updated phone records, including the time *since* Melissa was murdered." She handed one of the stacks each to Jo and Arnett, and pointed to one of the highlighted texts.

Are you free? We need to talk.

Jo looked at the names next to the sending and receiving numbers, and her mouth dropped. "Travis texted Dustin Heidami?"

CHAPTER FORTY-THREE

"Yep, the day you interviewed him the second time, before you even knew Dustin Heidami was relevant." Lopez's smile was triumphant.

Jo glanced down at the responding text: *I'll stop by after work.*

"So Heidami flat-out lied to us about being in contact." Arnett jabbed at the paper. "Rollins must have been warning Heidami."

"But why not do it after we talked to him the day before?" She cast her mind back. "We must have asked him something that triggered it."

Arnett's brow creased. "We needed to talk to Avery, but we'd also discovered his alibi was bullshit, and that he hadn't told us Melissa locked Avery in the closet."

Jo's hand flew up to her necklace. "And he seemed genuinely confused about why the closet incident mattered to us, but then he ran to text Heidami after."

"What would Heidami care, unless Rollins had reason to connect it to Louisa Pryzik's death?"

"Exactly," Jo said, then remembered the other sections Lopez highlighted. "What are these?"

"Turns out Heidami moved into his current residence shortly after Louisa's murder. It doesn't have a landline, but his previous apartment did." She pointed to the number. "That's his old landline."

Arnett scanned and flipped. "And they talked five times on that line. Son of a bitch."

"But then they don't have contact for almost a year, and nothing before Melissa was murdered," Jo said.

Lopez held up a finger. "That's not fully accurate, actually. They may very well have texted."

Jo grimaced at her oversight. "But we're lucky if phone companies keep text messages for more than a few days, let alone a few months."

Lopez touched her index finger to her nose. "I have a request in to both phone companies to see if anyone can resurrect any of them, but since it's not Easter time, we might be fresh out of that type of miracle."

"Well." Jo tapped a nail on the printout. "This still proves Dustin Heidami lied to us. And where there's one lie, there's usually more."

"You know, since he told us to talk to his lawyer and all, I'm thinking he can come to us this time," Arnett said. "I'm thinking we even send some uniforms over to the paper mill to give him a nice ride."

Jo half-smiled. "Wish I could be there to see it. Thanks, Christine, this is a huge help." She tapped the phone to call in a request to have Heidami brought in.

"Aw, shucks." Lopez grasped her hands together and ducked her head, then glanced back up with a twinkle in her eyes. "But if you like that, you're gonna *love* what else I have for you..."

Jo abandoned the phone. "Really. Do tell."

"Okay, first I have a caveat. Upstate Ursula was in here yesterday and caught sight of the analyses I was doing—"

Arnett threw up a hand. "Wait. Upstate Ursula?"

Lopez blinked at him. "Lieutenant Hayes."

He gaped back. "I don't get it."

She lowered her voice and glanced around. "She transferred in from upstate New York?"

"Sure, that part I get. But her first name isn't Ursula."

Jo laughed, and Lopez rolled her eyes. "Ursula is the villain from *The Little Mermaid*? She's determined to replace the king as ultimate ruler of the ocean?"

Arnett held up both hands. "My bad. I forgot to study up on Disney movie dynamics."

Lopez patted his shoulder. "Nobody's perfect. Just so as you know."

Arnett glared at her, and Jo hurried to intercept. "I'm guessing if you're telling us this, Ursula figured out it had something to do with me and wasn't happy?"

Lopez ran a hand down her ponytail. "No, not one bit. She started to blow her little stack, but I short-circuited it."

Jo's brows popped up. "Dammit. This is leaking over onto you now?"

A laugh exploded out of Lopez. "Yeah, right, like I'd let her cramp my style. I told her you'd proposed an extremely innovative solution to re-examining a cold case, and that I believe your approach has the potential to help with future cases, and for that reason I was continuing on as a test case to see if the analyses yielded results. Because if they do, we'll certainly want to use them in the future, and can point to the success when applying for future warrants. All true, if incomplete."

Jo watched the set of her jaw change as she spoke. "Did you have that look on your face at the time?"

Lopez gave a curt nod. "You *know* I did, and you *know* she backed off. Walked off grumbling something about making sure it didn't take away time from 'real' cases. I just thought I should mention it to you 'cause the last time I saw hair go up on someone's neck like that, it was a cat at Halloween."

Jo grimaced. "Thanks. And just to be clear, I don't want to put either of you in an awkward situation. If you want to set this case aside, I completely understand—"

Lopez threw up a hand to cut her off, eyes gleaming. "First piece of good news. It was super easy to track Bennie's cell phone's last ping to a tower." She slapped a map of San Francisco down in front of them. "That happened right here, at eight oh three on the evening of August sixth."

Jo peered down at the location. "About halfway between Ocean Beach and the Golden Gate Bridge. Is it the closest tower to the bridge?"

"It is not, which is a crucial catch. Because not only was I able to get *that* information, I was also able to get NELOS info, and—"

"NELOS information?" Arnett asked.

"Network Event Location System information. It basically tells you how far the target device was from the tower, and it's generally accurate within about ten to fifteen meters. Long story short, between the two of those sets of information, I can tell you the last time Bennie's phone communicated with the tower was somewhere in this area here." She motioned to the western end of a large park-like area labeled Land's End. "Since we know he went into the water before he died, the only spot that fits the distance from the tower and is on the edge of the water is right near here."

"Sutro Baths?"

"Sutro Baths." She reached for one of her keyboards and pulled up a shot of Google Earth. "There're several walking paths out in this region, but this one runs right along the water. And, look what's directly to the south of all of this."

Blood rushed through Jo's ears. "Ocean Beach."

"Ocean Beach. Good instincts, my fine detective friend. You were right—Bennie did *not* throw himself off the Golden Gate Bridge."

"What about the other supposed suicide, Jim Dornan?" Arnett asked.

Lopez grimaced. "No way to know, they only keep NELOS data for six months. We have the tower dumps for him, so I was able to get his approximate time of death, too, but not his location data."

"Damn—but the time of death is the main thing," Jo said.

"It is, and no worries, 'cause it only gets better from there. So what we're hoping is that if Moreno and Dornan, and thus Scherer, were murdered, their killer's phone signal should be in the same general area around the time of both of their deaths, right?"

"Right," Jo said, and Arnett nodded.

"So I got the cell tower data from the times of the last pings from Moreno's and Dornan's deaths, and eliminated all of the devices that were only in one or the other of those two data sets, because our theory is the killer would have had to be there for both. That part was easy-peasy. But, then I had to figure out how to get rid of all of the devices that were in *both* data sets, but for non-murderous reasons—people who just happen to live or work in the area, or who commute past that spot at the same time every night. Or, since both deaths occurred on a Friday night, people who come to their local watering hole to kick off every weekend, that kind of thing." She paused to check their faces.

Jo and Arnett nodded.

"So, since we agreed in the warrant to only analyze data anonymously until we'd eliminated non-suspects, I asked for additional data sets from the same cell tower for three *other* nights the week of Moreno's death, at the same exact time of night. People who reside or work there rather than just show up to kill people should also be present in those other data sets too —their devices should ping every day, or almost every day, in a given week."

Jo's pulse sped up. "But since our killer is long gone, their phone *wouldn't* show up in those data sets."

"Yeppers—that's the hope."

"Unless our killer lives close to the tower and kills close to home," Arnett said.

Lopez nodded. "If that's the case, we're sunk, because there's no way to pull their cell number out from the rest of the cell data. The only way this works is if our killer was near this particular cell tower *only* when killing their victims."

"Gotcha," Arnett said.

"So, I next had my program subtract out every device that was present at the time of both Moreno and Dornan's deaths, *and* was in at least two of those other data aggregates." Lopez paused dramatically, rubbing her hands together like an evil genius.

"You're killing me." Jo laughed.

Lopez grinned. "That left me with four cell phone numbers. A sufficiently small number of potential suspects to give us permission to research further."

"Wait a minute." Jo held up a hand. "That NELOS data you mentioned. Can we use that to find out which of the cell numbers was in proximity to Bennie?"

Lopez pointed at her and clicked her tongue. "Nice catch. I tried that, but unfortunately, none of them are clearly next to the location where Bennie's phone last contacted the tower. Not surprising because it took at least several minutes for the water to kill the phones, probably more if they were buried deep into layers of clothing, and during that time our murderer almost certainly hightailed it away from the scene."

"Damn." Another thought popped into her head. "What about that mystery number we found in Bennie's phone records, that he was talking and texting to? Did you happen to check to see if that was in the data set?"

"I did, and it wasn't, not in any of them."

"Double damn. Well, thanks for trying," Jo said. "Now I just have to dive into those four people and see if I can find any evidence that connects them with our deaths."

"Piece of cake, right?" Lopez laughed. "I'll search them, too, and see what I can come up with. I'll also start a warrant so we can check with Blizzard and see if any of these four are World of Warcraft players."

"Perfect. Still an uphill climb, but we're a lot higher up the mountain than we were before you ran all these analyses. Really, really impressive, Christine." Little electrical prickles ran up and down Jo's body, and she turned to Arnett. "I say while we wait for Heidami to come talk to us, we dive into these numbers."

CHAPTER FORTY-FOUR

Diana watched the ocean slide by as the plane banked its approach into LAX.

She'd spent the rest of the week tying up loose ends. Friday and Saturday she followed Mr. Handsome, who turned out to be Matt Soltero, Josette's neurologist boyfriend, and was pleasantly surprised to see that when he wasn't with Josette, he worked out and spent time with people who turned out to be his family. Sunday, she followed Sophie Belleau and confirmed Sophie's life was filled with her two sweet girls and contributions to the community. As they spent the afternoon helping at a food bank, Diana watched through the large plate-glass window that fronted the space. She couldn't take her eyes off the two precious little girls filling boxes with their mother. They were perfect, innocent and wholesome, all curly hair and big eyes and easy smiles. And Sophie was a paragon, really, almost an archetypal mother figure—she deserved far better than the sort of disgusting philanderer who'd impregnate another woman —and watching the family he was betraying so badly magnified the flames of her hatred for David Belleau, like embers thrown on a pile of leaves. So much so, she'd struggled to *not* kill him just for the satisfaction of it.

She also set up discreet cameras where she could get away with it—one near Josette's house, one outside of Matt Soltero's, and one across the street from the pregnant blonde homewrecker's house, all connected back to a burner phone.

By the end of the week, she decided she'd learned all she could from the direct surveillance. She needed to return home regardless—she normally never left Cleopatra for more than a few days at a time—and could figure out the rest of what she needed over the internet.

She turned her head away from the plane window and closed her eyes, at peace. Because what she did with everything she'd learned depended entirely on Josette Fournier. If she left Diana alone, Diana would leave her family to sort out their own problems. If not, well... she now had several pressure points she could use to apply leverage.

———

The plane landed uneventfully; she deboarded and navigated the terminal with experienced efficiency, then settled into the lulling rhythm of the stop-and-go traffic. When she finally pulled up into her driveway, darling Kenzie, her ten-year-old cat sitter, appeared from around the back of the house and pulled the side gate closed behind her. She ran up as Diana stepped out of the car and gave her a giant hug.

Diana kissed the top of her head. "Hello, my sweet! How's Cleopatra doing?"

"She's good! We just played for half an hour before she ran back in the house. But she's not eating all her food, so I think she misses you."

Kenzie had been fascinated with the hairless cat since moving into the house next door five years before, and Diana trusted her more than she trusted anyone else in the world. But Diana's trust necessarily had limits. Kenzie had a key to the backyard but not the house, and put out food and water on the back porch. When Cleopatra heard the shake of the food, she came out for cuddles and play, then went back inside when the mood struck her.

Diana smiled and tugged one of the auburn pigtails. "It's nice to be missed. We said ten dollars a day, right?"

The girl's brow creased. "You don't have to—"

"Hush now. You know the rules." She located her wallet and pulled out several bills. "It's good to be kind to people, but you have to know your worth in this life. We don't ever let anyone undervalue us, right?"

Kenzie took the money with a sheepish smile. "Right. Thank you Ms. Montauk."

"Thank *you*. Now go do something fun." She waved the girl playfully away.

As Kenzie predicted, Cleopatra was overjoyed to see her, and jumped onto her shoulder before she'd set her purse on the hall table. Diana reached up to stroke her. "Hello, my love."

She carried the cat into the kitchen and opened a can of tuna for her. As Cleopatra attacked it with delicate licks, Diana unpacked. Once they'd both finished, they curled up together on her red couch and she ran over everything in her mind. Most likely, she decided, she'd overreacted to Naya Moreno's Facebook posting. Josette wasn't following up on it, and Diana had abandoned the World of Warcraft angle so long ago Josette might as well be chasing the wind. But it was always better to be safe than sorry, and she was glad she'd gone and gathered what she needed.

She pulled up her current project to work on, but sat, drumming her red nails on the side of her laptop.

Because the vision of David Belleau kissing the blonde bimbo wouldn't leave her mind.

CHAPTER FORTY-FIVE

Back at their desks, Jo and Arnett dove into the four cell phone numbers from Lopez's analysis of Bennie Moreno's and Jim Dornan's deaths.

"Cell phone number one belongs to a Randy Murry." Jo pointed to a picture taken from his driver's license. "He lives in Sacramento, California, an hour and a half away from San Francisco, forty-five years old with a wife and two kids, both boys. He's an IT coordinator for a mortgage company that has branches in Rancho Cordova and San Francisco, and has been for ten years. I pulled up the location of the San Francisco branch, and it's on the other side of San Francisco from where our death occurred. However, when I plugged the business address and his home address into Google Maps, it does direct me to drive over the Golden Gate Bridge. So if he's got a favorite restaurant or something in that area he hits before he heads home, that would explain why he was there on the two days in question, but not there on other days."

"Or, he could have stopped off to meet up with our guys and kill them," Arnett said.

"True. I scoured his social media, but couldn't find anything that looked out of the ordinary. He loves to fish and takes regular trips up to Mount Shasta with his family. He likes NASCAR and goes to races out at a track in Sonoma. He's never been arrested for anything, has excellent credit, and has both a dog and a cat."

"The serial killers are always the normal-looking ones..." He shook his head, and pointed to a driver's license mug shot of his own. "I have Rita Flowers. Fifty-two, and lives in a town called Fresno, about three hours away from San Francisco, where she works for an agricultural supply company. She's got no work-related reason to go out to San Francisco, but both she and her husband, no kids, do enjoy both ballet and surfing, and from what I can tell, Fresno has limited amounts of both. Pictures all over her social media of trips to the War Memorial Opera House, and a variety of beaches, including Ocean Beach. Zero pictures of her murdering anyone."

"That's inconvenient." Jo shook her head.

"Ain't it just. Also never been arrested for anything, has mediocre credit, and two very large snakes named Pebbles and Bam-Bam."

"Some mother's children." Jo waved a hand at her eyes. "My second one is Garson Grey—and no, I kid you not. Thirty-seven. Lives alone in San Francisco itself, but over here." She pointed at the San Francisco map. "Called the Richmond District, just east of Ocean Beach and the Sutro Baths, and he lives in nearly the most eastern end of it, here. He's an artist—"

"With a name like that, what else could he be?" Arnett said.

"—and works out of his house. So he doesn't live or work close enough to our target cell tower to show up in all the data sets Lopez requested, but the neighborhood is close enough that our target area might contain cafés and such he frequents."

"Or he could be there killing our vics," Arnett said.

Jo pointed her pen at him in agreement. "I found multiple features in local papers about him because his art's apparently pretty good, although not great according to his mountain of credit card debt. He does have an arrest record, but it's exactly what you'd expect if you googled *stereotype of San Franciscan artist*—chaining himself to things during protests and possession of marijuana before it was legal."

"Can't say I've ever heard of a stoner serial killer," Arnett said.

"Someone has to be the first," Jo said.

Arnett's brows raised in agreement, then held up a picture. "And for our final contestant, we have Diana Montauk, thirty-eight. She's a software engineer who lives in Los Angeles. Single. She has no arrest record that I could find, and owes nothing to nobody as far as I can tell."

Jo waited, but he didn't say more. "And?"

"And—that's it. She and I are the last remaining social media holdouts. No Facebook, no Instagram, no Twitter, not even anything on LinkedIn. Google comes back with pages of results that have both 'Diana' and 'Montauk' on the page, but not together."

Jo straightened slightly. "That's strange in this day and age, and especially for a software engineer to have no digital foot-print, but not necessarily conclusive. You said she's thirty-eight?"

"Yep."

"Huh." Jo considered everything Lopez taught her about generational differences in social media use. "Thirty-eight would put her on the edge between millennial and gen-X, and the millennials are fifty-fiftyish about Facebook. But even those usually use something else. Not even TikTok?"

"Not that I could find. Definitely worth digging further."

Jo considered. "So what's our next move? If we want to dig any deeper, we'll need some sort of help, either to tap into personal records and communication or to do some surveillance. And asking Hayes is out of the question."

"I don't see a judge being overly willing to let us take that next step based on the data analyses Lopez did. We know she's brilliant, but for most people it'll look like witchcraft," Arnett said. "Same thing with surveillance. I can't see other police departments channeling resources into this when we're not even sure there was a crime."

Jo took a deep breath and inhaled slowly. "No, that's probably true. What I really want to do is go interview each of them myself, but I can't see how I can manage that with Hayes breathing down my neck."

"No." Arnett shook his head. "But I'm thinking if you turn on a little bit of the Fournier charm, we might be able to tap into enough interdepartmental goodwill to get at least SFPD to send officers out to ask for alibi information."

"If we ask about that, our killer will instantly know we're on to them," Jo said.

"True. But I'm not sure what else we can do," Arnett said.

Jo bounced a fist on her thigh. They were at a dead end with respect to leads, the investigation wasn't official so getting help would be difficult, and nobody was likely to believe there was a killer at all with the evidence they had. But, very real people were dying, and it was only a matter of time before the next victim turned up—she couldn't let the perpetrator continue to kill just because her lieutenant found strong female detectives in her unit threatening. But since she'd used up all her vacation time dealing with her father's recent battle with cancer, she couldn't just go herself on the sly. "You're right, shaking the tree looks like the only option we have left. If the inquiries trigger suspicious behavior, we'll at least know we're on to something and might be able to elicit cooperation at that point."

"It's worth a shot," Arnett said.

"I'll call San Francisco and Los Angeles, and you call Sacramento and Fresno," she said. "How much should we tell them?"

"I say keep it simple. We believe Moreno and Dornan were

killed, and we have reason to believe one of these four people did it. We'd like to have an experienced professional look 'em in the face when they ask about alibis for the nights in question, and we'll be more than happy to reciprocate however we can."

———

By the time they'd finished liaising with the other law enforcement agencies, Dustin Heidami and Tom Fischer had arrived, and had been escorted to an interview room.

"Mr. Heidami." Arnett strode across the interrogation room, slid into the chair across from Heidami, and bent forward toward him all in one motion. "I *really* dislike it when people lie to me."

The righteously indignant annoyance on Heidami's face morphed instantly into self-preservation. "I don't know what you're talking about. I never lied to you."

Fischer threw up his hand. "What are you referring to, detectives?"

Jo stood at the back of the room, sipping her coffee. "We asked Mr. Heidami if he knew the Rollinses."

Heidami crossed his arms and leaned back against his chair. "No, you didn't. You asked me if I knew 'them,' and from the context, I thought you meant Melissa and Avery. I never met either of them, and I don't believe Louisa or Raina did, either."

Fischer hadn't been expecting that—he shot a nasty glare at Heidami before recovering his composure.

"Ah." Arnett rubbed his hand across his chin and looked back toward Jo. "Mr. Heidami likes to play games."

Jo nodded over her coffee. "I see that."

Arnett turned back around with a wry smile. "You know what one of my favorite games is, Mr. Heidami? It's called 'let's arrest the suspect for obstruction of justice.'"

The blood drained from Heidami's face.

Jo raised her brows and tilted her head. "Detective Arnett *does* like that game. The last guy he played with won a two-year stay at the Oakhurst County Jail."

"We don't appreciate facetious threats," Fischer said, tone wary.

Arnett stared directly at Heidami. "We don't appreciate people who get in our way when we're trying to bring a murderer to justice. So how about we try this again. How do you know Travis Rollins?"

Fischer indicated he should answer, and Heidami shifted in his chair. "I met him at Tom's office. I was there signing some paperwork, and he came out of a meeting with Tom."

"How long ago was this?" Jo asked.

"I honestly don't remember exactly. Somewhere around nine months ago? It was before Christmas, I remember that."

Was he still trying to prevaricate? "Why do you remember that?" Jo asked.

"Because we talked about how the holidays were gonna be tough, having to deal with our girls' custody arrangements."

"Was this before or after Louisa was killed?"

Heidami squirmed in the chair again. "Before."

Jo's eyes narrowed. "So before October fifteenth, then."

Heidami's eyes widened—he must not have expected them to put that together. "Right, I guess so, yeah."

"So why did you lie to us?" Arnett asked.

"Because you were looking for a suspect, and I didn't want to be it."

"We suspect people who lie," Arnett said.

"Especially when you supposedly have a solid alibi," Jo said. "That makes us wonder if you somehow managed to slip out of work the day Louisa died."

Heidami glanced between them. "There's security all over that place. I'd never be able to walk off in the middle of my shift without anyone noticing."

"Maybe." Arnett shrugged. "Or maybe you've been there long enough to know how to avoid the hot spots."

"Or maybe you took off during your dinner break," Jo said. "You worked several hours of overtime the night Melissa Rollins was killed. You'd be entitled to a meal break."

Fischer's hand raised, and Heidami's mouth slammed shut.

"When was the last time you spoke with Travis Rollins?" Arnett asked.

"Last week."

That tracked. "Why did he contact you?" Jo asked.

"He was concerned about your visit."

"Why?"

He paused for a second before answering. "He said it was obvious you considered him a suspect."

"So why call you?" Arnett asked.

He shrugged. "I was the only person who understood what he'd been through with the custody battle."

"You have your phone with you, right?" Jo asked.

"I—I mean, yeah, of course," he answered.

"Can you show us the text exchange?" she asked.

"I deleted it."

Arnett shook his head and clucked his tongue. "Innocent people don't delete text messages, Dustin."

"There's no law against deleting text messages, Detective." Fischer's tone rang deliberately bored.

"Doesn't matter," Jo said. "I remember the message. It said 'we need to talk.' Not 'I'm upset and could use a friend,' but 'we need to talk.' He clearly thought something going on was relevant to you, too."

Heidami blinked. "I —I told you. We were worried what you were going to think, because it doesn't look good that both our ex-partners ended up dead."

Arnett turned back to Jo, brows raised. "He makes a good point. That really doesn't look good."

Jo nodded. "It really doesn't. Especially since, if that were the real reason for the call, he would have called you after our first visit, when he first found out Melissa was killed. But he didn't call you until our second visit."

Heidami looked at Fischer, then down at the table in front of him.

Silence pressed down on the room.

Finally, he cleared his throat. "We didn't think anything of it at the time. I made a joke, I know it was in bad taste, about how Louisa'd been bashed in the head with a frying pan the same way she'd done to Raina. I said it was fitting that she got a taste of her own medicine. Literally neither of us thought about it again until you told Travis that Melissa had been murdered the same way she abused Avery. And he freaked out because there was no way the closet situation could have happened by coincidence."

"Why did that require a desperate, furtive call you both lied about if neither of you had anything to do with the deaths?" Jo asked.

The heel of Heidami's foot bounced frantically under the table. "I know how it looks, but I swear. I didn't hurt Louisa or Melissa. I didn't like how Louisa treated Raina and I sure as hell didn't want her to have even partial custody. But I would never kill her. I'd never kill *anybody*."

"We'd really like to believe that," Arnett said. "But the thing is, once you lie to us, it's really hard to trust you."

"It seems to me"—Fischer's voice rang out a little too loudly —"that you're throwing everybody at the wall to see who sticks. First Mr. Rollins, now Mr. Heidami, and a few days ago you even accused me. Do you have any actual evidence, or are you just going to arrest all of us?"

"Mr. Fischer makes an interesting point." Jo slipped into the second chair across from Heidami, holding his gaze. "Because I see a clear conflict of interest here. If you're all suspects, how can your attorney adequately defend you when he's also responsible for defending Travis Rollins, and for defending himself? When the bus comes rolling around the corner, someone's getting pushed under it. *I* sure wouldn't be willing to gamble that my attorney would risk going to jail himself in order to defend *me*."

CHAPTER FORTY-SIX

Diana was distracted—so much so she blew right past the turn onto her street as she came home from picking up groceries.

The little girl inside her couldn't stop thinking about David Belleau. Which wasn't surprising—once she found a candidate that engaged the little girl's interest, the obsession only built. But there was another reason she was taken with him, and it worried her—because she felt protective of Josette.

As she spent time with Josette and her circle, she felt less like an observer and more like a participant. Ridiculous, because of course she knew she wasn't. She pulled up the few articles she'd found about Josette and read them repeatedly, as though she could glean some additional insight if she studied them often enough. The compassion in her quotes, even for people who committed crimes, and the outreach work she did in the community made clear Josette was the real deal, not one of those power-trip cops—she cared about the citizens in her juris-diction. She didn't just fight crime, she reached out to people in need to help them. Josette had the same priorities Diana did, and as odd as it sounded, she truly believed they could be friends. She didn't feel that way about many people—and she really didn't like watching David Belleau and his tart make a fool of her friend's family.

Diana swore when she realized she'd missed her turn, then flipped a quick U-turn and headed back to her street.

As she approached her driveway, Kenzie, playing in her own yard, spotted her and waved. Diana waved back and, as she parked and got out of the car, Kenzie trotted up the yard with a wrinkle in her brow.

Studying Kenzie's face over her shoulder, she reached into the car for her bag of groceries. "Hey, sweetie, what's going on?"

Kenzie screeched to a halt in the gravel. "You had a visitor. When you weren't home he came over to talk to us, and asked me to give you this." Her arm thrust out, holding a card.

The world slammed into slow motion as Diana reached for the card. She never got visitors, and that meant only one thing. "What did he want?"

Her face scrunched up. "He said he was with the police, but he wasn't wearing a uniform. My mom said he was a detective. He asked if I knew when you'd be home."

Diana's entire body was ice. "What did you tell him?"

"I said I didn't know. I told him you just got back from a trip, and I got to feed Cleopatra for you." Kenzie must have seen something in Diana's face, because a shadow passed over her own. "Was that bad?"

"No, sweetie. That's perfect. Did he say why he wanted to know?"

Kenzie plucked at the jelly bracelet on her wrist as she thought. "Nope. He just said he wanted to ask you some questions, and gave me the card."

"Thanks so much, I appreciate it. I have to start dinner now, but you can come play with Cleopatra later if you want to."

Her sweet face broke into a wide smile. "I can't, I'm going to a pizza party tonight for Tamika's birthday! I get to wear my new dress. Can I come play with her tomorrow?"

Diana forced a smile on her face. "Of course."

Kenzie twirled and ran off down the driveway. Diana watched until she disappeared out of sight, then hurried into the house. She dropped the bag on her kitchen counter, then stared down at the card: Detective Jose Del Rosario, LAPD. She turned it over, but there was nothing additional on the back.

She told herself not to overreact. That there was no reason to assume anything bad, this was probably just some routine inquiry, something strange had happened in the area, her alarm had had a malfunction, something like that. There was simply no way anyone could have connected her to the deaths in San Francisco. It just wasn't possible.

But they wouldn't send out a detective for any of that.

With a shaking hand, she poured herself a glass of water and drank it slowly, forcing herself to think calmly so she could choose the best course of action. What would an innocent person do in this situation? They'd be worried something had happened to someone they loved, or that they needed help. They'd call back almost immediately. And if she didn't call, he'd just come back and she'd have to look him in the face when she answered his questions. Better to be able to control the interaction over the phone.

Hand still shaking, she pulled out her cell phone and entered the number.

The voice that answered was brisk and efficient. "Del Rosario."

She kept her own voice calm, but with a slight edge of worry. "Hello, Detective Del Rosario. My name is Diana Montauk. My neighbor just told me you came to my house asking for me?"

"Yes, right. I have a couple of quick questions I need to ask you."

"Certainly. What is this about?"

"Just a routine inquiry we're doing to help out another department. We just need to know why you were in San Francisco on August sixth."

The world slowed again, and came into almost impossible focus. The light streaming through the curtains lit up every chip in her counter, and the ticking clock over her refrigerator struck like a drumbeat.

"Hang on one second please, my cat is tearing up my plant." She tossed the phone down on the counter, stepped a few feet away, chastised the absent cat, and made rustling sounds while she thought.

They knew she'd been in San Francisco? How? She always made day trips so she didn't have to stay at a hotel. Never made purchases with anything other than cash. Was careful what venues she went to. Always used a burner phone that she got rid of immediately after, before she even left the city, and only turned on her actual cell *after* she'd disposed of the burner. Used rental cars so she wouldn't even register on license plate readers.

But she didn't have time to worry about that now, she had to say something, and fast. The best way to go was stick as close to the truth as possible.

She picked the phone back up. "I'm sorry, Detective. She has the worst timing. You were asking about my trip to San Francisco?"

"Yes," he said, his voice a notch tenser than it had been before.

"I went up to see an exhibit at the Legion of Honor."

"Which exhibit was that?"

Thankfully, she knew the answer to this, since she'd seen the banners all over the building. "It was relics from Pompeii, frescoes and fossilized artifacts."

A pen scratched in the background. "That's a long way to go for an exhibit."

The room had turned uncomfortably hot—she crossed into the living room and turned on the air conditioning. "I spent my childhood in San Francisco, and I like to go up and visit every so often."

"You have friends and family there?"

She modulated her voice. "Sadly, no. Both my parents are deceased, and the friends I knew have moved away."

"Where did you stay when you were up there?"

"I didn't. I just went for the day."

He paused—he wasn't buying it. Despite the air conditioning, a thin layer of sweat broke out on her forehead.

"Gotta love those commuter flights," he finally said, tone lighter.

Was that purposeful? Was she reading him wrong?

She matched it regardless. "Thank you, American Airlines."

His pen scratched again, and she winced. A sheet of something flipped.

"And how about October twenty-third of last year?"

Electricity zinged through every inch of her body—they knew about October 23rd too. "I'll have to check my calendar, I don't remember that far back."

"You don't remember why you went to San Francisco, or you don't remember going to San Francisco?"

"I'm fairly certain I went to San Francisco sometime around that time, but I'm not sure about the exact date, and I don't remember what exactly I did on that trip. But I can dig up my records if it's important?"

He put a smile into his voice, but his tone was firm. "I'd appreciate that."

Her eyes squeezed shut—damn, damn, damn. She'd have to hop onto the Internet Wayback Machine and figure out what had been showing at the Legion that day. She hurried to cover. "That's no problem, but I have a conference call in a few minutes and groceries getting warm on my counter. Can I dig out my records and call you back with the information?"

"Sure, that'd be no problem. Can you get back to me tonight?"

She winced again. "I'm not sure how long my call will be, or how long it'll take me to dig into last year's records, but I'll call as soon as I can."

"Thank you very much, Ms. Montauk, I appreciate that."

"Not a problem."

The call ended. She stared around the room, seeing nothing.

Josette hadn't abandoned Bennie's murder at all. Quite the opposite—she'd outsourced it. Despite a week of surveillance, Diana had underestimated what Josette knew. She'd been foolish to think someone that dedicated would just walk away from a lead.

But—Diana had leverage now, and this is why she'd gotten it. There was no point in second-guessing what or why. She had to assume Josette knew everything, and act accordingly. No matter what else, they knew her name and where she lived, and that meant she had no choice.

It was time for plan B.

CHAPTER FORTY-SEVEN

SEPTEMBER 1ST

Jo's cell phone shrieked her out of a dream—one where she couldn't catch up with a gunman charging through a mall—she bolted upright, heart pounding, and snatched the phone up to her ear.

"Jo. I'm sorry to wake you at three in the morning." Marzillo sounded disturbed.

"Is everything okay? Are you alright?"

"I'm fine, I'm at a crime scene. It's technically Goran and Coyne's case, but I think you and Arnett should head over here as soon as you can."

Jo's hand flew to her heart, and she inhaled deeply. "Glad you're safe. Why do you think we should head over?"

"Because my vic has three fresh injection sites in her left cubital fossa."

"I'm going to guess cubital fossa means the interior side of her elbow?"

"Correct."

"And let me guess—you're in Greenfern?"

"Correct."

Jo threw off the covers. "Have you cleared it with Goran and Coyne, or do I need to do some finessing when I get there?"

"With the bump in crime due to the heat, they're practically salivating at the thought of handing it off to you."

A smile tugged at one corner of Jo's mouth. "Can you text me the address? I'll call Arnett and we'll get there as fast as we can."

Jo picked up Arnett in exchange for the large travel tumbler of coffee Laura sent out of the house with him. By the time they pulled up in front of a dilapidated beige cottage in Greenfern, her tumbler was empty and her brain fully awake.

Arnett jutted his chin toward the ivy-covered fence surrounding the property, illuminated by crime-scene flood-lights. "Low visibility, just like the other two scenes."

They checked in with the officer guarding the perimeter, suited up into their PPE, and made their way as quickly as caution allowed to where Detectives Eli Goran and Charles Coyne stood in the hallway. A relative newbie, Eli Goran was a tall, slender man with a medium-brown complexion who made a stark contrast with Coyne, a seasoned veteran who was short and stout, with pale skin, hair, and eyes. Both smiled, then gestured them over to Marzillo and Peterson.

Jo nodded as she surveyed the living room. Cozy and invit-ing, despite the worn furniture and abundance of ropes, anchors, and life preservers in the decor, possibly because of the peaceful-looking white brunette slumped on the couch as though she'd fallen asleep watching television. Only the syringe, lighter, and drug cooker on the coffee table, and the strip of blue elastic tied around her left bicep, ruined the effect.

"Fournier. Arnett." Marzillo turned to greet them, and Peterson shot them a careful two-finger salute that didn't touch his forehead.

Jo pointed to the syringe. "I'm a little confused. We seem to have a clear reason for the injection sites here."

"Bear with me." Marzillo rubbed her nose with the back of her forearm. "This is Gina Purcelli, twenty-eight. Her mother made the nine-one-one call just before midnight. Gina missed her habitual ten o'clock call, and her mother called multiple times to see if she was okay, but got no answer. She used her spare key to get in and found Gina in this position. She went to take her pulse, and realized Gina was in rigor mortis. The ME came, and based on the drug paraphernalia, he made a preliminary assessment that she most likely overdosed pending a tox screen."

"Seems reasonable," Arnett said, also looking confused.

Marzillo gestured to the cooker on the table. "Oh, I agree. I'll be stunned if she wasn't killed by an overdose of something, most likely heroin. There's no trauma to the body, no wounds or abrasions, she wasn't beaten, stabbed, shot, or strangled." She paused and bent slightly to point at Gina's fingernails. "Her nails are blue, her tongue is blue, and under that lipstick I'd bet her lips are, too. Lots of possible reasons for that, and underlying most of them is myocardial infarct, but since most twenty-eight-year-olds don't have heart attacks out of the blue, it's safe to say whatever was in that syringe stopped her breathing and her heart."

"Waiting for the punchline," Arnett said.

"No punchline. Maybe what we see here is exactly what we get. Maybe she miscalculated her fix, and overdosed. But it doesn't feel right to me. Primarily because of her arms and legs."

Jo leaned closer for a better view. "No tracks and no scars from tracks, at least not where I can see."

"Correct." She gestured toward Gina's sandals. "And then there's the question of the three injection sites, which is unusual."

"Couldn't find a vein because she was new to it?" Arnett asked.

Marzillo shook her head and pointed, careful not to actually touch the arm. "Except see this one right here? This one is fresh, it happened right before she died. You see hemostasis, the initial clotting that happens pretty much immediately to stop a wound from bleeding, but it hasn't moved into any sort of inflammation the way these two have. That means time passed between them and this one, so not just multiple attempts all at once. It's a very subtle difference, and the ME said he'll take a closer look when he does the autopsy. They're all from today though, so maybe she just shot up several times over the course of the evening."

Jo squinted down at the table, then around the room. "No, you're right, something about this feels off. She only has one bag of heroin, and the equipment is new. How many people decide they want to try heroin and shoot up by themselves the first time?"

"Maybe she was trying to kill herself and figured this would be a pleasant way to do it, but didn't inject enough the first time?" Arnett said.

"It's possible." Marzillo's face scrunched skeptically under the PPE. "It just felt odd enough I thought you two should have a look. I told the ME about the potential connection to your case, and he said he'd put a rush on the tox screen and any other tests we think will help. He also said he'd get you her medical history."

"Good call, it's best to assume this is related until we can rule it out." Jo pointed to a picture on the wall of a six-year-old boy in a kindergarten graduation gown. "She is a mother, so that fits with TMK, unless that's a nephew or some such."

Arnett shot her a glare. "TMK? Please don't encourage Lopez."

Jo shrugged. "She's right, it's good shorthand."

Marzillo smiled. "One of the two bedrooms is decorated for a young boy, so yes, I assume he's her son. But the RO is the one who spoke to Gina's family."

Jo frowned. "In the other two cases, the killer's method mirrored the way the children were abused. So if this is the same killer, why make it look like an overdose?"

"Maybe he was interrupted somehow?" Marzillo said.

"And yet we have three injection sites that seem to indicate two different injection times. Curiouser and curiouser." Jo shook her head. "Do you have a time of death?"

"The ME estimated sometime last night, probably between five and eight p.m., but that's very tentative until we can find out what killed her. The substance itself can alter the course of the decomposition, or our measurements of it."

"I remember that case where MDMA raised the vic's temp and you had to recalibrate." Jo stepped forward to look at the woman's feet, obscured by the coffee table. "Feet not bound, hands not bound, so there was no restraint of any kind."

Marzillo shook her head. "Nothing that we've been able to determine."

"Killer could have threatened her with a gun?" Arnett said.

She nodded, but slowly. "And you found fingerprints on the syringe?"

"Yep," Marzillo said.

"I'm guessing they wouldn't be stupid enough to leave their own prints there, so maybe they forced her to inject herself with something?"

"Or put her fingerprints on it afterward," Arnett said.

Jo glanced toward the front door. "And I'm guessing there's no sign of a break-in?"

"None whatsoever," Marzillo answered. "Front and back door both locked, windows all locked."

"Suggests she knew the killer," Arnett said.

"Just like the other two." Jo turned back to Marzillo. "I know you're still processing, but do we have any other fingerprints or anything else to go by?"

"So far, nothing. We're collecting everything we can, trying to see if we've got any fibers, hair, what have you that seems out of place. We found a glass and a bowl in the sink, so we dusted those for prints and took DNA swabs to be sure, but nothing anywhere suggests she had a visitor."

"Anything else we need to know?" Jo asked.

"Not yet. We'll finish up here and I'll have Lopez look at her laptop and phone asap."

"Thanks for the rush on the tests. I don't like that it's only been two weeks since the last murder," Arnett said.

Jo bent over again to examine Gina's face. "If this is related to our case, it feels like someone has an agenda, and it's speeding up for some reason. And the world is filled with child abusers."

CHAPTER FORTY-EIGHT

Bianca Purcelli swiped the tears off her cheeks with a crumpled tissue as she waved Jo and Arnett into her living room. "Please sit down. Do you want some coffee? I'll make you some coffee. I'll be right back." She disappeared through the tiny dining alcove behind the couch before Jo or Arnett could answer.

Jo sat on the brown-and-sage brocade couch that faced a small brick fireplace, then swiveled to glance around the room. Family pictures and doilies filled every available surface, displaying a large family of six children, some with children of their own now, all with the same dark hair, soulful eyes, and pale skin. Jo was still following Gina through her lifespan when Bianca returned with two cups of coffee, sugar and cream, and a plate of biscotti on a tray.

"Here, please, it's so late, or early now really, and you're working so hard, you need something." Tears reappeared down both cheeks, and she pulled a new tissue out of a nearby box before perching on the armchair.

Jo picked up one of the cups to be polite. As she set it on a coaster, she glanced around unconsciously for ashtrays. Because Bianca transported her instantly to her best friend Eva's nonni's house, a plump, welcoming woman who fit every Italian grand-mother stereotype by overfeeding them, pinching their cheeks, and constantly giving them coffee even as teenagers—but who also smoked like a chimney and swore like a sailor. "Mrs. Purcelli, we're so sorry for your loss. Will it be okay for us to ask you a few questions?"

"Yes, of course. I'm so sorry to take up your time." She glanced at Arnett's wedding band, then back to his face. "She was my baby, you know, my sweet angel. The youngest are always the hardest, don't you think?"

Jo kept her face neutral despite the strange contradiction, and the apology—bereaved loved ones didn't usually apologize to detectives. Bianca was upset by her daughter's death, but seemed almost to have expected it.

"I know mine was," he answered gently. "Can you tell us why you were so worried when you couldn't reach your daughter?"

"She checks in with me every night before she goes to bed, and she didn't check in last night," Bianca answered.

The response felt odd, even for a close family. "It's that unusual for her to miss a call? A twenty-eight-year-old woman?"

A flush of embarrassment crept up Bianca's face. "That was our agreement. She calls every night without fail at ten. She needed my help to get Rafael back, and I told her I could only help her if she was serious this time, and that she needed to show me she was committed."

Jo struggled to follow. Had she missed something? "Rafael was Gina's son?"

"That's right." Bianca stood and plucked one of the pictures from its location on an end table, then thrust it toward Jo. "That's my Gina, and her Rafael."

"She's beautiful, and he's adorable," Jo said, wincing inter-nally at the accidental use of the present tense. "She was trying to get Rafael back from his father?"

Bianca nodded, wiped at a fresh trail of tears, then sat the picture and herself back down. "Yes. He had full custody of Rafael, and now she just got partial custody back."

"What's the father's name?" Jo braced for the torrent of anger sure to come.

"Scott Rosen. He's such a good man, this is gonna break his heart. He tried everything he could to help her. We all did, my late husband most of all. But you can't help someone who doesn't want help."

Jo's brows rose—the pieces were coming together. "Help her how?"

Bianca stared at her, then at Arnett, then back again. "Oh. You don't— Oh. I'm so sorry. My daughter was an alcoholic. I just assumed—"

Jo shot Arnett a quick glance to be sure the pieces had slammed together for him too. If Gina was an alcoholic, was her death unrelated to TMK after all?

"Gina was an addict?" Arnett asked.

Bianca stiffened, and puffed out her chest. "No, not an *addict*. An alcoholic."

"She didn't use any other substances?" Jo asked. Alcoholics didn't always use other drugs, Jo knew, but they were far more likely to than not.

"She smoked marijuana sometimes, and she sometimes did LSD, that's what got her in the trouble. But those were rare, not all the time, and she never did anything harder than that. No pills, no methamphetamines, no cocaine, not once, *never*." She sliced the air in front of her with stiff fingers and her voice rose. "I know that sounds crazy of me to even say, but it's true. *Alcohol* was her problem. She's been struggling for years, ever since she had Rafael. She got hit hard with the baby blues, and started drinking to help her sleep and it just got worse and worse. We tried everything, Scott tried everything, but nothing worked until Scott went to the social workers and got custody of

Rafael. But her problem was only alcohol. Even the people at the rehab said it."

Arnett looked at his shoes, and Jo could read her own thoughts on his face. Nobody ever did drugs until they did them —and depending on the drug, that first time was sometimes one time too many.

"Sorry, give me just one moment." Jo took a long pause to do something she'd normally never do—sip coffee made by a stranger in a murder investigation. But she wanted to give Bianca a moment to gather herself, and she had to admit, she needed a moment to process everything, too. "Your coffee is delicious. Thank you so much."

Bianca smiled wanly and her voice calmed. "The secret is the beans you use. And you have to store them in the freezer."

"I'll try that." Jo smiled and set the cup back down. "Was Gina a diabetic? Or did she have any sort of allergies, the kind you need EpiPens for? Or did she have her blood drawn recently?"

Bianca shook her head vigorously. "None of those things, thank God, because she was afraid of needles. Absolutely hated them, and broke out in a sweat whenever she had to have blood drawn. Believe me, I'd have heard about it if she did."

Jo nodded. "So Gina struggled with alcohol addiction, and her partner left her with their son Rafael."

"He wasn't her partner for a while. I always hoped they'd get married because he's such a nice man, but she couldn't... well, she struggled after the baby. He moved out when Rafael was three, but he stayed very active in Rafael's life."

"Got it. But you said the LSD was what got her into trouble?" Jo asked.

The shame cascaded over Bianca's face again, bringing another stream of tears. "That was the last straw. She had some LSD, and she had it out in her bedroom. I guess they have little cartoons on them? Like stamps with cartoons or something?

Well, Rafael saw them, and was playing with them, and you know how kids are, they stick everything in their mouth. He had a couple of activity books with stamp thingies you have to lick to make them stick, and I guess he thought this was the same."

Every hair on Jo's body stood on end. "He licked the LSD."

The shame on Bianca's face shifted to anger. "She rushed him to the hospital as soon as she realized what had happened, and everything turned out okay, or at least that's what the doctors and nurses claimed. But you always hear about flash-backs, horrible things like that. They said it wouldn't happen to him, but I don't see how they can know that for sure."

"I'm sure they know what they're talking about. Children are so different from adults, and they heal so much faster." Jo prayed she sounded convincing as she pushed down her own nausea—she wasn't sure at all, and she'd be asking Matt about it the next time she saw him.

"But the reason it was the last straw was, who knows what could have happened? What if it had been Drano or rat poison? Scott had enough, and I'll tell you the truth, I did, too. If Scott didn't report her, I would have. But it didn't matter anyway because she checked herself into rehab. It all seemed to knock some sense into her, seeing Rafael like that and knowing it was her fault. Before that I think she convinced herself it didn't matter because she only drank after he was asleep, or on the days he was with Scott."

"How long ago did she go to rehab?" Jo asked.

"About a year ago. She went for ninety days and came out a new person. Not that Scott or I believed that because we'd heard all the promises before. But her job—she was a mortgage specialist—held her position for her, and she found that little cottage to rent because she wanted a nice place for Rafael, and she stayed sober and did everything we asked her to do so she could get custody back. And she talked to us and the social worker about getting partial custody of Rafael, and about two months ago we agreed. Part of the deal was that she called both Scott and I every day at the same time. We FaceTime so we can tell she's sober and everything's okay. And she's never been more than two minutes late until last night."

"So when she didn't call, you figured something must be wrong," Jo said.

Bianca nodded silently, and wiped her tears.

Jo took another sip of the coffee, fighting back the seeming injustice, then cleared her throat. "Please forgive me, but whenever we have cases like this, we have to ask. Do you know of anyone who was angry with your daughter? Anyone who might have wanted to hurt her?"

Bianca's brow creased. "Not that I know of. She didn't really have enemies, or friends. Always such a solitary girl. She didn't go out drinking, she drank at home. From what she told me, she got along with the people at work. Scott only ever wanted good things for her—I think he still loved her and I always hoped they'd get back together now that she was sober."

"He sounds like a good man and a caring father," Jo said. "We'd like to talk to him. Do you happen to have his contact information?"

"Of course." She got up and glanced around the room until she located her phone. "I left a message for him earlier, but he didn't answer."

"I'm not surprised, given the time. We'll just go directly to his house," Jo said.

"Oh, he's not home, he's in California. He took Rafael to Disneyland and he won't be back until Sunday morning."

Arnett's head shot up from his notebook. "When did they leave?"

"Monday morning, after he picked Rafael up from Gina."

"Since Scott and Gina weren't ever married, he wouldn't have needed a divorce lawyer, but did he get one to help with the custody issue?"

"He did. Gina told him she wasn't going to fight, but he thought it was good for everyone to make sure everything was done right. I told him I understood one hundred percent."

Jo nodded. "Do you happen to know who his attorney was?"

"Of course, I talked to him several times. Tom Fischer."

CHAPTER FORTY-NINE

I slowed only slightly as I drove by the street crossing Gina Purcelli's, and glanced ever-so casually toward the police cars there. Then I drove away at a carefully measured pace.

When I'd watched Gina Purcelli come out of the liquor store with her bottle of wine, I'd struggled to keep control of my emotions.

Righteous vindication that I'd been right about her all along.

Fear gripping my heart for Rafael's well-being.

Anger setting my scalp on fire—how could she care so little for her son? How could she be right back at it again?

Gratitude that I'd chosen to follow her that day. I could barely manage to watch her two nights a week, and had been considering dropping down to one. Thank God I hadn't—I might not have realized she was drinking again in time. I shook my head—who had she thought she was fooling with a single bottle of wine? She'd have been back the next day for another, and she'd have been guzzling hard alcohol by next week.

As I slowed to a stop at a red light I allowed myself a moment of self-congratulation. I pictured Rafael taller now, a full-grown man rather than a child, shaking my hand and *thanking me for releasing him from his hell. On his wedding day, possibly? Looking refined in a black tux, next to a beautiful woman elegant in her white dress. Or maybe after the birth of his first child, holding a son who looked just like him. He'd smile up at me and thank me for breaking him free from the cycle while a single tear slid down each of his cheeks.*

Yes, I liked that one best. I ran it through my mind's eye twice, then three times, before the light turned green and I continued away.

CHAPTER FIFTY

"I think I just got whiplash," Arnett said as they drove back from Greenfern. "She had me just about convinced Gina overdosed until she mentioned Fischer."

"And if Gina hated needles, my guess is she'd try something other than shooting up if she decided to branch out, regardless." Jo fired off a quick text to Marzillo asking her to note any alcohol she found in the house in addition to any other drug paraphernalia. "I suppose it's possible she got drunk and did something stupid, but I can't come up with a scenario that gets us from a drink to injecting heroin alone in her house. Did she just happen to have a single syringe and cooker in her house on the off chance she'd need it someday?"

"Maybe she got some sort of newbie starter kit from her new dealer." Arnett's voice dripped with sarcasm.

"Maybe someone was there partying with her, and when she overdosed, they bailed?"

Arnett nodded. "With only one glass in the sink? Who parties without leaving *some* trace, even a dealer who came to show her the ropes? I guess it's possible, but the scene doesn't match anything I've seen in over two decades on the job."

"No, you're right. Unless Marzillo and Peterson find something else on the scene to make me think otherwise, I can't make it fit. But no matter what, we need evidence, and fast, since our killer's accelerating." She put through a call to Lopez.

Lopez picked up immediately. "Hey, Jo, what's up?"

"You may already know, but Marzillo has a computer and a phone coming your way."

"Yep, she texted me earlier it's a rush job."

"Excellent." She caught Lopez up on their thinking. "So we're looking for any cross-over between the three cases whatsoever. Any phone calls between the families, anything to do with Tom Fischer or his office, any potential contact with Rick Burke. And, I think we also want to look for any evidence of a hired killer."

"I'm on it."

"Thanks, as always." Jo hung up.

"Let's hope she finds something impressive. I'm not sure evidence of contact is going to be enough."

Jo pulled up *The Greenfern Daily* archives on her phone, and did a quick search for the name Purcelli. "Yep, here we go, same twin pair of articles on Gina Purcelli as we saw with the other two cases. First one reporting the claims of dangerously neglectful behavior, then another reporting in very cold language that partial custody had been restored to Gina."

"Not surprised. But that's not gonna be enough, either," Arnett said.

"No, you're right. So far everybody's had facile answers to account for all of it, and each of them present enough reasonable doubt for the others that none of it will ever walk in court. What we really need is some sort of physical evidence from Marzillo."

"Or a confession."

Jo reached up to her necklace. "And, while two might be a coincidence, three is a pattern. I think we need to pull up every child-abuse article of Burke's and look into all of the families involved. Especially anywhere custody was taken away but then restored." Jo started to send another text to Lopez, but her phone rang. "Huh. Someone from LAPD." She answered the call.

"Detective Josette Fournier?" a middle-aged, efficient male voice asked.

"Speaking."

"I'm Detective Jose Del Rosario. I'm calling about Diana Montauk."

CHAPTER FIFTY-ONE

As Jo continued the call, Arnett pulled the car over on a suburban street, then dug out his notebook. "Thanks for calling us back, Detective, and for helping us in the first place," Jo said.

"Not a problem. Truth be told I was annoyed at first, but it got interesting pretty quick."

Jo shot Arnett a look—their eyebrows went up. "How so?"

"She wasn't home when I went to talk to her. The neighbor told me Montauk is a nice lady who's single and keeps to herself. No friends or romantic partners, she works from home but travels now and then. I left a card so Montauk could call me back."

Arnett jotted 'loner = profile' on his notepad, and Jo nodded her head. "Interesting," she said to Del Rosario.

"She called me back an hour later. Right off the bat it was odd. The second I started in, she had to go deal with her cat, but the noises in the background were strange. When she came back she told me she periodically makes day trips to San Francisco to visit art museums because she grew up there."

Jo squinted at Arnett. "Not too strange to visit if she grew up there?"

"Except she claims she doesn't have any family or friends up there anymore."

Jo's pulse sped up, and her focus zoomed in. "Okay, yeah, I see where you're going."

"She said she'd get me proof she was at the museum on the sixth, and check her records for October. But she didn't get back to me that night or the next day."

"Not good," Jo said.

"No, and I get cranky when people shine me on. So, I figured, everybody loves a bright-eyed-bushy-tailed visit from the cops at six in the a.m., so I'd stop on by today."

Arnett jotted *I like this guy* on the pad.

"But a double-homicide dropped right in my lap. Since I got the sense time was of the essence, I figured I'd let you know that this just may be the suspicious someone you're looking for. I'm happy to go see her again, but it won't happen today."

"Not a problem, we know how it is," Jo said. "Can you hang on a sec?"

"Sure."

Jo hit the mute button, and grinned widely at Arnett. "Have you ever been to Disneyland?"

CHAPTER FIFTY-TWO

As Arnett pulled back into traffic with a smile now matching Jo's, Jo sent a text to Lopez and Marzillo: *Arnett and I are flying out to California to interview Scott Rosen, Gina Purcelli's boyfriend, at Disneyland. Won't be at mandatory meeting today.*

Lopez fired back: *Slick. I'm jelly. Bring me back an Ursula doll.*

Jo laughed, but Arnett shook his head. "That's funny and all, but Hayes isn't stupid. And, she's not going to like the unapproved expense, which will make her dig into this hard."

"Hayes falls into the category of people where it's better to seek forgiveness than ask for permission." Jo waved him off. "If she tells me no and I go, I'm in trouble. If she gets angry after the fact, I can tell her I was doing my best to follow her instructions as per our little chat on Wednesday, because it's obviously very important we talk to Rosen. If she finds out we swung by the other address, well, I'll tell her it was all my idea and you didn't know a thing. And, I'll pick up the tab so the department won't be out a dime. Thank goodness it's still early, plenty of time to make arrangements for our flight and get our operational need clearance from the TSA."

They drove straight to Hartford, rushed through to the next flight to LAX, and were standing in line for a rental car by one thirty California time.

Jo checked the message notification on her phone. "Rosen returned our call. He says he's eager to help any way he can."

"Let's see if that includes chatting with us while he's in line for the Matterhorn," Arnett said.

"So who do we talk to first, Scott Rosen, or Diana Montauk?"

Arnett tapped on his phone. "According to GPS, both are just under an hour away, and they're in opposite directions. Encino's twenty-two miles away, Disneyland's thirty-four."

"Rosen knows we're coming and Montauk doesn't, so it would be kinder to let Rosen get back to his vacation sooner than later. And since she works from home, we have some flexibility."

Jo called Scott, who wasn't enthusiastic about talking to Jo and Arnett in front of his son. They arranged to meet inside Disneyland near the carousel so they could talk while Rafael was on the ride.

As they strode up Main Street toward Fantasyland an hour later, Arnett's head swiveled right and left, taking in the old-fashioned buildings draped with red-white-and-blue swag. "Did we just fall into a production of *The Music Man*?"

"It's very all-American circa the nineteen-teens, isn't it?" Jo tilted her head and considered. "You've never been to Disneyland before?"

"Nope. Mountain Park was good enough for the likes of me. No Mickey or Minnie, but we had Friendly Mabel and Slim Jim the Cowboy. And we took the girls to Six Flags."

Memories of the now-defunct amusement park in Holyoke tugged at Jo. "Oh, geez, I haven't thought about Mountain Park in years. Decades, even. I think I went once, maybe twice, when my mother brought us back on visits from New Orleans. By the time she divorced my father and moved us back here, the park was closed. I don't think Sophie remembers it at all."

"You ever been to Disneyland before?" Arnett asked.

"Twice. I think I was fourteen the first time? Too old to really buy into it on a childhood-wonder sort of level. I spent most of my time noticing the hot guys, much to my father's annoyance. Then I went once about three years ago with Sophie and the kids. David ended up having to stay home to work, so it was good I was there. Emily was far too young to go on most of the rides, so she stayed with me when Sophie and Isabelle went on some of the older rides. But despite the babysitting and my sister's antagonism, there was still a moment or two of Disney joy that snuck up on me."

"Like what?"

"Like when a life-sized Winnie the Pooh came up and hugged me."

"I'd pay solid money to see a picture of that."

"I'm sure one exists. And if my mother thinks it'll embarrass me, she'll tear apart the house to find it."

Arnett pointed to a cable car gliding by on rails. "That'd save us some time."

Jo glared at him. "Keep walking. We need to shake out the blood clots that accumulated during our time sitting on the plane."

Arnett grimaced. "Is it always this crowded?"

"My sister assures me that if you pay more, you can get into the park an hour earlier than everyone else."

"How much more?" Arnett's voice jumped an octave. "I saw the prices when we were out front."

Jo shook her head at him. "I think you're missing the point, which is the opportunity to experience Disney Magic."

Arnett shot her a look like she was speaking in tongues. "As far as I can tell, Disney Magic seems to mean roasting in the sun while you wait in never-ending lines."

"So, Bob Arnett is not a happiest-place-on-earth sort of person. Noted." She pointed in the distance. "There's the carousel. Pick a bench that looks comfy, and I'll text him."

As Arnett sat, Jo scanned the area for a man fitting Scott's description. A few minutes later a tall, brawny white man with thick dark hair, blue eyes, and a spray of tourist sunburn approached tentatively, tugging at the hem of the green polo shirt that topped his khaki cargo shorts.

"Scott Rosen?" Jo asked.

His face cleared, and he glanced back over his shoulder. "That's me. My sister says she'll just keep getting back in line with Rafael and her twins as long as we need her to. Rafael loves the carousel. I think it calms him."

"This is a lot for a six-year-old." Jo smiled.

"It's a lot for a fifty-something-year-old," Arnett muttered.

"We appreciate you taking time out of your vacation to talk with us." Jo gestured to the bench.

Scott's eyes filled with tears as he dropped down next to Arnett. "I can't believe this is happening. My first reaction was to go back home, but Stephanie, that's my sister, said we should stay. She said Rafael will never be the same once he knows, so I should give him the week to enjoy Disneyland before blowing up his world."

Jo glanced in the direction of the carousel as she sat, turned toward Scott. "No, you really don't want him to associate Disneyland with his mother dying if you can help it."

Scott bobbed his head. "What exactly happened? Bianca said she assumed Gina relapsed, but that couldn't be right because you didn't know about her alcohol problem?"

Jo gave a stripped-down version of what they'd found, then led him through questions about Gina's alcoholism and the demise of their relationship. His answers matched up with what Bianca had told them.

"So she didn't relapse?" A sort of hope seemed to spring into Scott's expression.

"We can't be certain yet. Do you think Gina was staying sober successfully?"

He met her eyes without hesitation. "She absolutely was, there was no way she could have hidden it. She called me every night at Rafael's bedtime between eight and eight thirty, then Bianca at ten, and she was at work every morning at seven. And Bianca and I know what it looks like when she's drinking. No way she could have fit it in."

"When you took custody of Rafael, you hired Tom Fischer to represent you. What exactly did he do for you?" Jo asked.

"Not a lot, really, because Gina didn't fight me. I had an initial consultation where he advised me about my rights and helped me with the DCF paperwork."

"Why did you hire an attorney if she wasn't fighting it?" Jo asked.

"Because I wanted to make sure I did everything right. Everyone said sometimes people change their minds and start fighting."

"Did Fischer know about the LSD incident with Rafael?" Arnett asked.

A hint of confusion flickered across Scott's face. "Of course."

"He advised you about your rights. Did he lay out a strategy for getting Rafael from Gina?"

"I'm not sure what you mean. I had already made the initial contact with DCF, but he gave me some general advice about how to approach them."

"I'm thinking more of strategies attorneys use to lay the groundwork for any case they have to argue to a social worker or a judge."

The confusion cleared. "Oh, I get what you're saying. Yes, he told me to make sure I didn't get into any sort of trouble she could use against me. He also wanted to know anything that might be ammunition against her. He said he's seen cases that start out amicable turn very, very ugly."

"So, the article in *The Greenfern Daily*, about the accusations of Gina's neglect. Was that his idea?"

Scott's face reddened. "I never would have allowed him to do that. She needed help, and she was as upset about what happened as anyone. I also wouldn't have wanted that to follow Rafael for however long. As it was, when I started getting calls about it from our mutual friends, I went down to *The Daily* and confronted the jerk who wrote it."

"Rick Burke?" Arnett asked.

"Yup. I went right up to him and told him to write a retraction. He said he hadn't written anything that wasn't true, and I told him she was putting her life back together and didn't need to have her reputation destroyed. He shrugged—actually literally shrugged—at me and said people were responsible for their actions, especially when kids were involved, and I should be thanking him. I nearly punched him right in the face. I didn't, but I *did* ask if he got off on ruining people's lives."

Jo hid her smile. "It's touching how much you cared for her."

A tear overflowed onto his cheek. "Alcoholism is a disease. People like Burke don't get that. Gina was a good person who ended up in a bad place because of a chemical in her brain that got messed up when she had a baby. Nobody gets pissed at diabetics or people with cancer when *their* bodies turn against them. And what she did, getting sober? Do you know how hard that is? Do you know how few people make it even to six months?"

Jo's only response was a nod. He wasn't talking to her, and he didn't need her to answer.

His voice thickened. "She didn't need me to hold her to account, even though I was ready to—when she realized what she did, she took responsibility and made her life *better*. If you'd seen the determination in her eyes you'd understand. I even asked her to bring wine for our celebration of the twins' birthday last Sunday, even though my mother was worried it would trigger her if she did, but I knew she'd be fine. She was her old self again and she was happy. I know I sound naive, but even if she had relapsed, she didn't deserve to die."

Jo nodded again. "I agree, she didn't. And we're going to try our best to figure out what happened to her. One more question. Do you know Travis Rollins or Dustin Heidami?"

His brow creased. "Travis Rollins. That sounds familiar. Why does that name sound familiar?"

"You've never met him?"

"No. Rollins—wait, isn't he the guy whose wife got murdered a couple of weeks ago?"

"Yes. He's also one of Tom Fischer's clients." Jo pulled a card out of her pocket. "If you think of anything else we should know, please call us."

"The other guy you mentioned, too?" An odd expression flashed over his face.

"Yes. Thank you again for letting us interrupt your vacation."

Scott's attention was still divided. "No problem."

————

"Scott's emotions read genuine to me," Jo said as they retraced their steps through the park. "And he doesn't seem to have any resentment toward Gina."

"Agreed." Arnett strode like a man escaping a hell hound.

"If there truly was no way she could get drunk between all those scheduled phone calls, could that be a reason to switch to heroin? Maybe she thought she could get high that way, but still be able to go to work the next morning," Jo said.

"Then why shoot up *before* she called her mother?" Arnett answered.

"Excellent point." Jo fell silent. "I'll tell you what, though— I'd've loved to see it when he confronted Burke, if he actually did."

"You and me both," Arnett said. "Not surprised Burke pushed back."

Jo pounded her fist into her thigh. "I seriously doubt we'll be able to glean anything new from Rafael's DCF file, but we should scour it anyway." She pulled out her phone as they exited the park and tapped the contact for DCF. The call went to voicemail. "No answer."

"You want me to try my contact?" Arnett asked.

"That would probably be faster."

The line picked up after two rings. "Renata Cruz."

Arnett identified himself and explained why they were calling. "We'd love to see the file if possible."

As keys clacked in the background, Renata's voice turned from efficient to grim. "You think this is connected to the Avery Rollins case?"

"That's what we're trying to figure out," Arnett answered. "The Raina Pryzik case, too."

The clacking stopped. "Found it. You want me to forward you what we have in the system, or do you want to see the physical file?"

"Both, if possible. And we'd like to talk to the social worker, if we could."

"That'd be Alison Choi."

CHAPTER FIFTY-THREE

Jo stared up at Arnett, whose jaw had dropped. "We just left a message for her."

"Everybody's gone for the day."

Arnett glanced at his watch. "Of course, it's five thirty there, I forgot about the time difference. How come you're still there?"

She laughed. "A supervisor's work is never done."

Jo tugged on Arnett's sleeve and mouthed the word "mute." He did, then looked up at her.

"That's two cases now Alison has been involved with," she said. "Ask her if Alison was ever involved in any way with the Pryzik case."

Arnett went back on the line, and asked.

"Let me check." More clacking came over the line. "No, not that I can see. That was Steve Brodlin's case, and his is the only name I'm seeing that notated the file in the system."

"Do the social workers ever help on one another's cases?" Arnett asked.

Jo heard caution creep into Renata's voice. "We try to avoid it, because it's too easy for things to slip through the cracks if someone who doesn't know the whole history tries to make decisions. But, it does happen from time to time, especially if a call comes in while someone's on vacation, that sort of thing."

"And would that be documented in the case file?"

"Absolutely. Every time someone looks at a file, the system automatically notes it."

"You keep physical files, could she have looked at that without anyone knowing?"

Jo could hear her confusion over the phone. "Technically she *could*. But the only way she'd even know the file exists is if she saw it in the system first, so I'm not sure how that would ever happen."

Arnett thanked her and hung up. "Do you think that's true?"

"Maybe." They reached the car, and Jo pulled open the passenger door to get in. "Cubicles don't afford much privacy, so who knows what she overheard? And maybe she's a friend of the family, knew what was going on somehow from outside of work? I don't think we can rule it out, but I think the more likely possibility is she's Rick Burke's source, or one of them. Wasn't his case worker her mentor?"

"Maybe he heard the Pryzik name through the court, and had her look it up." Arnett fired up the ignition. "And in terms of being the killer, it's like the angel-of-death doctor phenomenon—when a lot of your patients start dying, somebody's gonna notice. Why risk that with two of your own cases?"

"Killers don't always think those things through," Jo said.

"True. But we showed up at her desk and told her flat out we thought the deaths were connected. Would you go out a week after the police tipped their hand and kill a third victim when you know they'll find out the vic is one of your caseload?"

"No, not really the smartest move." Jo pulled out her phone and started texting. "But we have to consider it. I'll ask Lopez to start looking into her phone and financial records. When we get back tomorrow we can ask her about her alibis—I'd like to do that in person."

"Agreed. In the meantime, hopefully we can get to talk to Diana Montauk before the legendary LA rush hour traffic swallows us whole."

———

Diana Montauk's house turned out to be a peach-beige cottage on a semi-crowded suburban street. A five-foot-two, sixty-something black woman with an emerald-green tracksuit and short gray sisterlocks struggled to pull something from a Chrysler LeBaron in the driveway, but stopped to stare when they pulled in behind it.

"I know license photos are bad, but I'm pretty certain Diana Montauk was white in hers," Arnett said.

"And supposedly she doesn't have many visitors." Jo unbuckled her seat belt as she double-checked the house number.

The woman's arms crossed over her chest as they exited the rental car. "Can I help you?"

Jo shifted her blazer to show the badge on her belt, and pulled a card from her pocket. "I'm Detective Josette Fournier and this is Detective Bob Arnett. We're from the Oakhurst County State Police Detective Unit."

"Where's Oakhurst County?"

"Massachusetts," Arnett answered.

Her brows popped up. "You take the left turn at Albuquerque?"

Jo hid her smile. "We're looking for Diana Montauk."

"I had a funny feeling. But you won't find her here."

"She doesn't live here?" Jo asked.

"Not as of two days ago. I got a call practically in the middle of the night telling me she had an out-of-state emergency and had to move 'cross country. And that her stuff would be out by the end of yesterday, and the whole place would be sparkling clean." The woman reached back into the LeBaron's door and pointedly pulled out a 'For Rent' sign.

"You're the owner of the house?" Jo asked.

"I am." She extended her hand and shook Jo's with a brisk, firm grip. "Arletta Davis."

"Good to meet you. She packed up her belongings in a day?"

"She sure did. The neighbor told me there was a huge truck and about ten guys out here. She hired a cleaning service too. Hardwood floors polished, kitchen and bathroom reeking of bleach, she even paid to have the windows washed and the walls wiped down. The house is cleaner than when she moved in, and I'm not too proud to admit it."

"We'd like to have a look inside, if that's okay with you?"

"Sure, but there's nothing to see. Any chance you can tell me what's going on? Or am I happier not knowing?" She narrowed her eyes and tilted her head.

"We need to speak with Ms. Montauk in connection with a series of murders we're investigating," Jo said.

"Murders?" Arletta's eyes widened. "Damn. It's always the quiet ones."

Jo nodded and pulled up Diana's driver's license photo. "Is this the Diana you knew?"

Arletta peered at the picture. "That's her. Beautiful woman, great tenant. Always paid her rent on time and never bothered me to repair a single thing the whole ten years she lived here. Said it was easier to fix everything herself. Truth is, the way she dropped the bomb on me about moving out, I expected the place to be trashed when I got here, but it's fit to rent today."

Jo smiled. "That's good, at least, since she left you in the lurch without a renter."

Arletta waved her off as she strolled toward the house. "No, she didn't. She told me to keep her deposit and her last month's rent. That's one of the reasons I expected to find the place trashed."

"I don't suppose she left you a forwarding address?" Jo asked.

Arletta shot her a *you're-kidding-right* look. "She did not. Probably 'cause it would have killed the whole disappear-in-the-middle-of-the-night plan she had going on."

Jo swallowed a laugh. "Very true. What else do you know about her?"

"I know she has a cat, one of those hairless ones that looks like a sick alien plotting to take over the planet. And she worked from home."

"Do you know if she had family, or did you ever see her with friends?" Arnett asked.

"Nope, and nope. She minded her business and I minded mine."

"She must have given you references when she moved in. Can we see them?"

Arletta threw her another skeptical glance as she unlocked the door. "She gave me a stack of references, all named Benjamin." She looked down at the doorknob. "I'm assuming it doesn't matter if I touch it, since I already did, and since she had a whole cleaning crew in the day before?"

"Probably best not to touch anything else if you can help it." Jo pulled a glove out of her pocket and snapped it on. "Did you happen to see the names of the moving company, or the cleaning crew?"

"They were done before I got here." She stood back to let Jo push open the door. "But one of the neighbors might have seen."

"We'll ask around," Jo said.

"I don't want to rush you, but I need to get this sign up and hurry to an appointment. Can you just leave the key with the neighbor over there when you go?" She pointed to her right.

"I'll have to get the locks changed for the new tenant, anyway."

Jo took the key from her. "Thank you so much. If you think of anything else about Ms. Montauk, would you let us know? Even a tiny detail might help."

"At the number on the card?"

"Yes."

"I absolutely will. I'm not trying to play with murderers." She shuddered, then took off down the porch.

The mingled scents of floor polish and bleach slapped Jo as she stepped through the front door and surveyed the living room. "Ms. Montauk knew what she was doing. White walls, so any dirt would be visible and easily cleaned. Hardwood floors, so no hairs or other matter hidden in carpet fibers."

Arnett grunted, then squatted down and peered into the baseboards. "Unless the cleaning company she hired was incompetent, they had no problem eradicating any sign she was ever here. We'd be lucky to find a hair, let alone DNA or prints."

"Even if we do, we'll never be able to prove it didn't belong to one of the cleaners or movers." Jo strode into the kitchen and opened a cabinet. "As someone well versed in obsessive cleaning, I can safely say they did an excellent job. I can't even find any grime deep back in the corners."

"I'm thinking we should have a CSI team go over it, just in case they can pick up something our eyes can't," Arnett said as they stepped onto the back porch of the tiny backyard.

"Or, hope they can pick up something outside. At least we have her fingerprints from the DMV database."

"Given how little else we have, I agree," Arnett said.

Jo grabbed her phone and called Detective Del Rosario. After initial greetings, she caught him up on what was happening.

"Holy shit," he said. "Completely gone?"

"And the house has been hermetically scrubbed," Jo said. "So I have another favor to ask."

"Lemme guess. You want me to send a tech to go over the place," Del Rosario said.

"If it's possible. I'm fairly certain it will be quick, because your CSI won't have much to work with," Jo said.

"I'll see what I can do, because now she went and pissed me off and made it personal."

Jo grinned—that's the same reaction she'd have, too. "We appreciate it."

"I'll call you back as soon as I know," he said, and hung up.

They made their way back outside, locked the door behind them, then circled around the front lawn to the neighbor's house. When they knocked, a scattered-looking thirty-five-ish white woman with a frightened expression opened the door and introduced herself as Mikayla Burnett. Jo caught a glimpse of a ten-year-old version of Mikayla hovering just behind her.

Jo explained why they were there. "Did you know Ms. Montauk at all?"

"No. She always seemed pleasant enough, but she kept to herself. She let my daughter Kenzie play with her cat, and paid her to feed it when she was out of town. But I'll tell you what, I've learned my lesson." She reached back for the little girl and pulled her into her leg. "The cops show up looking for her and she disappears overnight? No thank you. I'm not letting my daughter go near anybody else until I have a background check done."

Kenzie's eyes filled with tears as her mother spoke. "Is Diana okay? And Cleopatra?"

Jo dropped into a squat. "We're not sure, but we're going to find out. You used to take care of her cat? So you've been inside her house?"

"No. Cleopatra had a cat door in the back and I fed her on the back porch."

Mikayla interjected. "I wouldn't have let her go inside someone else's house without me anyway."

Jo searched Kenzie's face for a sign that she'd gone in despite her mother's objections, but Kenzie's eyes were clear and Jo's hopes faded. "Did you ever get a glimpse inside?"

She wrinkled her nose and looked up. "A couple of times. I saw a really cool red couch and she had a pretty picture of a woman over it. But she was careful with her door so Cleopatra wouldn't get out."

Jo nodded. "Did either of you see the company name on the moving van that came, or the cleaning crew?"

"The movers were called Starving College Movers, and the cleaners were Industrial Comp inc.," Mikayla said.

Arnett jotted the names down as Jo pulled out another card. "Thanks so much, we really appreciate your help. If you think of anything else that you know about Diana, we'd really appreciate it if you'd give us a call."

Arnett shook his head as they returned to the car. "I'm just gonna say it. Over eight years later, trail as cold as an arctic winter, but you managed to find something. That's damned impressive."

But Jo grimaced as she tapped away on her phone. "I'll celebrate when we're sitting across from Diana Montauk in an interrogation room. I just sent a text to Lopez updating her, so we can track her. We have her DMV information, and we should be able to track her ID and credit cards. But based on this"—she motioned to the house—"she'll dump the car and use cash. So my biggest hope right now is the moving company that took her belongings."

CHAPTER FIFTY-FOUR

Diana pulled into the parking lot next to AJ's Last Chance, an-off-off-off-strip dive bar in Las Vegas. She took a deep breath, grabbed her purse, and said a silent prayer that Reggie still owned the place.

A middle-of-the-night disappearance required intricate planning, nerves of steel, and a complete lack of sentiment. The planning had been in place for more than ten years. She'd created an emergency identity for herself before her first kill; she scrolled through microfiche of newspaper obituaries looking for little girls the right age who'd died prematurely, then painstakingly obtained a certified birth certificate and social security card. But since her fingerprints were already attached to her true identity, she had to find someone—Reggie—to make a fake driver's license and a passport for the new one. With a blonde wig and a hefty payment, Kristen Dowdler from Wichita, Kansas was born anew.

Then she'd painstakingly created a life for Kristen. Bank accounts, a pay-as-you-go credit card, a PO box. She also worked occasional freelance jobs under that name, and fed all the accounts with cash when she traveled.

Her life back in LA revolved around the planning, too. She converted everything she earned, beyond the base amount she kept in the bank, into cash that she kept stored in a safe so her assets would be instantly liquid should she ever need to run. So once she did, she bought a car with Kristen's identity, a five-year-old SUV that would allow her to carry the few possessions she needed comfortably, and made arrangements to get rid of the car registered to Diana Montauk. Then she packed up her essentials in the middle of the night, paid the moving and cleaning companies exorbitant sums from the balance of Diana's bank accounts, destroyed her cell phone and her SIM card, and disappeared into the night leaving Diana Montauk behind her.

The nerves of steel had also long been in play—she'd spent the last ten years carefully evaluating every person she met and every situation she found herself in for the signs that it was time to pull the trigger. She'd forced herself to stay cool and not over-react through several close calls, most notably when Martin Scherer turned out to be a serial killer. And every time she killed a man she dealt with at least one moment that teetered on going horribly wrong, so the adrenaline rush that came with those moments now signaled the need to stay cool, calm, and surgically analytical.

She always thought the complete lack of sentiment was the easiest part—until yesterday. For years she avoided permanent attachments to anyone or anything except Cleopatra, who easily fit inside a carrier and could be transported anywhere. She had no more family and she didn't believe in romantic relationships, so all that was easy. Contracting from home meant her only co-workers existed over phone or video call. And she'd never made friends easily—trust wasn't something she had in over-abundance.

But when it came to Kenzie, she'd started to feel—what? Motherly.

It ripped her heart out to leave—like she was abandoning her own child. Which was ridiculous because Kenzie had a mother who took excellent care of her and loved her and Diana was just the weird neighbor who lived next door. She never should have allowed herself to bond with Kenzie, it left her too open to mistakes. She wouldn't allow that to happen again.

With a quick look at herself in the rearview mirror, she pulled herself together. Eyes magnified by liner and mascara, mouth downplayed with neutral lipstick, the exact opposite of her normal make-up. She hated it, and her newly blonde hair. But once she got settled into her new life, she wouldn't have to look exactly like the picture in the license—women changed hair color every day. For now it did the job it needed to do.

An odd, nostalgic sense of déjà vu hit her as she pushed through the door to AJ's Last Chance, including the same tangential curiosity about 'AJ's' identity. Was he an original owner? Someone's long lost love? Questions like that crept under her skin—everybody and everything had a story, and most people wanted desperately to hide theirs.

The blue *employees only* door was right where she remembered it: back hall, past the restroom doors whose *men* and *women* placards were so old they were nearly unreadable. The bartender gazed at her as she crossed the dim room; she dipped her chin in acknowledgment, then pointed it back toward the hall. He nodded and turned to the beer he was pouring for a regular who stared up at some game replay on a decade-old television.

She rapped on the blue door, three quick taps followed by three slow ones, followed by three fast again. After a long moment, the door opened and Reggie stood in front of her. Still short, pale, and handsome, the only hint that a decade had passed was the faint touches of gray in his brown hair.

He broke into a smile and motioned her inside. "Diana Montauk."

"I'm impressed." She genuinely was. She eased into a chair next to the desk dotted with orderly stacks. "Kristen Dowdler now."

"Don't be impressed. I make it a habit not to remember faces, but you—you're hard to forget."

She scrunched up her nose. "Not exactly what I need to hear at the moment."

The nostalgia squeezed her again, taking her back to the precipice she'd been walking when she met him. She'd spent nearly a year insinuating herself into the darker side of Las Vegas, building up enough trust to get the documents she needed. In the process she'd allowed herself to get a little too close to Reggie, and had almost ended up in his bed. He was the one and only time she'd been tempted—but the angry little girl inside her had other ideas.

His face turned somber as he slid into his office chair. "No, right. And if you're using your backup, you must need another one?"

"As soon as possible. I can't linger." She pulled two envelopes out of her purse and slid them across to him. "Here's the information for another girl my age, this one out of Maryland."

He opened the first envelope and scanned the contents. "Nadia Robinson. I love it when a customer makes my job easy for me." He reached for the second envelope. "My prices have gone up some since last time."

"I figured," she said. "That's twenty large."

His brows shot up as he verified the bills. "They haven't gone up *that* much."

She smiled. "I mean it when I say I need a rush. I also need a cheapo temporary for some errands I have to run while I wait. Nobody will be looking closely, and I plan to burn it when I leave town."

He gazed at her for a moment, as though he wanted to ask

something. If so, he decided against it. "I should have something that'll work. Hang tight."

A key chain rattled out of his pocket and he unlocked the door in the wall behind him. She glanced over the office as she waited for him to return, smiling at the half-naked-women calendars on the walls—very much *not* who Reggie was—and boxes labeled with various liquors and bar supplies. She considered them—she never drank more than a sip or two of alcohol, and even then only when she was pretending to lure a kill. But at times like this it was tempting.

Reggie reappeared and held out a license. "How about Grace Hawkins? Blonde hair, right approximate height and weight, and if you squint hard she could be your sister."

She took it and glanced down at it. "That'll work."

"You caught me at a good time. I should be able to pull the rest together for you by this time Saturday."

She nodded and stood up. "I really appreciate it."

His gaze flicked back and forth between her two eyes. "You need a place to stay tonight?"

She gave a wry smile. "You don't want what that might bring."

"I can take the heat."

"I don't want to be the reason you have to." She let the smile broaden across her face. "Besides, if something happens to you, who will I get my next passport from?"

He nodded, not smiling. "See you Saturday, then."

She turned, but then pivoted back. "Oh, I almost forgot. I also need a gun."

CHAPTER FIFTY-FIVE

SEPTEMBER 2ND

Jo slept on the plane back to Oakhurst, and was fully awake when it landed at three in the morning. After dropping off Arnett she hurried home, stripped off her clothes, and fell into bed to sleep in her underwear hoping for a couple more hours of blessed sleep.

For once, her brain cooperated. She woke the next morning energized, and raced through her morning routine. Apparently the same happened for Arnett, because when she walked through the doors of HQ, he was pulling off his suit jacket with one hand and inhaling a cup of coffee with the other.

"Don't even bother to sit down." She laughed. "Marzillo texted me as I was driving. She's got some results back from the first crime scene."

He grabbed his notepad and pen with his now-free hand. "We need to pow-wow with Lopez about Diana Montauk anyway."

Jo tossed her jacket over the back of her chair and grasped her mocha with both hands as they strode together to the lab. Lopez waited, sitting cross-legged in her office chair, tinkering with a phone.

"Boy, do we have a story for you," Jo started, then noticed the dark cloud on Lopez's face.

She shoved the phone away. "Can't find a damned thing on either the phone or the laptop."

Arnett's eyebrows raised. "You're in a mood. You accidentally grab a decaf Rockstar?"

"Never speak such blasphemy in my presence again." Lopez pointed a finger at him without looking up. "It's *your* case that's pissing me off, 'cause I've never spent so much time finding so much nothing before in my life. Gina went to work, she took care of her kid, she went to AA meetings, she watched movies. As far as I can tell, her mother was right, she was living a sober, boring AF life—and was doing well. Good job, bank account steadily rising, no drama. No angry texts or emails, no dirty pictures, she wasn't even on any dating apps. Guess she was taking that whole 'don't date anybody for a year' thing they do in AA seriously."

Jo nodded. Lopez's mother struggled with alcoholism, and had been attending AA for several months—not a topic Lopez generally discussed at work. "How about old friends? Anyone that might have an ax to grind, or might trigger her into old behavior?"

"Not that I can see. She's in contact with her mother, her ex, and two women she talks about AA with, so I assume they're new friends. One of them is a sponsor. There're several pictures of her with a couple of ladies at Denny's, I'm assuming that's a post-meeting coffee klatch. The only other contact I see is with Rafael's teacher, since school started back up." She took a frustrated pull of her Rockstar.

Jo patted her shoulder. "Thanks for going through all that. It was pretty unlikely this had anything to do with a personal issue against Gina, but we had to rule it out, just to make sure this one's related to the other cases."

"Hey, that's what I'm here for. And speaking of things that

are going nowhere, I heard back from our old buddy at Blizzard. None of the four people we found near our suicides in San Francisco are World of Warcraft players." Lopez slumped back against her chair.

"I'm not surprised, because she'd have been stupid not to use a fake name, but that's okay, because—"

Marzillo swept in, curly black hair stacked impressively high and wrapped with a bubble-gum pink gingham bandana, with matching bubble-gum pink cigarette pants sticking out from under her lab coat.

Lopez broke the moment of silence. "Okay, I'm starting to be concerned. First goth princess and now rockabilly queen. Did you inhale some toxic fumes at a crime scene?"

"I'm trying something new." Marzillo blushed, then turned into her office. "Nothing wrong with keeping things fresh."

"I personally love the retro-fifties look." Jo flashed a glare back at Lopez.

Lopez jutted an upturned palm toward Marzillo's back, eyes wide.

Jo mouthed the word 'Zelda'—one of the issues Marzillo's partner had cited for her recent infidelity was that the relationship had fallen into a rut.

Marzillo clicked on one of her computers. "I have a test result for Melissa Rollins. Two, actually, and an interesting finding from the Gina Purcelli scene. First, we did verify the presence of GHB in Melissa Rollins' system, so she was definitely drugged."

"That's both Rollins and Pryzik," Arnett said. "So maybe our killer gave Purcelli too much?"

Marzillo's brow furrowed. "I'd expect to see a different set of indicators if she'd overdosed on GHB, like vomiting. But, that doesn't always happen, so we'll need to get the results back to be sure. I'm hoping by tomorrow."

"You said there's a second test result?" Jo asked.

"I followed a hunch, and it paid off. Melissa Rollins had thiazide in her blood, which is a diuretic normally given for hypertension. But she didn't have high blood pressure, and she didn't have a prescription for thiazide," Marzillo said.

"So someone drugged her, nailed her into a closet, busted up the heat to make her sweat, and gave her a drug that made her process water out of her body faster?" Lopez asked. "That's not murder, that's torture."

Jo nodded. "Someone was very invested in making sure Melissa didn't just die, but that she suffered, the same way she made Avery suffer. Trapped and aware, inside a closet, and urinating all over herself. And that explains why you'd knock someone out rather than just kill them—our killer needed them subdued, but wanted them alive and aware of what was happening to them."

"If that's right, he knocked out Louisa, tied her up in the chair, then waited for her to come to before he smashed her on the head with the pan," Arnett said. "Is there any way we can verify that from her injuries?"

Marzillo sorted through the files on her desk and flipped to a set of autopsy photos. "I can tell you based on the bruising that she was alive when she was tied up, but I can't specify for how long."

"I'm not sure it matters, anyway—this is the only explanation that fits all the facts. Where things get fuzzy is when I try to extrapolate to Gina Purcelli. She didn't abuse her son exactly; it was more of an issue of neglect. The only real incident we found in the case was when her son ingested LSD. So I'd think our killer would try to kill her with LSD—but is that even possible?" Jo asked.

"It's not. You can't kill someone directly with an overdose of LSD, they'll just have a really unpleasant experience. Sometimes to the point of an accident or suicide, but not as a reaction to the drug itself."

Jo nodded. "So maybe the killer just wanted to simulate Rafael's abuse, to give her a scary acid trip. There were three injection sites, could the killer have injected her with three different things? Maybe first the GHB like the others, then when she woke up again, with a huge dose of LSD to trigger a bad trip, then heroin to cause an overdose?" Jo asked.

"Once she started feeling that bad trip, she'd be up off the couch freaking out," Lopez said. "Unless there was an interaction with the GHB that kept her incapacitated?"

Marzillo shook her head. "Possible depending on the amounts, but not likely. Kids mix those drugs all the time in the club scene. Very dangerous because LSD can mask danger signs with the GHB. But if that's what happened here, there wouldn't have been the need for a third injection of something."

"No way Gina would have just chilled on the couch, then," Lopez said.

"Agreed. Take a look at this." She picked a picture up from her desk and handed it to Jo, who shifted so Arnett and Lopez could see.

Jo peered down at magnification of what looked like an oddly shaped blue puffball on a gold strap. "This strap, is that part of the sandals Gina was wearing?"

"Yes, good recall. I pulled off the sandals to double-check for track marks, and when I did, I noticed this." She pointed to the blue puffball. "Some sort of a fiber. One that didn't match her clothes, the couch, or anything else I could find on the scene."

"This edge is distended, like it tore off of something." Jo looked back up at Marzillo as the implication hit. "You think something was tied around her ankles?"

"Possibly her wrists too." She turned to her computer and pulled up a window. "Something like this."

Jo shifted along with Arnett and Lopez to examine the picture. "Bed restraints with blue padding."

"Like they use in hospitals, designed not to leave ligature marks. I put a rush order on this one so I can compare the fibers. It'll be here tomorrow."

"So our killer drugged her with GHB, restrained her, then waited until she woke up—how long would that take?" Jo asked.

"Depends on the dose, which is tricky to get right. Most likely somewhere between one to two hours, but possibly as long as four," Marzillo answered.

"Okay, so the killer waits until Gina wakes up, injects her again but this time with enough LSD to really mess with her, and watches as she freaks out, unable to move, due to the bad trip. Then the third injection to actually kill her?"

"That would explain the three injections within such a close time frame, but all showing different stages of inflammation. But we'll have to wait for her results to be sure." Marzillo checked her watch. "I'll let you know as soon as the restraints come in. Right now I have to run to a meeting. I'll text you as soon as Gina's results come in."

They filed out of Marzillo's office, back to Lopez's desk.

"So. When you came in, you said you had a story for me." Lopez's eyes twinkled.

Jo pulled a chair over to Lopez's desk and recapped what had happened with Diana Montauk.

Lopez's mouth dropped open. "Gone? Like, completely gone?"

Jo raised a hand. "Not even a hair in the corner of the floorboards."

"You said she had a cat, there must have at least been cat hair? If not, I want to hire those cleaners, 'cause damn."

"She had one of those hairless cats," Arnett said with a shudder.

Lopez stared at him. "Of course she did. That's brilliant."

Lopez's meaning caught her off guard. "Oh—I didn't even

think of that. The perfect pet for a serial killer—no pet hair to track with you."

Arnett's eyes widened. "I'll never trust anyone with a hairless pet again."

"Oh hush, my cousin has one, and it's the sweetest thing." Lopez waved him off. "But anyway, the point is, that's pretty impressive Houdini skills—and that clinches it. Jo, I must take a moment to bow before your instinct and perseverance. I'm not worthy." She raised both hands, then bent at the waist.

Jo tapped her notepad. "Completely worthless unless we can find her."

CHAPTER FIFTY-SIX

Diana paced up and down across the dingy, cheap hotel-room carpet, trying to convince herself she didn't have to kill Josette Fournier.

After meeting with Reggie she'd cruised around looking for a motel that seemed to be the right kind of wrong: external doors, minimal security cameras, run-down just enough to know cash would be all too welcome. She brought Cleopatra and her essentials up to the second-floor room, pulled out the food she'd picked up as she'd cruised the area, and settled in to think.

Diana tapped her nails on her new phone as she considered. Since going to Massachusetts, she'd planned, if Josette continued on her trail, to threaten someone Josette loved—either Matt Soltero or Sophie Belleau—then kill David Belleau to send the message that her warning was serious. But Josette had tracked the untrackable before, and done it in a disturbingly short period of time. The smart thing to do would be to *not* mess around with a warning, but rather go straight to the root of her problem, and kill Josette. Deep down in the corners of her soul she knew she simply couldn't afford to have Josette searching for her for the rest of her life.

But every cell in her body rebelled against the very thought. Diana didn't kill righteous people; that went directly against everything she stood for. She was an avenger, a purveyor of justice, a protector of the innocent. And killing Josette would be *worse* than killing an innocent, because *she* was an avenger, too. They were fighting the same battle.

If she pulled that trigger, it would push her over a line she couldn't come back from.

Plus, when Diana checked the video footage from the camera across from her now-abandoned house earlier in the day, she discovered Josette hadn't come to the house by herself, she'd come with Arnett. That meant this wasn't something she was doing alone. He was involved in the search, and if Josette showed up dead he'd almost certainly alert the entire Oakhurst County State Police Detective Unit to what was going on. That meant she had to kill him too.

There had to be another way around it. Diana pulled out her computer, grabbed her cup of hotel-room coffee, and started in to double-check her searches on Josette et al., hoping for some inspiration.

Her eyes froze halfway down the first page of results. Josette was now investigating the death of a second child abuser, and that couldn't be a coincidence.

Diana spent the next couple of hours researching the two abusers and thinking through the implications of their deaths. Then she sat, silent, eyes searching the yellowed walls as Josette, David Belleau, and the child abusers circled through her mind.

She smiled as a potential tweak to her original plan—an additional type of leverage she could use—came to her. If it worked, she might not have to kill Josette.

There was a better way.

CHAPTER FIFTY-SEVEN

SEPTEMBER 4TH

While they waited for Gina Purcelli's test results, Jo and Arnett spent the next few days chasing down every lead available to them on both cases, well into their weekend. As it turned out, they weren't the only ones—Lopez texted late Saturday that she had an update, and they met her in the lab.

"I spent a fair chunk of yesterday researching Alison Choi," Lopez said when they settled in. "Not only did I find nothing sinister whatsoever, she was with her husband and daughter during both Melissa's and Gina's murders. And before you say they may be covering for her, she has an iron-clad alibi for Louisa Pryzik's murder: she was at an aunt's funeral in Boca Raton, with plenty of witnesses and a boatload of photos from the big family get-together that night."

"Everybody has an iron-clad alibi for one of the three murders here, like Travis' for Melissa's murder, and Dustin's for Louisa's. It's looking more and more like a team effort," Arnett said.

Jo nodded, playing with her necklace.

Lopez continued. "As for phone records, of course she has plenty of contact with Fischer, since he represented the fathers.

No calls whatsoever to Rick Burke or anyone else from *The Greenfern Daily*, and no unaccounted for numbers. Her personal line is clean—she mostly texts, and those were to confirmed friends and family. Her financial records are disgustingly regular, nearly identical amounts in and out every month, savings dipped into twice a year for vacation. I don't see how she could have killed any of our vics, and if she hired a hit man she's smart enough not to do it with her own phone or her own money."

"I think we can rule out a hit man," Jo said. "It's one thing to hire someone to shoot a person, it's another to get them to enact your revenge fantasy."

"True. No contract killer is gonna be willing to do this." Arnett waved at the files. "Maybe tie someone up and then beat them to death, but sit with them until they wake up so they can send them on a bad LSD trip? Inject 'em with thiazide, then nail 'em into a closet? No way."

"She could still be working with one of the others if she's using a burner phone." Jo drummed her fist on her thigh. "Which still leaves us needing proof."

"Switching over to our femme fatale, I nearly fell into a coma while checking Diana Montauk's email. All business all the time, all dry, not a hint of a friend or lover in her life. Same with her phone and her texts. And, you won't be surprised to hear she deactivated that phone. No active signal."

"Lots of psychopaths are loners," Arnett said. "Any luck with the moving company?"

"Oh, sure." Lopez's eyes flashed. "They had no problem sharing the destination of her belongings—because she paid them to throw everything into a Los Angeles dump."

Arnett's eyes squeezed shut. "You *have* to be kidding me."

"The manager actually said, and I quote, '*It was great, we didn't have to worry about breaking anything*,' then laughed like it was the funniest thing he'd ever heard. He gave me contact information for the team who handled the move, but predictably everyone claimed they hadn't kept anything of hers."

"If they did, they fenced it by now, anyway," Arnett said.

"The cleaning company wasn't much more help. She paid them well—three times their normal fee—to be certain the job was done by the end of the evening. She gave a long list of instructions about what she wanted done, including wiping down walls, waxing hardwood floors, etc., etc. Told them she'd be sending over someone to check. Paid both companies with her credit card."

Arnett jumped in. "A credit card she has automatically paid in full out of her checking account each month. She had enough to cover it all, but not much more. She has periodic direct deposits made from a variety of employers, and her bills are on autopay. She transfers over her surplus to her savings account, and makes withdrawals from that every month."

"Large withdrawals?" Jo asked.

"Depends. She keeps her savings account hovering between fifteen and twenty thousand dollars, and pulls out the rest."

"And no other accounts in her name?" Jo asked. "Retirement funds, anything?"

"Can't find any."

"So she either has some sort of expensive hobby, or she's stashing it away somewhere we can't find," Lopez said.

"Not a coincidence, I'm sure. She's been planning this for a long time. Dammit." Jo threw her empty Starbucks' cup into the trash like a rocket. "I tipped her off by sending a cop to her house, and now she's gone."

"What should we have done?" Arnett said. "Those four numbers were the only leads we had. And now there's no ambiguity—we know Scherer was killed, and we know who killed him."

Jo grimaced, and threw up a hand. "I should have gone there myself, that's what."

Arnett glared at her. "How exactly were you going to do that when Hayes told you explicitly to drop the case? You don't think she would have been suspicious if you asked her to sign off on a random week's vacation in the middle of murder season for no apparent reason? And we knew this might happen—it was a calculated risk."

"I never thought she'd *disappear within hours*," Jo said.

"What about the car?" Lopez asked. "Anything there?"

Jo laughed a dry, sarcastic laugh. "Oh, that's the best one of all. No hits on the ALPR system for her plates yet, so I double-checked the VIN at the DMV. Turns out, a title surrender just came through, so I called the guy she signed it over to. Any guesses what happened?"

Arnett's eyes narrowed.

Jo continued. "She sold it to a wrecking yard. Told them she'd always wanted to see a car shredded and would pay them an extra five grand if they let her watch. He vehemently assured me they checked the trunk for bodies before they agreed."

"You're bleeping kidding me," Lopez said. "This chick is next level."

Arnett rubbed his brow. "LAPD's team didn't find anything worth anything in the house. But her cell phone company is sending over her phone records. We'll scour those, and her credit card receipts, and we have alerts out on her. Something will lead to her. Nobody can disappear without a trace."

Jo bit her tongue—somehow she was certain that if anybody could, it'd be Diana Montauk.

A notification from her phone interrupted the thought, and she glanced down at it. Her personal account had received an email from a name she didn't recognize. She clicked on it.

She gasped. "Oh, God."

Arnett and Lopez both sprang up and bent to look at her

phone. She held it out, hands shaking, and Lopez grabbed it so they could read it.

Dear Josette—

For years I've gone to extreme lengths to make sure I was untraceable. Yet, somehow you discovered not just what I do, but where I live, and who I am.

What you need to understand now is that I'm not a murderer. I'm a protector. I kill bad men, men that hurt women. Martin Scherer was a serial killer. Bennie Moreno was a wife beater. I assure you all the others I've killed also destroyed women's lives in one way or another.

Why am I taking such a risk to tell you this? Because I need you to understand that you and I are the same, Josette. I've been watching you closely, and I've come to respect and admire you. We both do the same job: we both protect the inno-cent. The only difference between us is you're restricted by an inflexible system that has an immorality built into it. In your world, it makes no difference if someone deserves to die—if they've been killed, you must find and punish their killer. No matter if the world is better off being rid of their evil. And in the process of ignoring that, you become the very thing your soul loathes: you become the destroyer of lives.

Look at the cases you're working on now; I know you're too good at your job not to realize they're connected. Melissa Rollins and Gina Purcelli were child abusers, plain and simple. The system failed to keep their precious children safe, so someone stepped in to see that justice was done. I'm cheering for that person because I understand them. They're hiding deep in the shadows where you'll never see them, with enough distance to judge, yet close enough to see everything so they can destroy the next evil. Just like me.

I don't believe you truly want to put that brave soul in jail.

I think you know the right thing to do is to take the Rollins and Purcelli files and bury them deep in the farthest corner of your office drawers. And I believe you know it's right to leave me to my work, also.

But while I hope appealing to your better nature will persuade you, I realize you may need an additional reason to leave me alone.

By now you've noticed the two attached pictures, one of you holding hands with the very handsome Matt Soltero, and one of your brother-in-law, David Belleau, kissing a pregnant girl who most definitely is not your sister Sophie. Is Matt a good man or a bad man? I'm not sure yet. But David? He's most definitely not a good man, and both your sister and the mystery girl would be far better off without him. I'll need another victim soon, and either David or Matt will save me the trouble of finding someone new—but only if I need to kill two birds with one stone.

I honestly wish you nothing but the best—and I hope you wish the same for me. For all our sakes.

Diana Montauk

CHAPTER FIFTY-EIGHT

"Holy shit." Arnett scrolled up and down the message on Jo's phone. "She's been watching us? Is that really David?"

Jo tapped the picture on her phone and enlarged it with trembling fingers. "Yes, that's David. Custom-made wedding band that matches Sophie's with onyx stones. One of a kind."

Lopez pointed to her monitor. "Can you pull it up here?"

Jo reached over and logged in to her personal email account, then stepped out of Lopez's way. Lopez clicked and typed.

Arnett's fists opened and closed. "What did she do, fly directly here after she spoke to Del Rosario?"

Jo tapped on the other attachment and brought up the picture. "Oh, it's far worse than that. See that dress I'm wearing? That's from when we all went to dinner together, a week and a half ago. Before Del Rosario went anywhere near her."

Arnett stared at the picture. "How is that possible?"

Jo paced the length of Lopez's space. "Excellent question. We triggered something somehow, did something that got back to her. Maybe someone at one of the phone companies tipped her off?"

Lopez continued working at the monitor. "Anything's possible. Maybe she works for the phone company herself under a different name. Okay, I've hacked into her account—"

Jo took a step toward her. "Is that legal?"

"Sorry, can't hear you, I'm a little deaf in that ear," Lopez said. "The information on the account says Diana Montauk, and shows the same phone number and address as the one we have already, so it's a dead end. There's nothing other than a welcome message in the folder, so nothing we can latch on to there. My guess is she opened this account just to send you this message. And—she did it only about two hours ago. She must have scheduled delivery for now."

"Can you tell where it was sent from?" Arnett asked.

"Soon. I have the IP address and the service provider. I'll need them to get me a physical location for the IP address. They may ask for a warrant, but I suspect once I mention the person we're trying to locate is threatening a cop, we'll get fast cooperation." Lopez reached for her landline, but then paused to look back at Jo. "Are you okay?"

"Oh, I'm just fine. She severely miscalculated if she thought this would deter me." Jo narrowed her eyes. "Quite the opposite. I don't care if it costs me my job, I'm gonna find her long before she can even *think* of going near anybody I love again."

———

Jo listened with half an ear as Lopez talked to the service provider while the rest of her brain searched for solutions and sorted through emotions. Fear. Anger. Self-recrimination.

She'd underestimated Diana Montauk. This woman had been piling up victims from all over the country for at least eight years, probably longer, and had managed to stay so far under the radar nobody even realized crimes had been committed. That took brains, the kind of brains that probably knew Jo was

tracking her before Jo knew it herself. She should have anticipated that.

Heat shot up her neck and face at the memory of David in
the picture. He hadn't just cheated—he'd gotten another woman
pregnant. How could he do that to Sophie? How could he do
that to Isabelle and Emily, who'd now have a little sister or
brother in the world that they'd either never know about or that
they'd have to spend the rest of their life navigating because
they were the child of the woman who broke up their parents'
marriage—

And Matt. He didn't deserve to be involved in this—all he'd
ever done was care about Jo, apparently the worst sin a man
could commit.

I'll break up with him, that'll get him out of danger—

She squeezed her eyes shut. She was slipping back into old
ways of thinking, that she could keep people safe by pushing
them away or making sure she didn't care too much about them
or they too much about her. Her therapist had warned her how
easy it was to backslide—

*Once you tell him, he'll break up with you, anyway. Why
would he stay?*

She couldn't blame him if he did, that would be the smart
thing to do, and heaven knew Matt was smart—

Sophie—oh, God, Sophie. How could she possibly tell her
about the picture? How could she possibly *not* tell her?

No. She leaned forward in her chair, elbows on knees,
hands clasped in a fist in front of her face. She wasn't going to
let the old ways of thinking cripple her, not when her family
needed her. After years of blaming herself when her boyfriend
Marc and fiancé Jack had been killed in front of her, she'd
finally been able to let go of that blame and trust herself again,
to lay the culpability at the feet of the people who deserved it:
the people who'd shot the guns. She needed to keep her focus
where it belonged, on finding this woman, *today. Now.*

Lopez slammed down the phone. "Got it. Gamer Gecko in Las Vegas. An internet café."

"I thought internet cafés were dead?" Arnett asked.

"Gamer culture resurrected them. Great place to go if you need the extra speed, or for team play fun." Lopez dialed the phone again and put it on speaker.

"Gamer Gecko, this is Mike."

Lopez launched into a brief explanation of why they were calling. "I don't suppose you had a Diana Montauk use one of your computers today?"

"Don't think so, but let me check the list. Hang on."

They listened to beeps and buzzes and clanks in the background until Mike came back on the line.

"Nope. Nobody named Diana anything. You sure you got the name right?"

"I'm not, actually." Lopez put on a light-hearted, flirty tone. "I don't suppose there's any way you can just fax me the whole list of everyone who's been in today?"

"Sure, as long as you give me a valid law-enforcement agency I can verify." Jo could hear the shrug in Mike's voice, and when he was met with surprised silence, he continued on. "We make it very clear to our customers, don't come in here if you're trying to do anything illegal, 'cause we'll turn you over to the cops at the first sign of trouble. If they want to buy malware attacks or drugs on the dark web, they're in the wrong place."

Lopez gave him HQ's name, address, and phone number.

"Great. We'll verify, then fax over the information."

"Do you have video footage?"

"Yup. We have a camera on the front door and a camera on the arcade area. I'll get what we have for today uploaded and send you a link to it."

As Lopez thanked him and hung up, Marzillo appeared from the depths of the lab, startling Jo. "I didn't realize you were here."

"I got a notification my package with the bed restraints arrived. I came in to see if they matched the fiber I found, and they do. I also got the tox screen and other test results back on Gina Purcelli." She bent over a monitor and clicked on the associated mouse to pull the results up. "Positive for GHB, LSD, and heroin." She straightened up and glanced between their three faces. "What's wrong?"

Arnett caught her up, and she stared at Jo. "Martin Scherer? You found his killer?"

Jo nodded. "Yes. We're trying to track her from the email she sent, and any ideas you have about that would be very welcome."

The printer next to Lopez rumbled. "Hopefully that's the list from Gamer Gecko." Lopez grabbed the printout and skimmed it. "Twelve people, that's not bad. Four of them women, although we can't count on that." She stuck the pages back into the machine and pushed the button to copy them.

Jo waited, hand poised to retrieve the copies, her mind churning forward. "I'm thinking the fastest way to proceed is to eliminate any established residents of Las Vegas. Hopefully that'll cut the list down significantly. Then, with whoever's left, we update the nationwide BOLO we sent out for Diana Montauk with these names, and send one directly to Las Vegas Metro so we can find those names if they pop up anywhere in Las Vegas, especially in rental car records, hotels, credit card transactions, gas stations. We need some sort of visual ID, security footage, or someone who's seen her."

CHAPTER FIFTY-NINE

After several hours of throwing everything they could think of at finding Diana Montauk, they came up frustratingly short. They scoured Gamer Gecko's video footage, but due to the angle of the camera and the resolution, they weren't able to get anything definitive. They narrowed the list down to four out-of-towners, two women and two men, and started plugging their names into an array of searches. They found rental car records for two, and requested video footage.

Arnett stood, and turned to Jo. "It's late. We need to get food and sleep."

Jo didn't look up from the computer. "You all go. I'll keep on for a little while longer."

Arnett put his hand on Jo's shoulder, forcing her to look up. "Sleep deprivation isn't gonna help us catch her. We need to stay sharp, and for now we've done all we can do. If any of them use a credit card, enter a casino, or check into a hotel in Las Vegas, we'll be notified immediately."

She glanced around at the empty vending-machine junk-food packets littering their workspaces. "Fine. If we don't have any hits by then, I'll start in on one-call-at-a-time grunt work first thing in the morning." She took a deep breath. "I need to go have a couple of difficult conversations anyway."

She texted Matt on the way home and asked him to meet her. Once home, she circled through the house waiting for him to arrive, stomach clenched and gurgling. She wiped down kitchen counters that were already clean, straightened bed corners that were already straight, and dusted bookshelves that were already nearly dust-free.

When her front bell sounded, she jumped like she'd been shocked. She composed herself, trying desperately to ignore the little voice in her head screaming that she was about to lose him.

He pulled her into his arms as soon as the door clicked in place behind him. "Thank God they finally found a replacement at work. I was really hoping you'd call tonight."

Her heart broke as she stared up into his eyes, and she almost lost her resolve. "I'm glad you're here. But I have something difficult to tell you, and I think you might need a drink."

His expression tightened, and his hands dropped from her waist. "In that case, hit me with that calvados you keep up in the cabinet."

With her chest tight as a drum, she led him into the kitchen, pulled the bottle down, and poured two fingers for each of them in snifters. After handing him his drink, she sat down at the kitchen table, pulled out her phone and opened the email.

"You remember that killer I've been tracking, not the one with the mothers in Greenfern, but the supposed suicides off the Golden Gate Bridge?"

"The one you tracked to LA." He took a sip of the calvados.

"Yes. It turns out she tracked me down, as well." She slid the phone over to him. Time slowed as she watched his eyes flick back and forth across the tiny screen.

When they stopped moving, he continued to stare down at the screen for a moment before looking back up at her, brows raised. "Well," he deadpanned. "That's disconcerting."

Jo tossed back her drink, then met his eyes again. "I'm so sorry. Danger's a part of my job and that's my choice. But—" She stopped, unable to find words, then shifted gears. "I told you that my fiancé was shot in an alley in Boston. But I haven't told you that the first man I fell in love with, boy really because he was only sixteen, was shot in front of me in New Orleans." Her throat tightened, and she stopped to clear it. "Bad things happen to men I care about. If you're smart, you'll leave now and you won't look back."

Matt grabbed the bottle of calvados off the counter and poured her another tot. "Bad things happen to everyone. If you think I'm going to let some crazy bitch chase me away from the most amazing woman I've ever met, you've got another think coming."

Jo shook her head. "You don't understand—"

His hand shot up. "I understand just fine. I refuse to make my life choices based on fear. I knew you were a detective when I met you, and knew that came with risks. And any man who'd leave you because of something like this doesn't deserve you."

Relief crumbled the levee holding back her emotion, and tears spilled onto her cheeks. She reached over and slipped her hand into his.

He squeezed it. "But it doesn't sound like she's all that interested in me, anyway. David's the one I'm worried about."

Heat washed over her. "David. I'm terrified for him and I feel guilty for bringing this on him, but I'm also so angry about what he did to Sophie I could kill him myself. Did you see the photos? How could he do something like this?"

"I did see." Matt stopped to take a large gulp of his drink, then tilted his head. "But you can't really tell me you didn't suspect something like that was going on?"

His words slammed into her, and a thousand conversations reorganized in her mind, taking on new meaning. "My God, you're absolutely right. Sophie's been making cryptic comments about their relationship for months now, and all the signs are there. Late work hours. Disconnection. Why else would he be so ticked about the change in restaurant the other night? He must have been worried his two worlds would somehow collide." She threaded her fingers together over her forehead. "How the hell could I not see that? I mean, it's not like I do this for a living, right, pick up on signals people leak, suss out what it is they're hiding."

He rolled the stem of the snifter between his thumb and forefinger. "You couldn't see it for the same reason I'm not supposed to treat my own family. Same thing with psychologists. We're too close to evaluate in an unbiased manner. If I'm not mistaken, detectives aren't supposed to handle cases that involve family, either."

She puffed air through her nose.

He laughed. "I know, I know. It's inconvenient being human, isn't it?"

"Right, sure, fine, I'm human. The problem remains the same. What the hell do I do? This is going to destroy my sister. David and the girls are her whole life, quite literally. She made the decision to not work so she could devote herself to her family. Not to mention that I've only just managed to thaw out a little porthole in the iceberg that is our relationship so we've finally started really *seeing* each other. She doesn't like being less than perfect, and she *really* doesn't like me seeing her as less than perfect. Her pride won't allow her to admit this is happening."

"You have a picture."

"She'll claim it's doctored or—something. Because..." She paused and took a sip of the calvados to screw up her courage. "What if she doesn't *want* to know? Or what if she knows already but is ignoring it because she's clinging to the life she's invested so much in? If I tell her, she won't be able to ignore it anymore. What gives me the right to make that choice for her?

And then on the other hand, if she doesn't know and I don't tell her, and she finds out I knew, she'll never trust me again."

His brows popped up as he took a deep breath. "It's a hard position to be in. You're right, your sister is proud. But I've also experienced her to be smart, caring, and fair."

Jo examined the wood pattern on her kitchen table for a long moment. "When I was in my mid-twenties, I had a friend who struggled to find a relationship. We bonded over it in a strange way, actually, because I was so heartbroken over Jack. Finally she found one, and she was the happiest I've ever seen her. After they'd been dating about two months, he hit on me."

Matt winced, and took another sip of calvados.

"I went straight to her—I mean, within minutes. She told me I must have misunderstood him. She asked him about it, and he told her he'd been 'joking.' To this day, I'm not sure what that even means. But not only did she believe him, she ended our friendship."

"Got it." Matt nodded. "Either choice is a risk, and that leaves you alone with your moral compass. What would you want her to do if the situation was reversed?"

Jo's laugh was dry. "I'd want to know, no matter how much it hurt. And I don't think I'd be able to get over it if I found out she knew and didn't tell me. But the whole problem with me and my sister is we've never seen the world the same way."

He drained his snifter. "I think you're far more alike than you realize."

Jo lifted her snifter in a toast gesture, then drank hers down, too. "I hope you're right."

CHAPTER SIXTY

The calvados helped Jo fall asleep, but didn't keep her that way. She woke at five in the morning, a ridiculous hour for a Sunday, and forced herself to go for a long, cleansing run before returning to HQ. Nobody was awake in the west, and with the BOLOs they'd put in place throughout Vegas and Nevada, the hour wouldn't make much difference in catching Diana, but the exercise would allow her to focus more effectively.

When she walked into HQ, still in her exercise clothes, Lopez was already waiting.

"How did you beat me?" Jo asked.

Lopez waved her off. "I literally got here ten minutes ago. How did the conversations go?"

Jo rubbed her eyes. "The one with Matt went well. I haven't talked to Sophie yet. After what we just went through with Emily, I'm not looking forward to telling her another psychopath is threatening her family, let alone that she's about to be a step-mom."

"Good times." Lopez picked up a sheet of paper off her desk and handed it to Jo. "Speaking of. Montauk was kind enough to leave location data on the picture, and between that and the number on the house, I was able to find David's paramour. Chelsea Whitens, twenty-eight, just finished a PhD in English lit from Boston College, volunteers at a food bank in her spare time."

"When she's not banging married men," Arnett said as he entered the room.

"Whoa, Nellie," Lopez said. "She may not even know he's married."

"Fair enough." Arnett didn't look convinced.

Lopez continued. "I also checked the metadata and analyzed the picture to see if it had been altered in any way. It appears to be legit, and taken the day after your dinner."

Jo nodded, tapped her phone awake, and checked the notifications. "Looks like Las Vegas called while I was on my run."

"Links to video clips of the rented cars are also waiting in my inbox, along with copies of their driver's licenses," Lopez said.

Jo jotted down the information from her voicemail. They'd managed to find the hotel locations for two of the out-of-towners, luckily those who hadn't turned up in the car rental records.

"Check the video clips and IDs first? We may be able to eliminate them completely just from that," Arnett suggested.

One video wasn't clear enough to make a determination, but the other was definitive. "Distance between the eyes are completely different, same with the lip contours," Lopez said. "And the other one, from his license, is a sixty-year-old bald man. Hard for Montauk to fake that unless she's a master of disguise."

The next suspect turned out to be a teenaged boy on vacation with his family. He was small for his age, so the security footage from the hotel eliminated him quickly as a possible Montauk disguise.

The final name from the list, Grace Hawkins, had been

located at a seedy hotel called The Cactus Flower on the outskirts of town.

"Help you?" a woman's voice answered the phone, sounding like she'd smoked several hundred too many packs of cigarettes and had seen several decades too much of life.

Jo explained why they were calling.

"Yep, I was here when she checked in, 'cause I'm always here," the woman, who identified herself as Amber, said. "I own the place, and I'm lucky if I get a day off once a month. Hard enough without any extra trouble, so when someone shows up at my hotel wanting to pay cash and claiming they don't have a car to park on site when I saw them drive up in one with my own two eyes, I do a little double-check."

"How do you manage that?" Jo asked.

"I got friends and I'm not gonna tell you who they are, so don't ask. They ran her license and it don't exist, so I let the police know. 'Course, they got better things to do with their time than follow up on fake IDs, but I figure if it's someone causing trouble, they'll be interested. And look who's calling me."

"Any chance we can email you a picture and see if it matches the woman who checked in under that name?"

Amber hesitated. "What'd she do?"

Jo made a quick decision. "The woman we're looking for murdered several men."

Amber gasped, then gushed the air back out. "Oh *hell* no. Send it over."

Jo's palm bounced frantically on her thigh as Lopez shot over a copy of Diana Montauk's license picture, then while Amber pulled it up.

"Yep, that's her. She's a blonde now, but it's her."

Adrenaline sent electricity through each of Jo's limbs. "You're sure?"

"Positive. Dark brown eyes and pixie chin, and I thought at

the time blonde wasn't right for her. She's pale like me, and if I had hazel eyes like that, I'd pop 'em out with long, dark, sexy hair. Some people don't know what they got."

Jo was up, putting on her blazer. "How long is she staying with you?"

"*Stayed* with me. She checked out at the crack of dawn."

CHAPTER SIXTY-ONE

"Dammit." Jo smacked the table. "I knew I should have worked through the night."

Lopez shot her a scornful look. "And done what? Called every single hotel and motel in Las Vegas to ask about her? We'd have found you passed out on the desk in the morning only a tenth of the way through the list, and you still wouldn't have found her any faster. The only reason we found out at all is because Amber went to the police."

Jo waved off the logic. "So now we put out a national BOLO for this alias. But the driver's license is useless, there have to be about fifty thousand Grace Hawkinses in the United States, and since Amber didn't have a license plate or a credit card number, I'm not sure how we proceed."

"We'll put the word out," Arnett said. "Cops don't like people who threaten other cops, and she'll have every member of law enforcement across the country looking for her. She'll show up somewhere."

Jo slouched back in her chair, pen tapping the desk in front of her. "We also need to go back to the beginning and double-check our work. Talk to Diana's neighbors and landlord and talk to them again, see if they remember anything else about her."

"Behavioral analysis," Lopez said. "Go over her credit card records and bank statements to see if we can learn anything from that. An obsession with opera, some strange type of food she likes, anything that might help determine where she's headed."

"Same with her phone records," Arnett said. "Maybe we—"

Jo sprung forward. "Her phone."

Lopez and Arnett stared at her.

"You said she turned off service, right, and there's no signal from the phone, GPS or otherwise?"

"Correct," Lopez said.

"Las Vegas is in the middle of the desert," Jo said.

"True?" Arnett stared at her.

"Who drives across a desert these days with no cell phone?" Jo asked.

Lopez straightened up. "Nice—she must have a burner, or a new account."

Arnett shrugged. "Doesn't help us if we can't identify it."

Jo's pulse pounded. "But that's just it. We *can* identify it. We now have two places we know for a fact she was. We even have the exact time of transaction at Gamer Gecko, and we can get the exact time of checkout from Amber."

A grin spread across Lopez's face. "So we use the same trick we used before. We get tower data from near Gamer Gecko and near The Cactus Flower, and we see what number was at both."

"Exactly." Jo poked her pen into the air toward Lopez's stacks of files. "We now have a threatening communication from our suspect, so we shouldn't have a problem getting a warrant."

"And this should take far less time, actually," Lopez said.

"So we just need to get the warrant," Arnett said.

"Arnett and I will take care of it." Lopez gave her a pointed look. "Because I know you need to go have a conversation with your sister."

Jo's grin faded. "Do I have to?"

———

Jo's eyes didn't move from her sister's face as she stared out the dining-room window, watching Isabelle and Emily play. Sophie had turned red when she heard Jo's news, then completely pale when she saw the picture of David and the pregnant girl, and now she'd been silent for several long minutes since.

"Are you okay, Soph?" Jo placed her hand gently on top of Sophie's. "I know that's a lot to take in, and I'm so sorry—"

Sophie turned, zombie-like, toward Jo. "She's pregnant."

"It might not be his."

Sophie narrowed her eyes. "Don't do that."

Jo cleared her throat. "No, you're right, that's not likely."

Sophie nodded, and stared back out the window.

After another long silence, Jo got up, located the bourbon in Sophie's cabinet, and poured out a generous shot into a juice glass.

Sophie pounded it back as though it were water. "I figured he was cheating. I didn't know for sure, and I told myself I didn't want to become one of those women who spy on their husbands. But that was just an excuse to avoid dealing with it." She looked back over at Jo. "But I never imagined he'd be stupid enough to get someone pregnant."

Jo just nodded.

"I get how he could do it to *me*. Neither of us is perfect, and our marriage certainly isn't. But how could he do that to the *girls*?"

Jo shook her head.

"There's no way I can hide this from them. If this woman has his child, he'll always be attached to her just like he'll always be attached to me. He'll have to negotiate it all—what does he think that's going to do to them?" She turned back to Jo.

"I don't know. And I'm sorry you had to find out this way."

Sophie laughed dryly. "As opposed to what? Her showing up at my door with a baby in her arms? Or him telling me over dinner at the fanciest restaurant in Boston so I'd be forced not to react poorly? Or to a teenager showing up at Isabelle's or Emily's dorm room announcing he or she's their half sibling?" She shook her head. "No, believe me, this is best, hearing it from someone who actually cares about me and having a minute to compose myself."

Jo cleared her throat again. "Except for the psychopath threatening to kill him."

"Ask her if she needs me to buy her a plane ticket," Sophie said, face blank.

"You don't mean that."

"No, I suppose I don't. That would be too easy. He should have to stick around and pay to raise three children while dealing with the drama of two different *baby mamas*." Her lip curled derisively as she spat out the phrase.

Jo poured another shot for Sophie. "What are you going to do?"

Sophie laughed the dry laugh again. "You'd think that would be an easy answer, wouldn't you?"

"No, I really don't. It seems like the hardest question anyone has ever had to answer."

Sophie stared at her strangely. "You know, sometimes— many times—I envy you. You'd never find yourself in this situation, dependent on a husband, ten years since you've had any sort of job, completely unemployable. On nights when he 'has to go back to the office' you'd never be caught dead sitting here with a glass of wine convincing yourself your whole life isn't a sham."

Jo glanced out the window at the girls. "Plenty of nights

when I'm alone in my house late at night, I envy *you*. You have two beautiful daughters who love you, and you've done such an amazing job turning them into good people. That's precious, and it's not easy. Just because *he* screwed up, that doesn't make *any* of *your* life a sham."

Sophie nodded. "You're right, and I know it. When I feel that way I slip into the girls' bedrooms and just stare at them, wondering how I managed to bring two such amazing creatures into the world. Whatever I had to go through, or have to go through, it was all worth it because I can't imagine my life without them."

Jo stared at Sophie a moment longer, marveling at her sister's strength, before turning to the window again. "I can't imagine my life without them, either."

CHAPTER SIXTY-TWO

SEPTEMBER 6TH

That night after Jo crawled into bed, she found herself tossing and turning, unable to settle as Diana's email circled through her mind.

Not because of Sophie or Matt—they'd both handled the contents far better than she could have hoped. Something else, something on the tip of her brain, unsettled her. So she went through the letter line by line in her mind and hit on it almost immediately: *I need you to understand that you and I are the same, Josette.*

She'd pushed the claim aside when she first read the note, preoccupied as she was with Sophie and Matt. But now it rose to the surface, roaring. And the thought that Diana might be right broke her out in a heavy sweat.

I think you know the right thing to do is to take the Rollins and Purcelli files and bury them deep in the farthest corner of your office drawers. And I believe you know it's right to leave me to my work, also.

The little voice in her head whispered to her: Was she on the wrong side of justice when she chased someone like Diana, or The Mom Killer? Martin Scherer certainly deserved to die, she'd never argue otherwise, so was it wrong to put his killer in jail? Was it justice to put someone in jail for protecting abused children?

She thrashed over to the other side of her bed, and punched her flattened pillow back into shape. Yes, she told herself emphatically, it *was* wrong. Not that she didn't struggle with the restrictions of law enforcement and the way bad guys sometimes got away and good guys didn't. But every role in the system had a vital part to play, and hers wasn't to make those determinations—that was for judges and juries to decide. Her role was to find the truth as best she could, and integrity was crucial to that role. Because taking justice into your own hands, deciding you knew best what was right, well, that was a slippery slope that always ended badly.

Is it? the voice tugged at her.

"Yes, it is," she said aloud, trying to convince herself. Matt had put it well: *These situations require distance.* If you were too close, if it was about your ego, you were dead in the water.

Distance, being too close, staying far enough away—Diana had said something about that, too. She ran through the letter again, and found it: *I'm cheering for them because I understand them. They're hiding deep in the shadows where you'll never see them, with enough distance to judge, yet close enough to see everything so they can destroy the next evil. Just like me.*

The words haunted her through the night as she faded in and out of sleep, ping-ponging back and forth between the accusation that she was thwarting justice, and her self-reassurance that professional distance was key, the protective core around her integrity, even if—

She sat straight up in bed as the two thoughts collided out of her subconscious.

Enough distance to judge. The sort of murderer who killed serially, like Diana, wasn't killing someone they had a personal stake in. An effective killer of this type would be someone who felt they had enough distance to judge—but also, crucially, to *keep out of sight*, continuing their work and finding the next victim. Someone who was out of sight, but who could still see. Someone with distance, back amid the shadows, watching.

There was one person they'd talked to who fit those criteria perfectly.

CHAPTER SIXTY-THREE

River Holt was getting her daughter back.

River Holt, who'd burned her little Tammy five times on the stovetop, and who thought everyone was stupid enough to think the girl had done it to herself—supposedly while making dinner. If she'd actually let her six-year-old cook dinner, that was just as bad, regardless. But one person was that stupid: the moronic judge who'd given Tammy back to River.

I skimmed the screen for the twentieth time, hoping it was all a mad delusion. But no, there it was, in clear black-and-white pixels. Another judge making another bone-headed call. I smashed my fist into the table so hard I thought I might have broken a bone. Didn't idiocy ever take a vacation?

I couldn't let this stand. Couldn't let her get her hands back on that child. But I also didn't see how I could take out another abuser so soon. The detectives were everywhere, asking questions, nosing at everything. If I had even just a few weeks, I could make do, because the cases would go cold and the detectives would shift to something else. But I didn't have a few weeks, because unlike everyone else, I'd been watching River. I knew she was a flight risk. She had a slew of relatives in Quebec, and just recently she'd sent off a bunch of her belongings in two big orange U-Haul crates. So, no, I didn't even have days. I had mere hours.

And that meant I'd have to run once I finished this one. Live the rest of my life, such as it was, in another country. I'd been responsibly saving my whole life, thank God, and had funds enough to live somewhere cheap.

I stared at the screen again, regret tugging at my heart. I'd hoped to watch and protect my hometown for at least a few years more. But God was in control, and this was what he wanted.

I told myself it didn't really matter. Time was running out for me either way.

CHAPTER SIXTY-FOUR

Jo tossed and turned, ran on the treadmill, then showered as she waited for the rest of the world to wake up. As soon as the clock hit five thirty, she sent a text to Arnett as she drove in to HQ: *Have a theory. Need to get moving as soon as you're ready.*

His response came almost immediately. *I'm on my way in.*

She sent him back a thumbs-up, and strode up to her desk just minutes before he did.

"So what's the urgent theory?" he said, handing her a latte.

She chugged a good third of the coffee before answering. "Because each of TMK's victims were murdered in ways that mimic their alleged abuse, we've been looking for someone who has a vendetta against abusers. We've considered the fathers working together somehow, or Tom Fischer since he's touched all the relevant cases, or Rick Burke since he's reported on all of them. But nothing fits, and we certainly have no evidence."

"With you," Arnett said.

"From the beginning, there have been too many connections between these people. But they can't all be connected to the murders—that would be impossible to coordinate."

"I bet Tom Fischer could manage it."

"Sure. But if you're planning that carefully, you're gonna make sure everyone has their alibis sorted out and don't do stupid things like lie about when they picked up their pizza."

Arnett's mouth twisted skeptically. "I've seen too many criminals do too many stupid things."

Jo threw up a hand. "Fine, let's say you're right. But, something in Montauk's letter hit me last night in combination with something Matt said to me. This killer has an ongoing agenda to kill abusive mothers. To carry that out effectively, they have to be *close enough* to the situation—in this case, abusive mothers in Greenfern—to identify potential suspects, while also being *removed enough* from the situation to not be at all obvious to us. They have to be able to see, but not be seen. Everybody we've considered a suspect so far hasn't been hidden at all. But when I stopped and thought if there was anybody who fit that combination of criteria, the answer came to me immediately."

"And that is?" Arnett said.

"Renata Cruz. She's both Alison Choi's and Steve Brodlin's direct supervisor. Part of her job is to evaluate them, which means she oversees their work. She has her *eyes* on every case that goes through her team, without having her *hands* in any of them. She's far enough removed to delude herself that she's a fair arbiter of their cases. And," she concluded triumphantly, "if she showed up at their doors for some sort of random check, they'd open the door and let her in without question, even though they'd never seen her before."

"Okay, it's a good theory, but I don't see how it's any better than our others. And we still don't have any evidence."

A Cheshire-cat grin spread over Jo's face. "Except if Cruz is our killer, I may know how to get some."

CHAPTER SIXTY-FIVE

Alison Choi wasn't happy to see them back at her desk.

"How can I help you *now*, detectives?" She crossed her arms over her chest. "Have you come to arrest me despite the detailed alibis I provided for you?"

Jo couldn't blame her for being salty—she'd be, too. "I know it's not pleasant to have the police call you asking for alibis. But we have to make sure no defense attorney can claim we didn't do our due diligence by considering alternative suspects. We have to eliminate the innocent so we can make sure our net is nice and tight around the right person."

Alison's expression softened, and her arms found their way back to the desk. "No, right. I understand. Have you found the killer, then?"

"We think we may have, but we need your help to be sure," Jo answered.

She glanced at both of them. "How so?"

Jo gave her a quick overview of what they suspected and why. "Renata mentioned when someone goes into a file, the system automatically marks it. Can you look that up for us?"

Alison drew a deep breath. "I don't have permission to see those notations. But I'm pretty sure the people in IT can."

"Do you know anybody in IT you trust? Or someone who doesn't particularly like Renata?"

She bit her lip. "I think I might."

———

Alison hurried through the office at such a clip Jo lost her sense of direction after the third abrupt turn. After descending into the basement and passing a darkened section, Alison knocked on a keycard-protected door in the bowels of the building.

A tall, fifty-something white man with a scraggly blond ponytail and a watermelon belly under his Pac-Man shirt pulled open the door. He shot a surprised look at Jo and Arnett. "Alison. What's up?"

Alison's voice dropped. "Can we come inside, Johnny? This is important, and confidential."

Johnny stepped back, then walked them past five employees working at half-sized cubicles into a smaller office filled with boxes, components, and a desk.

As soon as the door closed firmly behind them, Alison spoke again. "These are two detectives from the Oakhurst SPDU. They have a favor to ask you."

"Oh, really." His eyes narrowed at Jo and Arnett. "Do they have a warrant?"

Alison shook her head. "That's why it's a favor. They can get one but it'll take a while, and they'd probably have to bring it to Renata, which is exactly what we don't want. They're entitled to see our confidential files in the course of investigations anyway, so I can't see how this could get you in actual trouble."

His face suddenly animated. "Well, hell, if they don't want Renata to know about it, that's all you had to say." He extended a hand to each of them in turn. "Johnny Himes, Head of IT here. What do you need?"

Jo's ears perked up at his rancor toward Renata, but she didn't have time to follow up on it now. "Alison said you might be able to track employee activity on files. Which case they open and when?"

"Of course. I know everything going on in my system at any moment," Johnny said.

"Do you store that information?" Arnett asked.

"We do. I can generate an activity log for each employee. I can also see everybody's emails and interoffice chat records."

Jo pulled out the list she'd prepared during her insomnia, flattened it on his desk, and pointed. "First we need to know whether Renata touched these files on these dates, the week before each murder. So, the Avery Rollins file during the week before Melissa Rollins was murdered, et cetera."

Johnny swiveled to his monitor and let loose a furious frenzy of typing and clicks. "Purcelli file first. Hang on a sec."

Alison gestured to the one other chair in the room, and Jo indicated with a wave that she should take it. She did, and pulled up next to the desk while Jo and Arnett peered over Johnny's shoulder. The screens flew by as Jo's heart played metronome.

He stopped, and pointed. "Right there. She looked at the Purcelli file twice on August thirtieth."

"The day before the murder," Jo said. "Can you provide a copy of that to us somehow? And is there a way to be sure nobody tampers with it?"

"I can print it for you. And the records are system created, they can't be altered." As his fingers flew, a machine hidden amid the boxes whirred to life. "Alison, can you grab that?"

She stood to retrieve it, and Johnny hunched back over his keyboard with an intensity that brought up Tour de France riders in Jo's mind. After another few minutes, he stopped again.

"There you are, my pretty," he cackled in a Wicked-Witch-of-the-West voice. "She pulled up the Rollins file twice on August fifteenth, and once on the sixteenth." He hit a key combo, and the printer whirred again.

"I don't suppose you can get a sense of whether she checks files regularly as a matter of course? So we can be sure this isn't just a coincidence?"

He typed and clicked and scrolled. "She does not. Looking over her general pattern of activity, she spends most of her time in employee files, and only opens actual case files when someone needs her to rubber stamp something, or she's doing reviews for some reason. See here? Those types of activities happen in clumps, and the Rollins and Purcelli files look nothing like that. I can print out her activity log for the entire month if you need to show these sign-ins are unusual. But fair warning, they'll make you go cross-eyed."

"Not a problem. We have a team member who lives to go cross-eyed over data," Jo said. "She'll love getting her hands on them.

"She single?" he said, eyes not moving from the screen.

"Sadly, no," Jo said.

"Damn. Nothing pops me a chub harder than a data geek." He shook his head. "This last one's gonna take a bit longer. Don't suppose you want to tell me what Cruz did while I'm searching?"

"I get the sense you're a smart guy. You really need us to say outright?" Arnett asked.

He chuckled. "Nah, not really. Just the hope you're gonna cart her out of my life is enough."

"Don't suppose you want to tell us why Renata's not your favorite person?" Jo asked.

"The usual. She thinks we're here to jump when she snaps her fingers, no please or thank you required."

Alison laughed. "And you caught her stealing your yogurt out of the break room fridge."

The back of Johnny's neck reddened. "Doesn't make the other stuff less true. But since she's so superior to everyone, you think she'd be smart enough to check the bottom of shit she steals before dumping the container in her office garbage."

"There's a special place in hell for people who steal coworkers' food," Arnett said.

"Truth." Johnny pointed backward toward Arnett, eyes still on his monitor. "Ha! Got it. She checked the Pryzik file twice on October thirteenth." He printed the screen and spun his chair around, face triumphant.

"Perfect," Jo said. "Now we'll go pay Renata a little visit."

"Not today you can't," Alison said. "She's out sick, which is really strange for her."

The hair on the back of Jo's neck stood on end. "What do you mean, strange?"

Her eyes widened. "She's only called in sick one other time all the years I've been here. She takes scheduled days off, but never calls in sick."

Jo exchanged a panicked glance with Arnett. "We called and asked her about the Pryzik file, so she knows we've connected the cases. Do you think she's running?"

"Or she's with her next victim."

CHAPTER SIXTY-SIX

I'd learned that seven in the evening, if I could manage it, was the perfect time for my visits. Late enough that mostly everyone was settling in, home from their jobs or errands and unlikely to notice my presence, but still early enough to give me time to do what I needed to do. But in this case I didn't have to avoid work hours. I could get in and out quickly because River Holt was an alimony mother who stayed home to take care of her child all day.

I knew the type well. My mother was one.

I scanned the street carefully as I pulled up and parked. Nobody in their front yards, no cars coming up or down the street —that was the best I could hope for. During my time watching her, I'd verified she had no alarm system or security cameras to avoid. I grabbed my work satchel and my clipboard and hurried up the driveway.

She opened the door almost immediately, in a faded black button-down tunic, faded red leggings, and a confused look on her face.

Her eyes flitted to the identification I held up. "Wait. We didn't have an appointment."

"No." I struggled to keep my face pleasant despite the rage

that bubbled up in me at the very sight of her. The long hipster haircut, the supercilious manner—even her pretentious name made me want to retch. "I find surprise visits are most effective."

I could tell she was tempted to tell me to go to hell, but knew full well she couldn't. She reluctantly stepped back and opened the door. "I'm not sure what more I can show you. I answered all of Alison's questions, and Tammy isn't even here today."

Of course not. I couldn't kill her while her daughter watched, now could I?

"The best time to do home inspections is when the children are away." I stepped into her living room and glanced around, not surprised to find clutter everywhere and clothes tossed over the furniture. I allowed my eyes to linger on the mess long enough for her to begin to sweat.

Then I glanced down at my clipboard. "Keeping an acceptably clean house was part of what you agreed to in order to regain custody."

Her eyes widened with fear. "But Tammy's not here this week—"

I threw up my hand to stop her. "I'll need to do a drug test, right here and right now. I'll need a urine sample, and I'll need to take some blood."

"I didn't agree to do that—"

I crossed my arms over my chest and held her eye. "No, you're right, you didn't. But if you refuse to give me these samples right now, I'll mark your case with 'refusal to cooperate' before I drive away from the corner, and we'll notify your husband that he now has full-time custody while the case is being reviewed. At least this way you'll have a chance to appeal the results and make arrangements, and you'll be able to see your daughter again before the decision is made."

I could practically see her brain calculating the possibility that whatever drug she'd used the night before would show up on the test, and how to explain it.

When she didn't speak, I reached inside the satchel for a plastic container. "You'll need to urinate in this."

Her arm snaked out slowly for the cup; she held it like toxic waste as she slunk into the master bath. Her eyes flicked back over her shoulder at me in a silent question—was I going to watch her? Luckily, I didn't care one whit if she had a clean back-up sample below her sink waiting to be added to the cup.

As soon as the door closed behind her, I prepped the syringe. You can learn anything on the internet these days, including how to administer shots and draw blood. The part you couldn't learn effectively was the balance of putting enough GHB in the bottom of the barrel syringe to do the job, but not so much that she'd notice it. I threaded the needle on, pulled back the safety and the cap, and drew the GHB into the very bottom of the syringe. Then I placed the cap back on and waited.

She finished and washed her hands for a long moment, probably hoping the extra time would somehow make it more likely she'd pass the test. After a good twenty seconds, I had to stop myself from screaming through the door for her to hurry it up.

She came out, looking like a rabbit caught in a hole. I gestured to the couch. "Please sit, and roll up your sleeve."

Her fingers pulled and tucked her sleeve out of the way. This was my favorite part, and I let myself enjoy it—tying the blue band around her bicep, feeling carefully for a vein, her fear so palpable I could almost feel the electric current of it on her skin. I made a show of swabbing the area, drawing out my anticipation, then inserted the needle into her arm.

As I depressed the plunger, adrenaline surged through me.

CHAPTER SIXTY-SEVEN

Jo's stomach dropped as Arnett's words hit her. Renata surely wasn't stupid enough to kill again so soon?

She turned to Johnny. "Can you get us a list of all the files she's looked at in the last, say, week? If she has another intended victim, she would have pulled up their case."

Within moments the printer whirred and buzzed again. He grabbed the printouts and thrust them at Jo and Arnett. "Here's all her activity for the last two weeks. This column shows what she's looking at, and if it's an employee file, it'll have a 'P' in this box."

Arnett took the sheets. "Shit. There have to be at least fifty non-employee names here. What're we going to do, go to each house?"

Jo shook her head. "No need. So far every woman she's killed lost custody of their child and regained it again." She turned to Alison. "That can't be all that common, right?"

Alison shook her head, popped up from the chair, and grabbed a pen. "None of my remaining families have that, so we can cross all those off the list." She took the sheets from Arnett and lined through several rows.

"Is there any way we can check through the rest quickly?" Jo asked.

Alison's face screwed up. "Each file has a summary update section, which should include the outcomes of the investigation, and any reversals. That would be the fastest way."

Johnny stepped away from his chair and pointed to his desk. "Use my computer."

CHAPTER SIXTY-EIGHT

As I injected the GHB, I made a show of pretending I'd hit the vein wrong and was struggling to get the blood flowing, then extracted enough to be certain she wouldn't be suspicious. After extracting the needle, I made another show of taping a cotton ball over the site.

"I'll need to look around the home." I stood and pointed to the stairs. "That's as good a place to start as any."

Better to finish up there first so I wouldn't have to drag her down a flight of stairs when she passed out. That had been my biggest fear with Melissa Rollins—that I wouldn't be able to orchestrate her passing out on the third floor. Luckily, I can always find a way to delay as needed.

She stared down at my blue surgical gloves. "Aren't you going to take those off?"

"I prefer to keep them on in unfamiliar homes," I said.

She didn't bother to hide her offense, but did manage to swallow it. "Whatever works."

She led me upstairs. I made notes as we progressed, and grew angrier with each room we entered. Tammy's room was the pinnacle—all pink walls and stuffed unicorns and rows of new books and toys in play cubbies. These monsters thought that would fool us, that if they dressed up a room to look like a play palace, we'd be tricked out of realizing it was really a chamber of horrors. I didn't even bother to hide my disgust.

Then, as we tramped back downstairs, I saw the first wobble. As we crossed through the hallway, she stumbled.

"Are you okay?" I asked.

Her head wobbled as she tried to shake it. "I dunno," she slurred.

Careful to touch her only with my gloves, I eased her into the kitchen, onto a chair. By the time her rear hit the seat, she was out, head lolling back on her neck, limbs twisting out at odd angles.

I rubbed my hands together despite the awkward friction of the gloves. This was going to be so very fun.

CHAPTER SIXTY-NINE

Alison worked quickly but methodically as Jo and Arnett watched over her shoulder, entering the file name, navigating to the proper screen, scanning the summary page. They skimmed along with her, but she knew the jargon and the shortcuts and finished faster than they did. With a clipped "Nope," she'd cross another line off the sheet.

Five lines.

Six.

Seven.

Jo glanced at her watch and did quick math. Each file only took about three minutes, but at this rate they'd need three hours to get through them all. The thought of what Renata could manage in three hours terrified her. "This is taking too long. Are there other computers Arnett and I can use, and split up the pages?"

Johnny's brows furrowed. "You have to have a system ID to log in. Come with me." He led them back into the main room. "Tony, Viola. Meet two of Oakhurst SPDU's finest. They need to use your computers, and your system IDs, to solve a crime. You okay with that?"

Both Tony's and Viola's eyes widened. They popped up like jumping jacks, scattering both chairs in the process. Jo and Arnett each grabbed one, and slid in front of their computers. Jo handed Arnett a third of the sheets, then started in on the remaining third.

Seema, Monica: finding, supported. Child relocated as final decision. Not what they were looking for.

Harper, Brooklyn: finding, substantiated concern, monitoring put into place. No.

Lassen, Stephen: finding, unsupported, no evidence of father's abuse. Maybe, but for now they were only looking for mothers.

Holt, Tamara: finding, supported. Custody given to father. Mother requested fair hearing. Finding, unsupported, child returned to joint custody—

"Alison," Jo called.

Alison flew out of Johnny's office, and instantly scoured Jo's monitor.

She nodded, expression grim. "That could be the one."

CHAPTER SEVENTY

This was both the best part, and the hardest.

The waiting was always stressful because that's when I was most vulnerable. No matter how much time I spent watching them, I could never be sure what might happen—a friend who dropped by, a package that needed a signature. A neighbor who'd spotted a strange car.

But, along with that was the cleansing ritual of it all. My method was always different, but there was still a ritual to setting up for the final act. Just like Preparation of the Altar during Mass—the placement of the crucifix, opening of the missal, the readying of the paten and the chalice for the host—all holy moments when a servant of God gathers what's needed to enact His will. The careful, reverential actions as offering to God's will —a transformation took place during all of it that fed my soul.

For Louisa Pryzik, arranging her in the right position, then putting on the restraints, was like preparing a baby for baptism, and placing the frying pan in front of her so it was the first thing she'd see focused her penance. For Melissa, it was nailing her into the closet—I reflected, somberly, on the parallel to Christ's nailing to the cross as I pounded those nails, five each on three sides to honor the mysteries of the rosary. For Gina it was arranging the drug paraphernalia on the table, and readying the drug injections, mirrors of the sinful sacrament she'd chosen for herself at her child's expense.

Meticulous movements. Extreme care to make sure I touched nothing and left no trace. And, of course, prayer before and after.

For River, I channeled my confirmation saint: St. Joan of Arc.

I secured her to the chair with heat-resistant flue tape, the kind you can buy anywhere.

I removed the Fatwood fire starter sticks from my satchel and arranged them at the base of her chair.

I doused the wood, the chair, and her clothing with zippo lighter fluid.

Then I gagged her so only God and I would hear her screams.

CHAPTER SEVENTY-ONE

"What's our ETA?" Jo hit the gas away from the DCF parking lot, scanning for pedestrians.

"Fifteen minutes. Hopefully five with sirens." Arnett reached to set up the portable.

Jo raced as fast as safety would allow, slowing only as needed through intersections, until she hit a stretch of curvy residential road that forced her down to thirty-five—and was dotted with stop signs.

"Dammit." She slammed her palms on the steering wheel as she stopped at the first, eyeing several more she could see in the distance. "Any way around this?"

He zoomed the GPS out. "Not that I can see. River Holt lives on the other end of this residential section. Heading around it would actually take longer."

She took off again, knuckles white around the steering wheel, silently praying for minimal traffic. Despite their siren, a PT Cruiser pulled into the four-way stop ahead of them. Then, realizing they'd just cut off a police car, the Cruiser slammed on their brakes, causing Jo to skid into a complete stop.

She glanced down at the GPS—River Holt was still five minutes away.

CHAPTER SEVENTY-TWO

River's eyes fluttered open, ending my period of reflection and prayer.

She stared at me like she'd never seen me before, and tried to mumble through the gag. "Wha?"

"I drugged you with a substance called GHB. It can interfere with short-term memory," I told her. "You don't know me. I'm here on behalf of your daughter, Tammy."

She tried to move, and fear bloomed across her face as she realized she couldn't. She mumbled something, panic edging her voice.

"I'll never understand how anyone can harm any child—let alone their own flesh and blood."

She tried to object—I didn't bother to try to understand her.

"If I had my way, every person who abused a child would not only die a slow, painful, terrifying death, they'd also rot in hell for eternity. Children are innocent, and powerless, and when the adults they trust turn on them, the damage to the very core of who they are, to their very soul, is inestimable. It's psychological damage that can't be healed or reversed any more than an amputated limb can be regrown."

She tried to speak again, her eyes pleading with me. I wondered—had Tammy's eyes pleaded with her the same way as she forced Tammy's little hand onto the stovetop?

"But God is forgiving, and requires us to be, too."

Her face relaxed, eyes slightly relieved.

I laughed. "Of course, many people misunderstand what forgiveness means. It isn't a get-out-of-jail-free card, and it doesn't remove responsibility for one's sins. True amends are required for true forgiveness. We must atone as well as apologize, pay a price for the suffering we've caused. In the Old Testament, God required blood sacrifice to cleanse sins, and espoused the philosophy of an eye for an eye. Not for the sake of revenge, but because of the lesson it taught—for every wrong you do, you will be required to pay a recompense. And only in the process of paying that recompense, may your soul be cleansed. Whether God chooses to accept your payment is up to him."

I watched the fear creep back into her eyes.

"So while I personally would be content allowing child abusers to suffer eternal damnation, God asks more of me. I am His agent, and I will extract the price you must pay. And only by doing His will can I right my own wrongs, and cleanse my own soul of its guilt." I raised my hand, showing her the long-nozzled utility lighter I'd been holding.

She suddenly strained and thrashed against her bonds so intensely I worried the tape might not hold. Thankfully, I'd been generous with it, and it held strong.

I tilted my head and considered. "I wonder—would it be more cleansing to have your feet catch fire first, or your face?"

The gag made her screams sound far away, as though she were falling into a pit. I waited for them to finish, but she started again, and again—she had no intention of stopping.

I flicked on the lighter, and bent toward the kindling.

CHAPTER SEVENTY-THREE

Jo turned off the sirens two blocks from River Holt's house—if Renata was there, they couldn't risk alerting her—but kept up as much speed as she could. She jammed on her brakes as she slid around into River's driveway.

Arnett's head twisted back behind them. "Pretty sure that was Renata's car parked back there."

Jo updated dispatch, then assessed the house in front of her. "The fences are too high, her only escape is out the front door or through the side fence gate. And I'm not sure we can afford to wait until backup gets here."

"No," Arnett said, expression grim. "Let's go."

Weapons drawn, they crept up the tiny porch of the sage-green colonial, then paused by the door to listen—an odd shuffling, crackling sound reached her. She pursed her brow pointedly at Arnett. He shook his head—he wasn't sure what it was, either.

She rapped on the door, hard. "Oakhurst County SPDU welfare check. Please open up."

The shuffling intensified, but otherwise nothing changed. Arnett called out the same instruction.

Jo jutted her head toward the window. Arnett pulled a punch out of his pocket, then with one swift motion smashed the glass and reached in to unlock the door. Jo thrust the door open, Beretta raised in front of her, and stepped in. Once she cleared the room, she motioned to Arnett. He leapfrogged past her toward the kitchen.

Something orange flickered on the visible wall of the kitchen. Jo jutted her chin toward it, and Arnett nodded acknowledgement. She rounded past him into the kitchen.

"Holy shit," she cried, and leapt toward the woman, tied to a chair, engulfed in flames. "Do you see a fire extinguisher?"

"No," Arnett said.

"Hang on." Jo ran back into the living room, grabbed the blanket draped over the couch, and raced to throw it over the burning woman. As she did, she shoved the chair back away from the wood burning underneath. Arnett kicked the wood away across the linoleum floor and stamped out the remains, then snatched a kitchen towel off the oven door and helped Jo put out the last remaining flames.

Jo jumped back up. "I'll pursue, you call the EMTs."

He nodded as he pulled the blanket back off the woman. "Hang on," he said to her. "I'm going to remove the gag from your mouth."

As Jo raced out the back door, the woman's screams filled the room.

CHAPTER SEVENTY-FOUR

I raced around the side of the house, praying the gate wasn't padlocked. It wasn't, but the old mechanism stuck, and took me far too long to force open. I clutched my satchel close and ran as fast as I could across the lawn, expecting to feel a bullet bite into my back at any moment.

The lawn ended—I rounded the shrubs, ran down the sidewalk. A siren wailed in the distance, and I glanced left and right, searching for some way to get off the road. There was a boat two houses down, with a tarp covering it—I could crawl under and hide—but no, with more police on the way they'd lock down the neighborhood and search every house.

Then I spotted salvation in the middle of the road.

I veered toward a shed in the next house's backyard, praying as I went, and slipped behind it just as the siren blasted by. Light flooded in from the high windows, and I saw everything with an instant precision I'd never experienced before—the hand of God guiding me to a crowbar.

I raced back into the street and struck the end into the manhole cover's notch. I shoved, and groaned—I'd expected it to *be heavy, but it was like lifting a car. I moved my hands as close to the end as I could grip for leverage, and shoved again.*

It moved—barely. But that was enough, I just needed it to shift slightly, then I could push it sideways rather than lift it. So I heaved again—it shifted, just enough to push slightly to the side.

"Hey!" a woman's voice called.

I didn't look up to find out if the voice was addressing me. Once I made it into the sewer, they'd never be able to track which way I went.

I tossed the crowbar aside and crouched next to the cover. I worked my fingers into the gap I'd created, and yanked. I shoved again, and had enough of a gap to fit my feet in. I dropped onto my rear and stuck my heels into the gap, then shoved with my legs—the metal screeched and groaned against the concrete, but it moved, sending up the sound of running water and the stale stench of sewage. I threw my legs over the edge, feeling for the metal ladder waiting inside.

"Freeze!"

My feet hit the rungs and I twisted to see who was yelling at me. A female detective, with a large gun trained on me. I grasped the top of the ladder with one hand—I just needed firm footing, then I could drop down inside.

"Show me your other hand, or I will fire on you!" the detective called.

I was so close, I just needed to push off—but her expression told me she wasn't bluffing.

What was the expression? Suicide by cop?

Far better than the agonizing death I was facing, regardless. When I first noticed the tremor in my hands, my doctor told me it was Parkinson's. Don't worry, he told me—treatments had advanced, and most people with the disorder lived a normal, or near-normal, lifespan. But the symptoms progressed more rapidly than they should have, and the treatments didn't work. Multiple

Systems Atrophy, the doctor told me. A rare form of Parkinson's with a much worse prognosis.

I'd never been so angry with God, even when my sister died. But I reminded myself He had a plan, and asked him to help me understand. I prayed harder and longer than I'd ever prayed before, and he finally answered—an abuse case popped up in my workload that looked almost exactly like my mother. I knew then —only someone with nothing to lose could act as boldly as required to save that child, and the others—that's what I'd been building toward all this time. I'd help as many as I could until the disease took over, and if they caught me and shuffled me off to jail in the meantime, I wouldn't be alive long enough to care.

But this, suicide by cop, was better.

I smiled at her. "I'm afraid you'll have to shoot."

CHAPTER SEVENTY-FIVE

The paramedics arrived within minutes. But to Jo, hunched over, repeatedly assuring River Holt that help was on the way, unsure River was even conscious now that she wasn't screaming, the wait felt like an eternity.

After surgery to remove the bullet from her shoulder, Renata made a full confession. She admitted to tipping off Tom Fischer about clients of special interest, and to providing Rick Burke with information about abuse cases, either directly or through Tom Fischer.

"I hoped the public shaming would keep other abusers from doing the same thing, and get members of the community involved in watching over the target individuals. Social control can be a strong incentive when it's used correctly, and whether they admit it or not, public outrage can sway judges," she'd said.

As much as Jo wished otherwise, she was right about that.

They went over all the details of each murder with her, and she confessed to two more: another abusive mother they hadn't connected yet, committed in between Louisa Pryzik's and Melissa Rollins murders—and, over thirty years ago, Renata's own mother.

Jo listened to all of it with a detachment that surprised her. "Here's something I don't understand," she asked when Renata finished her story. "These weren't your cases, you didn't have first-hand knowledge of them or the people involved. Like Melissa Rollins—her husband had a clear motive to lie, or at least exaggerate, about the abuse she committed. Yet you're so convinced she's guilty that you felt justified killing her."

She pushed herself up with her good arm and shifted her pillow behind her. "Was there a question in there, Detective?"

Jo swallowed the sarcastic response that rose up, and narrowed her eyes. "The question is, how can you justify taking a life when you aren't certain what happened?"

She stared at Jo with a serene smile. "I'm one hundred percent certain. Little ones don't lie about those sorts of things, and adults who refuse to hear them are complicit in their abuse."

"Children are humans, and humans lie. I've met plenty who've told lies that would turn you gray," Arnett said.

Renata turned the serene smile on him. "Maybe. But I've prayed long and hard on each of these cases. God directs me, I'm just his agent."

Jo's stomach clenched. Her relationship with God was complicated, she couldn't deny that. Her father was a morally devoted Catholic who felt no need to attend Mass regularly, and while her mother insisted she and Sophie attend once a week throughout their childhoods, she'd never asked for more than that. Then, when Marc died, Jo began to question whether God even existed. She'd talked to more than one priest about her doubts, and had been assured those doubts were part of faith's journey. One of the things those conversations and that journey had taught her was to be suspicious of anyone who claimed to have all the answers when it came to God—they were far more likely to be delusional than beatific.

Arnett's eyes narrowed. "What about repentance and

forgiveness? Isn't that the whole point of Christ's crucifixion, that He gave his life to take away our sins? Doesn't everybody deserve a chance to change their lives?"

Renata's entire body seemed to clench, and her demeanor shifted. "Not when a child's life hangs in the balance."

Jo shook her head. "Gina Purcelli went to rehab, quit drinking, and got her life back on track. What happened to her son was an accident, and she was trying to atone for it."

Renata jutted forward and jabbed a finger toward Jo, her face screwed up in a terrifying moue. "Ha! See! That's exactly where you're wrong, that's exactly what they all want you to believe. Gina was drinking again. It was only a matter of time before something ugly happened, and this time Rafael *might not have come out alive.*"

Jo exchanged a confused glance with Arnett. "We found no evidence Gina was drinking again. Why do you think she was?"

"Because I did my homework, Detective. I followed all of them and watched them while I was praying for them. And a week before I killed Gina, I watched her buy a bottle of wine."

Something jostled in Jo's memory. "The week just before?"

Renata flinched, then narrowed her eyes at Jo. "Yes. Why?"

An infinite sadness settled on Jo, along with a serenity of her own. She'd always believed it wasn't up to her to make these decisions, that no one person could determine truth when someone's life hung in the balance. This was why.

Jo met and held Renata's eyes. "The wine wasn't for her. She'd been invited to a family dinner at her ex's sister's house. He told us how proud he was of her that even though she brought it, she never gave the bottle a second glance once it was opened. She checked in every night with her ex and with her mother. There wasn't time for her to be intoxicated in between those calls and her job."

Renata's eyes widened and her face flushed red; her mouth moved in a silent question. But almost as soon as her self-righteousness disappeared it returned again, and her eyes blazed judgment. "People are what they are, and leopards don't change their spots. If she hadn't relapsed yet, it was only a matter of time before she did. And we all have to pay for our sins."

"And now you'll pay for yours." Arnett turned and walked toward the door.

Renata shook her head. "No. Now I'll be rewarded in heaven for my good deeds."

Arnett looked back over his shoulder, expression disgusted and scornful. "Keep telling yourself that as you spend the rest of your life in jail."

Renata leaned back against her pillow and closed her eyes, still smiling. "That's just it, Detective. Didn't the doctors tell you? I'm dying. Probably no more than another year to live, maybe two. That's why I knew if I was going to make a difference in the world, I needed to do it now. The only regret I have is I wasn't able to finish my list."

CHAPTER SEVENTY-SIX

SEPTEMBER 8TH

As Jo waited for the data sets to come back from the phone companies and for Lopez to analyze the data, she tied up loose ends and tried not to examine the similarity between Diana, Renata, and herself. All three of them had good intentions—but, she reminded herself repeatedly, the crucial difference boiled down to that single bottle of wine. The laws and regulations and restrictions that sometimes felt like they stifled Jo's ability to bring criminals to justice were there to prevent mistakes or bias or decisions influenced by evil. No one person could be trusted to see any situation clearly, no matter how well intentioned they were. Better a guilty man go free than an innocent man be punished.

Unless you were the child or the woman abused by that guilty man, or the next person to be murdered.

She pushed the thought away. No system was perfect, and neither was she. It was above her moral pay grade to make those decisions.

She'd just finished her first cup of coffee Wednesday morning when Lopez texted her. "She's got some results for us," she told Arnett.

They hurried in, and found her sitting cross-legged on her office chair, a huge, triumphant smile lighting up her face. "You guys, you guys, you guys, I have good news and bad news, which do you want first?"

Jo's pulse picked up at the excitement in Lopez's voice. "Good news."

"Nothing ambiguous this time—there's only one number that was at both The Cactus Flower motel and Gamer Gecko during the target times."

"Let me guess—a burner phone?"

"Yeppers, and I can't trace it because it was purchased several years ago, of course with cash, and of course any security footage is long gone. But that doesn't matter. What matters is, since we got the warrant to track the number once we found it, I can and I did." She pointed with a flourish at her screen.

Jo scanned the monitor. "Wichita?"

Lopez's smile got even wider as she zoomed the map in. "Wichita. But not just Wichita—the GPS information puts us within a half-block area. And according to the service provider, the number's been in Wichita for two days now, after a brisk drive from LA and a stop in Las Vegas."

Electricity shot through Jo's limbs. "That has to be her."

"Agreed. But the bad news is, the signal disappeared about an hour ago."

"She stopped using it?" Jo asked.

"Must have," Lopez said, and pointed to a section of the map a few miles from the houses. "The last signal we got for it was over here."

"So we don't know where she is, and the only guess we have about where she'll return to is a half-block area? We can't get any more precise than that with GPS?" Arnett asked.

"Sometimes GPS hits dead-nuts accurate, sometimes it flops around, it depends on the satellite, and there's no way of knowing which readings are which. She's been all over Wichita, which suggests she's staying for at least a little while. And her movements periodically return to this spot here on Hatch Road. I can narrow it down to these three houses." She referenced the addresses, jotted them down, and gestured to the other monitors in the room. "Divide and conquer?"

"Yes." Jo chewed on her lip. "But I'm not making the same mistake twice. We identify the property owners if we can, but we don't want to make contact. We can't risk tipping her off again."

"Right," Arnett said.

They each grabbed a monitor. "According to the records I can find, the owners of 2541 have lived there for twenty years," Jo reported.

"There's a rental listing for 2537, but it's not active. Looks like it was rented out about six months ago," Lopez said.

"I've got an open rental listing for 2539," Arnett said.

"So the most likely target would seem to be 2539—if she just rented the house, the listing wouldn't be down yet," Jo said. "But, she could be staying with friends at any of the locations."

"Should we send in uniforms to surveil?" Lopez asked.

But Jo was already standing again. "Yes, with the clear instruction that they should not make contact. I'm not losing her again. I'm going to Wichita. I'll let Hayes know why once I'm back."

Arnett stood up. "I'm going with you. But since this woman is threatening your family, don't you think Hayes would be—"

Jo and Lopez both sent him withering glares.

He shook his head. "No, probably not. Forgiveness rather than permission. Let's go."

CHAPTER SEVENTY-SEVEN

Jo and Arnett secured an emergency seat on a flight to Wichita, and arrived late that afternoon.

The city of Wichita's Crimes Against Persons Bureau were deeply concerned to discover that a potential serial killer had moved into their jurisdiction. Detectives Arnie Isenhard and Rich Kemp, two fifty-something lean white men, picked them up at the airport.

"We've sent out a team to surveil the houses, but haven't yet been able to determine which your suspect is staying in. We've got plain wrappers in place for backup," Isenhard told them as he drove. "I'm assuming you want to be in the surveillance van?"

Jo was torn. She'd studied Diana's license picture and the photoshopped version Lopez had created that put her in a blonde wig; she'd likely be able to identify her from across a football field, far earlier than anybody else in that van. But at the same time, the thought of not having her own vehicle made her itchy. Still, if the Wichita police were patrolling a perimeter around the houses, everything should be fine. "That works." She nodded.

Half an hour later he dropped them off at a van parked around the corner from the three target houses. The door slid open and silently swallowed them in.

"Daniella Marquez." A light-skinned black woman in her late thirties greeted them. "This is Sloan Matthews."

Jo shook her hand, then turned to the ruddy-cheeked blond man who looked to be in his late twenties. "I'm Josette Fournier, and this is Bob Arnett. What are we looking at?"

Marquez gestured to the equipment in front of her. "The houses are close enough together we were able to place a camera that gives a view of all three entryways. We have another at each end of the block so we can see approaching cars. Everything's quiet, but people should be coming home from work soon."

Jo glanced at the houses. "What do we know about the rear exits?"

Sloan rotated a laptop with a bird's-eye Google Earth image on it, then pointed to each house in turn. "Exits here, here, and here. Each yard backs up against the yard on the street behind it, so we have an unmarked team on that street too. Same on the end of Hatch, and on the other cross street."

Jo nodded. "Sounds like we just wait."

CHAPTER SEVENTY-EIGHT

Diana glanced in the rearview mirror as she pulled out of the Best Buy parking lot. Her right hand fluttered onto the bag of security cameras sitting on the passenger seat as she checked the final item off her to-do list.

She could finally breathe.

Despite making most of the arrangements online, she'd spent every daylight hour and a dangerously large chunk of her savings to finish her necessary errands. But that's what the savings were for, and now she could go home, cuddle with Cleopatra, and wait for the copious deliveries scheduled over the next week. Once she had a steady enough stream of income coming in under Kristen's name, she'd begin laying down the foundation for a new backup identity.

She'd also have to figure out what exactly to do about Josette Fournier. Hopefully, for everyone's benefit, Josette would be swayed by her note, but she couldn't assume that would be the case. So she'd spent her evening hours, when errands weren't possible, digging down deep into her research, using every trick in her arsenal to find out as much about Josette's past as she could. She'd learned a few interesting things, but her best hope was monitoring the current situation, and she wasn't sure the one camera she'd left behind would be enough.

She turned onto the street that crossed her own, and smiled out at the neighborhood. Quiet. Peaceful. Filled with older couples who walked together in the mornings, children who played in yards in the afternoons, and career women who jogged through the streets in the evenings. Safe. Reliable. Comfortable.

Something's wrong.

She slowed to process the voice in her head. This must be paranoia—she hadn't been around long enough to have developed reliable instincts about this place.

But, no, something prompted the thought, and better safe than sorry. She slowed, and she scanned.

A white panel van.

Not double parked with flashers on, making a delivery. Nobody running up to a nearby porch with a package. Fully parked, lights off, windows tinted.

If it belonged here, she would have noticed it before now. But possibly it belonged to a visiting friend?

She couldn't take that chance.

CHAPTER SEVENTY-NINE

Jo leaned forward as a red Ford Fusion headed toward the camera. "California plates."

Arnett and Matthews mirrored her posture, and Marquez radioed the other cars. "Possible ID in Red Ford Fusion, California plates. Stand by."

Jo stared with laser focus, willing the car to keep the slow pace as she watched, every muscle taut.

A ball of electricity tingled in Jo's chest as the woman came into view. Large sunglasses obscured half her face, but her hair was long and blonde, and the chin had the same heart-shape. "That's her."

"You sure?" Arnett's gaze flicked from the screen to Jo's face.

"Ninety-nine percent."

"Description of driver matches our suspect. Hold your positions," Marquez said.

The vehicle turned the corner onto Hatch Street, and headed toward the target houses. Jo held her finger up—if they showed themselves prematurely, Diana would speed away, but as soon as she turned into a driveway, they'd need to reach her before she barricaded herself inside.

But she passed all three houses.

"And you're sure it's her?" Marquez asked.

"Unless someone who looks just like her happens to be driving by with California plates."

Marquez gave a sharp nod. "Barton, Riker, pull her over as she comes to the end of the block. Stevens, Charlton, cover."

The Fusion slowed to turn at the end of the block. Then, the car shot through the intersection.

"Shit." Matthews climbed into the driver's seat. "Wait here, or pursue?"

"Drive," Jo yelled, "or move the hell out of the way so I can."

CHAPTER EIGHTY

As Diana approached the intersection at the end of Hatch, a car moved toward her, both occupants staring at her intently.

Her instincts had been right.

She floored the gas pedal and bolted through the intersection. Was Josette Fournier some sort of witch? How in the hell could they possibly have found her? But all that mattered was they'd been stupid about it, they hadn't gone inside the house and waited for her there, and if they'd done that they'd have caught her for sure—

And that meant they didn't know which house was hers. They must have tracked her to the neighborhood somehow, but not to the exact house. And the only way to do *that* was to track her phone. She slammed her hands onto the steering wheel—the damned burner phone she'd ditched that morning.

Sirens blared behind her as she approached the end of the next block. She had to make a choice, and make it fast, or she was screwed. A right turn would take her back to the highway, which was a trap—they'd see every move she made from a mile away, and would have backup to cut her off. A left would dump her at an air force base, filled with high-visibility wide-open fields and military fortifications she'd never be able to breach.

Neither option worked—she'd have to double back. But that was fine, they wouldn't be expecting that move anyway—for anyone else it would be suicide. She'd get in, grab Cleopatra, steal a car, and find a place to hide until the sun went down.

She made a quick left and thanked heaven the blocks were rectangular, not square. She could turn left again before they got her back in sight, and they wouldn't know which way she'd gone.

After whipping around the second corner, she pulled immediately behind a large SUV parked on the curb. She ducked down so her head wouldn't show, and waited. After a long minute, a siren approached, seemed to slow, then sped off and faded again.

She popped up to check the coast was clear, then grabbed her purse and bolted down the street. She counted the houses to find the right one, then made a sharp turn toward the house's backyard gate, hoping to hell that Midwesterners really were nicer and more trusting than coasties.

In this case, they were—the gate wasn't locked. She moved as quickly and silently as she could. At the back fence, she pulled a decorative statue of St. Francis out of sight behind the shed, then used his head to vault herself over into her own backyard.

She landed awkwardly, but did no serious damage, and scanned for police as she made her way to the back door. She listened for another moment, then pulled her new key out of her purse with one hand and her new Smith & Wesson M&P 22 out with her other.

With the gun at her side, she crept through the kitchen. Empty, and so was the living room, except for Cleopatra sitting in a sunbeam on the floor.

"Sorry about this, my love." She tossed the key and gun into her purse and scooped up the cat. "Back into the carrier for now." She crossed to the hall closet, pulled the carrier out of the door, and slid Cleopatra in. Then she paused for a minute, still in a crouch, to think.

What would the police do next? As soon as it was clear they'd lost her, they'd put out an APB on her and on the car. They'd contact the California DMV to find out who the car was registered to, and they'd have her new name. How long would it take them to figure out which house she'd rented?

She wasn't sure. She couldn't afford to linger.

CHAPTER EIGHTY-ONE

"We lost her," a man's frustrated cry crackled over the radio.

"How?" Marquez asked.

"She turned again before we caught up."

Marquez didn't miss a beat. "Barton, Riker, search east. Stevens, Charlton, west. Triton, Samuels, north, and we'll take south. I already put out the APB."

"How the hell did she disappear so fast?" Matthews turned the wheel sharply.

Jo'd been thinking the same thing. It just wasn't possible to be suddenly out of everyone's sight— "Unless she pulled over," Jo blurted.

Sloan turned down the street parallel to Hatch. "Spiral search outward?"

"Do it," Arnett said.

Jo's hands clenched, silently fighting the limited visibility and slow speed. If she were Diana, what would she do right now? She didn't know her well enough to judge—but she did know Diana was smart. She wouldn't try to outrun the police, and she'd realize her car was useless, so she'd abandon it asap. But then what?

She'd need another vehicle. But she'd also realize she needed to disappear, and not just for a day or two—

"There it is." Matthews yanked the van to the side of the road.

Jo was out of the van before it came to a full stop, rounding the front of the Fusion. She glanced around, taking stock. "She doubled back to her house."

"We still don't know which one that is," Matthews said.

"No, we don't, but we also don't need to worry about the element of surprise anymore. So we check all three."

––––––

"You call the others back," Jo told Marquez, and gestured toward the house in front of them. "We'll take the house behind this one."

As Marquez moved off with Matthews, Jo and Arnett circled the block. "Around back, so it's not obvious to the entire street?"

Arnett nodded. The gate to the backyard was latched, but not locked—apparently Diana hadn't gotten around to that yet. They moved cautiously toward the covered patio, to the back door.

Jo twisted the knob, not surprised when it didn't resist. She stepped inside to the left as Arnett stepped to the right—the kitchen sat empty except for a plastic bag on the counter. "Clear."

Arnett crossed the room. "Hallway."

They cleared the rooms as they went. Bathroom. Empty room to the left. Closet, empty except for a coat. Living room, devoid of furniture.

She paused to listen. No sound of any sort.

Had she been wrong? Had Diana just wanted them to think

she'd doubled back to the house? Had she really run off in the other direction?

Arnett gestured toward the window by the front door. "Matthews and Marquez are liaising in front of the house next door. I'll catch them up."

"I'll double-check in here, see if there's anything that might give us a clue."

He nodded, and moved out. As the front door swung closed behind him, Jo crossed the entryway and she caught sight of another door. The garage.

She pushed it open, and stepped in.

Diana stood directly in front of her, gun raised and pointed at Jo's head.

CHAPTER EIGHTY-TWO

Diana had been desperately hoping that anybody in the world other than Josette was on the other side of that door. Some anonymous officer or detective she could talk herself into believing was an abuser—she'd been surprised to learn through her Facebook groups that such cops existed. But no, here Josette was, in the flesh, where she had no right to be. And at the sight of her, Diana's brain kicked into survival mode.

"Put your gun down." Diana weighed Josette's reaction as she said the words, tracking her face, her stance, her gaze.

"You know I can't do that. And the house is surrounded. Even if you kill me, you won't get away—but I don't think you want to kill me."

Electricity pricked at Diana as she took in Josette's voice for the first time. Steady, calm, musical, with a filament of steel rebar—but also an undercurrent of...curiosity? Uncertainty?

Diana's pulse slowed slightly, and she allowed her glimmer of hope to expand. She tilted her head and stared into Josette's piercing eyes, searching for the sisterhood. It wasn't hard to find. She could read it in the way Josette's gaze flicked from one of her eyes to the other, and in the tiny wrinkles that deepened as she leaned in, ever so slightly, studying Diana, also searching for a kindred soul.

Yes—the opening was there. She had one last chance to reach her, to help her see the truth.

Diana lifted her gun higher. "If I have to, I will. But no, I don't want to kill you. And I don't think *you* want to kill *me*."

"Drop your weapon, Diana," Josette said.

The prickles returned at the sound of Josette's voice saying her name—she was well aware of the intimacy it signaled, even if Josette wasn't. Whisper a man's name in a lowered, sexy voice and they'd turn into a quivering mass before your eyes—blush when they whispered yours and their sense of power and control skyrocketed. Josette's choice to use Diana's first name was deeply significant, even if she herself didn't realize it.

And—Diana was certain Josette's gun had wobbled slightly.

Diana forced her posture to relax, and put on a friendly, conspiratorial smile. "Let's talk about Martin Scherer."

———

"How many women did he kill? If I remember correctly, the paper claimed at least five. How many more did you find?"

The icy calm of heightened sensation settled over Jo as she tracked Diana's every twitch and emotion, assessing the situation and calculating her response. Arnett believed Jo was searching the house, so he wouldn't expect her to emerge immediately—how long before he came looking for her? She could shoot Diana, but if she did, she'd have to shoot to kill—Diana wouldn't hesitate to return fire in an attempt to survive. And with Hayes already looking to kneecap her, a fatal shooting with no witnesses might be just the excuse she needed. Especially since the evidence they had against Diana so far was dangerously thin, mostly speculation and unproven cell-tower wizardry—they needed Diana in an interrogation room, answering questions and making admissions or mistakes they could use to prosecute her. She had to play this carefully.

"Isn't five enough?" Jo said.

"Five too many," Diana said. "So let's extrapolate. He killed five in, what, about five years? That means in the last eight years, he would have killed at least eight more. Eight women are alive because *I* killed *him*."

Jo forced herself not to stiffen. "We'd have had him in custody by the next day."

Diana smiled. "Maybe. Maybe not. Even if you had, the right defense attorney can get just about anybody off. You know that's true."

Jo watched Diana's expression, fascinated. Her eyes shone, nearly twinkled, with intensity, and Jo could feel the waves of hatred at the very mention of Scherer's name. Diana truly believed she was the avenging angel she claimed to be, and Jo found herself fighting back admiration. This woman had stalked the stalker, had outwitted the predator. And she was right—the system was far from perfect, that was no secret. She dealt with that reality in a different way than Jo did. But as much as Jo might not want to admit it, their motives were the same.

Words poured from Jo before she could stop them. "Why is this your responsibility? What happened to you?"

Diana's face flinched, but she continued. "Eight families that didn't have to suffer the loss of their loved ones. Eight husbands and countless children. And those five families who did lose their loved ones? How many of them, if they found themselves face to face with Martin Scherer, would have killed him on the spot?"

"No system is perfect. And putting justice in the hands of biased individuals is certainly no better."

Diana's eyes burrowed into Jo's. "I've had a lot of hurry-up-and-wait time these last couple of weeks, giving me plenty of time to delve into new interests. A couple of days ago I found an old engagement announcement in the archives of the Boston Globe. *Your* engagement announcement."

The words hit Jo like a two-by-four in the stomach, knocking the breath from her. She struggled to keep her gun steady as Jack's face materialized before her, his warm blue eyes gazing up toward the sky, blood pouring from the bullet hole in his temple as she desperately worked compressions on his chest.

"I also found your fiancé's obituary, which led me to a series of news articles. I'm so sorry for your loss. He seemed to be a wonderful man—he didn't deserve to be slaughtered in an alley like an animal."

Jo forced her eyes back in focus and stared into Diana's again, surprised by what she found there. Compassion. Empathy. Pain. Anger.

"They never found the man that killed Jack. The system didn't get him justice," Diana said.

Jo's throat went dry. She stayed silent, afraid her voice would give away her emotions. She needed to stay in control.

"No system is perfect." Diana's head tilted, and her eyes narrowed. "But imagine turning into an alley one day and finding the killer there in front of you. Late at night, with nobody around, no security cameras, no way anybody will ever know what happened if you kill him."

But Jo didn't have to imagine. She'd gone to that alley hundreds of times, hoping to find him, every chance she got. In the mornings, at noon, at night, along with nearby alleys and alleys on the opposite sides of the city. She'd played out every scenario—finding him and turning him in, killing him with her bare hands, tight around his throat as the life faded from his eyes. Played them over and over as she walked by herself in the dark, hunting for him, not realizing until years later that she half hoped the man would kill *her* this time, too.

Jo's voice came out strong and clear. "I'd turn him in to the police."

Diana's brows popped up, and the corners of her mouth dropped, as though she was considering this alternative. "And what if he disappeared again before the police arrived? Or what if they arrested him, but he got bail and disappeared? How many more people would he have killed trying to get his next fix? How could you live with yourself knowing they would have lived if you'd taken the shot?"

Jo felt her blood drain into her feet, and prayed for the strength not to faint.

───────

Diana watched the color leave Josette's face—she'd hit her mark. Now all she had to do was bring it all home.

"You can't make that choice, you're sworn into a system that prevents it. But *I'm* not. I can protect against the evil that falls through the cracks. I've sharpened my skills and I know people. If the man who killed your fiancé is still alive, I can find him, and I can fix it."

Diana watched Josette's eyes flick back and forth and her jaw clench as a battle royale exploded across her pale face. Diana could practically hear all the rules Josette had been taught to value fighting desperately against the deep-seated desire to get vengeance for her fiancé and to protect other innocents from his killer. All it would take now was a tiny push from Diana.

"I know you couldn't avoid bringing in Renata Cruz because everyone was too involved, but Arnett never needs to know you found me here. I can slip out the—" She stopped short.

Because Josette's face had changed, hardened somehow—like a light had gone off in her eyes when Diana mentioned Renata's name.

She struggled to bring Josette back. "I can stop the abusers. I can make it right."

Josette sank ever so slightly into her stance, and raised the gun another inch. "Drop your weapon. Now."

Diana's hope faded, and the smile slid from her face. She'd been so close—Josette had been seconds away from lowering her weapon. What had changed? She'd said the wrong thing, or overplayed something—but what?

Not that it mattered. She'd tried, and she'd failed. Josette stubbornly refused to see the truth. That meant the time had come to make the hard final choice she'd been desperate to avoid—pull the literal trigger, or the figurative one. Neither option had an easy happy ending.

Live to fight another day, her father's voice whispered to her.

It had been one of his favorite expressions, a life lesson he'd encouraged her to embrace. That sometimes the smart thing to do was walk away, regroup, and try again better. The memory of those clichés had pissed her off for years because after her mother broke his heart, he flung himself into the San Francisco Bay. *So much for living to fight another day, right, Daddy?*

But she'd come to realize that only proved his point. Some choices couldn't be unmade. And you couldn't come back from shooting a cop.

That dropped her to her final, very risky, option. Good defense attorneys got people off every day, and one of her first self-protective moves upon reaching Wichita was to identify the best defense attorney in Kansas. The police didn't have any concrete evidence against her—if they had, they'd have carted her in to the police station in Los Angeles. So she'd thought carefully about what she could tell a lawyer, spent hours combing through the details, putting together a well-constructed story about fleeing California because of a stalker boyfriend on the police force who sent an e-mail to Josette in an attempt to frame her for his own crimes. That should be more than enough to create reasonable doubt in skilled hands. And if it didn't? Well. Ted Bundy escaped from jail twice. Countless criminals got off on technicalities. She was smart, and she was still drawing breath, and those were advantages she'd learned to exploit very effectively.

"You're right." She released her hold on the gun. "I'm putting it on the floor."

Josette's eyes narrowed. Diana wouldn't have expected less —Josette was smart, too, and the smart thing was to be suspicious. So Diana moved slowly, bending at the knees with her hands held high, then carefully lowered her hands to the floor.

"Step back from the weapon." Josette's voice rang strong.

Diana stepped back.

Another voice rang out. "Against the wall."

Diana's head snapped to the door, where Arnett had appeared and gestured with his head toward the side of the garage. She stepped toward it, watching back over her shoulder. Josette didn't lower her gun until he came forward to cuff Diana and read her her rights.

Diana continued to study Josette's face as he read the Miranda warning, still trying to figure out what had gone wrong. Was that sadness she saw in Josette's eyes? Disappointment? Regret? Whatever it was, it most certainly wasn't triumph or arrogance, and that rekindled the smallest spark of Diana's hope.

"Do you understand the rights that I have just read to you?" Arnett said.

"Yes," she answered.

"With those rights in mind, do you wish to speak to us?"

"I have a request," she said.

Arnett snorted. Josette's brows creased. "What's that?" she asked.

"My cat is by the wall in her carrier. Will you make sure she's taken care of until I'm released?"

CHAPTER EIGHTY-THREE

SEPTEMBER 10TH

Jo stood over the cast-iron pan, continuously stirring the butter, oil, and flour roux for her shrimp etouffee, encouraging her mind to focus on the eternal etouffee roux controversy: dark roux, light roux, or no roux?

A dark roux gave deep, rich flavor, but took ages of careful stirring. A light roux gave a nuttier flavor, and required far less time—but didn't have the robust color and always felt like a cheat. Using no roux was just plain crazy as far as she was concerned, but there were plenty in her family that would say the same thing about the diced tomatoes she added in. To each his own.

Cleopatra rubbed up against her leg, breaking Jo's steadfast concentration on *not* thinking about Diana. She stroked the cat affectionately. Cleopatra had turned out to be the perfect house guest—quiet, friendly but not cloying, and, of course, didn't shed all over Jo's floors and furniture.

Jo still couldn't figure out why Diana put down the gun. After ensuring Cleopatra had a safe home, Diana had asked for an attorney and refused to say another word. The only clues Jo had to what happened and why were in the email Diana had previously sent, so she'd spent the two days since streaming its content continuously through her mind. Completely ridiculous, because it was all very simple—Diana was a psychopath, a serial killer, and that was all. One that had almost manipulated her into second guessing her own moral code.

And yet, some very real part of her screamed bloody murder at the sight of Diana in a jumpsuit and handcuffs, in the back of a transport vehicle. Why?

The more immediate concern was Lieutenant Hayes. Given that Jo had succeeded in apprehending a murderer nobody even knew existed, who'd killed at least thirteen victims nobody but Jo had detected, Hayes couldn't very well punish Jo for going behind her back. In fact, Jo, Arnett, and Lopez would most likely receive commendations for the work they'd done. But Jo didn't need finely tuned intuition to know it wasn't as simple as that. All she needed was one look at Hayes to know she was seething inside—her hatred for Jo had only intensified, and eventually there would be a reckoning.

Jo sighed and tried to focus on the roux.

Her doorbell rang—Matt was early. The answering flutter in her chest made her smile as she crossed through the house to let him in.

He glanced down at the pan she was still stirring in the entryway as he bent to kiss her. "You know, that'll cook faster if you put it on the stove."

"Exactly." She craned her neck to meet his. "You can't turn your back on a roux for a hot second or it's over. Especially the way cast iron holds heat."

"Whatever you're doing, it's working. That smells amazing." He followed her back through the kitchen. "Ah! You haven't diced your tomatoes yet? Are you feeling alright?"

"You did all that whining about how there's never anything for you to help with when I cook, so I left them."

His eyes widened playfully. "And the world didn't instantly

end? I thought it made you itchy to start cooking before you finished your mise en place?"

She shot him a teasing death glare. "It does. But I'm not the only one that matters. I can listen and I can grow."

She smiled and leaned in for another kiss—one that lingered and filled her mind with his soft lips—until she almost burned the roux.

They chatted about their workdays as they finished preparing the meal, and continued the conversation as they ate. He told her how work was slowly returning to normal now that the hospital had brought another neurologist on staff. She told him Diana was now in Massachusetts to be tried for Bennie Moreno's murder, and the ADA was busy putting together a case for that and the rest of her alleged kills.

"So you're safe," she finished, only half-joking. "She won't be showing up to take you out."

"David must be relieved." He smiled wryly. "How's Sophie doing?"

Jo pushed away her empty plate. "Still trying to figure it all out. David says he wants to save the marriage."

Matt's brows raised. "What's his plan for the baby?"

"He seems to think they can all pretend there is no baby. He told Sophie he doesn't see why Emily and Isabelle need to know about it."

Matt let out a low whistle. "That's some heavy denial."

"David's used to having the world revolve around him. If he doesn't like something a certain way, that thing changes. But Sophie's done expending time and energy to create that for him."

"What do you think? Will she let him stay?"

Jo fiddled with her napkin. "My instincts have never worked when it comes to Sophie. She surprises me every time I turn around, especially lately. Same with my father and mother.

I guess I just don't have enough distance to judge correctly." She smiled a half-smile.

Matt squeezed her hand, then stood up and gathered their plates. "Coffee?"

"Always."

He rinsed the dishes and put them in the dishwasher, then pulled out her moka pot. She leaned back in her chair and watched as he moved through the motions of filling the well, putting in the grinds, and setting the flame to heat the water at just the right speed. There was an alchemy to it, a patience and a grace of movement that stirred something in her.

Is Matt a good man? Diana had asked. An over-simplified question, because there was good and bad in everyone. But Jo understood the spirit intended—was Matt the sort of man who would hurt a woman? Was he the sort of man who'd abuse or cheat or neglect? But no abused woman, or man, ever thought their partner would beat them. No one thought their partner would cheat on them. But it happened, far too often. The only way to protect yourself was not to be in a relationship in the first place, a method Jo herself had tried.

The coffee bubbled up through the spout in the center of the pot, spitting like an angry volcano. When it finished, Matt divided the liquid into two cups, added a dash of milk to hers, and brought them both to the table.

Jo lifted her cup, watching him over the rim as he closed his eyes to savor the smell, then slowly sip.

Trust is a choice.

She set her cup back down. "Matt," she said softly.

His eyes opened, his gentle smile still in place. "Yes?"

"What do you think about moving in together?"

A LETTER FROM M.M. CHOUINARD

Thank you so much for reading *Her Silent Prayer*. If you enjoyed the book and have time to leave me a short, honest review on Amazon, Goodreads, or wherever you purchased the book, I'd really appreciate it. Reviews help me reach new readers, and that means I get to bring you more books! Also, if you know of friends or family who would enjoy the book, I'd love your recommendation there too—word of mouth means so much to authors. And if you have a moment to say hi on social media, please do—I love hearing from you!

If you'd like to keep up to date with any of my new releases, please click the link below to sign up for Bookouture's newsletter; your email will never be shared, and they'll only contact you when they have news about a new Bookouture release.

www.bookouture.com/mm-chouinard

You can also sign up for my personal newsletter at www.mmchouinard.com for news directly from me about all my activities; I also will never share your email. And you can connect with me via my website, Facebook, Goodreads, and Twitter. I'd love to hear from you.

When I first wrote *The Dancing Girls*, I considered the story complete. I was open to writing a series that featured Jo Fournier, and I'm so glad my editor and publisher wanted that! But, if I'm honest, I never for a minute thought I'd write about Diana Montauk again. To my mind, she'd played her role: she spoke to the damage of sexual abuse in young girls, warned that privilege in society isn't inviolable, and reclaimed power for victimized women in a way that raised a serious moral quandary about vigilante justice. Allowing her to slip away at the end of the book, never to be seen again, was the plan.

Then people started asking me when Diana would be back.

Luckily for me, one of the first people who asked me this was my then-editor, Leodora Darlington. I was intrigued by the idea of bringing Diana back, but both Leo and I believed firmly that it had to happen at the right time and in the right way. In *The Dancing Girls,* Diana and Jo form two sides of the same coin—strong women who are fighting for justice as they see it. They have similarities: both are smart, both are compassionate, and both have dealt with more pain in their lives than any living being should have to. But, they're different in important ways, too, and if *The Dancing Girls* highlighted the similarities, I wanted any future book with Diana to highlight the differences, and to offer at least a tentative answer to the question raised in *The Dancing Girls* about vigilante justice. In order for that shift to make sense, Jo had to grow and change in some important ways. I dropped some hints in the intervening books so readers would know I wanted Jo and Diana to clash some day, all while paying close attention to where Jo took me and where Diana would fit best. My next editor, Maisie Lawrence, agreed with me that the fifth book in the series was the right place for this to happen.

Will Diana return again? I'm honestly not sure. That depends on whether she has something else to teach Jo—or maybe on whether Jo has something to teach her—and on what that something is. It also depends on *you*—I'd love to hear your thoughts on whether you think she should return, and why (or why not).

Thank you so much for reading my books. I am more honored than I can say that you choose to spend your time and money with Jo and me.

Michelle

www.mmchouinard.com

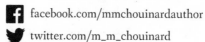

facebook.com/mmchouinardauthor
twitter.com/m_m_chouinard
instagram.com/mmchouinard

ACKNOWLEDGMENTS

First and foremost, thank *you* for reading my books! And to everyone who takes the time to review them, blog about them, or tell a friend about them—I'm deeply grateful. Your support means the world to me.

The amazing team of people at Bookouture take my words and do magical things to them. Maisie Lawrence's input helped in the early stages, and Sonny Marr's and Rhianna Louise's incredible expertise poked and prodded and tweaked and twizzled it into something worth reading. Lauren Finger, Alex Holmes, Emily Boyce, Nicky Gyopari, and Jane Eastgate (whose gift for detail and continuity continues to astound me) helped edit and produce it; Kim Nash, Noelle Holten, Sarah Hardy, and Jess Readett tirelessly promoted it; Melanie Price and Alex Crow helped market it; Rhianna Louise and Alba Proko made the audiobook a reality; and Jenny Geras, Laura Deacon, and Natalie Butlin oversaw it all. So many amazing hands making it all happen!

I couldn't do what I do without the help of experts to guide me along the way. Thank you to the NWDA Hampshire County Detective Unit, and to Leonard Von Flatern and Detective Adam Hill for their invaluable expertise and patience answering questions about strange scenarios. Any errors/inaccuracies that exist are my fault entirely.

Thanks to my agent, Lynnette Novak, and Nicole Resciniti: you advise me, guide me, and support me. Thank you!

Thanks also to my writing tribe, who encourage me, educate

me, write with me, critique me, lift me up, and make me laugh. This includes Writer's Bloc, BSW, my fellow SinC brothers and sisters (especially the drop-ins), my fellow MWA members (especially the Monday and Wednesday crew), D.K. Dailey, Karen McCoy, and my fellow Bookouture authors. Writing can be so solitary, I am truly thankful to have friends like you.

Thanks also to my furbabies, who never complain when I read my writing out loud, never keep track of how much coffee I drink, and who keep me writing, because I literally can't get up when they're covering my lap.

But as always, my deepest debt of gratitude is to my husband. Without his support, I never would have had the courage to write. Love you always!